Also Available from Mia Kay and Carina Press

Soft Target

MIA KAY

HARD SILENCE

carina press™

carina press™

ISBN-13: 978-1-335-00619-6

Recycling programs for this product may not exist in your area.

Hard Silence

This edition published by arrangement with Harlequin Books S.A.

www.CarinaPress.com

Printed in U.S.A.

To my mother. This book is not about her.

Chapter One

Body Found In Well.

The Lewisville Clarion headline was brief, and the story wasn't much longer. Beau Archer's remains had been found in an old well on his property in Virginia. The man had gone missing twenty-eight years ago and, without family to keep it open, the investigation had gone cold.

Abby Quinn read the story three times, scrolling through the online version of the small-town paper in the hopes of finding more information. When she didn't, she wavered between relief and regret.

Beau Archer, her first stepfather, had stumbled into her life when he'd married her mother in Atlantic City. He'd taught Abby to ride a bike. She could still hear his boots pounding on the hard-packed dirt of the country road in front of his house, his heavy breath in her ear. He'd whooped with laughter when she'd turned at the end of the lane and made her wobbly way back to him. Then he'd taken her for ice cream.

A month after that memorable bike ride, his *loving* wife Wallis had shoved his lifeless body down a well.

He deserved more than one paragraph in the newspaper, but at least now he'd get a headstone.

Toby—her third Toby in almost twenty years—whined through the screen door, reminding her of the time. She deleted the alert email, cleaned out her trash folder and cleared her browser history. It was time to get to work.

Walking out onto her front porch, Abby let the door slap closed behind her as she stood and enjoyed the brisk Idaho spring morning. Past the security light illuminating the yard, the still-early lavender sky met the dark hills on the horizon.

Stretching her muscles, she winced as pain lanced from her neck down her left side. Most days she could ignore it, but she'd pushed too hard yesterday. She'd felt the muscles cramp as she'd fixed fences and then stayed at the computer, perched in her chair squinting at code until late in the evening.

And then the nightmares, and the news about Beau.

Already halfway to the stables, Toby looked over his shoulder to see if she was following. Abby swore the border collie was smiling. She could always count on her dog.

"Work. Yeah, I know," she grumbled good-naturedly as she tramped down the steps and toward the paddock. At the outer edge of the light, she faced the darkness beyond and hesitated.

Nineteen years, sixty-nine hundred mornings, and she still gritted her teeth and held her breath when she stepped into the shadows. But she did it.

She did it again when she swung the stable doors open. Reaching around the wall, she turned on the lights before she stepped inside.

On either side of the aisle, her horses poked their heads over the stall doors, blinking under the bright lights, chuffing and huffing hellos.

"Good morning, George," Abby whispered as she put a calming hand on the palomino's velvety nose. "I told you I'd be back this morning." After a year of working to earn the animal's trust, it was rewarding to look into eyes no longer hazy with disappointment. Still, the minute the gate opened, George trotted into the misty dawn, as though afraid someone would slam the door and trap her inside.

The other horse remained quiet in his stall. "Good morning, Hemingway," Abby whispered as she stroked the giant black gelding's nose and danced her fingers through his forelock. He was becoming such an elegant animal. "How are you, handsome? Ready to work this morning?" He dropped his head to her waiting hand. "I'll take that as a yes."

She forced her left arm up, ignoring the persistent pain, slipped the halter over his head and scratched his ears until he quieted. "No saddle today, I promise. Let's get used to this first." She opened the door but let the lead rope dangle as she walked away and let him follow. He needed to know she wouldn't tug and pull. His clopping tread reminded her of Beau and her wobbly bike ride.

Shaking the memory free, she stood in the stable doorway. The pasture was cloaked in fog, and dew silvered the grasses not already trampled. It was like looking through a soft-focus lens. In this moment, right before sunrise, the world was fuzzy, tinted green, blue and gray. The birds chirped quiet, sleepy greetings. Hemingway froze when she picked up the rope.

"I won't hurt you." Abby took one step, keeping the lead slack, and waited. When the animal moved forward, she took another step. They inched through the paddock and the gate to the edge of the field.

"Good boy," she murmured as she offered him a carrot and stroked his graceful neck. "See? No pain."

Leaving him there, she went back into the stable only to run out when an equine scream ended in canine yelps and snarls. All that remained of Hemingway were his thundering hoof beats and the waving grass.

Abby knelt next to Toby and ran her hands over him, checking him for injuries. The dog's shame gave way to a plea for a belly rub.

"I know you want to herd him," she scolded as she gave in and scratched his chest, "but he hates to be crowded right now." She stood and sighed. "Let's go get him."

Hem's trail was marked in the dew, and easy to follow. The tall grass swallowed Toby in a gulp, and Abby waded through the swaying fescue to the river, her bag of carrots and apples bouncing against her hip. Stepping carefully on the slick rocks, she hopped to the Simons' pasture and continued up the hill.

Off to her left, a covey of quail clattered clumsily into the sky, scaring her as much as she'd startled them. Toby shot off, intent on catching the slowest prey. Abby trudged on alone.

The giant gelding was stopped at the fence, munching on Deb Simon's newly budded shrubs. He watched her approach with one dark, wild eye.

"Shh." She touched his neck and pursued him when he flinched away. When he quieted, she rubbed his sweaty coat and stared down at the ragged plant. "I hope you haven't killed that. I'll never find a replacement." At least the Simons were gone for the summer. It would be enough time to determine the damage and do some shopping, if necessary.

Comforting pats grew to long strokes as Abby ran her hands over the horse's shoulder and then down his back. When she reached his ribs he stepped away and tossed his head. She kept a steady grip on the lead rope. "Quiet. I need to see if you've reinjured yourself. It won't hurt. I promise." She hoped she was right.

She got farther the second time. "Good boy, Hem." He moved away again, and she started over.

It took four tries before she could run a light hand over his bones and feel the spots that were once jagged pieces. The horse shook beneath her, but he stayed still. "Good boy. I know it's scary to trust someone, but you're a brave man." She pulled an apple from her bag. "You're going to be good as new."

The horse ignored the treat and stared over her shoulder, his nostrils flaring at a new scent. They weren't alone.

Abby's skin tingled as her muscles tightened. If she faced the intruder, she risked chasing Hem again. She tensed and moved her weight to the balls of her feet and whistled for backup. Toby came at a run. The dog was too well trained to bark, but his eyes stayed glued on their observer. Abby kept her focus on her dog.

Instead of growling, he wagged his tail. He'd seen whoever it was before. Convinced it was safe, Abby turned to face their audience.

"Hi, Abby."

Jeff Crandall stood on the Simons' porch, barefooted, in a wrinkled T-shirt and faded jeans. Lounging against a newel post, he was sipping a cup of steaming coffee, holding it with one hand while the other was shoved into the front pocket of his jeans.

Abby swept her gaze from him to the yard. She'd been so intent on the horse, she'd missed the car parked in front of the barn Hank Simon used as a garage. The silver Audi roadster with Illinois plates was the sort of car she only saw in magazines, and it would have easily fit in her horse trailer.

Maggie Harper's reminder echoed through Abby's scrambled brain. Jeff was renting the house for the summer, something about a project related to his job with the FBI.

He descended into the yard and started toward them with an easy gait, frowning slightly like he always did when she caught his eye. She'd seen that look for so many years, from so many people—teachers, doctors, ministers…stepfathers.

Would she ever get used to him appearing without warning? For the past year, since Gray Harper had asked for his help figuring out who was stalking Maggie, Jeff had come and gone with predictable unpredictability, always keeping her on edge.

Abby slipped her hand under Hem's mane and stole his warmth, using it to ground her.

Disheveled in the early morning sun, Jeff looked less like an FBI agent than ever. His salt-and-pepper hair hung to his shoulders, but it stayed swept back out of his face. That was good—otherwise it would've been caught in his well-trimmed mustache and beard like Velcro.

Abby kept herself safe by reading facial cues, and the beard hid Jeff's expressions, which was another cause for worry. Then he'd get close enough she could see the mischievous twinkle in his green eyes, and she'd leave abject fright behind for a frisson of nerves. Like now.

"Hi. Jeff." She stroked Hemingway's proud neck, letting his presence soothe her while she crafted one syllable at a time.

"How have you been?" His smile was now so big his coffee cup couldn't hide it, and her nervousness faded to curiosity. What could be so funny this early in the morning?

Hemingway nudged her hand for the apple he'd ignored earlier, pushing at her baggy shirt. When she shifted, wet denim slapped her calves. Her. She was the early morning comic relief.

"Fine. Thanks. You?" She'd spent her adult life practicing pleasantries, learning both how to make polite conversation and when to stop. Everyone in town had become accustomed to her limits.

Jeff wasn't from here, though. He took the deep breath that always signaled a long conversation, and she panicked. *Not now. It's always more difficult in the morning, like my tongue forgets it shouldn't move. And with Beau's headline—*

Hemingway snorted and tossed his head, slinging the lead until it snapped against the brim of her cap. Abby grabbed for it on reflex, then flinched and dropped her arm, curling it against her as pain lanced from her shoulder to her waist.

"I got in late last night," Jeff said as he caught the rope.

"Go easy," she snapped.

"Of course," he said before he shifted his attention to the horse. "Quiet, boy," he murmured, his words complementing his firm grip on the rope and his careful removal of the halter. "No one's going to hurt you. What's his name?"

Hemingway, because he was so beat up he reminded me of a war-horse. You should have seen him. His coat was dull and brittle, and his ribs were broken. He screamed every time I touched him. It took him weeks to look at me. "Hem."

"Him?"

The horse had abandoned the shrubbery for fescue, munching on the correct side of the fence, and Toby had bounded off in search of feathered quarry. It left her with nothing warm, and her voice faltered in the cool air. "H—. Hem-ingway."

Jeff's bright, teasing smile softened to one she'd never seen before. "Nice name. It fits him."

"I thought so." Abby stared after the animals who were now making their way home. "I should—"

"Coffee?" Jeff asked, lifting his cup.

The smell on the breeze made her mouth water, and her fingers twitched in vain for something to hold. She hadn't had time for a cup this morning, but she shouldn't stay. "We should—"

"It's the least you can do since he woke me."

Embarrassment heated her skin. Not a great start to neighborly relationships. "He did? I'm sorry."

"I made too much anyway," Jeff said. "It takes a while to get accustomed to making it for one person again."

Slinging the halter over his shoulder, Jeff stepped on the lower course of barbed wire and lifted the upper one, making a hole for her to crouch through. "Stay for a minute. Let him calm down."

It would've been rude to leave him standing there holding the fence, and to refuse an offer…and to waste coffee. Abby bent double, slipped through the fence and straightened in time to see Jeff's smile fade.

They walked in silence to the back door, which he held open. He had a habit of doing that, whenever he visited and wherever they were, and it always made her feel both dainty and terrified. She stared at the pristine kitchen floor and then pointedly at her muck-covered boots.

"I'll bring it out," he offered. Tilting his head, he stared down at her, frowning again. "Cream and sugar, right? I think I saw powdered creamer in the pantry. Will that work?"

She nodded and sat in the nearest chair while he went inside. When she saw her shadow stretch across the porch, she snapped straight and whipped the cap from her head. Then she ripped the rubber band from her ponytail, hissing as strands tore free. Blinking the tears from her eyes, she raked her hands through her hair—only to realize they were filthy. Scurrying to Deb's garden sink, Abby scrubbed her nails and then squinted into the window to check her reflection. Jeff poked his head in the window, ruining her view. She jumped backward, and his snicker drifted through the thin pane separating them.

He backed out onto the porch, a coffee cup in both hands, and let the door swing closed behind him. "What was that about?"

I hate things popping out at me. Abby wrapped her fingers around the hot cup he gave her. "Cleaning. Up."

"You look fine. Relax." Stretching his legs in front of him, he sipped his coffee. "What have I missed?"

They found my stepdad's remains in a Virginia well.

"Not. Much." Despite the breeze chilling her skin and the forbidden words building in her throat, she needed to talk to him. He'd remembered how she took her coffee, for pity's sake. "What have. You been. Doing?"

She sounded like a moron. Or like one of those people in the hallway at the nursing home who talked only as much as their oxygen supply would allow.

"I've spent the last few weeks in Tennessee with my family, but they kept me from writing and now I'm behind. Gray arranged for me to rent this place as a retreat."

Abby knew the questions she should ask. *What's your family like? What are you writing? How was your trip?* Those questions had been surrendered when she'd allowed Toby his freedom. "You. Drove?"

He nodded. "It gave me a chance to see places I normally fly over. I made a few notes about spots to visit later."

"Where?" she asked.

"There's this great little lake in northern Arkansas for fishing, and the prettiest resort overlooks it. The Colorado foothills would be a great place to hike in the summer, and I'd love to spend more time in Utah." He'd been talking to the horizon, but now he swiveled to face her with those sparkling eyes. "I never thought parks without grass and trees could be appealing. Have you been there?"

I have three books on the Arches National Park at home. I've always wanted to photograph there and watch the angle of the sun change the colors. She shook her head. "What are you wr-writing?"

His smile made her glad she'd put her effort into the

question. "I'm rewriting a training manual for the basic profiling class I taught last summer," he explained, "and creating a new class on indicative behaviors and past trauma. If I have enough time, I'm going to revise the material I use for teaching evidence techniques." He toyed with the handle of his mug. "It's what I do in Chicago. I lead a group of evidence techs, and I train agents on evidence discovery and recovery."

She knew that. She'd listened to his conversations every time he'd visited Gray and Maggie. And like then, questions she shouldn't ask clamored in her brain. Fingerprints, DNA, Luminol, excavation, tool marks…

Abby stood. "Have to go. Thanks for. Coffee."

He set his empty cup next to her half-full one. "Do you need help?"

Yes, please. Can I tell you a story? The words bubbled on her tongue, but Abby swallowed them as she shook her head and backed toward the steps, grabbing the halter from the porch railing. Rather than climbing the fence, she hurried toward the gate at the far end of the yard.

He caught up with her and held the gate. "I'll walk with you. I'm still stiff from the drive yesterday."

She walked in front of him and onto the well-worn path, forcing herself not to flee.

"The trail's easy to follow. You visit with the Simons a lot?"

"No," she lied. Hank and Deb had taught her almost everything about running a farm, and she'd repaid them with as much kindness as she could risk, but Jeff didn't need to get used to seeing her all the time. "I don't. Visit."

The sun and breeze had evaporated the dew, and now

the long grass tickled her fingers. They caught up with Toby and Hemingway at the river. Hem submitted to the harness and trailed behind Jeff across the river and up the bank to her paddock.

"Why don't I help with your chores?"

Abby arched an eyebrow. Didn't he have work to do?

"Don't look at me like that. I used to help on my grandparents' farm all the time." He stood still, waiting.

He shouldn't be here. She slid her hand under Hemingway's mane. "You have work. Of your own."

"I'll catch up later. I need the exercise, Abby."

She looked down his lean, fit frame. He didn't need the exercise.

"Fine," he sighed. "I like to procrastinate."

Send him away.

He grinned. "And maybe I'll fall flat on my ass and you'll get a laugh. Either way, one of us will have a great Saturday morning."

"Feed or milk?" she asked.

"Feed." He winked. "I hate cows."

After setting Jeff to work feeding the horses, Abby trekked through the yard to the smaller barn.

"Good morning, Jane," she said before she blew on her hands and pulled the short stool next to the patient dairy cow. "Sorry I'm late. What story would you like to hear this morning? How about *Jack and the Beanstalk*? No, probably not a good idea since he trades the cow. *The Princess and the Pea*, then." She wasn't sure why the cow liked fairy tales, but telling one always meant milking went faster.

"Finished with the horses. Now what?" Jeff asked

from the doorway as she was filling a saucer for Eddie, the barn cat.

"Chickens or garden?" she asked.

He looked over his shoulder, as if expecting the vegetables to attack from behind.

"Chickens," he said as he reached for the bag of corn, seed and pellets.

Abby carried the milk pail to the back porch and then walked through the garden, picking what had ripened. She did the same for the greenhouse before turning on the sprinklers and soaker hoses.

Her gaze went to the chicken coop. Jeff stood in the center of the yard, scattering feed and grinning at the birds clucking around him, all while dancing away from her territorial rooster. When he turned his attention toward collecting eggs, she went to the porch and found a clean jar and a basket. Then she scurried into the house. Rummaging through her cupboards and fridge, she gathered supplies before pouring cold milk into the jar.

She walked back to the porch as he came through the door. He'd made his shirttail into a bowl for eggs.

"I always forget to grab a basket," Jeff said, grinning as he placed them on the table one at a time.

"You're dirty," Abby scolded.

"It'll wash."

She rinsed the eggs in the outdoor sink, trying not to think about having someone new here, this close to the back pasture, to the hallway, to the attic.

"Thank you," he said. "Some of my favorite childhood memories involve summers with my grandparents. They've moved to town now, and it's not the same."

Nodding, Abby searched for something with which to dry her hands. If he wasn't here, she'd just wipe them on her jeans, but her jeans were dirty and that wasn't how a hostess was supposed to behave.

Jeff offered his handkerchief. She blinked at the bright white square and shook her head.

"I blow my nose on it, Abby. It can handle a little dirt."

Her fingers hovered over his. "Did you use it today?"

His laughter filled the tiny space. "No."

She plucked it from his hand without touching him. "Thank you." Drying her hands, she folded it and put it in the basket with bread, butter, jam, milk, berries, and a few of the clean eggs. She thrust it between them. "For you. For helping."

"This is too much."

"I didn't make the jam."

"Well then," he snorted. "That makes it even."

She pushed harder. "You haven't. Shopped. Yet."

"You know—"

Toby's bark drowned out his sentence and Abby froze. Without thinking, she looked over his shoulder into the woods, half expecting to see Wallis spring from the shadows like the grim reaper she was.

A honking horn joined the dog's yipping. Recognizing Lex's traditional greeting, Abby jogged to the front yard, Jeff close behind.

The veterinarian leapt from his truck and sprinted to the back of the trailer he was pulling. The trailer he only brought for… Abby broke into a run, reaching him as he slung the door wide, muttering, "Sorry. I know I should've texted, but I couldn't stop with him."

She peered around the door and sucked in a breath. The iron gray horse inside was skin and bones, and *skin* was the proper term. Most of his coat was missing, and his mane and tail were ragged and dull. He groaned as Lex walked him backward.

Abby's chest tightened as the horse emerged into the daylight. Scabbed-over wounds split and oozed across his back and down his sides, and now she realized his mane wasn't ragged—it was singed. Someone had burned him.

The horse stared at her, its dark eyes dull and ancient, until even the weight of his head was too much. He swayed on his feet as he shivered in the breeze.

"Jesus," Jeff muttered. "Why not put him down?"

Anger rose in her throat. All he saw was the mistreatment—the bony angles and scars, the dirt and weariness. Where would she be if people had thought that about her? *Just throw her away. She's not able to care for herself. She'll be a drain on every resource we have.* The emotion must have shown on her face.

"Whoa." He held up his hands. "He's safe. I left my gun at home."

"He needs to be off his feet," Lex ordered.

Abby ran to the stable and into the last vacant stall. Swinging the support from the wall, she hooked the sling into place and tugged the pulley from the ceiling while making sure the floor was clean and dry.

"As if your stable would be dirty," Lex said with a grim smile as he led the horse around the corner. "Grab your medical supplies and get back here, I'm going to need—"

"She's one-armed this morning. I can help," Jeff said as he stepped into the stall.

Abby looked at his flimsy shoes and his T-shirt covered in chicken shit. He'd done enough. "No."

"I need him, Ab," Lex snapped before he faced Jeff. "Lex Waters. Vet."

Jeff reached under the horse, straightening the sling. "Jeff Crandall. Neighbor."

Abby stood there, blinking at Jeff's words. He'd noticed she was hurt. No one but Maggie and Faye ever noticed. She didn't need more people helping her. He had to leave. She didn't *ask* for him to be here. "Jeff, he'll step—"

"He's not moving an awful lot right now," he replied. "I'm fine."

At the sight of a large needle and a thick IV line, Abby backed out of the stall and retreated to the storeroom at the back of the stable. Needles, skin, punctures… She knotted her fingers into a fist to stop their shaking before she gathered every medical supply she could find. Keeping her eyes averted from the men bustling around the horse, she arranged everything within easy reach on the shelf inside the stall, thumping and banging bottles as her anger built. "Who would—"

"I'm filing charges, so don't get your dander up," Lex said.

As they worked to make the poor beast comfortable, he gave her the rundown on injuries and treatment. He ended with his customary warning. "Don't get attached to him, Ab. He's going to have a hard road."

She touched the coarse forelock and imagined what it would feel like healthy, saw the horse grazing in the field next to the others. It was too late, she was already attached. She nodded anyway.

"Yeah, right," Lex said as he checked his watch. "I've got appointments this morning. I'll come back this evening and check on him." He looked past her and smiled. "Nice to meet you, Jeff. Thanks for your help."

"Glad to do it."

Both men walked toward the paddock, leaving Abby inside the stall, finally alone with the horse in her care. She stroked his nose and let him grow accustomed to her. His eyes were clouded by pain and fatigue, but she imagined she saw relief in their depths—as though he realized she would take care of him.

To earn that faith, she checked the dressing around the port and the large-bore IV pumping nutrients, fluid and antibiotics into his system. Her assessment moved to the wounds seeping through ointment. Right now, he was covered in more medication than hair.

Kneeling, she went to work on his hooves. The chains around the sling creaked. "I won't hurt you." She kept her movements slow and steady as she dressed one, slipped a cover over it, and moved to the next. "Good boy. You'll feel better soon."

She was working on the last leg when soft footfalls echoed through the stable. Lifting her eyes to the doorway, she watched the shadow approach—long and straight. Why was Jeff still here? He shouldn't be here.

She returned to work. Behind her, Toby sighed and curled up in the sunshine.

"Hey, Toby." Despite Jeff's warm greeting, the dog didn't move. "Still on the job, huh?"

Proud of her partner, Abby was nonetheless embarrassed the dog was virtually shackled to her all the time. He hadn't signed on for that when he'd whined at her from his cage at the Humane Society.

"Okay, Toby," she whispered.

His tags rattled, and she smiled at the sawdust-covered floor. She could at least let him enjoy a belly rub.

She stood, trying to relax as she stroked the ragged mane and felt the horse's breath rattle through his chest. The big stallion wasn't going to go easily; he'd had plenty of opportunities already.

Jeff explored her small stable, stopping to stare at the nameplate on the gate across the other stall. "George? Which author?" he asked.

"Elizabeth," Abby said, surprised he'd caught on. Of course, he'd met Hemingway first, so it wasn't that hard.

"And your new guy?"

She stared at the scarred and filthy, but still proud, horse. "Butcher."

"Perfect," Jeff said as he peeked into the stall. "And Toby? Who's he named for?"

My dog. My Toby. I've had five of them, counting him. My first one was just a puppy. He was black with a white collar. That's all I remember. I had to leave him with Papa because Wallis didn't like dogs. I hope someone found him and loved him. My second Toby was a birthday gift from Buck. He's buried under his favorite tree not far from my garden. I carried him... She gulped. "Toby."

He frowned again, but this time she wasn't giving in. Cleaning her hands on her jeans, she walked toward the door.

Jeff retrieved his basket from the top of a hay bale, and they emerged into the quiet paddock, blinking in the sunshine. Toby huffed a sigh and trotted after them, his collar jangling. Their shadows stretched across the ground.

Now what did she say? "Thanks."

"It was fun." Jeff lifted a finger to his brow. "See you later, neighbor Abby."

He walked over the hill, disappearing from view and ending the break in her day, taking his smile and smooth voice with him. Rather than being relieved, she was…disappointed.

She'd battled that feeling since he'd waited with them in the emergency room while Maggie Harper had been in surgery. Abby had sat on the edge of the crowd, watching her friends and fighting her fears that her nightmare had come true. Jeff had taken the seat next to her and answered her questions, assuring her that Maggie's attacker was in jail.

But the maniac who'd come after Maggie hadn't been the attacker Abby was expecting. The whole incident had just been a reminder of what *could* happen if Wallis ever came back to Fiddler.

It had also been the first time she hadn't felt alone. Jeff had stayed on the edge of the crowd, too. She'd chalked it up to being in an unfamiliar setting until she'd watched him watch *them*.

He did that a lot—observed, or at least it felt like he did, because he was always looking at *her*. And he was always talking to her. The residents of Fiddler saw her every day, so they knew to expect the silence. Visitors generally avoided her altogether. But Jeff had become a hybrid of resident and visitor.

Rather than making Abby nervous, it made her feel normal. He never finished her sentences, and he didn't treat her like she was stupid. He just stood beside her and talked in his silky drawl and exuded the warmth she'd come to associate with only him.

And just when she got used to seeing him, actually

looked forward to it, he left—went back to his life in Chicago. Just like he was going to do again. Just like he should.

She turned and kicked a piece of gravel into the grass, only to retrieve it and toss it back into the driveway. The wind rustled through the trees, the chickens clucked, and Jane's bell clanged as she munched on the sweet grass near the barn. Farther away, up the hill, Jeff's door squeaked before banging closed.

Toby lifted his head toward the noise, and Abby followed his gaze.

"He's going to be our neighbor, Toby," she whispered. "But not for long. We'll stay on our side of the river and he'll stay off the List." She brushed her hands on her jeans. "You help me remember that, all right?"

At the end of the day full of neighbors, animal rescue, and working on clients' websites, Abby dropped into her favorite, worn chair on her back porch. Evening descended as bird songs melted into the thrum of frogs and the chirping of crickets. A whip-poor-will called for its mate and finally, when all seemed lost, got a far-off reply.

Despite her reluctance this morning, she'd been proud to have Jeff here, proud he could see the things she'd built over the years. Like this porch, which was now weathered and creaky but still solid. It looked like it had been original to the house. Beau would be pleased with her carpentry skills.

The sun turned tangerine, and night air took its first sharp bite. Beau's ghost had stayed with her all day and now it brought a nostalgic mood with it. Abby let her memories free. She'd built all sorts of things on his workbench, standing on a stepstool he'd made just for her. Was it still there, used by whoever now owned the house in Virginia? Or had they chopped it into kindling?

She'd wanted to take it with her, but Wallis had hauled her from bed in the middle of the night and told her to pack. Then they'd gone outside and… Abby slammed the door on that closet in her brain, but other memories, later memories, seeped through.

After Kentucky, after four deaths in six years, they'd headed south to avoid suspicion. South. Mosquitoes, sand, sticky air and fishing.

A great little lake for fishing. Isn't that what Jeff had said this morning? Fishing. She'd been ten when Wallis had married Ron, and Abby's new stepfather had taught her how to fish in the lake adjoining his property. They'd spent hours on the bank under the shade of large trees. He'd told her wild stories until her cheeks had ached from giggling.

She picked up her food and held the door for Toby, following him into the house. He curled onto his pillow with a sigh while she put everything in the refrigerator. The half-empty jar of jam reminded her that she'd have to trade eggs to Jean Miles for more.

In her office, Abby sent an email to Jean, checked her inbox, and made a list of new projects. Somewhere between appointments, chores, clients, therapy sessions, and photography jobs, she needed to design the calendar for the animal therapy program and finish her donations and the preparations for the Humane Society fundraiser.

It would leave her with time for a hike later in the week and maybe a few hours to work with the shelter dogs. She needed to see which could be trained as service dogs for use in the veterans' outreach program.

Her gaze roamed across the calendar. Almost every hour was filled in for the week. It was going to be another row of long, busy days. Her eyes drooped as she rubbed her aching feet. What it would be like to have a day off, a lighter load?

No. It did her no good to think about it. She hadn't chosen that life. She had a job only she could do.

Abandoning her calendar, she climbed into the attic and pulled the box from the corner. Keeping her back to the wall and one eye on the crawl space door, she searched for the correct notebook and the right page. Once she'd found it, she carried the records downstairs.

Over the years, it had become more difficult to write the letters. Forensic developments dictated changes in her process and, after mailing so many, she'd begun to believe no one would ever listen.

Until Beau.

She had to keep trying.

One part of her process had remained simple. The actual text never changed.

The first, to the Franklin County, Alabama, sheriff was completed from memory. *Ron Thomas's body is buried in The Dismals, under the large tree next to Temple Cave.*

The second, to the Tunica, Mississippi, postmaster was brief. *Please post this for mailing.*

Wallis had met Ron, Abby's third stepfather, in Tunica, Mississippi, so his letter needed to be postmarked there. She kept hoping someone would put it together. Ron gambled in Tunica, the letter came from Tunica—maybe they'd read the letter and search harder. Maybe they'd find Wallis and Ron's marriage license at the county records office.

Last summer, the printer repairman had given Abby a lesson on humidity and protecting her paper. He'd also given her a large sealed bag to keep it dry. Now it protected paper from fibers, hair, and trace evidence. She laid out her latex gloves, hairnet, distilled water, and a sponge. No DNA, no fingerprints, no minerals from the water. The letter to the sheriff was addressed and stamped, then slid inside the envelope to the postmaster, which was also addressed and stamped.

Finished, she sealed the package in a sandwich bag. She'd drive to Baxter early in the morning and mail it.

Someone would pay attention.

Chapter Two

Jeff woke and stared at the unfamiliar ceiling, disoriented by the silence and by the large bed with the squishy mattress, mountains of pillows, and colorful quilt. Idaho. He was in Idaho.

He struggled from his down-filled nest and walked into the bathroom, the floorboards squeaking with every step until he reached cool tile and bright lights. Thankfully the shower was easy to operate, the water was hot, and the spray was just this side of painful. By the time he was done, dripping a puddle onto the bath mat, he was awake enough to rummage through his toiletry kit for a comb and scissors. He looked in the mirror and a droopy-eyed reflection stared back. He wasn't awake enough to *use* the scissors.

Coffee. He needed coffee.

After mopping the water from the floor and hanging his towels to dry, he put on sweats and a T-shirt and padded down the hall. The house was a warren of hallways and small rooms that kept the interior dark and cool. It reminded him of his grandparents' home, where he'd played hide-and-seek with his sisters.

The pictures in the hallway caught his attention. The Simons looked like a nice family. A large, multigenerational clan who loved to spend time together. Much like his own. *That one's Christmas. Maybe the grandchild's first one, given her lack of hair. Is it a she? Hard to tell in those clothes. Oh yeah. See that one. Birthday cake. Candle. She had curls now, and icing was smeared through them. First birthday. Granddaughter's first birthday. Not that long ago, given the mother's haircut and clothing.*

Jeff shook his head. They weren't crime scene photos, but he was treating them like a case. Profiling his hosts.

"Get a grip, Crandall." Jeff's admonition echoed through the empty house. He abandoned the photos and went into the kitchen.

The house was in mid-remodel and the kitchen had been updated and expanded so that it, the dining room, and the den were one large space. A wide expanse of windows provided a view of the valley. Jeff admired it while his coffee brewed.

Past the wide porch with Cape Cod blue newel posts was a yard like the one he'd played in growing up in Tennessee. The house was surrounded by foundation plants, which gave way to the lawn, which stopped at the shrubs and the fence line, and beyond that was a sea of fescue.

The tall grass glinted in the pink sunrise and rippled in the early morning breeze, sweeping over the hill toward the river. His gaze followed the waves to Abby's ranch, dark except for the security light bathing the front yard in a sterile glow. Another light shone over the stable doorway.

A truck bounced up her driveway, the lights swinging drunkenly. The garage door opened. She was out early for a Sunday. He checked the time. Out late, maybe? There were plenty of times he'd dragged home at dawn after a wild night.

How did that jive with the woman he'd found standing at his fence yesterday? Much like then, he poured his coffee and stared at the mangled shrub, half wishing to find her there with her long ponytail, tight jeans, and the baggy shirt he could see down when she bent over.

He opened the refrigerator and pulled out the basket she'd given him yesterday. Cutting a thick slice of bread, he spread it with butter and jam before taking a healthy bite. Crumbs fell into the sink as he relished the smooth, rich butter and the sweet bite of the strawberries. Did someone who cooked like this, who worried about his groceries, party until daybreak?

She was a study in contrasts, quiet but able to speak volumes with one glance. Shy but funny. Hardworking but worried about getting his handkerchief dirty. Stubborn but softhearted. Imprisoned by bars made out of one-syllable words.

She managed to escape using Toby, or a horse, a cow, or even a cup of coffee. Without them, she floundered.

Could he help her? Should he try? All he ever dealt with were criminals and killers. It might be a nice challenge to work on something that didn't involve a body.

Jackass. He would have enough challenges doing what he was paid to do, finishing a job and getting home and back to his caseload. If he wasn't going to write, he could have stayed in Tennessee where his mother had cooked his favorite food and his aunt had brought him ready-made dates. Small-town girls with their own rules, ones that included marriage and babies and family dinners.

Despite her silence, Abby was just like them. And he avoided girls like that. Too many headaches.

Turning his back on the view, he strode down the hall and past the steep stairs that led to the second floor. The formal living room was almost obsessive in its neatness. The white carpet didn't even have footprints in the pile. However, the formal dining room had been repurposed for a study. Judging by the color scheme and the photos, it was Hank Simon's domain. And for a while, it would be Jeff's.

He sat in the wooden office chair, kicked his feet onto the desk, and looked at shelves full of books that didn't belong to him, trophy fish he hadn't caught, and plaid curtains.

After starting his laptop, he lifted his binder full of notes from the nearest chair and found where he'd left off yesterday afternoon. The cursor blinked.

"Dammit all to hell." He put both feet on the floor and typed the two words that had been lurking in the back of his mind since he'd left Abby yesterday. *Selective mutism.*

Capable of speech but doesn't speak to certain people or in certain situations. *Bingo.* He flipped to a clean page in his notebook, picked up a pencil, and listed Abby's symptoms.

OCD. Everything was in order. You could eat off the floor in her stable. And yesterday had been the first time he'd seen her rumpled and out of sorts. *Check.*

Intelligent. Her eyes crackled with it. *Check.*

It could be tied to shyness, but that didn't sound right. She was quiet around people she'd known for years. She was more at ease with him, most of the time.

Another possibility was social anxiety. Fear of rejection didn't ring true. People in Fiddler loved her. But fear of not being good enough? That could be. Her best friend Maggie could buy the state of Idaho, and she did spend most of her time with the Junior League crowd.

He read further. She could have been treated as a child. Why hadn't her parents insisted? Where were her parents, anyway?

Without treatment, her silence would have become self-fulfilling. The longer she'd gone without speaking, the more difficult it had become. He looked at all the forms of the disorder, and only two fit—symbiotic and reactive.

Symbiotic mutism indicated a controlling parent, usually a mother. Since Abby's mother wasn't around, that wasn't a relationship he could observe. The other indication was a child manipulating their environment and the people in it. Many people used silence strategically, benefitting from the bribes others gave to make them talk, garnering attention. But that didn't make sense. Abby went out of her way to stay invisible and independent.

However, silence was also an effective method of pushing people away, of isolating yourself. Living out here would reinforce that behavior. She was so busy farming she only had time for friends on her terms.

Reactive mutism made him nauseous. He imagined Abby as a child, with pigtails and serious eyes. Surely no one had hurt her. Maggie would know. Gray would have said something.

He stood and paced the room, stopped and stared out the window. The drive was lined with evergreen trees. Blooming dogwoods sparkled in the sunshine.

His mother loved dogwoods. He should call her before she started to worry.

He refilled his coffee and walked outside, inhaling deeply as he slid his earpiece into place. He calculated the time difference and how long it *should* have taken him to get here. If he'd driven exactly the speed limit and only for eight-hour days. Yesterday would have been too early. This morning was possible.

He dialed his mother's number.

"Hi, Mama."

"Jeff! Are you all right?"

"I'm fine, don't worry. I just wanted to let you know I got here."

"Just now? You made good time."

"Yes, ma'am." He cringed at the lie, but if he told her the truth she'd worry.

"You must've left Billings early. Did you get enough—"

"Don't worry," he repeated. "How's everything there?"

His mother launched into the rapid-fire gossip delivery she'd developed over years of rushing details between demands on his time. Jeff listened the way he'd learned to do, plucking facts from the stream like fish. Her upcoming retirement, his grandparents, his sisters, their husbands, his nephew. "Jason cries every time Clay leaves the house. He wants to go with his daddy. You were like that. Remember?"

"Yes." Sometimes he wondered how much he actually remembered and how much he recalled from her repeated stories. And the stories grew more frequent in the spring. God knew his own thoughts grew repetitive and wistful as the anniversary of his father's death approached. "How's Cass?"

"Wild as a March hare. I'm not sure what to do with

her. None of the rest of you came home from college like that."

Ruth had met Clayton in college; Janice, the bookworm, had gone straight from undergrad to grad school; and he'd gone right from college to grad school to Quantico. All three of the older Crandall siblings had been eager to make their old man proud of them, even if he'd never see it. As the only one of them without memories of their father, Cass had always been her own person.

"I'll talk to her."

"She won't listen, but you can try. Thank you, dear. Are you sure you'll be okay? Have you seen your house?"

"I'm standing in the yard now, waiting to unpack. It's a huge farmhouse, with a great big yard and dogwoods lining the drive. I won't even need the upstairs. It's quiet, and there's a porch where I can write and get some fresh air when I need it."

"Won't you get lonely?"

He sighed. If he were eighty and she were a hundred, he'd still be her little boy. "Gray and Maggie are, like, ten minutes away. And I have a neighbor within range if I fall and can't get up."

The squeal and slap of Abby's screen door drew his gaze to her yard. She was already halfway to the stable, down to check on Butcher, no doubt. Toby stayed at her heels. Was her shoulder better today? Did she need help with the horse, or with chores? Should he check?

You aren't here to be a farmhand. Not even a neighbor, really.

But he was a neighbor, and she needed help. Whether she'd ask for it or not.

"Son, are you conducting surveillance on your neighbor?"

"What?" He looked over his shoulder at his mother's question, half expecting to see her behind him.

"I've asked you the same question twice without an answer." Her laughter didn't help his embarrassment.

"No. I've just realized the time. I need to get ready for church."

"Church? Thomas Jefferson! Did you say the c word?"

"I'm not a heathen. I think I can go to church without lightning striking. Besides, it's sort of a thing here. Church, Sunday lunch, and sleepy afternoons."

"Before you go," she said, her glee vanishing, "the district attorney called. Kyle Davis is up for parole. They want me to go to the hearing at the end of the week."

"Do you want me to come home and go with you?"

"No. I've been thinking." Her voice thinned and shrank. "It's been over twenty years."

After years of looking out for her, he recognized the reluctant tone. What was wrong with her? There was no time limit on what Davis and his friends had taken from them. "You have to go. Take Ruthie with you." He'd text his sister and make sure she had it covered. Kyle Davis should never see the light of day.

"He didn't even pull the trigger, Jeff. He was just behind the wheel."

"He was *there*," he spat.

"I didn't mean to upset you. Don't worry, we'll take care of it. Go to church, and be sure and tell Gray hello. Love you."

Jeff exhaled a shaky breath. "Love you, too, Mama. Talk to you next week."

He was still shaky and tense an hour later as he stood at the back of the little Methodist Church. Chatter bounced and echoed from the slate floor and stucco walls, and sunlight was fractured by leaded windows. The kaleidoscope of color and noise made him dizzy.

Glen Roberts, the chief of police, met him at the door. "It's nice to see you again." He lowered his voice. "There's nothing wrong, is there?"

One of my father's murderers is up for parole and my mother wants to let him have it just because he didn't pull the trigger. Jeff looked over the man's shoulder and saw several concerned stares. A few of the conversations ended so they could hear his answer. His students didn't pay this much attention to what he said.

The last time he'd been in Fiddler he'd testified against the woman who had killed a beloved resident and had almost killed Maggie Harper. He might not know all the congregants' names, but they knew him and they were worried his scowl meant more trouble.

Loosening his jaw, he took a deep breath and faked a smile. "I'm on sabbatical to re-write classroom material," he said, speaking loud enough to be heard by the back rows. He knew word would travel fast. "Everything is fine. Maybe we could do some fishing while I'm out here."

"I'd like that, thanks." Glen clapped him on the shoulder before he moved away.

The group at the front of the church greeted him like the old friend he was becoming. He slid into Gray and Maggie Harper's pew, taking the seat in the middle and his place in the conversations swirling around him.

Late arrivals claimed his attention. Abby stumbled to a stop and stared down at him before perching on the edge of the pew, nodding even though her mouth was set in a grim line.

"Hello, neighbor." Jeff didn't bother hiding his smile. It was perverse, but he enjoyed that look on her face—the color in her cheeks, the snap and crackle in her eyes—like she wanted to tell him off but the words were too big for her to say. It's what kept him opening doors for her, what had kept him at the farm too long yesterday, and part of what kept him here, sitting in her usual spot. The other reason was something he'd never admit aloud.

Abby dressed for church and the change was always incredible. Today was no exception. Velvet-brown eyes and high cheekbones were framed by hair that reminded him of coffee, chocolate, and chestnuts. Bright blue earrings winked between strands, and her long, simple dress matched them.

"Move in, Ab," Lex teased from behind her. As she slid closer, her fingers worried the edge of the printed order of worship. Jeff got the first hint of her perfume.

A younger man reached over the pew and grabbed Jeff's hand, pumping like he was priming a well. "Carter Garrett. I work with Abby."

Jeff muttered a greeting while he focused on the smell. Gardenias, with just enough fruity notes to banish thoughts of his grandmother and prom corsages. Abby looked past him to Maggie, her irritated expression melting into a small smile, her eyes twinkling. Her wave was really just a lift of her hand, but the thin bracelet around her wrist sparkled in the light.

The choir filled the loft, and she faced forward, forcing him to do the same.

He knew from past visits that she'd follow along in the hymnal, but not sing. She'd read the liturgy, but not respond. She'd shake his hand and smile when they passed the peace to their neighbors. It was all a prelude to the prayer.

His mother would have scolded him for not paying attention, but watching Abby pray fascinated him. Her knuckles whitened in her lap and her shoulders tensed with the effort, as if she could will God to grant her silent request.

And she was especially silent today. Someone had stolen all her words before she'd arrived. Where had she gone this morning? Who had she seen? The two best suspects were the men who had arrived with her.

Carter Garrett poked a finger in Abby's back until she swatted him away without looking. That was a sibling sort of torment. Jeff knew from experience.

On Abby's other side, Lex sat at an angle, his body acting as a barrier to isolate him on the end of the pew. There didn't seem to be an attraction there, either.

What the hell? Sorry, God. But why do I care who's attracted to her?

"Amen," Reverend Ferguson intoned.

Rather than get caught staring, Jeff pulled his head to his chest, slammed his eyes closed, and counted to three before he opened them again.

After the service, Abby walked away without a backward glance, moving through the crowd and nodding as she shook hands. Everyone greeted her, but no one talked to her.

"How's the house?"

"Huh?" Jeff looked over his shoulder. Gray Harper was at his elbow, and Jeff realized how much he'd missed his wingman.

"House?" Gray repeated, his grin widening.

"Should be fine. Can I still have it until October?"

Jeff turned, determined to wipe the smile from his friend's face.

"Will you need it that long?" Gray stared pointedly at Abby. "Or longer?"

"Screw you," Jeff mumbled. "You could've told me she lived next door."

"What's a wingman for?" Gray asked. "Are you coming for lunch?"

"Yeah. It's kinda fun watching you be all domesticated."

"Screw you," Gray said as he walked off.

Jeff walked down the aisle alone, recalling the facts he'd filed away and putting them to familiar faces. The smiles he got were rewarding. He enjoyed the residents of Fiddler, and he liked it that they all liked him.

Nearly all of them, anyway. Abby was at the back of the church, ignoring him as she knelt beside elderly Faye Coleman. The older woman's tasteful dress was accessorized by a brace on one leg, but she sat straight in her wheelchair and her smile never wavered. As he approached, her green eyes snapped and sparkled. She reached a weathered hand for his, and caught him in a strong, hot grip.

"Welcome back, Jeff. Maggie says you're here for the summer?"

"Yes, ma'am." He looked up as an orderly approached, the white name tag and nursing home's logo prominent on his blue jacket. Faye followed his stare.

"Back to the cell," she grumbled as she patted Abby's hand. "Come see me and bring some berries."

As Faye was escorted out of the church, Jeff offered his hand for Abby to use as she stood.

Her nails were short and well shaped, and her fingers were long and softer than he'd expected. How did she keep them that way? What would they feel like—?

Get it together. You're in church. Maybe his mother had been right to worry about lightning strikes.

He snatched his hand away and started toward the door, unable to resist shortening his stride so Abby could fall in beside him. At Bailey's, his favorite Chicago bar, all it took was a glass of wine and a smile to get a woman to chat like her tongue was loose at both ends. And the girls at home in Knoxville had asked him so many questions it had felt like a job interview. Abby just walked while he floundered for something to say.

"Are you going to lunch at Maggie and Gray's?" He didn't look at her. She did better if people didn't stare.

"Yes."

Once outside, she was swallowed by one group while he was captured by another on his way to the parking lot. A cloudless blue sky lorded over the soft green of budding trees. Despite the bite of the breeze, Jeff lowered the convertible's top to let in the fresh air and sunshine.

His friends put him in the middle of the lunch convoy to make sure he didn't get lost, as though he hadn't navigated across the country on his own or driven to Gray and Maggie's without help numerous times. In the car in front of him, Gray had one arm slung around Maggie's shoulders. At a flat spot in the road, he planted a kiss on her hair.

The sweet image made a spot in Jeff's brain itch.

The same spot had chased him from Chicago, where his best friends were newlyweds, and again from Tennessee, where one of his sisters was newly married and another was a new mother. And now, here he was, staring at another newly minted couple. It was great…for them. That life wasn't for everyone.

It wasn't for him. No wife would put up with midnight research sessions when he couldn't sleep, piles of trash when a rabbit trail of an idea didn't pan out, or books scattered across the furniture and photos of crime scenes taped to the walls. No woman would tolerate broken plans and erratic schedules. He didn't have to worry about coming home to a fight or, worse, a too-quiet house like so many of his fellow agents had experienced.

The itchy spot was a reminder of that, not jealousy.

Let it itch.

Chapter Three

After lunch, they sat in the fresh air, filling the Harpers' outdoor dining space with baseball commentary and laughter.

Jeff settled back and listened to the conversations around him. Every time he was here, the crowd grew larger. Couples were now joined by single friends and relatives. Old friends welcomed new ones. Good-natured ribbing mixed with stories from the workweek, bets on the game, and discussions of upcoming projects. Everyone took turns holding the youngest member of their group: Toni Marx, Gray and Maggie's toddler goddaughter.

Eventually everyone else drifted away, heading to their own homes, leaving only him and Abby.

She was sitting with Maggie. The Harpers' cat, Felix, was in her lap, and she had *that* look on her face. Like she wanted to say something but had reconsidered. Before he realized it, Jeff was on his feet and walking toward her.

Gray fell into step beside him. At least he remembered one thing about being a good wingman.

They sat, and the women shifted. Maggie curled into

Gray's side. Abby leaned away, grasping the opposite arm of the sofa and tucking her feet under her.

"What are you talking about?" Jeff asked, angling so that he faced her.

"*The Story of Edgar Sawtelle*." Maggie sighed. "We read it for book club, and it was awful. It was Hamlet with dogs."

"Exactly." Abby's smile widened. "And the. Dogs. Lived."

"But everyone else died." Maggie shook her head. "What was the point of it? Because I couldn't get through the pages of details. And it didn't end happily."

"It did for the dogs," Abby said with a sly smile.

"You are horrible," Maggie laughed. "You know I prefer happy endings."

"Those are. Relative."

As Abby talked, her ministrations to Felix changed. Instead of stroking ears to tail, she now limited her attention to the cat's head, rubbing and scratching its chin and throat, and then rubbing the top of its head before taking an ear between her thumb and finger. The animal was in heaven.

Jeff had never before been jealous of a cat.

"What do you mean by *relative*?" he asked.

Abby blinked at him and tilted her head, much like Toby would've. "What does. Happy. Mean? Who. Decides?" She kept his gaze. "Edgar avenged his father. The dogs were free of cages. Of any kind. Isn't that happy?"

"Ab, Edgar died," Maggie pressed.

"But he did what he'd set out to do." Abby stood her ground, even though she blushed to her hairline. "He died. Satisfied."

Damn. He was shocked by the depth of her answer, and embarrassed that he was shocked. He of all people should know that small town didn't mean small minds.

They were all too quiet, suddenly. Jeff recognized the bleak look in Gray's eyes, the echo of it in Maggie's. They were stuck in the past, reliving their losses. He felt the same shadow on his shoulder, snagging his clothes as it tried to drag him backward in time.

Abby's gaze darted to each of them, her lips moving as if she were trying to gobble the words from the air. Regret shadowed her eyes. He didn't want her to feel guilty for expressing herself. For talking to him.

He cleared his throat. "Maggie, has Gray ever confessed about the geisha?"

Her smile banished the gloom settling over the group. "No. Were you there?"

Jeff nodded, waggling his eyebrows. "We were in Japan for a conference—"

"Crandall," Gray warned. "Quantico."

Maggie smacked him on the shoulder. "That is so not fair."

Laughing, Jeff tossed his hair out of his eyes and watched them play. There. He'd done his good deed for the day.

"What. Happened at. Quantico?" Abby asked.

Jeff blinked, hearing Gray's choked laughter as the blush heated his ears. "Umm…nothing. Nothing at all." He picked up his plate. "Why don't I help carry in dishes?"

When he'd finished busing tables, Jeff spotted the cat curled into a chair. Wherever she was, Abby was alone.

He found her in the hallway, staring at a photograph. As he approached, she shifted on her feet, leaning away from him. He mimicked her posture, invading her space just to tease her.

The candid photo had been shot from a distance. Gray and Maggie were in shadows, her adjusting his tie, his hands on her waist. It was a simple act, but the love they each harbored, their uncertainty, had been captured with one click.

“When was this taken?” Jeff asked.

“At Nate’s wedding,” she murmured.

“I’ve worried about them, you know?” He smiled into her frowning face. “I’ve seen them both bloody on the floor. I get to worry. They’ve been through a lot, and you hope they’re happy, that they don’t have any regrets.” He looked back at the photo. “This puts my mind at ease.”

Few people would have paid close enough attention to catch this moment. The photographer had a good eye. Jeff read the neat calligraphy in the corner of the mat. *A. Quinn.*

“You took it?”

She nodded. “It’s when *I* stopped worrying if he made her happy.”

He blinked at her, watching her profile. The hesitation had vanished from her speech. She’d shifted on her feet again, closer to him this time, almost close enough to touch.

“Wait until you see her landscapes,” Maggie said from the top of the hall. Abby stepped away, but her scent lingered. “She’s got a booth at the art auction they’re doing at the Humane Society on Saturday. It’s not too late to buy a ticket.”

Art? The town had three thousand people in it and most of them worked in a quarry. How much *art* could there be? But he'd buy a ticket just to see more of her work. He refocused on Abby, hoping to return to their conversational bubble. "Can I buy one from you?"

She nodded and scurried up the hall, away from him. Apparently she was going to sell him one now.

"Thank you. For lunch," she said as she passed the kitchen. "Time to go."

"Me, too," Jeff said.

"You kids have fun," Gray drawled.

Jeff flipped his friend the bird as he held the door for Abby. He'd started doing it because it was the polite thing to do. He'd kept doing it because he loved teasing her. But beyond that, Abby Quinn had a world-class behind.

Catching up with her at the truck, he reached for the door handle just as she did. Her fingers curved over his. Gasping, she snatched her hand away.

"Do I scare you?" he asked, genuinely worried both by her expression and by the tingling in his fingers. Teasing her was one thing, frightening her would be quite another. And grown men did *not* tingle.

"Nervous," she breathed. "You're always. Behind me."

"I like the view," he drawled as he opened her door. She was frozen in place, her eyes wide and her features slack. He winked. "How much for the ticket?"

Though she wouldn't look at him as she rifled through her bag, he thought he saw the corner of her smile. She handed him a ticket. "Ten dollars."

After he made his payment and slid the ticket into his wallet, he helped her into the truck. Her fingers shook in his.

"Thanks."

"Sure." Despite wanting to stay close to her, he stepped away. "See you over the fence, neighbor."

He jogged to his car and slammed the door, but by the time he looked up she was already at the highway. He raced down the lane, heedless of the gravel pinging against the paint, and then onto the pavement, risking a ticket to catch up to her.

When she hit the brakes and whipped onto a dirt and gravel country road, he followed, staying clear of the billowing dust. The race was on. His laughter bubbled free.

Once home, he changed clothes, grabbed his laptop, his notes, and his iPod and went outside to the wide porch and the patio table. He put his earbuds in, cranked the volume on his favorite playlist, and perched his glasses on his nose.

Movement over the top of his computer caught his attention, and he lost focus on his outline. An Abby-sized dot was in her front yard, weeding her flower beds. He squinted to get a better look, and then caught himself and yanked his attention back to his notes.

She walked to the barn. Jeff gritted his teeth and refocused, but she was in there for a long time. He pulled his earbuds free and strained to hear a distress call. Instead, Abby emerged atop her palomino, George, and trotted off. Toby ranged the field in front of her. Jeff changed chairs, put his back to the valley, and scowled at his lack of progress.

When yips from the returning party caught his attention, he looked over his shoulder in time to see Abby in the paddock. Maybe she'd go in now and he could focus. But she didn't. Her laughter floated up the hill, making him look again as she disappeared around the side of the stable.

Golden sunlight heated the porch, birds sang, and the wind ruffled his notes. Why waste a beautiful afternoon working?

Sunday was for fishing.

Jeff searched the office and the garage, but found nothing. He was about to give up when he saw the cabinet on the porch. Inside hung neat rows of rods, reels, tackle, nets and waders. He shouldn't need waders. He could fish from the shore. He plucked a fly rod from its resting place and chose a hand-tied fly from the shelf. In a fit of wishful thinking, he grabbed a net and a stringer, too. Tugging a borrowed cap low over his sunglasses, he loped across the yard and through the gate.

As he neared the bottom of the valley, the waterborne breeze chilled his skin. The birds got louder and unseen animals scrabbled and crashed through the brush. Under all the noises was the constant whisper of water rushing unhindered. Further downstream was the faint argument waged between river and stone, upstream it skipped over branches and exposed roots.

Jeff came around the last corner and stopped, shocked at the sight. Across the stream, Abby stood with her rod raised in midcast. Her eyes were wide under the brim of her cap. Toby lounged under a tree, too tired from his patrol to chase squirrels and rabbits.

"You fish?" He was still for another minute as he took in the familiar gear. "You *fly*-fish?"

There it was again—the hesitation, the parted lips, and then the gulp. She nodded. He quieted on his shore, reading the water—where it rushed or pooled, where his fly would go. Balancing the rod with one hand, he slid the line through the fingers of the other, then cast. Soon the only sounds were the snaps of casts and the lures dropping on the water. The rush of the current was interrupted by the thrash and splash of a snared fish, and it wasn't his catch. Jeff turned in time to see Abby smile as she snagged a keeper.

His first fish was larger.

As sunset encroached, she hooked her second fish. He watched the path of the water and cast again—he wasn't going to lose to a girl. Behind him, he heard the rustle of gear and the scratch of paws in the grass.

He kept his attention on his line. "Good night."

When there wasn't further movement, he turned to see her crouched with her camera at the ready. An engine purred at the top of her hill, and Toby scrambled to the crest to greet the new arrival. She stayed put.

"You have company, I think."

"Lex." Abby explained as she lifted her camera. Jeff followed the direction of the lens and caught the moment when the sunset made the water burn. The trees darkened from green to umber.

"Wow," he whispered, "that is something."

When he turned back, she was halfway up the hill, almost invisible in the shadowy twilight.

"Jeff?" The chain stringer rattled. "Would you. Like."

He waited but kept his focus on the fly even though he couldn't see where it landed.

"Tocomefordinner?" The whispered words bumped together. He wished he could see her face.

"I would. Thank you." He snapped his line back and eased his grip on the rod. "I'll bring my fish. What time?"

"Seven." The word shook.

"Can I bring anything else?"

"No." The answer came from farther away.

Jeff grabbed his net and retrieved the stringer. He had thirty minutes to clean his fish and get ready for dinner.

Half an hour later, he coasted to a stop at the end of the gravel drive. A yellow square of light flooded the paddock from the stable. A companion glow created a carpet runner down the front steps.

Before he could knock, Abby peeked around the wooden door and beckoned him in. The screen door opened with a swish, and he let it bounce closed against the fingers he put behind him.

Classical cello drifted through the living room, and lamplight banished darkness from the corners. Neutral paint coated the walls, complementing the clean lines of furniture crowded with wildly patterned pillows. Brightly colored hooked rugs dotted the hardwood floors. Toby was curled on a dog bed in front of a low fire.

Abby had returned to the kitchen, working at the island. She'd changed clothes again, this time into a sleeveless T-shirt emblazoned with "Boys are Better in Books" and a long skirt. Her toes peeked from under the hem.

Lex was setting a table surrounded by upholstered chairs. He moved around the space with the accustomed ease of a frequent visitor. Maybe Jeff had read them wrong. He refused to be disappointed by that.

With a smile, Abby extended her hand for the fish. Jeff surrendered it and watched as she added it to the griddle with the other two. She had tea instead of beer. Had he ever seen her with alcohol?

He snooped through her cabinets until he located heavy, unadorned drinking glasses. Opening the freezer for ice, he found everything stored in neatly labeled, vacuum-sealed bags. No meat, except for fish. Pescatarian. In the fridge, the store-bought items stood out in stark contrast to the homegrown ones. The tea was in a gallon jar with a spigot. His grandmother had a similar one she'd used to brew tea in the sun. However, his grandmother had never put fruit and cinnamon sticks in her tea. He sipped it. Or honey.

He carried the drinks to the table as she ferried trout and roasted vegetables from the stove. Lex brought the salad.

They took their seats, and the handcrafted plate in front of him was beautiful without food on it. It only got better looking as he added dinner. Instead of digging in, he savored every flavor of the farm-grown vegetables and fish that had been swimming only an hour earlier.

"Lex, I don't remember you from the fall, but I didn't meet everyone. Were you here?" He hoped the question didn't sound like an interrogation.

The other man shook his head. "I got here in January. Fred Saunders sold me his practice when he retired. What brought you to Fiddler?"

He glanced at Abby, somehow surprised she hadn't filled Lex in. "Work."

"What do you do?"

"Professor." Jeff didn't say *FBI* to strangers. It made people nervous. "No family?"

"Just my parents in Missouri." Lex gripped his fork. "My wife was set to come out here, but she changed her mind."

"About moving?"

"About everything." His mouth twisted into a wry smile. "What about you?"

"My family's in Tennessee."

"Where?" Abby asked.

Her interest pleased him more than it should. "Outside of Knoxville. I grew up there, and my sisters still live there. Ruth is an attorney, Janice teaches history, and Cass just graduated from college with a degree in Art, of all things."

"What's wrong. With art?" she asked.

"Nothing," he said, grinning around a bite of bread. "It's just hard to make a living at it. Isn't it?"

She nodded. "What about your parents?"

He swallowed and reached for his tea. "My mom teaches English at a community college. My father died when I was a teenager. He was murdered in the line of duty."

"He was a cop?" Lex asked.

"Highway Patrol. He'd pulled over a speeder, only to find it was a group of bank robbers on the run from their last heist. He didn't even have time to draw his weapon."

Abby put her hand over his and squeezed his fingers, and he looked up into her sad eyes. She didn't say anything trite, didn't offer any platitudes. She'd lost someone, too. He'd bet his next paycheck on it. He squeezed back.

She left the table and returned with dessert—mixed berry shortcake and fresh cream. The delicious flavors distracted him from the sad conversation.

Sighing, with a goofy smile on his face, Lex carried his plate to the sink. Abby stood, and Jeff followed suit. Dinner was over.

"I'm going to go out and check on our boy," Lex said as he gave the cook a one-armed hug. "Thanks, Ab."

Jeff carried his plate to the sink and started the dishwater. "I'll help you clean. It'll go faster."

She shook her head and gripped a dishtowel in her fist. "We shouldn't distract you."

"Please let me help you." He wasn't sure if he meant dishes or something else. But he watched as she hesitated. No further words came. *Baby steps, Crandall.*

"It's the least I can do in exchange for dinner."

Her skin tinted pink. Averting her eyes, she nodded.

He washed; she rinsed and dried. Side by side, elbow to elbow, with the thumping dishes accompanying the classical melodies. They worked in silence, but somehow it didn't bother him. Maybe it was the music. Maybe it was her humming along. And it did go faster. Dammit.

"Dinner was delicious. Thank you."

She walked him to the door. "I'm glad you liked it."

What did he do now? Hug her? Shake her hand? Nod? He opted for the same one-armed hug Lex had given her, pushing the door open with his other hand. "Good night."

She shook in his grasp. Did she shake with Lex, too? But she nodded and smiled, and waved as he walked down the steps to his car. Motion lights lit his path, and Lex waved from the stables. Jeff climbed behind the wheel. Abby was still in the door, the light casting her in silhouette as he backed away.

He was home reading an article on positive reinforcement of a curiosity, the laptop a bright square in the dark, when his phone rang.

"Has Harper recruited you to move to Hickville yet?" The question was a laughing greeting.

Jeff pushed away from his desk. "No way in hell. What's up, boss?"

If he concentrated, he could hear Bob Myers's office chair squeak. It was Sunday, late by Chicago time, and Bob was still in his office at the FBI. It was one of the perks of being the Special Agent in Charge. Or the director of the lab. Those hours were one thing Jeff didn't miss about Chicago.

"How are you coming along?"

"I'm right on schedule," Jeff lied. "Why?"

"We need your help on a case. The Bureau of Land Management in New Mexico found a body in the Sandia Mountains. They ID'd him as Ray Finch, a local who's been missing for fifteen years."

Jeff stayed quiet. Bob wouldn't sidetrack him for one body.

"And the police chief in Lewisville, Virginia, found another one in a remote well. They're assuming it's a guy by the name of Beau Archer, since he once owned the property. He's been missing since eighty-seven."

Jeff grabbed a new notebook and plucked the pencil from behind his ear. "How did they find them?"

Bob hesitated, and Jeff recognized the hitch of excitement. "In Virginia, the local PD received a note with Archer's name and the exact details of the dump site."

Adrenaline coursed through his body. He knew it was wrong. These men were lost to someone. Still, the case sounded like fun. "But no note for Finch?"

"Nope."

"Are you sure they're related? There are a lot of years between them."

"Two men dumped in remote locations, each with a hole at the base of his skull."

"Gunshots?"

"Hammer. Our guys—*your* guys—think it was a roofing hammer."

"Shit." Jeff leaned back in his chair and stared into the darkness. "Send me what you have and who to contact. I'll see what I can do."

"Keep Quantico happy," Bob cautioned, "and check your email. I sent everything earlier this afternoon."

Wallis Riker scowled as she read *The Lewisville Clarion* headline blaring across her screen. It was already two days old. She and Hale had been out of town on a cruise. He'd won enough to keep her in the boutiques and had enjoyed seeing her model everything. They'd had a good time. She deserved a good time.

Then she'd come home and seen the alert in her email.

Why had anyone gone to that well, and how much had they found? After almost thirty years, it was surely just bones. Maybe not all of them, either. All sorts of critters—creatures—prowled those woods. She'd covered her tracks, filed all the right reports, said all the right things. If they found her, if they came with questions, she'd know what to say.

How frightening to have him die so close to home! He must have sacrificed himself to save us. He loved us so much. My poor daughter would have been heartbroken. I'm glad she's not alive to hear the news.

Chapter Four

The rain washed blood from Ron's pale, bloodless skin and plastered his hair to his head. Sightless eyes stared into the flashlight's glare from the depths of the hole. His macabre grimace widened as he reached for her. And he was crying, whimpering. She couldn't get away. He pursued her as if he was trying to emerge, or pull her back down with him.

Abby woke, already upright, kicking the sheets tangled around her feet, pushing Toby away. He was fighting to get to her, just like that other dog so many years ago. Overcoming her nightmare, she pried her hands from his fur and dropped her head to her knees. The dog snuggled closer, and she let his soft head help calm her racing heart.

"Sorry, boy," she rasped.

Once her breaths didn't echo through the room, she stood and made herself walk down the hall and around each corner in the dark until her knees no longer wobbled. She'd fought fear for years, and she wouldn't lose the battle just because of a nightmare.

Toby's nails clicked a reassuring agreement. When they reached the porch, his sharp gaze searched the dark, seeing things Abby could only hear. Small creatures, non-lethal. She was safe.

"Go play. You earned it."

He stopped on the top step and smiled over his shoulder before he bolted for the tree line.

Early morning was her favorite time. Buck had always moved around early, and he'd welcomed her tagging along. A man of few words, her last stepfather had never pushed Abby to talk. Instead, he'd explained things without waiting on her to ask.

A yellow square shined atop the hill, a beacon in the dark that drew her attention to the Simons' house. Was Jeff a night owl or did he leave the kitchen light on all the time? In the quiet, the squeal of a rusty spring answered her question. Jeff was awake.

Before, that noise had been her cue to lift her hand in a wide wave, knowing Hank waved back as if they were on adjoining lots instead of acres apart. Her hand was halfway up before she dropped it back to the arm of her chair. She'd managed to keep away from Jeff for most of the week.

Please let me help you.

She'd been ready to pull every skeleton from her closet. He'd been talking about doing the dishes.

Sunday had been enjoyable. His soft drawl had added a lilt to the routine liturgy, and he'd interceded at lunch when she'd stuck her foot in her mouth. However, instead of contradicting her, of making light of her opinions, he'd changed the subject.

And after learning about his father's death, she knew why. Loss had touched each of them in different ways, all of it violent. She, Jeff, Maggie and Gray were their own unique survivors' club, even though they had no idea of her membership qualifications.

Maybe she didn't qualify. She was a living victim, an escaped accomplice. A keeper of secrets and the teller of lies.

And why the hell had she invited a *profiler* to dinner? Or Lex, for that matter? She shouldn't have people here, just like she shouldn't go to Sunday lunch at Maggie's, and she shouldn't do…anything she'd been doing. It was too risky for them. She ought to go back to the way things were when she'd spent all her time and energy supporting herself.

But it was too late. When Maggie had finished college and returned to Fiddler, dragging Charlene and Tiffany in her wake, it had signaled the rebirth of parties, lunches and fun. There hadn't been a way to say no; they'd just ignored her. And, God forgive her, she liked being included.

Abby dropped her head to the back of her chair. She didn't deserve to be happy, but she wasn't going to disappoint the people who'd sacrificed their time to help her, and she wasn't going to turn her back on any more innocents—be they humans or animals. If her job was to keep everyone safe, she was going to succeed at it.

Her nerves prickled under her skin. If she wasn't going to sleep, she should work. Inside. She'd come out here again when the sun came up. She whistled Toby to her and went back into the house, arming the security system before she locked the door.

Once the sun rose, she left her computer and the programming code that had given her a headache. After rushing through her chores, she went to the stables.

When she entered Butcher's stall, he raised his head and the sling creaked. His eyes seemed brighter. Lex kept telling her not to get her hopes up, but she couldn't help it. The horse was getting better. He was.

"Good morning, old man," she whispered as she stroked his nose. "Let's get you cleaned up."

The vet had his way of doing things, and she had hers. He'd thought her homeopathic approach was nuts at first, and she couldn't tell him she'd learned from jockeys and trainers across the country at the racetracks where Wallis had hunted her prey. Instead she'd shown him with dogs first, since she'd had more experience with them, and then with George. They'd come to an agreement on combining their approaches. So far it had worked well.

She hung a new IV bag full of fluids, vitamins and minerals and then washed Butcher down with water, witch hazel and vinegar. While his coat dried, she knelt at his feet and put a hand on his leg.

"How about it?"

He picked his foot up without her needing to lift. He *was* better. She conditioned his hooves one by one, checking for areas Lex should examine and finding few worries.

By now, the horse's spindly, brittle coat was dry. Time to rub. Sighing, Abby stretched to loosen her muscles. Her left ribs pulled, and the scar in her hairline twinged in sympathy. Wallis's final blows had left indelible reminders of her deadly promises, as if Abby's memories weren't enough.

Pushing that dark night away, she stripped down to her tank top and jeans, and went to work, rubbing mineral oil into Butcher's coat and skin, taking care around his wounds, feeling for muscles that relaxed and spots that made him flinch. She finished by dabbing antibiotic ointment on the worst burns and aloe vera on the others. Every day she used more aloe and less medication.

Ears, mane, teeth, tail. By the time she was finished, she was exhausted. But then Butcher pushed his nose into her hand, and her weariness faded. Tears blurred her vision.

"You're welcome, fella. I'm sorry someone hurt you, but you're safe now. You're going to be fine."

Wiping her eyes, she opened his doors so he could get some sunlight and air. "One day your view will change. I promise."

She cleaned stalls and cared for her tack and equipment. Then, sure everything was finished, she went to her darkroom.

Panic set in until her eyes adjusted. This wasn't a closet. It wasn't punishment. It was her sanctuary. Her hands shook as she poured solution and fumbled with film. She couldn't develop yet. She'd make a mistake.

Instead, she looked at the photos hanging overhead. Melody Solomon and Kyle Monroe smiled at her from their engagement photos. She'd done Melody's senior pictures, and then the prom photos for their first date. They were a cute couple. Working their wedding would be fun. They'd have cute children, too. They'd be good parents.

Abby unclipped the photos and put them in the file, then put the file on top of the cabinet. Every drawer was an alphabetized, photographic history of life in Fiddler—of everyone around her moving forward, of all their happy moments. Some of them they'd posed for, some of them they never knew she took.

Sure she was calm enough to work, she opened the film canister, unrolled the negatives and lost herself in the photos she'd taken over the past week. Hiking shots transitioned to Lex working in the stables, deep in concentration, then to Toby standing guard at the front door, then to fishing. Then to Jeff.

The black-and-white portrait came to life in the developer. His hair, gray at the temples, his salt-and-pepper beard. His mirrored sunglasses, and his broad white smile as he snagged his fish. Not posed, not wary on the witness stand, not exhausted and worried in the emergency room. He was *himself.*

After hanging it to dry, she walked to the counter and plucked a new file folder from the shelf and her pink Sharpie from the tin can full of grease pencils and ink pens.

Crandall.

Cursing the nightmare that had woken her too early and kept her running all day, Abby stood in her booth at the art auction and surveyed her handiwork. She'd raided her Humane Society office back by the kennels for a chair and a lamp, and the table was fashioned from spare boxes and covered with a half-finished quilt top. Toby's bed lay in the corner, and she had a book ready in case no one stopped. Her photographs were arranged neatly across all three walls.

Her shoulder ached and sweat trickled down her neck, but she was ready. She was also surrounded by people and noise as they prepared their displays. Everyone had questions, and they were running her volunteers ragged.

Abby stepped into the breach, loading a cart with all

the surge protectors, extension cords, duct tape, pens and nails she could find and roaming the aisles, helping without having to talk, grateful when the noise subsided from panic to organized work.

When she got back to her cubicle, Maggie Harper and Tiffany Marx were waiting on her.

"We've come to help," Tiffany said as she surveyed the space. The tiny blonde was a dynamo, whether she was organizing preschool or helping with Sunday lunch.

"I'm. Already. Finished."

"Tell her what you did, Tiff," Maggie sighed.

"Don't act like that," Tiffany scolded. "This is a good thing." She faced Abby, her blue eyes wide but her smile trembling. "I have a friend who owns a gallery in Boise. She's seen the picture you gave me and Michael, the one we have over the fireplace, and she keeps asking about it. So I invited her tonight."

A gallery. I'd love to have my work in a gallery. Abby looked at the framed photos, imagining them under lights against clean walls like the ones she'd seen during college field trips.

And she saw the hand-cut mats, the frames she'd designed from found objects based on each subject, the temporary pegboard walls, her ragged tablecloth, and secondhand, worn furniture. Her shirt was sticking to her, and her hair was hanging in her eyes. *A gallery owner? Here?*

"I didn't tell you because I wanted it to be a surprise, and," Tiffany continued, blushing, "I thought you'd say no."

"Luckily, she told me," Charlene Anderson drawled as she joined them. Impeccably dressed as always, her four-inch heels adding to her already impressive height, she had a garment bag dangling from her fingers and a shoebox under her arm. "Come on."

The three of them pushed her into her office.

"Put this on," Charlene ordered.

"I smell," Abby objected. Charlene's clothes were always too nice to sweat in.

"Then go wash up in the bathroom and change in there. There's a bra in the bottom of the bag, and I bought you new underwear, too."

Abby blinked at the three women who'd appointed themselves as her non-wicked stepsisters. Maggie shooed her out the door. "Go. I'll do your hair. Char will do your makeup. Hurry."

In the bathroom, Abby slid the bag from the hanger. The clothes were far too fancy for a silent auction that was basically an arts-and-crafts swap meet, but they were perfect for a gallery show. After peeling off her dirty clothes and washing her hands, she slipped into new underwear and the strapless bra that was necessary because the black blouse hung low on her shoulders. The cream skirt was long with a deep slit up one leg and a black lace panel. She wobbled on the spike heels of the strappy black sandals.

She could do this. She'd been more dressed up for weddings. She'd be on a level surface, not in the paddock. And she wouldn't have to move. Much.

The three women smiled when she rejoined them. Maggie pushed her into a chair. "We'll leave your hair loose. I brought dry shampoo."

Charlene winked at her. "You look like a million bucks. Don't worry."

They were done in minutes, and Tiffany added the final touch with a necklace and a cocktail ring. Abby walked across the room a few times so they could check the outfit and the shoes, and then they all went out together.

No one noticed the change, although Toby might have stared too long. *Great. I get dressed to the teeth, and the only person who notices is my dog.*

"Where are the guys?" Tiffany asked as shoppers began to mill through the booths. "They can't spend all night outside."

"Calm down, Smurfette," Nate Mathis, Maggie's twin brother, drawled as he walked up with his wife, Faith, under his arm. "They're right behind us." He winked at Abby. "The girls have been at it, I see."

Blushing, she nodded.

"What's the occasion?"

"Tracy Hoover is coming to see her," Tiffany said.

Abby's knees trembled at the name. The Hoover Gallery was one of the best in the Northwest. It had a national reputation for showcasing western art and landscapes by top-tier artists. Oh God. She couldn't do this. That woman would take one look and laugh all the way back to Boise.

"She's here," Michael Marx whispered as he hurried to the group. "Right behind me. She stopped to look at a quilt."

Kevin Anderson and Gray Harper ambled up behind him. Kevin whistled softly. "Char picked well. You look great, Abby."

Gray squeezed her shoulder. "You can do this. No doubt in my mind."

Abby looked around the small space at everyone's smiles. This is why she'd added them all to her List of People to Protect From Wallis. For so long it had only been Maggie. Then it had grown to Nate and the rest of the Mathis family. When Wallis left, Abby had added every family in Fiddler who had taught her to take care of herself. As she'd needed less physical help, she'd begun to list the people who befriended her or encouraged her. She'd added Lex after his first visit to the farm.

A cloud of expensive perfume warned them of Tracy's approach. Abby took a deep breath and smiled at the blonde in casual clothes that had probably cost more than her first truck. "Hello. I'm Abby Quinn."

"Tracy Hoover." Her smile was wide, and her handshake was firm. "I have to tell you how impressed I am. There are some beautiful pieces displayed, and everyone has been quick to tell me you're responsible for organizing the entire event."

Organizing was a stretch. She'd gone to meetings with blueprints and diagrams and then set up an email loop to simplify communication. Her volunteer coordinator had stepped in when email wasn't enough. *You can do this, Abby. Don't sound like a moron.* She fought the words clattering against her teeth. "I'm glad you're en-joying. Yourself."

Oh God, this is awful.

Tracy walked into the booth, lifting her glasses as she examined each photo. "These are beautiful, Abby. Tell me about them."

She couldn't, not without Toby, and he would get dog hair all over Charlene's skirt.

Jeff walked around the corner, his eyes widening, as Tracy smiled over her shoulder. "Where was this taken?" she asked.

In my front pasture. I can't take pictures in the back. No one goes back there. My stepfather is buried…

Jeff put his hand on her waist. "That's the tree between our houses, isn't it Abby?"

"Y-yes." She soaked in the warmth surrounding her, his smell. "It's always the first to get the sun in the morning when the fog burns off."

"And this one?" Tracy asked.

Abby walked further, flailing for Jeff's hand. He grasped her fingers and then linked them together. "That's in the foothills just north of town, right off the hiking trail."

"This tree is interesting." Tracy pointed at another. "I always like to see the structure left when the leaves fall."

Abby nodded. "And the weather patterns the dead ones differently."

"It does." Tracy stopped at a photo in the corner. "This one is beautiful."

"I took it last weekend," Abby explained as she looked at the golden fishing line snapping across the umber trees. "Fishing."

"Wow," Jeff whispered in her ear, heating and tickling her skin. "I never saw you take it."

Tracy turned back to her and extended a card. "Call me and we'll set up an appointment. If your entire portfolio is like this, you'll pack my gallery."

"Thank you, Tracy. I hope you'll stay and shop."

"Wouldn't dream of leaving until I see if I win my bids. And the food looks amazing," she said as she left the booth, still smiling. "We'll talk soon."

Charlene held her finger to her lips as she tiptoed forward and looked down the aisle. Gray craned his neck to look over the top of the neighboring walls.

"She's gone."

Those two words broke the dam.

"I knew she'd love them," Tiffany squealed, bouncing as much as her high heels would allow. "I knew it!"

And then Abby was smothered in hugs. Despite the attention, she still noticed when Jeff released her.

"Badger," Gray said as he took Maggie's hand. "I want you to see something."

"You, too, Nate," Faith said as she peeled away. "Come on."

Michael pulled Tiffany one way. Kevin tugged Charlene the other. She and Jeff were alone, on opposite sides of the small space.

"Well," he drawled. "That was subtle."

She rolled her eyes, laughing. It had been years since she'd laughed. "Thank. You."

"Glad to help." He looked around her makeshift store space. "They belong in a gallery. Do you—"

"There you are."

At the words, Abby turned to see Celia Hughes approaching, arm in arm with an unfamiliar man.

"Abby, this is Doctor Tom Beckett from the VA. I asked him to come down for the benefit and see the facility. Is this a good time for a tour and to talk about your plans for the veterans' outreach?"

Tom Beckett had nice eyes. That was a good sign for animal therapy. But his hands were cold. She looked over her shoulder and reached for Jeff. "May I introduce Jeff Crandall? He's visiting this summer."

And he wants to help me, but I can't let him because it would be too dangerous.

Jeff squeezed her fingers and smiled.

"Jeff," she said. "Celia is the social worker at the hospital. We do animal th-therapy."

I started therapy to help me talk about the right *things. Toby reminds me who, what, will get hurt if I tell—*

"Doctor Beckett," she continued, looking into Jeff's green eyes for courage, "wants us to start animal therapy with his patients."

He tucked her hand into his elbow. "Lead the way to the kennels, Abby."

As she looked into his warm smile and twinkling eyes, her heart hammered as her stomach plummeted. Despite her best intentions, Jeff's name went on her List.

He kept her close throughout the tour, stepping in to ask questions when talking became too much for her. And then they shopped together. It got easier to see people staring. Poor Abby Quinn is all dressed up and has a date.

But she was in borrowed clothes, and he wasn't a date. He was a security blanket.

When they returned to her booth, every photo had a Sold note stuck in the corner.

"You have an amazing eye and an incredible talent," Jeff said from behind her.

Her skin heated. Sure everyone complimented her on her photos, but they *knew* her. He didn't. And she wasn't the only talented person in Fiddler. She waved her hand behind her, indicating the stalls they'd worked their way through. "So do they."

"Not like this."

No. He didn't get to belittle the people who'd helped her, who'd taught her to sew or fix her roof. The people who'd hired her to help in storefronts or given her credit when her clients hadn't paid. She swept her hair over her shoulder, hissing as the necklace pulled the shorter strands tight.

"Stop. Let me."

She didn't need his help. He *shouldn't* help her.

"Don't rip it or you'll hurt yourself. Move your hands."

Their fingers bumped together, and she recoiled as if he'd burned her. "I'm tougher than I look," she grumbled.

Tough, sure. That's why his breath on her skin made her fingers twitch. That's why so many people close to her had—

"You *look* beautiful." He rolled the chain and teased her hair free, his fingers tormenting her until her toes curled.

"Charlene brought me clothes so I could impress Tracy," she whispered. "Thank you."

"For saving your hair or for the compliment?" he teased.

"Both."

He rested his hand on the curve of her shoulder, keeping her still. It wasn't necessary. She couldn't move even if she wanted.

"Why are you pissed at me?" he asked.

She glanced over her shoulder. He was close enough she could see the sea-green flecks in his irises. "Is their work less pretty because it's useful?" She nodded down the row, indicating spaces full of pottery, home goods, quilts, jewelry, and clothing. "My work just hangs there."

"That isn't true." Jeff pointed to the one of the

gnarled tree. "I could stare at that one for hours. It looks like driftwood, but we're too far inland. How did its branches get twisted and stripped of their bark? Or this one, where you've caught the light as it spills through the fissure and shows off the layers in the stone. What caused it to break? How long had it been whole? And how long did you sit, waiting for the right moment?"

He saw too much. He was the most unmanageable person on her List. She made herself step away from him.

He pursued her, slipping back into place behind her. "But you're right. I don't tend to think of functional things as art. Art is in museums or galleries, on the walls."

Abby shook her head. "Everything is designed by someone."

"True," he agreed. "But not everything makes you *feel* something."

He pointed to the misty tree. "I've watched that same tree emerge from the fog when I'm up early. It makes me peaceful, sort of like a meditation before I start writing. And the fishing one. You caught the exact moment I felt at home here. I hate that someone else bought it."

"They didn't," she whispered. "It's a gift for you."

Now he turned her to face him. "You don't have to do that. I already bought one." He nodded toward the tree they shared.

"I want to give it to you. For letting me hold your hand."

"Yeah," he snorted. "That was really hard to do."

"Please accept it."

"If you'll let me take you to dinner."

She couldn't do that. Why couldn't he just be happy with the picture? "You don't have to—"

"I want to," he smiled as he mimicked her earlier plea.

No. No. Thank you. I can't. You shouldn't be seen with me. It's dangerous.

He leaned closer, his hair tickling her nose. "I'll wear a flea collar if it'll make you more comfortable."

He made her feel lighter than she'd felt in years. Would it be so bad? He was leaving anyway. Maybe Wallis would never find out.

"Yes. Thank you. I'd love to go."

I have a date. Abby repeated it all the way home, each time feeling her smile widen. *I have a date with Jeff. Not a security blanket, not a come-with-me-so-I-can-talk date, not an appointment. A* date *date. Like a normal girl.*

It wasn't until she was home, with her borrowed clothes hung carefully in the closet, showering behind a clear curtain and keeping one eye on the doorway, that the reality hit her.

She wasn't a normal girl. He asked too many questions, and his warmth and his smile made her forget she shouldn't answer. *Can you imagine the conversation over dessert? I moved here twenty-three years ago when my mother married her sixth husband in eight years. Where is she? Gone. No, I don't miss her. She's a monster. Where's my last stepdad? Grab that flashlight and I'll show you.*

Maybe she could suggest they eat here. She could have dinner ready when he came to get her. She could pack a picnic, and they could hike. No, they couldn't hike at night. Dinner here would be best.

She sighed. It would be best if he stayed the hell away from her. She should just pin a note to her door quarantining herself. *I have a crazy mother. Go away.*

But he wouldn't. He'd ask, and she'd tell him. And then there wouldn't be any more friends, no more home, no more gallery show, or warm hands to hold.

And didn't that make her sound like a selfish bitch? She couldn't be selfish. Not with him.

Chapter Five

"We have a third set of remains," Bob said.

"Shit," Jeff grumbled as he sat his coffee cup on the desk and dropped into Hank's leather chair. "Where?"

"Alabama. Someplace called The Dismals." Bob snorted. "That's fitting."

"Note?"

"Yeah. Tying it to a man who's been missing since 1990. Ron Thomas. I'm emailing you what I have. The local PD will forward copies of their reports." Bob's chair squeaked. "How's your manual coming, Professor?"

"Fine." Jeff looked at his stack of finished work. It really was fine. He was caught up, maybe even ahead of schedule. "I might be done sooner than I thought."

"You don't sound so happy about that."

"Just tired," Jeff lied. "I went for a hike yesterday."

"Hike? Dude, are we paying you to go for long walks in the woods?"

"Screw you." Jeff laughed. "Did you miss the 'ahead of schedule' part of this conversation? I'll be back to punching a clock before you can miss me more than you already do."

"Well, the girls miss you," Bob teased. "They've

taken to hanging out in the lab bugging your techs for information. Trish Phillips almost quit over it. She couldn't get any work done for answering your phone."

"Tell her to forward my calls."

"I did. To Amanda. She's making up all sorts of nonsense just for laughs. Right now, everyone thinks you're skiing in the Alps."

His front doorbell rang, making Jeff jump in his chair. No one ever came to the door. He looked out the window. All he could see was a horse halfway up his front steps. The bell rang again.

"Is that the doorbell?" Bob asked. "People are stopping by? Shit. They *are* going to end up keeping you. What is with that place?"

"Relax," Jeff replied. "Apparently it's Mr. Ed." The bell rang again. Twice this time. "I'll look over your information and get back to you. Bye."

He stepped into the hallway, fumbled with the locks, and opened the door. Abby was standing there, her arm raised to knock. Hemingway was looking over her shoulder.

"Good morning," he said. "Why are you bringing me a horse?"

"I'm. Training. Him." She blinked. "Glasses?"

He frowned, trying to follow. "Huh?"

She touched the bridge of her nose. "You wear. Glasses?"

"When I work, yeah."

"I won't. Keep you. About our. Date."

As she shifted from foot to foot, she switched the lead rope from hand to hand, and Hemingway's head weaved every time she fidgeted. Toby sat at her feet. She was trying to cancel, and she'd brought reinforcements.

Shoving his glasses into his pocket, he stepped out onto the porch. "Why are you training him? Isn't he broken to ride?"

"Broken," she whispered, turning her attention to Hem and sweeping her hand along the arch of his neck in long, slow strokes. "Isn't that an. Awful. Word?"

With the horse stretched across his steps, Jeff could match the scars to anatomical structure. Someone had fractured Hemingway's ribs and gouged his flanks.

"It is," he agreed. "So you're teaching him what?"

"To trust that I won't hurt him."

Something moved under her shirt, contorting and squirming like a B movie alien. A pitiful mewl was muffled by the denim. "Do you have a *kitten* under your clothes?"

As if on cue, the animal wiggled its tiny head out between Abby's buttons. At the same time, Hemingway yanked his head and stepped backward, rocking her on her heels. Jeff grabbed her hips to keep her from toppling off the porch.

She was the weirdest woman he'd ever met, and it should have been funny. But, with her in his arms, all he could think of was unbuttoning her shirt and carrying her in the house. Spending the afternoon closeted away with her while Hem ate Mrs. Simon's shrubs. It's all he'd been able to think about since Saturday when she'd grabbed his hand.

He saw the same desperation in her eyes now. He could let her off the hook, or he could push her out of her comfort zone. Not much, just enough.

Inching closer, he flicked the shirt button that was halfway undone anyway, and slid his hand under the tiny kitten. Abby's breathing hitched, but she stayed put as his fingertips grazed her stomach. Sweet Jesus, he hadn't even kissed her yet. He could remedy that, right now.

Kitten in hand, he was halfway to her mouth when another wet nose poked his wrist. Two kittens.

"Are there more in there? Do I need to search you?" *Please say yes.*

"Just the two. Someone dumped them last night. I found them by the road on my way up here." She backed up and rearranged her clothes.

Left with no other recourse, Jeff stared at the two silver tabby cats he held in one hand. Their eyes were barely open. "Do people dump animals on you a lot?"

"They know I'll take care of them or take them to the shelter."

"How do you take care of them? I mean, horses, dogs, chickens, cows, cats. Isn't it expensive?"

"I have a job," she said as she struggled to keep Hemingway still.

He was embarrassed to realize he'd never asked her *anything* about her life. He plucked the lead rope from her hand. "Stay for coffee."

"I can't. I don't—"

"Visit. Yeah, I know." He shoved the kittens at her and tramped down the stairs leading the horse with one hand and remembering not to pull. When they reached the gate, he slipped the halter off. Hemingway nudged his hand in thanks and walked into the field, content to graze.

"What are you doing?" Abby snapped as she rushed behind him.

"He's had enough training for the day, and I'm not

going to stand there and watch him break your neck. Come in the house."

She held up the kittens, one in either hand. "They aren't litter trained."

"I have dozens of boxes," he countered as he turned her toward the house. He kept pushing her, gently but consistently, until she was curled into an oversized chair in his living room, next to a box full of kittens and holding a cup of coffee. He sat opposite her.

"You work for Carter, right? He said something about it that first Sunday."

She frowned. "Carter works for me."

It was his turn to be confused. "Doing what?"

"Web design and. Programming. He's my. Salesman."

"And you're the designer," he concluded. "Where did you learn to do that?"

"College." She shook her head. "See? This is why we shouldn't date."

"What does that mean?"

"You think I'm a moron," she said. "I have dual degrees in Computer Science and Fine Art, and more software certifications than you can count. And I finished my MFA last year." She frowned again. "What?"

"I should've pissed you off months ago," he teased, hoping she wouldn't clam up on him and trying to alleviate his embarrassment. "And I never said you were a moron."

"You didn't have to *say* it."

He had to give her that one. He'd seen her in work boots, listened to her stammer, and assumed she struggled to make ends meet. "I'm sorry. But I wish you'd said something."

"Why?" She unfolded her legs and put her feet on the

floor. “You don’t say, ‘Hi, I’m Jeff Crandall and I’m a forensic scientist with a Masters in Criminalistics and a PhD in Criminology and I work for the FBI.’”

“How did you know all that?” *How did you say it without tripping over the words?*

“You said it when you testified at the trial.”

Once. Almost a year ago. And she’d just recited it like she was reading his CV.

“Ed Geary was on the jury, and until you said PhD he’d been more interested in trying to clean the spot in his tie.” She sat her coffee cup on the table. “I can’t—”

No. She wasn’t going to back out. He wasn’t going to let her. “How’s Butcher coming along?”

“Better. Jeff. I can’t—”

He liked the way she said his name. “Let me walk you home.”

She gathered her kittens and shook her head. “I can get there.”

“Hem will pull you into the river and those kittens will claw out your intestines trying to stay dry.” He held the door for her.

“Jeff,” she wheedled.

“Abby.” He kept the door open and glared at her from under his brows.

Shaking her head, she stalked past him, down the steps and across the yard. He caught up with her and opened the gate, just in time to see her blush. When Hem crossed the river on his own, Abby scowled over her shoulder.

Jeff hopped across on the stones, intent on reaching the paddock. By the time he got there, Abby was already in the stable, settling the kittens into a straw bed. He carried Hem's halter to the back and hung it with the rest of her tack. Then he stood next to her and waited.

"I'll be right there with you," he finally said. "Just some little roadside place. Nothing fancy. You have to eat anyway."

"Fine. Will you go home now?"

"Yep." He dropped his forehead to her hair, still warm from the sunshine. "See you for dinner on Friday. At seven."

Jeff left the stable and strode up the hill and home to his office. After flopping into his chair, he stared at the ceiling. He'd never worked this hard for a date.

She never stopped surprising him, never stopped pushing him, and it was exhausting. But her smile, her voice, seeing her think, made it worth it.

Knowing she'd paid such close attention to him was a bonus.

Facing his computer, he typed in the one word he'd kept at the front of his mind since she'd recited his credentials and told the jury story without hesitating once. *Hyperthymesia*: exceptional, uncontrollable, autobiographical memory. Every day spent dealing with the present and reliving the past. If she had it, no wonder she'd isolated herself and stayed quiet. It must be maddening. And there wasn't a treatment. She probably worked herself into exhaustion just to get some rest.

Did she fumble with words because it always a struggle to remember what was *now* and what was *then*? Is that why she didn't want to go to dinner? He remembered her laugh from Saturday, the look on her face when she'd said yes.

She wanted to go, but she was afraid. Life was too short to live it in fear.

When his email alert dinged, he opened Bob's message and downloaded the attached files. The pictures tiling across the screen dragged him back to reality. Dirty bones piled into a muddy hole, roots reaching to reclaim their grisly trophies, worms and bugs burrowing new escape routes. Something the poor bastard in the hole never had the chance to search for.

Ron Thomas had been another big guy—long femurs indicated at least six feet tall. Thick bones, healthy. His killer, or killers, would have to be mountainous. Just like the others.

He'd lived in a small town. Atwood, Alabama. Ray Finch had lived in a one-horse town in New Mexico. Beau Archer had lived miles from the nearest town, somewhere in Virginia. Like Finch, Ron Thomas hadn't been found near his home.

Ron didn't have a family. No parents living. No siblings, no aunts, uncles, or cousins. Just like the others. They'd each been married at their deaths. Ron had been married to Liz. Beau had been married to Betty. Ray had been married to Allie. The authorities had lost track of their wives. Ron and Beau had each had a stepdaughter but no one remembered much about them. Ray had been childless.

As his printer whirred, Jeff stared at the growing pile of paper. It was no way to think. He needed to spread out. He needed supplies.

After programming directions to the nearest Office Depot into his phone, he slid behind the wheel and settled in for the hour-long drive. Honestly, how could anyone live this far from major necessities? What had brought Abby here? Had she grown up here, like the Mathises?

Not everyone had, and Fiddler wasn't someplace you just stumbled onto. Charlene Anderson, Tiffany Marx and Gray Harper had relocated for friendship. Even he had come because Gray had needed his help. Only someone you liked would get you to somewhere this remote.

Jeff almost missed a turn and pulled over at the first wide spot in the shoulder. Rifling through his bag, he grabbed a pen and an envelope. Then, shading his eyes to stare at his phone, he searched for information on the burial sites and scribbled notes.

The Dismals and Sandia had websites. They were beautiful, but remote. No one would follow a stranger there. Beau had been found on his property. He wouldn't have invited a stranger home.

They had been killed by people they trusted.

Putting his notes away, he continued to think until the Hastings city limits forced him to consider traffic and navigation. When he reached Office Depot, he loped across the parking lot and grabbed a cart, eager to get home.

He went straight for paper—printer paper, glossy sheets for photographs, legal pads, file folders and sticky notes—then to Sharpies, pens and highlighters, relaxing into the familiarity of color coding. He added all his favorite tools and a roll of butcher paper to protect the office wall. An oversized United States wall map and a box of colored pins finished the pile.

Satisfied, he took his place in the cashier line and waited. And waited. The woman behind him spent the time on her cell phone. Behind her, another shopper sighed. Further back, a child whined and demanded candy.

The front door swished open and the breeze carried the scent of gardenias. He looked over each shoulder, expecting to see Abby behind him. She wasn't, but there was a scented candle on the impulse-buy shelf. *When the hell did candles become office supplies?*

His fingers twitched and flexed at the memory of holding her, of feeling her hips flex in an effort to keep her balance. Her muscles were hard and lean. But her skin? God, it had been difficult to tell which was softer, her or that damned kitten. Her voice was soft, too, even when she was upset with him. And he liked her upset with him. Her hesitation disappeared, and she said exactly what she thought when she was irritated.

Smart, spunky, soft, sexy as hell…

The door opened again, dragging the fragrance on the breeze once more, and his mouth watered. He shifted his feet as his body followed his thoughts and his jeans became uncomfortable. He pushed the cart forward. This was the longest line he'd ever seen. Why couldn't they get another cashier to help? And what was the guy in front of him buying, anyway? Box cutters, zip ties, trash bags, bleach, rubber gloves…

Photos from past cases and excerpts from his recently edited chapters pinged through Jeff's brain. All the guy was missing was rope, but he wouldn't need rope if his victim was already dead.

The suspect pushed his cart to the door, and Jeff shifted to the balls of his feet. Should he leave his cart and follow the guy? Maybe call the Hastings PD? There were a lot of women in here; office-supply shopping seemed to always be relegated to women. What if the asshole with the box cutters was waiting in the parking lot when one of these shoppers came out with her hands full?

"Sir? The line's moved. It's your turn."

"Thanks." Jeff turned to see a pretty blonde with a hand basket full of sticky notes and legal pads. She was in tight pants, an even tighter jacket, and three-inch heels. Her sunglasses were propped on her head. She looked good enough to eat and slow enough to catch. Yeah, he'd make a call from the parking lot. He could follow the guy and keep the dispatcher on the phone.

One last look would get him a physical description. Tall, strawberry blond, trimmed beard, shaggy hair, jeans, work boots, and a uniform. A janitorial uniform. Shit. He was profiling a *janitor*. Heat bloomed under Jeff's skin as he pushed his cart forward.

He took twice as long at the register as the janitor/axe murderer, and managed to hold it together until he reached his car. Yanking open the trunk, he tossed the bags inside.

Damn it. He spent too much time with dead people and criminals. It wasn't bad enough he had photos of them taped to the walls at home and on the pages of his teaching materials, now he was seeing them in line at the store.

He threw the map on top of the bags and pushed the trunk lid down, but it wouldn't close. He snatched it from the pile and watched the pedestrians and drivers in the parking lot. What would it be like to go through life *not* knowing what lurked in the shadows? To never know how easily, how quickly, life could change?

"You sure had a load of things to buy. Are you setting up an office?"

The woman with all the sticky notes was standing beside the neighboring sports car, her driver's door open, and leaning against the roof. Her hair gleamed under the sunlight, almost as bright as her smile.

"I'm setting up shop in Fiddler for a few weeks," Jeff muttered as he pitched the map into his backseat. *I'm supposed to be on friggin' sabbatical. I'm supposed to be writing.*

"I go through there on my way home. I work for my dad in Baxter. They keep promising a supply store over there, but it never happens. Baxter's too small. There's a great truck stop on the way to Fiddler. They do breakfast all day. Maybe we could stop for coffee?"

Seriously? She was hitting on him? She'd known him five minutes and he already knew what she drove, her route home and where she'd stop. A truck stop. A place with a motel attached. Where nameless, random drivers passed through on their way to unknown locations. With large sleeping compartments behind the seats. He could be anyone. Take her anywhere.

Did no one have common sense anymore?

"Thanks, but I've got a long day ahead of me." Jeff smiled as he slid behind the wheel. "You be careful driving home, ma'am."

Jeff drove away, watching in the rearview mirror to make sure the blonde danger magnet got into her car and pulled out of her parking space. The spot in his brain itched again. The woman had been hitting on him, and he was more worried about her safety. Apprehension frittered at the edge of his brain, making him think about turning around and chasing her down, taking her up on her on her offer. He could do that...but he didn't.

When his phone rang, he answered out of habit, "Crandall."

"Hello, Agent. It's Colonel Eric Freeman from the Idaho State Police. We met a few years ago at a seminar on blood splatter?"

Jeff stifled his sigh. Only he could spend a sunny day with the top down, the sun heating his hair, dealing with serial killers, suspicious janitors and blood splatter. "Colonel Freeman, I'm sorry but—"

"Don't worry about not remembering. And call me Eric. Your SAC gave me your number."

Of course Bob gave out his number. Because rewriting three manuals and tracking down an interstate killer wasn't nearly enough to do. "How can I help, Eric?"

"We're building a new lab, and our team is sort of at loggerheads. I could use an expert opinion, and maybe a little guidance. Any chance I could buy you lunch and pick your brain? Maybe in a few weeks?"

Jeff pulled in his professional enthusiasm. If he missed anything about Chicago, other than his friends, it was his lab. But he didn't have time for a four-hour round trip. "In Boise?"

"No. The ISP's headquarters are in Hastings."

That was more like it. He resisted the urge to reschedule his day and stay in town. "Sure. Shoot me an email and we'll get it scheduled."

They disconnected the call, and Jeff's phone buzzed in his hand. What now?

"Hello?"

"Hi, Jeffy."

"Ruthie," he grumbled at his sister, one of the few people who ever dared call him that. "How's the mother of my favorite nephew?"

"Tired. I don't know how Mama did this four times."

"That's why God makes them cute and helpless, sis," Jeff said. "How did the hearing go?"

She was quiet for a long time, and the prolonged silence chilled him through. "Ruth Anne?"

"The board just called me as a courtesy. Kyle Davis was granted parole."

Jeff's knuckles whitened on the steering wheel. Suddenly he was thirteen again, sitting at the top of the stairs in the midnight darkness, worried about getting caught out of bed while he watched his mother open the door. Reverend Steele and Captain Graves had been standing in the rain, their words drowned out by the thunder and his mother's wail. He'd given up his hiding spot to catch her as she sank to the floor.

"How's Mom?" He managed to squeeze the words past his tight throat, but he couldn't talk and breathe at the same time.

"Worried about us."

"I should've come home. I should've—"

"It wouldn't have mattered," Ruth said. "He's been a model prisoner—drug treatment, twelve-step program, getting his GED, college, helping other inmates learn to read."

"Because he wanted something. How could you—"

"Hey," Ruth barked. "*I* didn't do this. We did everything we could. We had your statement. Captain Graves came up from Florida. The current commander of the Highway Patrol testified. We tried, Jeff. They disagreed with us."

"So all that *we'll always honor your dad's sacrifice for the state* was utter bullshit."

"I hated to call you with this," Ruth said. "I know

you're trying to get finished and back to work. Don't let it distract you."

One of his father's murderers was free to walk the street, to feel the sun and laugh with his family, and *he* was supposed to stay on task?

"We can't do a damn thing about it, Jeff. We lost this round. Vince Baker's hearing is next year. We'll try again then."

"Yeah, thanks," he muttered as he exited from the interstate onto the road that would lead to Fiddler. "Love you, Ruthie. Thanks for calling."

He hung up. The fluffy white clouds he'd admired this morning now drifted across his day, creating shadows and gloom. Twenty-three years and he still felt the weight of his father's disappointment and his mother's grief. *Sorry, Pop. We tried.*

Pressing his foot to the accelerator, riveting his gaze on the yellow line in the asphalt, Jeff kept driving until he was home.

In the garage, he scrounged for a hammer and finishing nails, hoping Mrs. Simon wouldn't mind a few small holes in her wall in the name of justice. Striding through the house, he avoided looking at the smiling family photographs.

He unrolled the butcher paper in the hallway, using the length of the wall to estimate the measurement. Satisfied, he cut paper, carried it into his office, and tacked it up. *Hammer. Not a distance weapon. Up close and personal.*

Something about whacking the nail, hearing the crack, feeling the nail sink in, made him feel better. *Had Ron Thomas's killer felt this same release of tension?*

Drywall dust drifted to the floor, dirtying the immaculate space. Bashing someone's head in would be messy. No one could wander around in bloody clothes. Cleanup would be necessary. So would extra clothes. *You'd have to scout the location first, put clothes in the trunk and remember your weapon.*

Starting with the oldest case, he flipped open the Archer file and taped the contents to the butcher paper. He scribbled notes as he worked.

The full skeleton of Beau Archer had been exhumed and reassembled at the coroner's office. Empty space represented where tendons and ligaments had once held the large bones together. The only flaw in the bones, other than long-healed breaks and dental work, was the jagged hole at the base of his skull. *Had he been prone when he'd been struck? Who got someone that big to kneel, and how?*

Had he been restrained? Wouldn't he have struggled? Not if the killer was armed. *But, if I had a gun, wouldn't I just shoot him? Why go to the trouble of the hammer, and the mess?*

If a man that size had struggled against restraints he'd have damaged his forearms or wrists. There'd been a case in Kansas City a few years back where the victim had been a five-foot-tall, hundred-pound woman. She'd cracked both her right radius and ulna as well as her left thumb. Beau Archer would've broken something.

So he hadn't been restrained. He'd sat still for this, or he'd never seen it coming. No one sat still for death, especially not a violent one. Had he been unconscious? No. An unconscious victim didn't react, and chances were this killer liked the reaction. Why else kill at such close range?

If Archer didn't see it coming, he'd been focused on someone else. Bait, maybe, someone who'd been used to lure him to his death. Or maybe he'd been outnumbered—two against one. If not a lure, maybe an accomplice.

The original article on Archer's disappearance was short. Betty and Beau had been married for almost two years when he'd gone to Atlantic City for a weekend poker tournament. He'd never returned, and Betty was worried he'd met with foul play.

The *Clarion* editor had provided the photo that had run with the story, nearly thirty years ago. Archer was in the Carhartt jacket that was synonymous with rural life. His wide smile was framed by a mustache and goatee, and his head was bracketed by a pair of skinned knees. Most probably those belonged to his stepdaughter, the little girl Betty Archer had brought into the marriage. The girl whose name no one could remember, and a thread no officer had pursued.

Who could blame them after so long? Betty and her daughter had stayed for two months after Beau had gone missing, and they'd taken everything with them when they'd left. Other than the little girl's knees captured as she sat atop her stepfather's shoulders, there weren't any family photos. No one knew where they'd gone, and a later search for Betty Archer had been fruitless.

He went back for another file, pushing the office chair out of his way and into his stack of books, which tumbled to the floor. Jeff halted his research and stared at the bookshelf. Surely Hank wouldn't mind if he moved a few things around.

He made room for his library, and then tackled the desk—rearranging the lamp, stashing Hank's ledgers in a drawer, and running the computer cords through previously hidden holes at the back of the rolltop desk. Dragging in a deep breath, he took a minute to enjoy the lack of clutter.

But now the focus was on the grisly photos on the wall. That was wrong in this place full of a family's happy memories. He retrieved the picture he'd bought at the art show from his bedroom. Returning to his office, he lifted one of the Simon family photos from its hanger and propped it against the wall behind the door.

In its place, he hung Abby's photo of the fog-shrouded tree. Straightening it, Jeff stroked the silvery, worn barn-wood frame. He didn't even question whether she'd made it. Straightforward, strong lines, rescued scraps made into something beautiful, picked because it enhanced the picture rather than distracting from it. And it was soft when you didn't expect it to be.

He went back to work, laying out the other cases and making notes, looking for patterns and similarities. They didn't go to the same places, have similar jobs, or know the same people. The rest of it was like the memory game he'd played with his sisters as children. Two files had commonalities, but the third didn't.

His stomach rumbled, and he looked up to find the house dark and shadowy. Dinner was a turkey sandwich, chips and beer eaten over the sink. He'd begun eating this way in high school because he'd always been hungry and he didn't want to leave a mess for his mother. He still did it in his apartment kitchen, staring at the wall while he chewed and let cases rumble in his head.

The view here was better. Moonlight tinted the tree branches and the tops of the grasses in the field. In the valley below, Abby's stable roof glowed a dull silver, and the security lights lit the yard and the paddock. But the house was dark. Was she out somewhere? Was she asleep already?

Exhaustion weighted his neck and shoulders, pushing his chin to his chest, but his brain continued to spin on the case.

What he knew had nothing to do with the victims, and everything to do with their killers. And after his review of the remains he was certain he was looking for two people. An organized, patient murderer and an accomplice who helped control and subdue the victim. The notes on Archer and Thomas might mean the accomplice had developed a conscience. Maybe the murderer had died. But why wasn't there a note on Finch? Did the accomplice feel guilty over Archer and Thomas but not Finch? Had he "earned" it somehow?

Archer's burial site was different than the rest, but he was also the first victim. Maybe the team had grown nervous about leaving Archer so close to his home.

He walked back to his office, still thinking, and pulled the ancient chair in front of his computer. The seat was lumpy, and the arms wobbled. Maybe he'd buy Hank Simon a new chair to make up for the nail holes in the wall.

Jeff yawned as he typed the email to Bob. *Serial killer, probably a team. It's possible that the alpha partner has died and the beta has now taken the lead. You'll have more bodies. Focus on locations similar to Thomas and Finch, on landmarks and parks.*

Trudging to the master bath, he rummaged through his shaving bag in search of his toothbrush, then his toothpaste, and his dental… Forget it. Opening a drawer, he tipped the bag upside down and shook the contents until everything rattled and clattered out into a pile.

In the bedroom, he dug through his suitcase, shoving clothes aside to find pajamas and then refolding his shirts to keep them unwrinkled. The front compartment refused to zip closed over the pile of dirty laundry he'd shoved in there over the last few days.

Again, the dresser drawers were empty, and there was a hamper in the closet. The Simons had made a space for him in their home, so why disappoint them? He tossed his dirty clothes into the hamper and stacked his clean ones in the drawers. Then he stored his suitcase in the closet.

The last step to moving in was hanging Abby's gift over the dresser. The light caught it just right, glinting against the pattern carved into the dark frame. He could hear the whip of the pole and the plop as the lure hit the water. As he drifted to sleep, his fingers twitched against the imaginary bite of the line.

Chapter Six

Abby gulped and dialed the phone. She couldn't cancel now, could she? Maybe there was a rule, like canceling a dentist appointment. Maggie answered on the third ring, and she lost her voice.

"Abby? Hang on. Let me turn this down." The blaring music in the background faded to a whisper.

"Hi."

"You sound awful. What's wrong?"

Abby plopped into the nearest chair and summoned Toby by snapping her fingers. "I have a d-date."

The music stopped altogether, allowing Abby to hear the smile in her friend's next word. "Really? With whom?"

"Jeff." Abby ruffled Toby's fur.

"Wow. Umm, when?"

"Seven."

"Tonight? You have date with Jeff at seven tonight?"

"Yes."

"Ab, that's two hours from now. Do you want me to come help?"

Yes, please. Come tell me I'm not an idiot for doing this. Or tell me I am an idiot, and stand next to me while I send him away. Better yet, come sit on my porch and send him away so I don't have to do it. Abby's gaze shot to the hill. Jeff would see Maggie's car in the driveway. He'd think she was making a big deal out of this. "No. This way is fine."

"All right. Where is he taking you?"

Where? I don't know where. He just said dinner, Friday at seven. "Umm..."

"He didn't tell you? God, I don't know why men think that's acceptable. They have no idea how many decisions we make based on where. What if we're too dressed up and we don't know until we open the door? Then everyone feels like an idiot—"

"Not helping."

"Sorry. What did he say?"

Abby slid to the floor and wrapped her free arm around her dog. "He wants to thank me. For a pic-picture." She sucked in a deep breath. She had to get it together. She couldn't stutter every word all night. "And for dinner. M-maybe it's not a date."

"Maybe not."

The comfort was cold. *Not* a date would be takeout burgers in the middle of the week. Even Abby knew Friday at seven was a date.

"Wear something you're comfortable in. You'll be fine," Maggie reassured her. "It's just Jeff."

Just Jeff. Abby rubbed a hand over her stomach, where her skin still tingled whenever she thought about his touch. Worse, she forgot to be quiet when he was around. It was addictive to watch his eyes sparkle, to see him smile, to listen to him talk. How was she supposed to spend a whole evening with him, listening to him, and *not* talking?

"Abby?"

"Yeah?"

"Have fun, relax, and be yourself." Maggie's smile coated her words. It helped. "Call me tomorrow and tell me how it went."

She hung up and sat with Toby, listening to the clock tick away precious minutes. *He'll run screaming if I'm myself. Everyone would. So, what would a normal girl do?*

Fifteen minutes later, after she'd formulated a plan, she pushed herself from the floor and into the bathroom. She wouldn't borrow trouble, instead she'd take one step at a time.

As she applied lip balm, the clock chimed seven o'clock. The tread of her boots on the hardwood gave her courage. Heavy black leather, cluttered with buckles, they made her feel braver just looking at them. She shook her head at Toby, sitting next to the door, under his leash.

"No, boy. I think this is one time when three's a crowd."

Should she wait on the porch? No. In the movies, the women opened the door. She'd wait in here.

Seven-oh-five. She got a glass of water and kept her gaze on her feet as she returned to the living room. Perched on the sofa, she listened for his car in the driveway.

Disgusted with herself, she pushed back and made her spine curve against the couch cushions. She dialed up a playlist to hide the ticking of the clock and picked up the Dumas book she'd borrowed from the library.

One page later, one page she'd have to read again on another day, she carried her empty glass to the kitchen and put it in the dishwasher. Forgetting her resolution, she stared out the window at her empty driveway. It was seven-fifteen.

He'd forgotten.

Her phone rang, shrill in the quiet, and she stared at it like a skunk she'd startled. How did he know her number?

She connected the call and whispered, "Hello?"

"Abby?"

All that worry for nothing. He wasn't coming, and he wasn't calling. "Hi. Doctor Morgan. How are. You?"

"I'm fine, dear. Is there any way you could come to the hospital?"

Hospital? Was Jeff late because something had happened? "Of course. Why?"

"We have a little boy down here who's had a hell of a time of it today, and he's not really talking. I was thinking—"

The warmth of a dog working its magic, soothing aches, reminding you there are sweet things in the world. Unless he's cold beneath you and his blood is mingled with yours.

"There's a. Beagle. Puppy," Abby squeaked. "At the. Shelter. I could. Bring. Him."

"Best thing for a boy is a beagle," Doctor Morgan said. "How soon could you be here?"

There was no reason to wait around. It wasn't like she had plans anymore. And she wasn't going to feel bad about it. "I'll leave now."

She hung up and stood. So did Toby.

"No," she said as she scratched his head. "You stay here. It's someone else's turn to work. And you don't need to steal his thunder."

Instead of taking the farm truck, she backed her SUV

out of her garage, looking in the review mirror and seeing only the house on the hill. The lights were on. He was home. She'd spent all afternoon worrying herself silly and he was *home*. Why the hell had he tortured her with the threat of a date if he was going to do *this*?

And why did it matter? It's what she'd wanted anyway. He was safer up there.

Abby focused on dodging the ruts in the driveway. Buck would have a fit that she'd let it erode like this, but she liked the obstacle course. It slowed down visitors so she could see them coming and have time to hide. Unless she was on the road when they arrived. Like now.

The headlights blinded her as the driver closed the distance, and she froze like a deer—waiting on her slaughter. Abby's heart thudded as her lungs screamed for air.

The little silver sports car drew even and stopped, and she stared down at the shaggy man behind the wheel. Dread replaced fear, but at least it was safe to roll down the window.

"Were you coming up to tell me off?" Jeff asked, his smile visible in the twilight.

"Going to town," Abby replied. "Doctor. Morgan. Called."

"He called me, too. Why don't we go together? I'll drive." He pulled forward, toward the house. "You can leave your car."

Dumbfounded, she craned her neck out the window to stare at his taillights as he stopped at her front door. She ought to just go and leave him waiting, but she couldn't leave him here alone.

"Dammit to hell," she muttered as she wrestled through a three-point turn and drove back to her garage. Jeff was waiting next to his car, standing beside the open passenger door.

"I lost track of the time." He swept his hand toward the seat and dipped his head until his bangs obscured his glasses. "Let me make it up to you."

The collar of his jacket was sticking up and his jeans were rumpled and bunched around his shoes, one of which was untied. He was the epitome of the absent-minded professor.

"We're both going to the hospital anyway," he wheedled. "It'll be less awkward."

Tell him no.

"After we're finished we can decide about dinner."

Go away.

"Please, Abby," he said as he dropped his hand. "I know I've fucked this up. I really am sorry."

"I have to pick up a dog," she warned him. Maybe he wouldn't want a puppy in his fancy car.

"Okay." His smile widened.

Dammit.

She stepped around him and ducked into the passenger seat. When he clicked the door closed, she slid her fingers against the supple leather seat as heat seeped through her jeans. Navigation, Bluetooth, a steering wheel loaded with controls. Jeff opened the driver's door, and the aluminum trim glinted in the light.

"Buckle up," he said.

She reached for the seat belt and stopped. "There's no backseat. I can't put a pet carrier in here."

"Are you bringing a Great Dane?" He smiled when she shook her head. "Then he'll fit somehow. Don't worry."

Once she was secure, he crept down the driveway,

slaloming around the ruts. “You should fix your driveway.”

“You should drive a sensible car,” she snapped, fighting the urge to snuggle against the leather.

“Sometimes sensible is overrated. Where are we going?”

“The Humane Society.”

They made a right onto the highway, and the car leapt forward. The acceleration pushed her back into the seat. Despite herself, Abby grinned.

“What were you saying about *sensible*?” Jeff asked, humor soaking his words.

Heated upholstery was no match for his laugh. Her muscles relaxed and her nerves calmed. “Why did Dale call you?”

“Most people hear *FBI* and *profiler* and think I’m some sort of shrink, a human lie detector.”

“And you’re not.”

He shook his head. “I don’t care about fixing criminals. I care about catching them. Don’t get me wrong, I’m really good at interrogations, but the trick is to never ask a question if you don’t already know the answer. It’s why I like evidence.”

“You’re going to. Interrogate. A little boy?”

“Of course not. The kid didn’t do anything wrong. I honestly don’t know how I can help, but I hated to tell Dale no.”

He liked catching the bad guys, and he was good at it. He liked helping. *Can I tell you a secret? Can I show you what I keep in my attic?* The words crept up her tongue. *My mother is a—*

They’d reached the Humane Society, and Abby

opened her door while the motor was still running. "I'll be right back."

"I'm not letting you go in there alone," he grumbled as he stood.

"I'm. Used. To. It." She scurried up the walk, anxious to get away before she told him everything. His long strides thudded behind her. He was too close. He shouldn't be this close.

"Don't. Chase. Me." She fought for the words even as she tried to outrun the comfort he offered.

"Then don't run," he said as he grabbed her hand.

The simple contact stopped her where his words wouldn't have. If he knew what he was chasing, what he was touching, he'd never do it. No one would. They'd banish her. She deserved at least that.

She tugged her fingers. He tightened his grip. And she did the most selfish thing she'd ever done—she held on.

They entered through the back door and the dogs came to life when she disarmed the alarm. Yipping and whining, they stood at the doors of their kennels, tails wagging. She hated to ignore them, but she was in a hurry.

"Not tonight, guys. We'll play tomorrow," she promised as she went to the end of the aisle.

The beagle puppy was standing on the door, his hello more of a warble than a bark. She gathered him into her arms and dissolved into giggles as he licked her face and snuffled in her ear.

Jeff was standing two kennels away, staring at her like she was from another planet. He was used to more sophisticated women. *See, this is why we shouldn't date.* Maybe he'd get the point and just take her home.

And maybe she'd remember it was for the best.

She picked up a small upholstered pet carrier and stashed the puppy inside.

This time, as they left the building, she didn't scurry away. As they walked side by side, Jeff twined his fingers through hers, holding on lightly as if she were breakable. It was the prettiest lie, and she let herself believe it.

He held the door for her, waiting patiently while she dithered over where to store the beagle. Finally she put the bag in her lap. After closing her door, he loped around the car and slid behind the wheel.

"Will you two be safe like that?"

She nodded, unable to say anything, and he put the car in reverse.

The drive to the hospital was too short for conversation, and he didn't seem to be in the mood for it. He was probably trying to figure out a way to get out of dinner. She'd smell like dog. That's just what a man looked for in a date, *eau de beagle.*

Dale Morgan greeted them at the nurses' station with a grandfatherly smile and an outstretched hand. "Glad you could both come."

"What's happened?" Jeff asked as they started down the hall, weaving between gurneys, wheelchairs, and staff.

"The boy's name is Evan Gaines," the doctor explained. "Chief Roberts and Max brought him in a few hours ago. Poor guy was hungry, filthy and exhausted. They found him under the porch, curled back into a corner with a hatchet. They had to pry it away out of his hands."

"Jesus," Jeff muttered. "And his parents?"

"The family moved here from North Dakota a few months ago. Andy, the dad, was hoping to get work with Mathis, but he couldn't pass the drug test. Laura, the mother, had been waiting tables at the truck stop. But Andy took his frustration out on her, and she missed too many shifts. They've been living hand-to-mouth ever since. And now Laura's in the morgue, Andy's in jail, and Glen Roberts thinks Evan is the only witness."

They'd reached the end of the hall and Abby grabbed Jeff before he rounded the corner into the room. "Wait," she whispered.

Kneeling, she unzipped the carrier and lifted the beagle. Praying he'd run for the boy in the bed and not down the hall, she sat him on the floor and pushed him into the room.

Jeff knelt next to her, his hand on her shoulder.

Thankfully, the puppy smelled food and boy and went in the right direction. After a few minutes, he whined for attention. The sheets rustled. The puppy barked as his nails scratched the floor. The giggle was faint, but unmistakable.

10, 9, 8, 7, 6, 5...

She touched Jeff's knee, so close to hers, and he looked at her. She had to focus on her job rather than his long, dark eyelashes. "Give me five minutes with him," she whispered into his ear.

4, 3, 2, 1.

She stood and walked into the room.

"There he is."

Evan Gaines was a redhead and his freckles stood in stark relief against his pale face. Deep circles ringed his eyes. No, not circles. Abby's stomach knotted, even as her hands clenched into fists. Evan's eyes had been blackened. Burns and scratches mottled his neck and arms. He was skin and bones.

Oh you poor baby. I know what you've been through. How you just wanted someone to love you and they hurt you instead. How you tried to be good, how you tried to stay out of the way. My mama locked me in a closet. Did your daddy do that?

Did he make you watch... Focus, Abby.

"Do you want 'im back, ma'am? I didn't take him, I promise. He just showed up."

"I know you didn't take him. He. Wandered. Away." *Focus.*

"And he looks like he's having fun with you."

As if to help, the beagle pounced on one of Evan's legs curled under the sheet, forming a makeshift play-pen and leaving room for Abby to sit on the bed.

"I'm Abby," she said as she handed off a tug toy she'd taken from the kennel.

"I'm Evan." His pale face erupted in a smile as he got the puppy to grab the other end of the toy. "What's his name?"

"He doesn't have one yet. What do you think?"

"Tug." Evan looked up at her. "Is that okay?"

The eight-year-old had the oldest eyes she had ever seen, and everything about him was dull and lifeless. His fingernails were brittle and broken, and white nicks marred the nail beds. His teeth, what teeth he had, were dirty along the gum line and the edges. Their surfaces were as clean as an eight-year-old could make them. There was a thin scar along his hairline, and another on his eyebrow.

"I think it's a great name." She held her breath. "Are you hurt, Evan?"

He shook his head. "I got scratched up climbing through my window. And I was hungry, so the nurses ordered pizza. I like pizza."

The years melted away, and Abby was warm in Faye's car, speeding away from her lonely, cold house toward a *home*. Someplace where she was safe, clean and fed. She stroked the beagle's silky ears and joined Evan in playing with the puppy. From the corner of her eye, she saw Jeff standing in the doorway. "Evan, this is my friend Jeff. Can he join us?"

The little boy's eyes widened. "Will you stay here?"

"Of course." Abby smiled. "I know he looks like a bear, but he's a nice guy."

He nodded, and Jeff walked to the bedside chair. "Hi, Evan."

"Hi." The little boy's eyes narrowed. "Are you a cop?"

"Sometimes. And sometimes I'm a teacher."

Evan looked up, squinted his eyes and wrinkled his nose, as if smelling a lie. "You can be both?"

"Yeah. But it gets confusing. I never know whether to arrest people or grade their papers."

"You're friends with Abby?" Evan asked, looking from Jeff to her, seeking confirmation. She remembered that feeling—expecting grown-ups to lie, to trick you into answering questions.

She nodded. "We go fishing together. Do you like to fish?"

The frail shoulders lifted. "My dad takes me, but I have to play on the bank while he tries to catch dinner. He always ends up cussing and throwing things."

"What's he throw?" Jeff asked.

"Cans and bottles, mostly."

"Where's he throw them?"

"At anything in the way."

"What's your mom do while you and your…dad are gone?"

"I don't know. She used to ask about going with us, but Dad said she was bad luck. She always tells me to be quiet and stay out of the way."

"What else do you do?" Abby asked.

Evan shrugged again. "Not much. I can't go anywhere after school, and sometimes Mom keeps me home because," he looked between her and Jeff. "I'm not supposed to say."

Her heart broke at those words. "Because she doesn't want people to see your bruises?"

He nodded. "She said they'd take me away from her, and they can't do that. We protect each other."

Jeff's fingers knotted in the sheets, and Abby covered his hand with hers, but he didn't relax.

"Is that why you had the hatchet?" she asked. God knew, if she'd been able to get her hands on anything sharp, Wallis would have been nothing but a long-ago memory.

"Yes. I used to keep it under my bed." Evan talked to her but played with the dog. "But then a few months ago, Dad chased me through the house for pushing him away from Mom, and I had to hide. Mom told me to put my hatchet in my hiding place so I'd have it if he chased me again." His voice shook. "I shouldn't have put it where I couldn't reach it."

She knew that guilt well. Six people were dead because she'd done something she shouldn't. No matter how hard she'd tried to be good, it was never good enough. Never.

She lifted his chin and stared into his big brown eyes. "She's happy you're safe."

Just like Buck's happy that I'm safe and still on his farm where he wanted me to stay.

Tug curled into Evan's lap with a wide yawn. The boy stroked the animal's long ears.

"She's dead, isn't she?" Evan looked Jeff in the eye. "I kinda figure she is because she's not in here telling me not to get Dad into trouble."

"What happened today?" Jeff croaked.

"Dad got the mail and took the check. Mom was mad because we needed food and she said he wouldn't buy enough. And, when he came home without any grocery sacks, she yelled at him. He got really mad."

"And you hid under the porch?" Jeff asked.

"Nah. I stayed in my room and waited to see if she'd need me. When it got quiet I opened the door just enough to see what was going on. Dad was standing over Mom, and she was on the kitchen floor. It was all bloody."

The dog toy fell off the bed. Careful not to disturb the beagle, Evan slid from under the sheets to retrieve it. The movement revealed more of the little boy's body and the old bruises mottling his skin. Underneath those, his vertebrae and ribs stood out in sharp relief.

For months, I stood in my room staring at bruises just like that, watching them fade while I wrapped my ribs so I could do chores. Faye fed me six times a day, claiming a good wind would blow me away.

Abby bit back her words, choking on a sob as she gripped Jeff's hand. This time, he held on just as hard.

"Are you tired?" Abby asked as Evan got back into bed and she covered his thin, scratched legs.

"A little. Is Dad getting out of jail?"

"Nope," Jeff said.

"What happens to me?"

"For right now, you're going to stay here," Abby said as she straightened his sheets and pulled his blanket up to his chest. Children should be warm.

"Will you bring Tug to see me again?"

"We'll come tomorrow," she promised as she put the puppy in the carrier.

Evan looked at Jeff. "Will you come, too?"

"Sure. Maybe not with Abby and Tug, but I'll be here."

They walked out of the room and closed the door.

"Shit," Jeff whispered. "That poor kid."

"What if his dad makes bail?"

He took her free hand and coaxed her down the hallway and outside. "I doubt they'll give it to him, but I'll work with Glen and Dale on reports to take to the hearing. That asshole will be staring at the sky through a grate in the floor."

Once they were back in the car, Abby stared out the window. At eight years old, Evan Gaines was braver than she'd been in her whole life. He'd put his dad in jail. Where was Wallis? The searches on her name never revealed anything, but maybe she'd died under an alias. Maybe she was overseas. Maybe she was in jail in Singapore or North Vietnam—or Siberia.

The light came on and her door opened. Jeff offered her his hand. "This is new. You're usually racing me out of the car."

"I was thinking," she muttered, blinking up at him. "Why does me opening my own door bug you?"

He bent and lifted her hand, helping her to her feet. "Because it deprives me of touching you."

Her knees shook at his words, and she tightened her grip on the pet carrier in her other hand. "You're teasing me."

"I never tease about that. You have great hands, strong and soft at the same time." He matched his stride to hers. "How do you keep them that way?"

"Mineral oil, hoof conditioner and Bag Balm," she quipped. "Doesn't every girl you know use those?"

His laughter danced up her skin. "I've never checked for Bag Balm. Although," he tilted his head and waggled his eyebrows, "I can think of a few other uses for it."

She unlocked the door and turned off the security system. "Trust a guy to think of *that*," she snorted.

"Hey! I never said what I was thinking," he chided, his glee echoing through the empty building until the dogs began barking. "Maybe you're the one with her mind in the gutter."

She put Tug in his kennel and watched as he curled up in a corner. Jeff stood behind her, his hand on her back. His thumb stroked in an arc, and her whole world narrowed to that spot.

"You're so warm."

"No one's ever paid me that particular compliment," he said as he moved his hand to her stomach and pulled her closer.

"Then they've never been cold." She dropped her head back, resting against his shoulder.

He touched her hairline and she knew he'd found the jagged scar most people missed. No one was generally close enough to see it. Jeff always saw too much.

"I fell." The age-old lie slipped over her tongue, and it made her feel slimy. He tightened his hold, keeping her close when she tried to wriggle free.

"I could do with a drink and cheesecake. How about you?" he asked.

It felt incredible to be held like this. To be close to him. "I could," Abby whispered. "Thanks."

Chapter Seven

When they passed the road home, she lost her nerve. Panic gripped her empty stomach and squeezed, and her fingers twitched with the urge to open the door and jump.

"It'll kill you, you know?" Jeff said from behind the wheel. "If you bail out at this speed, you'll be a greasy spot on the asphalt."

"How did you know?"

"You're about to break my fingers," he teased, and then kept hold of her hand when she struggled to pull it free. "Relax, Ab. After all we've been through tonight, we've earned this."

Taking a deep breath, she forced her fingers to relax. What did normal girls talk about? Work. He liked his work.

"How is your. Writing?"

He squeezed her fingers and smiled. "Good. I'm ahead of schedule, which is great because—never mind. What you did with Evan tonight, letting the puppy go first, was genius. What gave you that idea?"

Years of having adults bribe me with shit, thinking it would make me talk. As if I'd endanger their lives for a candy bar.

"A grown-up with a puppy is a bribe. Children aren't stupid. Traumatized children especially."

"Why *especially*?"

"They've spent years. Keeping. Secrets. Sur-surviving." This was a dangerous conversation. They needed to talk about his work. "Did you always want to be in the FBI?"

He shook his head. "I'd planned to follow Dad into the highway patrol. After he died, I was more convinced than ever, but I saw my mom's face when I talked about it. The older I got, the more she worried. So I found a way to catch the bad guys without being in the line of fire." He flicked the blinker and made a left-hand turn. "How about Italian? Every time I drive by here, they're busy. The food must be good."

Abby looked out the window at the parking lot beside the repurposed house. She didn't even need to read the sign. Romanelli's.

They couldn't eat here. As Jeff got out of the car, she looked down at her clothes. She was dressed for a casual date. So was he.

"Waiting again," he teased as he opened the door and offered his hand. "Good for you." He frowned as she stayed put. "What?"

"They take. Res-reservations." She forced the words out. "Not. Casual."

"Well, damn. Every other place is closed by now, and the restaurants in Hastings will be closed by the time we get there."

"I could cook," she offered.

He shook his head. "That's not a treat for you. Shit. What a colossal mess. I'm sorry, Abby."

They were both exhausted, hungry, and disappointed. And Sera Romanelli made the best dessert in the state. If they had a hope of salvaging this, it was up to her. She took his hand. "We can try."

I can do this. She silently chanted the words with every step. Jeff held the door for her and she walked through and straight to a smiling Clio Romanelli at the hostess stand.

"Ciao, *cara mia*!" she said as she wrapped Abby in a tight hug. "We didn't expect you until Sunday."

"I'll still be here then." Abby rushed the words before the warmth left her. "But any chance. There's a. Table. Now?"

Jeff stepped forward. "I didn't know to make a reservation, ma'am. Abby's had a rough night of it, and I was hoping to treat her." He offered his hand. "Jeff Crandall."

"Clio Romanelli. And if you're taking care of Abby, I'll find you a table even if it has to be upstairs."

Once they were alone, Jeff leaned over. "What's upstairs?"

"Their house." She smiled at the waiter approaching. "Hello, Giovanni."

"Ciao, *sorella*." He beckoned them. "Follow me. Do you want your usual?"

She nodded.

"What's the usual?" Jeff asked.

"Bruschetta, chestnut pasta, a green salad and iced tea," Gio explained.

"I'd like that as well, please."

"Does Sera still have panna cotta?" Abby asked. She was rewarded with Gio's nod. "Could you set. Aside two?"

"I will."

Gio left them and walked to the kitchen.

"So you come here a lot?" Jeff asked.

She shook her head. "I did their. Website. And they buy my extra eggs and cream. They treat me like family."

Gio proved that point by delivering the bruschetta and drinks, plus a plate of mozzarella. "Papa said you needed more cheese."

They dug in, and Jeff rolled his eyes as he swallowed. "Jesus, that's good. I'm glad you could get us in."

"This is the only pull I have, other than getting a discount at the farm supply."

He choked on his tea, and then settled in for another bite. "How long have you lived here?"

"Twenty-three years."

"You moved here?"

"Yes," she said around a mouthful of tomato and feta, "from Tacoma."

She heard the words leave her mouth, felt the air chill her skin. *It's okay. Nobody died in Washington. It's not a secret. It's on my records at school.*

School. Buck had taken her into town and registered her for junior high. Wallis had slammed dishes and drawers for days afterward.

"So you grew up in Washington?" Jeff asked.

This was normal date chatter. She knew he'd grown up in Tennessee. He'd told her. He just wanted—

He can't know.

She shook her head. "We. Bounced. Around. A lot."

"After your father died?"

How did he know her father had died? She hadn't said anything. She didn't tell. She didn't—

He put his hand over hers. "Sorry, professional hazard. You were so kind about my dad, I sort of guessed. I didn't mean to freak you out."

See. There. Not my fault. He guessed. And he still didn't know particulars.

"When did he die?"

"I was four."

"Damn. How?"

I don't know. I didn't see it. All I know was the floor was all red like when I'd spilled Kool-Aid, and I was worried Mama would think I'd made a mess, but Papa was there. He was so still, and Mama was so mad. Her voice made me cry.

"Abby?"

She looked away from him, trying to catch her thoughts and to stop the words. And there, in the corner, with her back to them. There was a lady with chestnut-brown hair, just like hers, cut into the severe style Wallis had always liked. An expensive bag sat at her feet, which were clad in designer shoes, and she reached a manicured hand for her napkin. Diamonds glittered under the lights.

Only the best, Abby. I deserve the best, and I'm going to have it. No one's going to stop me.

Oh God, oh God, oh God. She should've known better than to try this. Wallis always knew. She blinked across the table. She'd told Jeff a secret. She was here with him, holding his hand, enjoying dinner with her friends. They were all in danger, because she'd been happy.

I'm sorry. I'm sorry.

"Darlin', what's wrong?"

She stumbled to her feet. "I have to wash my hands."

"Ooh-kay." He smiled up at her. "I'll be right here. Hurry back before I eat all the mozzarella."

I'm so sorry.

Careful not to cause a scene, she slipped down the hall to the ladies' room, dodging Gio as he came out of the kitchen.

"Pasta's on, *sorella*. Hurry before it gets cold."

I'm so sorry.

Clio came out behind her son, and her bright smile vanished. "What is it, *mia figlia*? Are you ill?"

The woman's kindness brought tears to Abby's eyes. Wallis couldn't hurt these people. Not because of her.

"Is he mean to you? Should I call Chief Roberts?"

"No." *No one else needs to be involved.* "He's fine, Clio. I'm just…just…"

Clio pulled her into the kitchen. "I'll go get Jeff."

"No." *Wallis will see. He'll be hurt. So you will you... all of you.* "I need to leave."

The woman never blinked. "Marco, take Abby home now. Leave through the back."

"Yes, Mama."

Abby snatched cash from her wallet and stopped for one moment. Grabbing a pen, she scrawled a note on an order pad and shoved it at Clio. "Give this to him in five minutes."

Then she ran for the door.

All the way home, she watched the rearview mirror. If Wallis caught up with them, she'd jump out of the tow truck. She might be a greasy spot, but Marco would be safe.

Greasy spot. Jeff's words, the memory of his laughter, brought tears to her eyes. *Stupid, Abby. How could you be so stupid?*

He'd be sitting at their table, watching his food get cold, waiting on her to come back. He'd wanted to do something nice for her, and she'd ruined it. He'd hate her, but he'd stay away now.

"Abby?" Marco whispered. "You're home."

She blinked out the windshield, expecting to see carnage and mayhem. Everything was how she'd left it.

"Do you need me to wait, *sorella*?"

Sister. She'd always wanted siblings, and now she had a whole Italian family. "No, Marco. I'm fine. Thanks." She opened the door and leapt from the truck. "Go home."

He waited until she put the key in the lock and opened the door, and then he backed away. Abby went inside and changed the security system from *Away* to *Perimeter* and shoved the deadbolts home. When she slid the grate over the dog door, Toby sat next to her and whined.

"Sorry, boy. You can't go out until tomorrow. I don't want her to get you."

Keeping the lights off, she grabbed a knife from the block on the counter, curled into a corner, and waited. Sure enough, twenty minutes later, lights seesawed through the trees as a car bounced up the driveway.

As the security lights blared to life, she closed her eyes and tightened her grip on her weapon. And dropped it when the pounding knock thundered through the house.

"Abby!"

No! He wasn't supposed to be here. He should be mad at her. Why didn't he just go home?

He banged on the door, hard enough she would've sworn the wood cracked. "I know you're in there."

The screen door slammed shut, and she sagged with relief. But Jeff prowled the porch, his footsteps thudding and his shadow looming in the window. He was like the big bad wolf, looking for a way in, not knowing something much worse than him was waiting inside.

"Goddammit!" He battered the door again. Toby flattened against her legs, bristling and growling.

"Go away," she said, wishing her voice didn't quiver.

"What?"

"Go away." She could do this. She'd practiced being mean for almost twenty years. She pushed the air from her diaphragm. "Leave me alone."

"What the hell happened?" He'd stopped trying to get in, but she could see his silhouette. He had braced both hands against the door.

"It was a bad idea." Her voice cracked.

"Dammit! Things were fine. What happened?"

My mother...my mother...my mother...

Abby stared at the trees, looking for more headlights. None were coming. Yet. He had to get out of here.

"Leave!"

"No. Not until I see you."

She struggled to her feet, tripping over Toby as he wrapped himself around her shins. Wiping the back of her hand across her cheek, Abby flinched as the knife scraped her chin. She tested the spot with her fingers, grateful they came away clean. He'd never believe she was fine if she was bleeding. She pulled the curtain aside and blinked against the glare.

"Baby," he groaned. "Please let me help you."

He couldn't help her. It was dangerous. She had to be mean.

"Stop. Pushing. Me," she shouted, forcing her eyes

to narrow, making her brow furrow. "Go. Away." She lifted one corner of her lip into a snarl. "Leave. Me. Alone."

He shook his head.

"I. Don't." *Want you.* "I. Don't." *Need you.* She tried to say the words, to keep her mask in place, but she couldn't.

"Please, Jeff. I'm sorry. I can't." A tear rolled down her cheek, but she didn't dare wipe it away. He'd see the knife in her hand. "Please leave me alone."

He backed away from the door, then walked down the steps. Then to his car.

Abby watched him go. Watched the night descend. Saw the lights crest the top of the hill.

She was alone. Just like she'd wanted to be.

Sliding down the door, she put her head on her knees and wept.

Chapter Eight

Jeff stood on the curb, next to his car, and stared at the rambling house that filled up most of its lot. What yard there was had been pounded to dirt, and toys for several age groups littered the space. A tire swing hung from a too-scrawny branch. It wouldn't hold much weight, but then there wasn't much room to swing anyway. The whole area was ringed by a chain link fence.

Trudging to the door, he knocked and half smiled at the cacophony on the other side. His smile widened when a harried woman opened it, shaking her head.

"Mrs. Perry? I'm Jeff Crandall. I called about seeing Evan."

"Doctor Crandall," she said, smiling back. "You aren't exactly what I expected."

"I never am," Jeff said as he displayed his badge.

"Thank you. What's your password?"

"Beagle," he drawled the word Evan had picked.

Evan squeezed under her arm and flew out the door. "Hi!"

"Hey yourself." He caught the still-thin boy in a hug. "Ready to go?"

"Yep."

Mrs. Perry looked at them from under her brows. "Back by three for chores."

"Yes, ma'am." Jeff nodded.

They walked to the car, and he climbed behind the wheel.

"Can we put the top down?" Evan asked.

"If you'll buckle your seat belt."

Once they were on the road, Jeff consulted his GPS. "How about pizza and the arcade?"

"Could we get burgers and go to the park?" Evan asked.

"Sure."

After the drive-thru, it took a few minutes to locate the nearest park. Jeff eyed the concrete and gravel skeptically. "Let's keep looking."

"There's one next to the zoo," Evan offered. "I saw it yesterday with Abby."

Jeff programmed the GPS. "Really?"

"Yep. She took me to the zoo, but I don't think she liked it very much. She said animals shouldn't be in cages."

"Sounds like her," Jeff muttered. *So that's where she'd been all day.* He pulled into traffic. "Is she okay?"

"Don't you guys hang out?"

"We've both been busy this week," Jeff lied. He'd been busy making himself *not* conduct surveillance on his neighbor. She'd been busy hiding from him, to the point of skipping church and lunch on Sunday.

"She brought Toby to play with us," Evan said. "She can't bring Tug because he's too little. She don't talk much, huh?"

"No, she don't—doesn't," Jeff agreed. *Not unless she's warm and safe.*

They found the park and spread their fast food feast across a picnic table under a tree. Jeff used their shakes to hold down the burger wrappers while Evan dumped their fries into a huge pile.

"Hey!" Jeff mock-scolded. "How am I supposed to know if you eat more than me?"

"Eat fast," Evan joked as he shoved fries in his mouth.

They sat, chewing and watching the baseball game on the neighboring field.

"He's going to hit a home run," Evan guessed as he pointed at the batter. "He swings hard."

"He swings *too* hard," Jeff contradicted. "He'll strike out because all he wants is a home run. Baseball is all about the score, not how hard you hit. You can't score if you're not on base. Bet you a fry he strikes out."

Two swings later, Evan handed him a fry as the batter trudged back to the dugout.

Evan scooted closer on the bench. They sat side by side, watching the game until the teams packed up to leave.

"How are things at Mrs. Perry's house?" Jeff asked as they walked back to the car.

"It's okay." Evan shrugged. "She's nice and all."

"Are the other kids mean to you?"

"No," Evan said. "I just don't like it. Couldn't I go home with you?"

Jeff lost his breath. "Evan—"

"I'd be good, and I wouldn't make any noise. I'd play outside all day and not get in the way. I wouldn't even argue about taking a bath. *Please?*"

Shit. This is why he preferred to deal with dead people.

"Evan, I want you to listen to me very carefully." Jeff stopped, fumbling for the right words. "You can't come with me." He held up his hand to stop the argument. "But it isn't because I don't want you to. I'd like nothing better, and I wouldn't make you promise to stay outside all day and stay out of my way." He was going to find Andy Gaines and kick his ass for being a sorry father. "But I don't live in Fiddler, remember?"

Evan wiped his nose and nodded. "I could go with you when you left."

Jeff pulled his handkerchief free and cleaned Evan's face. "I couldn't keep you, buddy. I'm not at home much, and I don't have a yard or anything. You'd get pretty bored all cooped up like a chicken." He waited until the little boy nodded. "But it doesn't mean I won't come visit you for as long as I can. Okay?"

"Can you come tomorrow?"

This kid was going to break his heart. "I have to go on a trip for work tomorrow. But I'll come as soon as I get back." He stood. "Let's get you to Mrs. Perry's before she sends out the SWAT team."

They drove back in silence, the fun drained from their day. Jeff walked Evan to the door and rang the bell, then he knelt to eye level. "It makes me happy and sad at the same time that you want to come with me."

Evan wrapped him in a strangling hug. "Me, too."

He disappeared into the house, and Jeff looked at Mrs. Perry. "I'll be out of town for a few days, but you can call, or he can, if something comes up."

"Thank you," she said as she shut the door between them.

He was trudging back to his car when his phone rang. "Yeah, what?"

"Two-fer," Bob said. "One in Illinois, one in the Eldorado National Forest out in California. That one has a note. If they're right, his name's John Parker. He's been missing since 1992. The one in Illinois they think is Abe Snyder. No one's seen him since 2006."

Jeff hooked his phone into the hands-free system and closed the top on the roadster. "How old is the note on Parker?"

"They got it last week."

Something didn't add up. Archer, Thomas and now Parker had all been dead for more than two decades. Why were they suddenly getting tips on twenty-year-old murders? "Do me a favor. Send local agents to check with the PD on Archer, Thomas and this new one. Make sure I have the whole file on each of them."

"Sure."

"I was leaving tomorrow for Alabama and Virginia. I'll add Illinois and California to the itinerary."

"Keep your receipts, and—"

"I know. Keep Quantico happy," Jeff grumbled. "I'll let you know what I find."

He hung up and stared at the road. Five bodies. Five. And no discernible pattern in timing or in locations. The only clues were their manners of death and their dump sites. He was missing something. He could feel it.

Jeff skirted the edge of Fiddler, eager to be home and make his notes and… What? Sit on his porch and stare at his neighbor's dark house? If it wasn't for seeing Abby in the yard, he'd think she'd left town in the middle of the night.

How had things gone so wrong so quickly? They'd been having a pretty decent time, considering he'd been late and they'd spent the first part of the night at the hospital with Evan.

When she'd held that beagle and giggled as it licked

her chin, her laugh had captivated him. Just like the freckles across her nose. And talking to her had been a revelation. Her hesitation and stammer had been replaced by intelligence, wit and humor. She got to him every time she opened her mouth. Like a trout lure, teasing him forward and making him want more.

As if his thoughts had conjured her, she passed him on the highway, headed to town. He slowed and watched her pass. She never looked his way.

He turned onto the county road toward home and pulled into his driveway, but it was blocked by a bright yellow SUV. Frowning, he parked behind the trespasser and walked up the steps. The girl waiting on him was wearing a T-shirt with a hedgehog on it, and her long legs stretched from beneath khaki shorts that were too short.

Shit.

He caught his youngest sister as she barreled into him. “Hey, Cassie. What brings you to Idaho?”

“Mom was being impossible.”

“Like how?” His mother was never impossible. Cass was a different story.

“She wants to know what I’m going to do next. She’s laying out graduate school brochures and job postings with my cereal. She’s even talked to the school board about me being an art teacher during summer session.”

He raised an eyebrow.

“Jeff, I just got finished with school—early, even. Can’t I take a break? Do I have to make a decision right this minute?”

“Well, if you’re going to grad school, you’ll have to start applying to make fall enrollment. And if you want to teach it would be best to get to know people in the district before they began offering contracts.”

"You sound just like her," Cassie huffed. "What if I don't want to do that?"

Shit. He had enough drama without adding his family to it.

"Let's skip that part for a little bit. I've had a long day. So you two had a fight and you hopped a plane to Idaho?"

"Mom said you had a big house, so I thought you wouldn't mind the company. Can I stay?"

Her suitcases were next to the door. He'd never been able to refuse her, and she'd used it against him since she was five years old. If she'd been able to find the spare key, she'd already be unpacked.

"For a few weeks, but you need to call Mom and tell her where you are. She's probably worried sick."

She kissed his cheek. "Thanks, Jeffy."

He held the door for her since she was already on the phone. "Hi, Mama. Don't worry—"

"Your room's upstairs," he said, pointing and then following her up, careful not to knock into the walls and ruin the paint. He stopped at the front bedroom and put her suitcases in the doorway. "You're on your own for sheets and towels. Find them up here and don't make a mess."

She pushed the phone at him. "Mom wants to talk to you."

He took it and walked downstairs, ignoring his sister's protest. "Hi, Mama."

"I'm sorry she surprised you," his mother sighed. "If you don't want her there, send her home."

"Do you need me to keep her? It sounds like the two of you could use a break."

"Would you mind?"

"No, ma'am. I'll keep an eye on her."

"Thank you, dear. How are you liking Fiddler now that you're there for a longer visit?"

"It's the perfect spot to catch up. I'm getting a lot done. And Bob sent me a case."

"Oh, Jeff. I was hoping you'd get a real break. You haven't had a vacation in years."

"Working keeps me sharp, and I'm only consulting," he lied, "so it's still like a break. Don't worry."

"I'll try not to. I'll talk to you next week. Love you."

"Love you, too, Mama."

Jeff walked into the kitchen, where Cass was waiting at the table and returned her phone as he sat. "We need to make a plan. I'm scheduled to leave town tomorrow for work. Will you be okay here alone?"

"Yes," she said, rolling her eyes. "I don't even know anyone here to invite to a wild party."

"So much the better," Jeff grumbled. "And don't roll your eyes. Do we need to take your rental back?"

"No. I worked in the library for the last few semesters. I've saved enough to pay for it. Besides, it would be inconvenient to have only one car, especially if I get a temporary job."

That was almost responsible.

"What? You thought I came out here to mooch and distract you?" She kicked him under the table. "Ye of little faith."

The disappointment underlying her words stopped him, and he stared across at her. Where Ruth and Jan looked like their mother, he and Cass looked like their father. Once Jeff had started going gray, some people actually mistook him for Cass's dad. It was a role he became used to assuming with her, after their father's death.

But the woman sitting across from him was an adult,

despite the inky-black braid and the Doc Martens. And he remembered what it had been like to be her age and have everyone trying to tell him what to do.

"How about we go to dinner so you can see the town and pick up a paper?"

"Don't you need to work?" Cass asked, raising an eyebrow. "Or are you still procrastinating?"

"I can work later. If we don't hurry, every place will be closed. C'mon."

"You have two options," he explained as they crossed into the city limits. "Burgers or everything else."

The wind caught Cassie's laugh and pulled it away. "That's a large choice."

"Not really. It's the burger joint or the diner," Jeff explained as he turned down the street with Herb's Drive-in at one end, The Diner at the other, and the grocery store in the middle.

"Diner," Cass decreed. Jeff found a parking spot a block away, between vehicles that towered over the convertible.

After stopping for a paper, he ushered his sister down the steps to the basement-level entrance into the restaurant. His eyes adjusted to the darker interior. High-backed booths with dark tables and navy blue leather upholstery ringed the room. Matching tables were scattered throughout, and those were surrounded by upholstered parson's chairs. Dark hardwood floors soaked up the light from the wrought iron chandeliers overhead. Every table was topped by a small bouquet of flowers.

"Diner?" Cass's eyes widened as she looked around. "I was expecting linoleum and a jukebox."

"Everyone does," an eavesdropper chirped.

Jeff turned just in time for Tiffany Marx to scoop him into a hug. She continued talking over his shoulder. "The Young family owns several of the buildings, and everyone wanted the storefronts but no one wanted the basements, so they built this place."

She moved past him and offered her hand. "I'm Tiffany Marx."

"Cassidy Crandall."

"My baby sister," Jeff offered belatedly. "She surprised me this afternoon."

"Can't you say younger sister?" Cass's whine diluted her request for recognized maturity.

"I know how you feel. My older brother does the same thing. Are you staying?"

"If I can find a job."

"Oh! Lex is looking for a receptionist for the summer. Zelda's going on a European tour and Mediterranean cruise. Are you allergic to animals?"

The women were still talking as they walked off, leaving Jeff to follow behind and wonder how a two-week visit had become the whole summer.

"This is Cassidy. She's staying with Jeff, and she needs a job."

Jeff heard the rushed explanation, saw Lex's widening smile, and then Abby…sitting next to Lex. His arm was stretched behind her along the back of the upholstered bench. She knotted her napkin around her fingers while she managed pleasantries.

Her dark eyes settled on him. "Hello."

Jeff nodded a greeting then turned to his sister. "Let's get a table. The hostess is waiting."

He walked away without making sure his sister was following, barely aware of the muted conversation behind him. The hostess showed him to a corner booth and out of habit he took the seat against the wall. It gave him a full view of the room, including Lex's table. Jeff fought the urge to switch sides.

"Lex seems like a good guy, and he's kinda cute in a serious sort of way. It might be fun to—"

"I don't think you should work for him. If you're already talking about his looks, it wouldn't be appropriate."

"So I can only work for old, ugly guys? That's going to seriously hinder my employment chances." She looked over her shoulder. "Is he married to Abby?"

"No."

"Are they an item?"

"It's none of my business," Jeff growled. He looked up from the menu in time to see Abby staring at Cass. Lex touched her hand, stealing her attention.

Once they'd ordered, Jeff faced his sister. She glanced over her shoulder.

"Stop staring."

"I will if you will," she said.

"I'm not."

"How many times has he touched her?" she asked.

Five. That one there makes six. "I'm not paying attention."

Cass tossed her napkin at him. "Liar."

Their food arrived, and they ate in silence. He hoped the subject was dead. He should have known better.

"Have you gone out with her?"

"None of your business."

"You *have*," she teased. "So why is she sitting with Dr. Do Me?"

Jeff sipped his tea. "I swung too hard."

Cassie's eyes widened. "You *like* her."

Across the room, Abby snatched up the check. It wasn't a date. And she hadn't smiled at all. She certainly hadn't laughed. That shouldn't relieve him, but it did. "I blew it."

He shouldn't want to run to the door and open it for her. And it shouldn't make him happy that Lex *didn't* do it.

"I think this was a business meeting," Cass offered. "They were sitting like that so they could both see the computer and the photos were of him working."

"She's probably designing his website," Jeff said as he paid their bill.

They got to the car. Lex drove past them, alone. Abby backed her SUV onto the street and went in the opposite direction, toward home.

"Do you want a tour of town?" Jeff asked, trying to remember his responsibilities.

"I want you to catch her," Cass urged. "Get in. Get in."

Using all his surveillance skills, Jeff kept a respectable distance as he tailed his neighbor home. As they passed her driveway, he slowed to a crawl and watched as she drove up her driveway in the dark. *Why would she turn off her headlights to go home?*

"Tell her you're sorry," Cass said as she put a hand on his shoulder. "Fix this."

Once they were home, she went upstairs to her room, carrying the paper with her. Jeff went to his office. After adding the two new victims to his wall, he printed what little information he'd been sent. It was a grim pattern—filthy bones, tattered clothes, ragged holes. Two more large men hidden away for years, waiting on fate to expose them.

He sat back in his chair and stared at his notes and then turned toward his computer, intent on working. Instead, he stopped in midspin and stared at the photograph of the tree, silvery in the fog, hanging where it could remind him of the beauty in the world.

Abby.

Every time he closed his eyes, he saw her wide, wild stare from the other side of her front door. She'd been terrified. Not of him, but she had very definitely pushed him away.

Why? And how did he fix it?

He should apologize. Whether her panic was his fault or not, they'd had a lousy date. He'd caused that by general lack of planning and time-management. Showing up on her doorstep unannounced risked compounding the disaster. Besides, he was leaving tomorrow.

Flowers. He pulled his computer into his lap and searched for the only florist in Fiddler. Of course it had a website, and of course Abby had designed it. Roses—maybe they would break the ice and they could start over when he got back.

Until she panicked again. And she would if he couldn't figure out why.

Jeff stared at the vacant spot on his wall and then at the roll of butcher paper leaning in the corner. It would be easy to diagram, all he had to do was—

Geez, Crandall, get a grip. She's a bad first date, not a criminal.

Still, he taped the brown paper to the wall and got a marker.

What did he know? Deceased father, absent mother, animal lover, teetotaling, vegetarian, intelligent, rescuer, creative, selective mute, reader, photographer, OCD. She'd lived in Tacoma before she'd moved here.

What did he guess? Hyperthymesia and agoraphobia.

Relationships. He snorted and shook his head. Everyone in town, but the closest were Maggie, Charlene and Tiffany. Faye. Carter and Lex. The Romanellis.

He taped her note at the top of the chart. *This was a mistake. I'm sorry. Please leave me alone.*

Bullshit.

Remains Found. The remains of Ron Thomas, a missing Atwell man, have been found near Temple Cave in Dismal Falls.

Wallis skimmed the remainder of the article to make sure her name wasn't mentioned. Once she reached the end, she deleted the alert, closed the browser, and leaned back into the desk chair, careful to keep her back straight and her shoulders square. One hand curved around the glassy, smooth mug. It was lipstick-red lacquer, and coffee heated the surface as the scent of Irish cream tickled her nose. The other set of fingers tightened around the chair's buttery leather arm. Hale had custom ordered it for her last birthday.

Damn that bitch. Wallis tightened her grip on the mug as she ground her teeth together. *She's been an obstacle since the day she was born.*

The crash of pottery brought her husband from his office. "Are you all right? Stay there, you'll cut yourself. I'll get a towel and a dustpan."

She kept her feet curled away from the mess on the floor and stared at the top of her doting husband's sandy-blond head. His hair was thinning, and she wasn't sure she cared.

"I'm sorry, Hale. I must've put it too close to the edge of the desk."

Ruined red shards clanked together in the dustpan. "It must have had a flaw in it, given the way it shattered." He looked up with a smile and ran a gentle thumb along her chin. "We're lucky it didn't cut your pretty face. I'll have a talk with the artist. She should have tested it better."

"You take such good care of me," she purred.

"Let me finish work and we can go for a drive and watch the sun come up."

He dumped the ruined mug and towel into the trash and returned to his office. Sure she was alone, Wallis unwound her feet from the base of the chair. Her beatific smile dissolved as she drummed her fingers on the desk.

The sharp tapping reminded her she was hitting her nails rather than the pads of her fingers, and she angled her hand until the noise was heavier. Tapping her nails ruined her polish. She'd had enough of ruined nail polish in her life—manicures cracked by washing dishes or bathing children, or ruined by digging in the garden. She hadn't done those things in decades, and she was proud of it.

She knotted her delicate hand into a hard fist and struck the table, careful to keep it quiet enough Hale wouldn't hear. First Beau and now Ron. *That* was no coincidence, was it? But then they'd found Abe, too, and *she* didn't know anything about him. After all these years, maybe it was time for the earth to vomit a few of her secrets. As long as they didn't tie everyone to her, she'd be fine. Maybe it was a coincidence.

Maybe.

Chapter Nine

Abby squinted in the sunshine and propped her foot on the bottom rail of the fence surrounding her paddock. As she watched George and Hemingway in the pasture, sweat trickled down her spine, soaking her shirt, and her shoulders ached from mucking out the stables and the barn. Behind her, Jane's bell clanged as the cow grazed in the grass that made her milk so sweet.

It had taken two days to realize Wallis hadn't been in Romanelli's, that she wasn't coming to wreak havoc and revenge. Slowly the color and sound had returned to Abby's world, and the fear had faded. In its wake had come a renewed commitment to her original goal…and a profound embarrassment.

She sneaked a glance at the house on the hill. Jeff had pushed his way into her life and made her warm, made her laugh—made her talk. And moved himself from the last spot on her List to the middle, behind Toby, Faye, Maggie and Gray.

And when she'd been unable to face him, he'd met someone else. Cassidy. Even though she knew it was for the best, Abby couldn't stop the disappointment.

She heard the engine before she saw the car. Shading her eyes with one hand, she frowned as the bright yellow van crept into view. Why on earth was the florist coming here? The delivery guy must be lost again.

She shook her head. Despite having lived in Fiddler his entire life, the kid still got turned around outside the city limits. It drove his grandmother nuts.

He stopped in the yard and emerged with a vase of roses, their deep red dark even in the sunshine. Someone was getting pretty flowers once the driver got his bearings.

"Hi, Abby," he said as he thrust the bouquet at her. "It's about time someone sent you these."

Me? She balanced the gift in one hand while she used the other to search her pockets for a tip. She didn't have anything. "Come up to the house."

"No need. I'm glad to come out here for something other than directions." He waved as he left. "Have a great afternoon."

The flowers' musky sweet scent filled her nose and clung to the air as she carried them into the house and sat them on the table. The sunlight through the window caught the facets in the vase and cast rainbows across the cabinets. They were beautiful. The weariness left her muscles and she felt her face soften and her lips curve into a smile. No wonder women loved getting these. She felt more feminine just having them in the house.

The card was a stark white square atop the mounds of soft red curves. Abby pulled it from the stand and looked down at Toby, who was staring at their present while his tail thumped on the floor. Even he seemed happy with the surprise.

The message was simple. *I'm sorry. Jeff.*

She stared at the words, and then the gift. "I can't accept these, Toby. It wasn't his fault, and keeping them will bring him back over the river." She put the card back into its plastic pitchfork. Even that was too much evidence to have lying around.

Without giving herself a chance to regret it, she picked up the flowers and stomped down the stairs and across her paddock toward the river. Holding the vase tight, she hopped from rock to rock and inhaled, memorizing the scent and the heavy glass in her hand. Toby and Tug scampered up the hill in front of her and wormed their way under the fence.

"Down." She whispered the command. Toby obeyed, but Tug was far too young to understand. She momentarily regretted bringing him home at all, then pushed it aside. It would crush Evan if someone adopted *his* dog while he was living at Mrs. Perry's. She scooped the puppy into one hand and talked to Toby. "Stay. We're going to have to make a quick escape."

Standing on the edge of the yard, she eyed the house like it was haunted. "I can do this. It's the right thing to do." She took one last look at the roses and acknowledged the unfairness of this whole thing.

Wrestling with Tug, she pushed herself forward and rehearsed her speech. *Thank you, but I can't keep them. Please don't ask.*

Her foot was on the bottom step when the back door opened and Cassidy walked out. She was in a dress, and her dark hair gleamed in the sunlight. Her makeup was flawless and, even though Abby couldn't smell anything other than roses, she'd bet Carter's paycheck that the woman didn't smell like horseshit.

"Abby?" the girl said, her smile wide. "It's nice to see you. Are you looking for Jeff? He had to leave town this morning. Poor guy. His plane left early, and he really didn't want to go."

He wasn't sorry about their botched date. He was sorry he'd tried at all. Abby bobbled the vase as she surrendered it, but managed to keep hold of both it and the puppy. "I can't keep these."

"But—"

"I. Can't." Abby persisted, shoving the flowers forward. "Please."

Cassidy wrapped her hands around the vase, and her manicured nails stood out next to Abby's dirty ones. God, this couldn't get any worse. Once her hands were free, she stepped back into the yard and kept hold of the squirming puppy.

Don't stand here like a moron. Leave. She spun on her heel.

"Hang on a minute. Abby?" Cassidy called after her. Abby broke into a sprint, only to fumble with the gate. It gave the other woman a chance to catch up. "Abby, wait. He should've—"

He should've left me alone, stayed on his porch, and not held my hand. He should've gone somewhere else to work. He should've been ugly and mean with no sense of humor. Abby swiped a tear away as she yanked on the latch. Relief flooded her as the gate swung free and, with a snap of her fingers, she called Toby to her. "I have chores to do," she called over her shoulder as she escaped into the open field.

Once home, she stashed Tug in his kennel and she and Toby went to the house. It still smelled like roses. She had to get out of here.

In the shower, she stood under the hot spray and used the sweetest-smelling soap she owned, until mounds of suds covered her feet and her skin stung and her cuticles ached. Once out, she wiped the fog from the mirror and attacked her hair, drying it by sections until it was sleek and straight, and then put on makeup the way Maggie had taught her.

She picked her blue dress, the prettiest thing she owned, and walked under a cloud of perfume. She changed her truck keys for the SUV keys. Farmers drove trucks. Women drove their SUVs to volunteer at the Humane Society. And she was a woman, dammit.

Before she left, she broke her own rule and opened all the windows in the house. Maybe by the time she came home, the place wouldn't smell like silly romantic dreams.

They arrived at the animal shelter, and Toby trotted down the hall to her office and his waiting dog bed.

"Wait 'til you see what we got today," Bridget Simpson gushed, a wide smile on her face.

"Is it an. Elephant?" Abby joked. Of all her volunteers, Bridget was the most fun to watch with the animals.

"Almost as good," Bridget teased back before looking her up and down. "You look pretty today. I'm glad you're feeling better. I was starting to worry."

Abby shooed her toward the kennels. "Thank you. I'm fine. Show me our new pet."

Bridget kept walking and talking, shouting over the din that always marked their arrival. "I was hoping I'd be here when you saw her. Abby, she's just beautiful. I can't believe anyone would get rid of her. I mean, I never see them in shelters, just on rescue pages and I—"

They'd stopped in front of Tug's old kennel. Curled

in the back, quiet and graceful even in her fright and confusion, was a fawn greyhound.

Blood rushed through Abby's veins, and her heart stuttered before it raced away, taking her breath with it. She lost the rest of Bridget's conversation, and the yipping madhouse of the kennel faded, as she reeled back in time until she was an eight-year-old in Wheeling, West Virginia.

At first glance, she'd loved the dog track in Wheeling with the beautiful and graceful hounds chasing the mechanical rabbit. Then she'd seen how the dogs were treated behind the scenes, what happened when they were too spent to run. She started spending her days at the kennels with the trainers, walking the dogs, stroking their lean muscles, comforting them as she could. It had kept her out of Wallis's way.

Then Walter Pine had married Wallis and they'd moved to North Carolina.

Walt—her second stepdad and the least attentive. He'd been a nice guy, but completely wrapped up in his wife, which meant Wallis had been happy. While Abby had missed the dog track, she'd enjoyed being left to her own devices, and she'd been able to go to school. Then she'd met Connie Dempsey, her first real friend.

Boone, North Carolina, would have been a good home. But she'd opened her mouth.

A chill crept across her skin, and Abby fought it back. Gritting her teeth, she kept the story from escaping and focused on the greyhound in front of her and on Bridget's ramblings.

You can do this. Don't fall apart again. There's no reason to be afraid. Wallis isn't here. She doesn't know. No one knows. Breathe, Abby. Breathe.

"You're right, Bridget. She's. Beautiful. Has Lex seen her?"

"Not yet. We have an appointment with him tomorrow."

"Thanks." Abby forced a smile and pretended her knees weren't shaking under her dress. "I'm going to my office."

Keeping her steps soft, but her strides long, Abby hurried to the other end of the building and closed the door.

Connie and Walt. The anniversary of their deaths was later this week. Of all the letters she wrote, theirs was the most difficult. It would have been easiest to write the truth: *Walter Pine did not kill his stepdaughter. I'm his stepdaughter, and I'm very much alive. Check the little girl's grave. Please give the Dempsey family peace.*

But she couldn't do that. It would cause a huge stir, and Wallis would know. She couldn't even leave hints about the bodies. Walt was buried. As far as she knew, the bullet that had killed him was rattling around his coffin. So she could only say part of the truth: *Walt Pine was not a killer or a child molester, nor did he commit suicide. Please reopen the case.*

But no one ever listened. As far as they were concerned, the case was solved and a monster had taken himself off the streets. They didn't know anything about monsters.

Connie. Every time Abby thought about her friend, her heart squeezed tight. Connie had seen a real monster in her life. It had been the last memory in her young brain, and she must have been so afraid. Connie should have gone to fourth grade. She should've learned her multiplication tables, been on the swim team, gotten her driver's license, and gone to prom. She should have grown up, gotten married, and had kids. She should be begging Abby to come home for their high school reunion. Instead, her age-progressed portrait was plastered all over North Carolina in case a miracle occurred.

No matter how many lost stepfathers Abby uncovered, she'd never be able to make up for her little redheaded friend. Evan Gaines reminded her so much of Connie.

Her phone rang, and she smiled as she recognized the number. "Hello, Celia."

"Hi. I need to move our meeting tomorrow."

"Is everything okay?"

"No. I've just gotten off the phone with Evan Gaines's grandparents and they can't take him."

"Why can't he stay at Mrs. Perry's?"

"He was supposed to be a temporary placement. She specializes in challenging kids, and the state needs her to take one more. Since Evan's not a disciplinary problem, we have to find him a new spot."

It was wrong to punish a little boy for being good, to keep him in limbo when all he wanted was a home and people who cared about him. That's all she'd ever wanted, and she had it. Could she offer him the same?

"What about me? Could I foster him?" Abby faced her computer and did a Google search for Child Protection Services and foster parenting applications. "I have the forms right here."

"Umm, you can try. You'll have to meet with CPS and have a site visit."

Her printer was already whirring. "I'll get everything turned in as quickly as possible."

As the morning faded into afternoon, Toby slept in the corner while Abby researched, gathered information and completed forms. The pile of printed documents grew larger and larger, and her stomach sank lower and lower.

The minute she opened her mouth, they'd deny her application. Who gave an eight-year-old to a woman who couldn't talk? She needed an attorney. And she only knew one. She dialed the phone.

"Hi, Maggie. Can I talk to Gray?"

While she waited on him to pick up, her mouth shaped into a smile. She had a new goal. One that had nothing to do with death or fear. This was about life and hope for a little boy. About her ability to do something good for someone while they could benefit from it rather than after the fact.

She couldn't save herself, but maybe she could save Evan.

Chapter Ten

At the end of the week, Abby carried blankets, a six-pack, and her camera to the river as the sun set. Every year, this was the only way she could find to honor Connie—to remember the times they'd sat under the stars.

Night came slowly, and Abby drank her beer as she watched it creep into the valley. Frogs thrummed and crickets chirped, and the fireflies came out to play.

She lay down on the blanket and stared up at the stars winking down at her. There. The one that looked pink was Connie. Pink had been her favorite color. And that one was Beau, and that one was Ron, and that one was John. The one there, all alone, was Walt. That fuzzy one there was the Toby Wallis had killed. The twinkly one nearest the horizon was Buck. And the brightest one, in the middle, was Papa.

Raising her camera, she focused on that one and adjusted the lens. She could see the wispy clouds in front of it and the drifts of stars behind it. Then she couldn't see anything. Putting her feet flat, she pushed her back against the ground and prepared to fight. The autofocus adjusted, revealing—not a monster—but gray hair gleaming in the moonlight.

Moving the camera, she blinked up at the obstruction. "You're in my shot."

"Sorry," Jeff muttered.

He wasn't sorry enough to move. Instead of taking the picture, she sat up, put her camera on the blanket and grabbed her ale. The sour apple flavor reminded her of Jolly Ranchers. She blinked up at him, waiting on his anger.

"Look, I don't mean to ruin your evening or *push* you. Just tell me what I did to piss you off so badly you'd refuse an apology."

Her skin heated. *Shit. See? This is what happens when you try to be normal. People find out you're weirder than they thought.*

"Why would you. Apologize. To me?" she asked, cursing that he'd approach her tonight when so many memories clanged against her tongue, begging to be told. "I'm the one. Who ruined. Everything."

Without waiting on an invitation, Jeff sat next to her on the blanket. "Are you? I—" he ticked the items on his fingers "—didn't let you cancel, didn't make reservations, forgot our date, took you to the hospital for an emergency, and then asked you to talk about something very painful." He looked at the bottle in her hand. "I thought you didn't drink."

"Only on special occasions." She smothered her belch and put the empty in the six-pack.

"It looks like a very special occasion."

She stared at the Jack Daniel's bottle in his hand. Buck had loved Jack Daniel's. "You seem to be having one of your own."

"Anniversary. You?"

She wove her fingers through the yarn fringe on

the blanket. She'd attached it after the satin border had given way during the first year she'd been here alone. "Anniversary."

"Your father?"

"My best friend." Abby preempted the question she knew he'd ask. "She was murdered." The last word tightened her lungs.

"How old were you?"

You can do this. One word. Just this one. "Eight."

"Did they catch him?"

It wasn't a him, it was a her. And no, they didn't. She got away, and she's out there, and I can't tell anyone. Every nerve in her body begged her to tell him. He'd find her monster. Just like he'd found Maggie's monster last year.

But Wallis would escape. She always did. And then Maggie would have a new monster to fear. So would Faye, and Evan, and even Jeff. He'd pay for his good deed. So Abby glued her lips together and shook her head.

"Do you know how frustrating that is?" Jeff asked. "To be talking to you and have you just stop?"

"Then why spend time with me?" she countered. "Go home." Though she used her best glare, he stayed put. "You can't *help* me," she persisted. "I'm not a. Victim. You can save." *It's too late for me.*

He took a sip of whiskey. "Can't I just like spending time with you?"

No he couldn't. He should go away. "Jeff—"

"I need someone to talk to, Abby. If I was back in Chicago I'd be out with friends, where I wouldn't be stuck in my own head." He looked across at her.

"What about Cassidy?"

"She's out with Carter." His smile widened. "She's my sister. Didn't she tell you?"

Not his girlfriend. She stared back, her skin heating even as her heart thudded. She ought to stick to her resolution. One last rebuff, after he'd confided in her, would permanently exile her. Taking a deep breath, she rehearsed the damning lines. *I don't care. Go away and leave me alone.*

"Is this the date your father died?" she asked.

"Twenty-three years ago today," he said. "It's weird. I've *not* had him longer than I actually did have him, but it never gets easier. I was still looking for him in the crowd when I finished my PhD. Hell, I even dreamed Mom had him stuffed and put him on the sofa like a pillow. He's missed all the experiences that made me who I am, but he's colored all my decisions." He sighed. "I feel like he's looking over my shoulder, and I don't want to disappoint him. And I have. One of his murderers was just granted parole, and I wasn't there to fight it."

She nodded. She felt a similar weight every day that Wallis walked free.

"Maybe it was meant for us to hang out together," he murmured, nudging her. "My dad, your friend, same day. That's a big coincidence."

If this was Fate in action, she had a sick sense of humor. Still, it was comforting to share this loss with him, knowing he'd experienced something similar. Even if she couldn't talk about it.

"What was her name?" he asked.

"Connie." That was safe enough. No last name, no location. Just a little girl who'd died.

"Did you grow up with her?"

Abby shook her head. "I met her my first day of third

grade. The desk in front of her was empty, so I sat there. We were wearing the same shoes."

"So you became instant friends?"

She nodded. "We used to stay on the playground until she had to go home, swinging so high the chains buckled and we'd drop like we were on a roller coaster. Her braids would bounce against her back, and she'd whoop and laugh and start again."

"I always liked the seesaw," Jeff whispered. His breath brushed her ear. When she turned her head, they were almost nose to nose, and his arm was warm against her back. This close, his smile was blinding. "You looked cold," he explained as if reading her mind. "My younger sisters were Brownies. Were you and Connie?"

"No. But she'd found an old handbook at the library, so we were working through it. One night we camped in her backyard and her dad showed us the stars while we roasted hot dogs and marshmallows."

He shook out her extra blanket and covered their legs. The flannel trapped his body heat against her skin and concentrated his scent.

"What constellations did you learn?" he asked.

She pointed at the sky. "Big Dipper. Little Dipper. Perseus—"

Jeff pointed to her left, and drew a design. "There's Cassiopeia." Then another. "Andromeda." Then he pointed to her right. "And there's Hercules." His fingers tightened on her hip. "You know, that thing you're doing with your hand is driving me crazy."

His words made her focus on the hand resting on his thigh. His well-worn jeans were silky soft, and she was rubbing the inside seam between her fingers. He shivered as her nails scratched the fabric. She yanked her hand away.

He pulled her back to him and placed his hand atop hers. Underneath were large solid muscles and bone, above were long, gentle fingers. Everything about him was comforting and *not* at the same time.

"I'm sorry I ran," she whispered.

"You worried the crap out of me," he replied. "And, what? You thought I'd just move another woman *in* within the week?"

There wasn't anything to say. She'd thought exactly that. Hoped for it and resented it at the same time.

"I'm not as shallow as people think, Abby. Not as fickle either."

"We can't date," she warned him—and herself. Dating was full of minefields for both of them, and she was just beginning to navigate her side of it. The side where she liked having him here, enjoyed talking to him, even liked him holding her doors. It was already going to be painful when he finished his work and left.

"Of course not," he said.

Fireflies crowded the field in front of them. Abby reached for her camera and Jeff released her other hand. Hoping the whir of the shutter wouldn't ruin the shot, she clicked. Again. Again. Rapid shots, grabbing as many glances as possible, wide views of the sparkling field, close-ups of single bugs.

When she finished, Jeff was staring at her, his beard a dark smudge in the night. "We used to catch them and put them in a jar. I remember lying in bed and watching them flash on my bedside table as I went to sleep. Did you do that?"

She nodded. Ron had helped her gather them once.

They'd had so much fun chasing each other around the field, trying to get new bugs in the jar while keeping the others from escaping.

"What about pulling the lights off and making rings?" he asked.

"Once," she said. "And then I found out it wouldn't grow back. That I'd. Killed. The bug for something that faded right away." She'd cried so hard Ron had worried about her for weeks afterward. It's one of the reasons he'd wanted to take her to The Dismals—to see the Dismalites in the canyon, lights that lived on and on.

Fireflies always made her think of Ron.

A coyote yipped in the distance, followed quickly by another set, and then a third. The smaller animals in the surrounding woods alternated between freezing in quiet panic and scrambling noisily for cover. The breeze grew colder. Abby abandoned her plan to sleep under the stars and gathered her things. Jeff stood and folded one blanket. She folded the other before he plucked it from her hands and added it to his load. Then he shoved her pillow under his arm.

"I'll see you home."

He shouldn't do that. Abby reached for the bedding and he stepped away.

"Otherwise you'll have to make two trips." He moved again when she tried to take the pillows, and his smile widened, glittering in the dark. The man's charm should be illegal.

"Fine," she huffed, refusing to smile. "C'mon." They walked in silence, except for the rattle of bottles and the bump of the camera against her stomach, and Jeff balanced the blankets while he wrestled with the screen door. Abby unlocked the house, disarmed the alarm, and went inside with him on her heels until he dropped the blankets on the sofa.

"Thank you," she said as she walked him out.

He stopped at the threshold. "Did you like the roses?" he asked in a quiet voice. His long thick lashes hid his eyes. He'd probably never had to ask another woman that question, and she was embarrassed by her poor manners as much as she was frightened of the truth.

"Yes," she whispered. "They were. Beautiful."

Before she could move away, he lowered his head and his breath fanned across her cheek as his lips touched hers and his beard tickled her chin. Abby returned the kiss on impulse, shaping her lips to his. They were softer than she'd expected. He kissed her again, angling his head as he stepped closer.

They couldn't do this. She put her hand on his chest, and he stopped.

His soft cotton shirt soothed her skin but did little to hide the powerful muscles underneath and his heart thudding against her palm. Even without cologne, he smelled good—clean but salty, with a hint of the river and outdoors, and sweet woodsy whiskey.

"Sorry," he muttered as he stepped backward.

She'd never felt this warm, this safe. She curled her fingers into his shirt and his chest hair teased her through the fabric. Jeff came back to her, curving his hand around her waist, and Abby's world centered on his slow, wicked smile.

This kiss was different. His lips were firm and the contact was brief before he nibbled her lip and swept his tongue across it. He tightened his hold on her as he delved deeper, coaxing her mouth open, sliding his tongue across hers. His mustache pricked her skin, and when she flinched he backed away, sucking her top lip into his mouth to soothe it.

She wanted to taste him again. Curving her hand around his shoulder, she urged him back to her, this time opening her mouth under his in invitation and sighing at the taste of whiskey on his hot tongue. His muscles gathered under her hand, tempting her to explore, and his groan rattled through her when she did.

"Damn," he muttered as he pulled his lips free. His breath heaved through his lungs, pushing his chest against hers. His thumb traced an arc across her stomach, from her waist to her rib cage and back, and Abby swore she could feel sparks along the path.

"What are we doing?" she panted.

"Not dating," he replied, his voice strained as he stepped away. He cleared his throat. "Good night. Lock the door behind me."

She did, but she lifted the curtain and watched until he'd disappeared over the hill toward the river. She counted to ten and cracked the door open, straining to hear and then smiling as his screen door squealed on its hinges. He was safe, too.

Shutting the door, she twisted every deadbolt and armed the security system. She turned to see Toby staring at her from his bed, his head cocked to one side.

"Don't look at me like that. You heard him. We're not dating."

Chapter Eleven

"I was beginning to think you were dead," Cass croaked from the kitchen table as Jeff shuffled to the coffeepot.

"Are you sure you aren't?" he teased. "What time did you get in?"

"Umm, three? I think." She wagged the sugar spoon at him. "Don't look at me like that. It's not like you don't stay out until all hours."

"That's different. I'm—"

"Don't you *dare* say grown up. I am sick and fucking—"

"Watch your language," he scolded. "I was going to say I'm a guy." And a grown-up.

"You're the *same* guy who taught me self-defense before my freshman year," Cass said, the last word ending on a yawn. "What did you do last night?"

"Not much," he lied. "Do you want breakfast?"

"I'll make it. Did you see the box in your office? It came while you were gone."

He hadn't. He'd come home from his trip around the crime scenes, grabbed a bottle, and gone for a walk. And he'd returned with the taste of apple ale on his tongue, so hard his sheets had tormented him.

From one kiss.

"Thanks. I'll go look through it. Yell when it's ready."

He took his coffee to his office. After moving the box out of the way, he unloaded the pile of brochures and notes from his trip and powered up his laptop. The photos from each scene were waiting in Google Drive, and while they printed he tacked the information from each site under the proper victim.

The grainy photos went up next. While they gave him the information he needed, they weren't as good as Abby's.

Abby…

Reversing course, he went to the other wall and marked through *agoraphobic* on his board. She wasn't afraid of crowds. And she wasn't afraid of him, thank God, but she was fearful enough to arm her security system just to walk to the river. And she'd seen way too much death at too young an age.

What else had he learned last night? She'd been poor, most likely. All her stories involved activities that were free. Even at eight, he'd gone places. His memories were of little league and summer camp. And no one had cared where she was. Connie had had to go home. Abby hadn't. She hated being cold. Her mother should have made sure she was warm.

What kind of mother didn't take care of her child? Jeff reined himself in. For all he knew, the woman had been working three jobs to pay for counseling services. Besides, the thought of Abby cold and alone, neglected, losing someone else at such a young age, left a bitter taste in his mouth.

Slugging back coffee, he scratched his chest and turned back to his bony victims, scribbling snippets from his notes next to evidence and details.

"Wow."

He whirled to face his sister, who was setting a tray, complete with fresh coffee, on his desk. "I told you I'd come—"

"Dude, I called you, like, three times." She grabbed an empty chair. "We can eat in here."

He walked back to his desk. "We don't have to. It's full of dead people."

"It's okay," she said as she stared at the wall. "That doesn't look like a manual."

"They asked me to help on an interstate multiple murder case," he explained as he chewed his toast.

"Serial killer?" Cass asked, her eyes sparkling. "Really?"

"Don't get that way," he scolded her the way he did new recruits. "Victims are lost to someone, although these guys don't seem to have anyone at all."

She looked at the five columns. "So what connects them?"

"Manner of death and where they were found, with the exception of the first guy. He was found on his property."

Cass carried her plate with her as she read. "What are you missing?"

"How they knew their killer," Jeff said, joining her at the board and lapsing into teacher mode. "They're from all over the place. None of them had the same job. All of them married late, but they don't have anyone in common."

She paced the line, looking over her shoulder when she reached the end. "All of their wives' names are variations on Elizabeth. Except for this one—Allie."

He nodded. "I noticed that, but Elizabeth is an incredibly common name. And some of the Elizabeths had a child, but some didn't. I can't assume it's the same woman."

Cass turned again, and Jeff panicked. "Come back over here and tell me about your first week of work."

Her mouth fell open as she read. "You're profiling your girlfriend."

"She's not my girlfriend."

Cass arched an eyebrow and waved her free hand at the board. "Really?"

"It's nothing. I have to find a way to answer my questions, and she won't talk about her past. Even last night—" Shit. He squinched his eyes closed, knowing he'd said too much.

"Last night? When you did *not much*?" Cass teased. "You told her I'm your sister, right?" She grinned when he nodded. "Good. I'd like to get to know her better if she's gonna be my sister-in-law."

"Cassidy Renee," he warned. Her giggle diffused his agitation, just like it always did. "You will pay for that one day."

She sat on the edge of the table. "We were all wondering what had happened to you."

"Don't sit on that," he said. "It's not ours." He walked back to the desk, glad to hear her following. He didn't want her reading too much into his habits. "What do you mean *all*?"

"The family," she said. "You haven't mentioned a new girl in a while. And you're always home these days, even when Janice calls you on Friday nights."

"So it's bad that I'm home?" he asked, ignoring that his insides felt like he was teetering at the crest of a roller coaster. He wasn't sure what was worse—that they'd noticed, or that they were all talking about him.

"It's just atypical," Cass continued. "And I heard Aunt Sophie brought you an entire group of women, some of whom looked like Miss America, and you didn't flirt once."

"I didn't flirt with them," he gritted the words out, "because country girls come with all these…strings. They don't understand casual." He scowled at her. "What?"

"First off," Cass pontificated, grinning. "I don't see a lot of skyscrapers around here. Second, no woman does casual, and if you know some who do…"

She was filtering. Cass never filtered herself. "Spit it out, baby sister."

"Women might say they're good with casual, but if they like a guy, they'll pretty much throw that out the window and pursue him. So why are you sleeping with women who don't like you?" She tilted her head. "Or are you picking them because they don't like you?"

His stomach hit the bottom of the coaster. That was just a little too sharp, a little too close to the truth. "Well," he countered, "if that's your argument, then Abby fits right into my normal pattern."

Cass shook her head. "You didn't see her when I opened that door. And you've said it yourself." She pointed at the wall. "She tells you to go away because she's scared of something. And it's not you."

Fuck. How had he let this conversation get this far? "We're not dating, Cass. She doesn't want to, and I'm not staying. That—" he pointed at the board "—is because I'd like to help her."

She propped her feet on the table, then removed them

when she met his gaze. "All right, Mr. Profiler. Let me give you a situation. A guy talks a woman into going out with him, and she goes but ditches him at the restaurant, has a panic attack and tells him to go away. But he doesn't. He sends her roses. And when she returns them, he chases her down to find out why, and ends up kissing her."

He was glad his beard hid his embarrassment. "How did you know that?"

"Lucky guess, big brother," she said, her grin widening. "But you're not dating."

Jeff leaned back in his chair, crossed his arms, and refused to say anything else. Cass had always been too smart for anyone else's good.

She stuck her tongue out at him and went back to his row of victims. Stopping this time at the first one—Beau Archer. "Did you see this?"

He walked behind her and read over her shoulder. It was Betty Archer's statement about why she was taking her daughter and leaving town. "She was afraid. So?"

"So?" Cass persisted. "If I'm married and my husband goes missing, my first reaction isn't that someone's going to come after me. Unless I know he was mixed up in something nasty." She tapped the words *Atlantic City*.

"He owed someone money," Jeff theorized.

"Maybe they all did," Cass said as she put her empty plate on the table.

They worked in silence, alternating between the map, the computer and his notes, and soon had every possible gaming location worked out. Jeff ruffled his sister's hair. "I guess I'm glad you're smart after all," he grumbled. "And just because you *might* be right on this, it doesn't mean you're right about everything else."

"Yeah, yeah," Cass grumbled back. "Did you open your box?"

Jeff blushed. He'd been so busy thinking about Abby he'd forgotten.

Cass shook her head and grinned. "But I'm not right."

He ripped the tab on the box and lifted the thick file. It was the information on Ron Thomas from Alabama. The documents on top were duplicates of what he already had, but behind that was something that chilled his blood even as it made it race in his veins.

Sixteen other letters, spaced a year apart, each saying the same thing. *Ron Thomas's body is buried in The Dismals, under the large tree next to Temple Cave.*

"What has you so excited?" Cass asked. "Don't deny it. I can see it in your eyes." She flipped through letter after letter. "They all say the same thing."

He nodded. "Exactly the same thing. Obsessively so." He checked the postmarks. "And timed obsessively, too. I'd bet your fancy degree they arrived on the date he died."

He went to the map. Ron's letter had been mailed from Tunica, Mississippi, which was within driving distance of Atwood, Alabama.

His phone rang, and he picked it up while still staring at the file. "Yeah?"

"Working?" Gray Harper asked.

"Of course. What are you doing?"

"Sitting on my back patio with a beautiful woman. You should try it."

"Wanna loan her to me?" Jeff teased. "Or are you worried she'd see the error of her ways?"

"I'm shaking in my shoes," Gray snorted. "What's on your agenda for today?"

Jeff looked around the room now crowded with paper and notes. "Nothing. Why?"

"Can you meet me at the hospital, at Celia Hughes's office? I've been hired to put forward an application to foster Evan Gaines, and I know you're interested in what happens to him. I think you should be there, and Celia agrees."

"Who wants him?" Jeff asked, dread pooling in his gut. He should be happy—Evan would have a family. The boy could move on and leave burgers on picnic tables behind.

"Privileged information," Gray said. "The meeting's at eleven."

Jeff checked his watch. It was ten now. "Thanks for the notice, asshole." He hung up and looked at Cass. "I have to go to a meeting. Don't mess with anything in here while I'm gone."

At five 'til eleven, Jeff strode down the hospital hallway, raking his fingers through his hair to make sure it was both dry and untangled. After that, he tugged the hem of his jacket, straightened his collar, and checked his fly. Then he prayed that whoever wanted Evan was a nice couple who wouldn't mind an eccentric sort-of uncle.

Knocking once on Celia's door, he let himself in.

Abby was sitting next to Gray. She looked over her shoulder with a tentative smile. Her thick hair was loose and she'd traded jeans and vintage cotton for gray dress slacks and a deep red blouse that reminded him of the roses he'd sent. She'd added makeup and tasteful jewelry. She looked like any woman he'd see at work, except ten times more beautiful, and he wondered what it would've been like to lie in bed this morning and watch her get dressed.

He took the empty seat next to her and narrowly avoiding stepping on Toby's tail.

"They called you, too?" He checked his watch. It was eleven. "Where are they?"

"Now that we're all here—" Gray grinned at him "—Abby's asked me to represent her in her emergency application to be Evan Gaines's foster parent."

Jeff looked at the woman between them. She blushed until she was almost as red as her blouse.

"We've completed all the necessary forms," Gray continued, "and Abby's provided her financial statement, her tax returns, all her background reports and a detailed plan for Evan's care. She's passed her home visit."

"Are you sure, Abby?" Celia asked. "He's an active little boy."

"He needs room to run and fresh air." While she talked, Abby grasped the chair with one hand and stroked Toby with the other. "I work from home, so he won't be alone."

Celia turned to him. "Jeff?"

Stomping on the glee he felt at having the kid close by, Jeff focused on being responsible. Abby couldn't even go out to dinner without a panic attack. Having Evan with her every day could push her past panic and straight to a nervous breakdown. If that happened, the boy would be in a third home in less than two months. He'd get labeled as trouble.

He could feel everyone staring at him—even Toby was waiting. *No.* The word was on the tip of his tongue when he saw the plea in Abby's velvet-brown eyes.

He looked over her shoulder at Gray, mentally cursing him for this ambush. “Can I speak to your *client* alone?”

“Okay with you, Ab?” Gray asked before he stood and followed Celia to the door. “We’ll go get coffee.”

“You do that,” Jeff drawled, and he swore he heard Gray’s laughter ring down the hallway.

Once they were alone, Jeff put on his glasses and reviewed her financial statement. Her photography business made a modest profit. She gave dog-training classes, and her farm even made a little money. But her web business showed ten years of steady increases. She had savings and investments, but no mortgage. She actually had very little debt at all. “When did you have a home visit?”

“Thursday.”

“Why didn’t you talk to me about it last night?” he asked. They’d talked about murder and death, about loss and childhood. But not *this* child.

“You didn’t. Ask.”

“I didn’t know to ask. But we’ll play this your way. What’s your plan?” She reached for Toby, and the dog put his head on her knee with a sigh. “He wants to live with me, Jeff. I want him to live with me.”

“He wants to live with me, too, but that doesn’t mean I’m the right choice.” He tossed the file on the desk. “Abby, he’s not a stray animal you can rehab. He’s a very active little boy. Have you thought about what having him with you all the time will do to you?”

“His grandparents can’t take him, and the state is going to move him because there’s another child who needs Mrs. Perry’s attention more than him.”

“But why you?”

"If Andy doesn't go to prison, the state won't fight him for custody. Evan will have to go back to that monster."

A pit opened in Jeff's stomach. He'd love to spout the law-and-order line all agents started out believing—that right would always win—but he knew better. There was a recently paroled felon in Tennessee who proved that point. "Let's share him."

"That's worse than calling him a stray dog."

"No it isn't. He'd get what he wanted," Jeff reasoned. "Both of us. He'd live with you. You'd be the responsible one, and I'm the…uncle next door."

"That would make us brother and sister," she teased.

"Yeah, that won't work." He leaned close enough that her hair tickled his nose. "Because that lipstick is inspiring some definite non-brotherly thoughts."

She blushed again, and his cock thumped against his zipper. "Why do you want him?"

"I want him to be happy and make it to fourth grade."

The grade her friend Connie had never seen. "Abby—"

"I know I can't keep him, that he'll be adopted by a family with two parents. But if he can stay at Mrs. Perry's, then he can stay with me." She stared at him, her gaze earnest. "Can't he?"

God help him, he nodded. "I'll be your backup. We'll figure it out as we go. Agreed?"

The kiss on his cheek was so light he thought he'd imagined it—until her breath warmed his skin. "Thank you."

The door opened, and she jumped away from him like he'd burned her. He was too stunned to move at all.

Gray handed over a cup of coffee, and began shaking

in silent laughter as he brushed his cheek. Jeff shifted in his chair, gaining control over his body as he searched for his handkerchief and then wiped his face. The telltale lipstick smudge stained the white cotton. Abby looked like she wanted to sink through the floor.

"We've reached an agreement." Jeff struggled to keep his voice level. "If Abby's application is approved, I'll be there to help."

"*If* I need it," she reminded him.

He stared at her. "Regardless. I'll see Evan as my schedule permits. And we'll be honest about the arrangement. No getting his hopes up about either of us keeping him. He was old enough to understand the situation at Mrs. Perry's. This is just another foster home."

She nodded. "Agreed."

Celia looked between them and smiled. "Thank you both. I'll call the court and set a hearing date, and call Gray with the details."

After the meeting, Jeff walked Abby to her car and opened her door. Toby leapt in while she pressed a piece of paper into Jeff's palm. "Phone number."

He pulled out his phone, added her information, and then texted her his number. "There we go. Official and everything," he said as he closed the door.

He watched them drive away before striding to his convertible. Gray was lounged against it, shaking his head, his smile wide.

"I never thought I'd be around when this happened to you."

"Just because you're happily married doesn't mean the whole world wants to be. All we're doing is sharing a little boy."

"And lipstick," Gray quipped as he walked away.

"Screw you," Jeff grumbled as he started the car. Ever since Gray had eloped to Vegas, he—

Damn.

Hitting Bob's number, Jeff listened to the phone ring as he navigated the busiest street in Fiddler and then around the square.

Bob answered the phone, laughing. "Harper just spent five minutes trying to convince me you're, like, a foster dad."

"I am," Jeff muttered. "His name is Evan, he's eight, and his dad's in jail for killing his mother. And I think the proper term is co-parenting. Abby Quinn is his foster mother."

"Abby? The brunette who doesn't talk?"

"Yep. She's my neighbor."

"Fuck," Bob sighed. "They got you, too."

"They did not," Jeff griped. "Listen. My files are missing marriage certificates. Can't anyone find them?"

"No. All anyone knows is the guys came home married."

Because they'd married in different states. Just like Gray and Maggie had married in Vegas and filed the certificate in Nevada before they'd left. "I'm going to send you a list of cities," Jeff barked as he turned on the road toward home. "Have Amanda start there." He hung up.

Passing Abby's driveway, he went up the hill. Cass was fidgeting in the doorway as he bolted up the steps. "What?"

"It's a woman," she blurted as she pushed open the screen door and got out of his way.

"Slow down." He put up his hand. "What makes you think that?"

She was already halfway down the hall. “Come see.”

In the room, she stood in front of his board and pointed at each site. “With the exception of Archer, they’re all near campgrounds. Someone would have noticed Guido and Sonny marching a nervous dude into the park. They would have stood out. But no one mentioned anything.”

Jeff nodded. That information dovetailed into what he’d just realized. “They went in as a family. No one would notice a family setting up camp for the weekend.”

Cass nodded as she darted to his Archer file and flipped it open. She displayed the oldest tip. It was on notebook paper, and the date was neatly written in the corner. The brief message was written in blue ballpoint ink, and the letters were neat, rounded and evenly spaced. It was a young woman’s handwriting. Jeff looked at his board of victims, at the skinned knees bracketing Beau Archer’s photo from the file. A daughter.

Betty Archer and her daughter. Who’d vanished without a trace.

“Now what?” Cass asked, her bright eyes shining.

“Now you go upstairs and read something light and fluffy, or get on Twitter and gossip. Mom would kill me if she knew I had you profiling murderers.” Jeff shoved her out the door. “Get away from this room while I think.”

Once it was quiet, Jeff closed his eyes and sat in his chair, stuffing each item from his day into its own box until only the case remained. The common traits of serial killers were, for him, as easy to recite as the alphabet, even if female killers weren’t common. And he had a pretty good hunch he was looking for mother and daughter, and that the daughter was the one with the conscience. And, if he held with his earlier theory, she'd graduated to killing on her own.

Underachiever? Possibly. They'd have to be transient and easy to ignore. Most jobs fitting that bill didn't require anything but a pretty smile.

Unstable families and domineering mothers? Jeff stared at the grisly photos littering his temporary office. That was sort of obvious.

Criminal histories in their families? Again, obvious—at least for the beta daughter. Betty—the alpha mother from hell—would have been a doozy to live with. Once he had marriage certificates, it might be easier to check Betty's background.

Abused? Betty was probably abusive. How could any person capable of this level of violence exempt their children? Her daughter probably fought for her life every day.

Hate their mothers? The daughter would more than likely despise Betty, the mother who had dragged her across the country and kept her on the fringes of society.

OCD? He looked at the stack of seventeen identical messages. Oh yeah.

While the rest of the traits might not fit as the investigation progressed, this list was enough to start him down an ugly path. Betty had been a monster, whether born that way or made that way was still a question. But she'd *made* a worse monster than herself. Her daughter, the beta, would be deadly.

He flipped through the file, checking dates. Archer had been dead almost thirty years, but the letters hadn't started until seventeen years ago. He drew a line down the board and labeled it 1999. Something had happened then to trigger her guilt on the earlier victims. Jeff opened an email to Bob and typed the list of cities to search for marriage licenses, urging him to find Beau Archer's first. He added the fateful lines.

Mother/daughter team. Mother more than likely dead or institutionalized within the last twenty years. Daughter possibly following in her footsteps.

Chapter Twelve

"Can we go fishing when we get home?" Evan asked. "Or maybe for a hike? Or could you show me how to ride the horse?"

Abby reached for Toby, but he shrank away from her toward the door. It had become a troubling pattern this first week. They were both talked almost to tears.

She tightened her grip on the steering wheel. "We have to do chores."

"What about after?"

"Laundry and dinner," she reminded him. It was the whole reason they'd come to town for a second grocery run in a week.

How did such a small person eat so much, talk so much and dirty so many clothes? Despite all that, the little boy was a welcome addition to her life. So much so that it was hard to imagine what it had been like without him. Though he'd become the star of her nightmares. Last night Wallis had chased him across the field under a bloodred sky.

Abby looked in the review mirror. "Listen. For a. Second."

He looked up at her, waiting.

"You and I are out here alone. So if. Something. Bad.

Happens, if I tell you to run or if you get scared. You run to Jeff. Okay?"

"Yes, ma'am." He went back to staring out the window, watching the world slip by. "Will it?"

"Not if I can help it," she promised. "But Jeff will keep you safe. No matter. What."

They got home, put his new clothes in the washing machine, and started the chores she'd had to skip this morning to get Evan to the dentist on time.

Milking came first. Poor Jane would be miserable if she had to wait much longer. "I'll milk. Why don't you take care of the chickens?"

After milking Jane and putting her in the barn for the night, Abby stared at the chicken coop and the small mountain of feed in the middle of her delighted, *stupid* chickens. "Did you. Feed them?"

"Yeah. I thought they'd want dinner."

We haven't fed them dinner all week. Why aren't you paying attention? Why do I have to explain things so many times? Where's your head? Listen to me! The ghosts of harsh words snapped and crackled through her brain.

"They don't need dinner, Ev. They're full of bugs."

"Wouldn't they rather have corn?"

Apparently they would, because she practically had to kick them out of the way as she scraped the feed into the yard. The mice would think they'd died and gone to heaven. "Did you get the eggs?" There was no sense in feeding the snakes, too.

"I forgot," Evan said as he ran to the coop.

"Be careful," she called after him.

Three eggs hit the ground before she could get around the corner. Evan was standing still, his arms full of eggs, and yolk running down his shirt. "There are too many."

Careless. He's careless, her ghosts snarled. *I'll show him what happens to careless—*

"Let me show you." She straddled the mess, lifted his shirttail, and put the intact eggs inside. "That's what. Jeff does when he. Gets them." She leveled a gaze at him. "A basket. Is better."

"We need to wash them off," he called over his shoulder as he galloped away.

"Walk," she croaked as she followed him to the house. He met her at the door, naked from the waist up. "I put them in the sink, and I was really careful. I even put my shirt in the wash."

"Was the. Washer. Still. Running?" she asked, hoping against hope.

His smile faded, and her heart fell at the thought of his filthy shirt tossed in with already clean clothes. "Don't worry. We'll just wash. Ev-everything again. Thank you for changing." She walked past him and into the house.

"What about the horses?"

"I'll do it later."

She trudged into his bathroom and started a bath, making sure to test the water temperature. Earlier in the week, he'd run a bath that was icy cold, and she'd worried that his every sneeze was a symptom of pneumonia. When she'd told him to make the next one warmer, he'd almost singed his hair off.

She turned off the water, careful not to overfill the tub. She was tired of mopping after bath time. Evan was already waiting with his dirty clothes on the floor and a towel around his waist.

She closed the door and then yelled through it, "Use soap."

She added the rest of his clothes to the washer, restarted it and shuffled to the kitchen, where she stared into the refrigerator. She was too tired to cook. Admitting defeat, she got out the peanut butter and jelly.

Evan came out of the bathroom wearing his new pajamas. The hems on his bright cotton pants legs rolled up, hiding a large portion of the Iron Men flying in various formations. He was in a red T-shirt rather than the matching long-sleeved top. He'd slept in it the first night and woke screaming because he'd become tangled in it and thought his father had caught him under the porch.

He galloped across the floor and climbed into his chair. His smile faded as he looked at the sandwich, but he ate half of it and waited on her to finish so he could help with the dishes.

He dragged his chair to the sink and climbed into it, putting him at eye level. "Do I have to go to school?"

"Yes."

He was silent for a long time. "What if they tease me?"

"Then you call me or Jeff, and we'll talk to your teacher." She looked into his wise, dark eyes. "Someone will always tease you."

"Did they razz you about not talking?"

"Yes. And it made me sad. But school is too. Important. To let mean people keep you away."

"Okay," he sighed as he rinsed a plate. "Will you read to me?"

Careful to school her face into a smile, Abby groaned on the inside. "How about listening to a CD?"

"You can't talk no more, huh?"

"*Any* more. And I am tired."

His lips trembled. "Did I talk too much?"

She wrapped him in a hug, and her stomach twisted at the frail bones under the shirt that hung on him even though the saleslady had assured her it was the right size for a boy his age. She felt bad for stealing his warmth, but she did it anyway. "No. How else are you going to learn to do things? We talked about this. Remember?"

"Uh-huh." He grew solemn in thought and brightened almost immediately. "Can Jeff come read to me?"

No. I don't want him judging how I'm taking care of you and seeing me frayed around the edges. It's exactly what he predicted would happen.

Evan was staring at her with hope in his eyes, and she couldn't disappoint him. She'd have to swallow her pride. "Call and ask him, and remember your manners."

He leapt from his perch and scrambled for her cell phone. Sitting next to him, she watched him work the buttons the way she'd taught him earlier in the week. She triggered the speakerphone so she could be sure of Evan's interpretation.

The phone rang…and rang. Maybe Jeff wouldn't answer. As Evan's face fell, Abby felt guilty for hoping.

"Hello." The baritone greeting was flavored with a smile.

"Hi, Jeff. It's Evan." Even though they spoke every night, the little boy still started every conversation that way. "Would you like to come visit?"

"Now?"

"Uh-huh. It's time for bed, and I can't sleep without a story, but Abby can't read to me because she's talked out for the day, so I want you to come do it."

Abby didn't know what made her more embarrassed—Evan's description of their predicament or his bad manners.

"Evan, *ask* him and say *please.*"

"Oh right. Would you please come read me a story?"

"I'm not sure—"

"But I said please." Evan's voice shrank.

Abby put a hand on his head. He was so small, so frail, and his hair was baby soft. "Remember what we talked about," she whispered.

"Abby?"

She deactivated the speaker and picked up the phone. "H-hello?"

"What did you talk about?"

"That please doesn't always get you a yes."

"Good lesson."

Two minutes of listening to his rich voice, and she was suddenly as eager to see him as Evan. "You don't have to—"

"I don't have anything to read to him except the DSM Five."

"He has a book."

"I'm on my way."

She took thirty seconds to listen to the silence, then she stood. "He's coming. Let's finish the dishes."

As they rinsed the last plate, Toby and Tug erupted in a duet of barks and yips that all but drowned out the rap on the door.

"Jeff!" Evan squealed and leapt from his stool. The wet plate slipped from his hands and crashed to the floor. He froze where he stood. Abby dropped to her knees in time to see a tear fall from his chin.

"Are you hurt?" When he continued to cry, her panic bubbled. What had she done? What had she said? She surveyed the ruined pottery, vaguely aware of the slap of the screen door and Jeff striding through the kitchen. "What is it?"

"I broke it," Evan whimpered. "I'm sorry."

God, she remembered that feeling—never knowing what would set Wallis off. Abby scraped the pottery from between them and tugged him into her lap, wrapping him in a tight hug while she blinked away tears. "Honey, it's just stuff. It's not important."

She took the paper towel Jeff shoved over her shoulder and used it to dry Evan's tears and clean his slimy hand. Then she kissed the top of his head. "Go wash your hands and brush your teeth, please. Then Jeff can tuck you in."

Evan nodded and stood, and Jeff followed him down the hallway. Finally alone, Abby covered her mouth with a shaking hand. It helped keep Wallis's ugliness in, but it meant she had to hear it in her head. *Worthless, whiny, unlovable, useless, helpless, good for nothing...*

She covered her ears, but her teeth chattered and her throat constricted.

She closed her eyes. Wallis had been wrong. Always. She could do this. She could be the type of mother Evan needed. Even if it was only temporary.

"Abby?" Jeff's quiet question was timed with his hand on her shoulder. She forced her eyes open to see his cautious smile. "Why don't you go outside and get some air?"

"Dark. Room," she choked out before she fled through the door.

Ignoring the horses still in the paddock and even Toby jogging behind her, Abby ran into her darkroom and closed the door.

What had she been thinking, having the little boy living with her? Having anyone here? It was too much of a risk. Wallis would never let her get away with it. Buck would have approved, though. He would like her rescuing Evan just like he'd rescued her. Buck might not even mind she was keeping his death a secret if it helped someone else.

Abby's tears renewed, her guilt making them hotter. It wasn't right to leave Buck in a pasture. He deserved a final resting place where he could hunt, fish or ride. Maybe her past Tobys were there, sitting on a covered porch or chasing the wind through the field.

Too bad she'd never see it. Because no matter how many things she accomplished, no matter how many good deeds, or how many beautiful photographs, she'd done too many things—and not done enough.

She blinked at the photos surrounding her. Other peoples' lives, all of them moving forward. And she couldn't. Her home belonged to a dead man, her boy belonged to a dead woman, and her past belonged to the skeletons in her closet. Even Jeff was borrowed.

She was staring at someone else's engagement photos when the room went dark. Her heart climbed into her throat to escape her shrinking lungs. Forcing herself to breathe deeply, she reached for the flashlight she kept on the shelf next to her desk. *You're fine. This happens all the time. Remember?*

The flashlight was gone. Her whimper echoed through the quiet, still room.

Stay in there and think about what you've done. This is your fault, you stupid girl, Wallis had hissed as she'd shoved her into the closet and locked the door. And the days had bled into one another like shadows.

Be quiet. If anyone hears you, I'll have to hurt them, too, and it will be your fault. And if they take me to jail, no one will know where you are. You'll starve.

Abby slid to the floor as the dark pressed on her skin and the room shrunk around her. Animals scratched and scurried. Rats? She drew her knees tighter to her chest. She hated rats.

Someone else was moving in the barn. Had Wallis returned?

Fighting her panic, Abby sucked in a ragged breath. *Don't be silly. The horses are in the stable wondering why you've not put them up for the night, and the scratching is tree limbs against the stable walls. You have a job to do. Get out of this room.* She inched forward on all fours, banging into stools, tables and cabinets until she reached the far wall. There was a sliver of light at the bottom, acting like a lighthouse in a horrible foggy storm.

Pulling herself up the wall, Abby flailed until her knuckles banged the doorknob. Her relief was short-lived. It wouldn't open. Fear clawed up her throat, and she beat it back. It was fine. She was home.

Shadows moved from the wall, pointing their fingers at her. Not her home. Not her family. Not her life. Her life was forfeit.

As the shadows closed in, she banged on the door, choking out a scream.

It opened, and the light blinded her as she fell into a pair of strong arms, sobbing in relief.

"Shh, baby," Jeff crooned. "You're fine. Please don't cry."

"The light went out," she whimpered as she tightened her hold on his neck. "My flashlight was gone."

"It's okay." He kept repeating it until the tension left her muscles. Realizing she was strangling him, she released him and dropped her arms. He didn't let her go, giving her little choice but to cuddle into his lap.

"Are you claustrophic or nyctophobic?" he asked, his question rumbling through her and soothing her nerves.

She frowned at the new word. "What's that?"

"Afraid of the dark."

She took a deep breath and practiced the word. "Nyctophobic. I like it." She sniffed as her heart banged against her ribs. "It doesn't sound so childish."

"What about *hyperthymesia*? Have you heard that one?"

"Celia and I have talked about it." She looked up at him. "Don't diagnose me. It makes me feel weirder than I am."

"You aren't weird. You're rare. And you've had a rough day. Evan gave me a rundown. Why didn't you call me sooner?"

"You were. Working."

"And you wanted to prove you could do it on your own," he groused. "Abby, I'm not judging you. Ever. This is a lot to do alone."

"What if I screw him up?" she whispered. "What if I make him like me?"

He leaned back and looked into her eyes. "Then he'd be a smart, self-sufficient kid."

"Who can't have a normal conversation."

"You do well with me, and with him," Jeff said. "And this goes both ways. What if I fuck him up? I'm going to worm my way into his life and then go home." He held her steady. "He's not afraid to be up there alone?"

"Not if Tug is with him, and he keeps his hatchet

under the mattress." She interrupted his objection. "It's so dull it's a club, but it makes him feel safe. Did he wash up and brush his teeth before he went to sleep?"

"The kid has a hatchet in his room, and you're worried about hygiene. He brushed his teeth, but we forgot about his hands." He kept hold of her to delay the argument. "As far as I know, no one has ever died from snot. Are you sure about that book? Maybe his nightmares have something to do with the werewolves and vampires."

"His dreams are about real monsters." She curled closer, content to be quiet and warm—until her worries bubbled to the surface. "I don't know what to do about his diet. The only vegetable he'll eat is French fries."

"Kids eat crap, Abby."

"He can't live on fries. He even turned his nose up at peanut butter and jelly. He hates it here."

"Use strawberry jelly. He likes that best. And he doesn't hate it here. He's just fallen asleep telling me all the things he's *helped* you with this week."

"It was a disaster," she admitted.

"He'll learn. You just have to keep explaining it."

"I can't," she said as she wiped her eyes. "God, I hate being like this."

"How about notes?" he asked. "We can put scoops in the different feed bins so he can measure things correctly. And we'll put a list of chores on the fridge."

She nodded. "I'll get everything together."

"And I'll replace the light in your darkroom."

He fixed her workspace and they put the horses in the stable before retracing the steps necessary for every chore. Jeff held the flashlight while she printed simple instructions Evan could read on his own and put all the tools he'd need within reach.

By the end of it, she sat with him at the kitchen table, exhausted but relieved. "How did you know to do this?"

"My mother was…distracted after my father's death. I ended up taking care of my sisters much of the time." He winked. "I can do a mean French braid, too. Have you called Tracy Hoover about the gallery show?"

She shook her head. "There isn't enough time in the day. And I can't leave Evan alone while I'm in the darkroom."

He took her hand. "Why don't I take him tomorrow? We'll come back here after school and do chores until you've finished for the day."

Abby sagged in her chair. "Thank you."

"I have an ulterior motive," he purred as he leaned closer. "I like seeing you smile."

He never moved from his chair as he kissed her, and he didn't touch her except for holding her hand, but the kiss made her languid and boneless just the same. Her lips clung to his, and she clasped his hand, using it to anchor her in place.

"What are we doing?" she asked when he lifted his head.

"Fucked if I know," he whispered. "But I think I like it."

Chapter Thirteen

In this morning's news...the body of Steve Peacock, a fixture on the poker circuit, has been found in West Texas. Foul play is suspected. Sources say the FBI has been called in to investigate and that it may be related to a string of cross-country murders.

Wallis stared at the television, hovering the sweetener packet above the grapefruit on her plate, feeling the paper yield under her fingers. *Damn.*

Steve. Her first high-roller husband, a step up from the cardsharps and hustlers, who'd been a step up from the weekend gamers who spent most of their energy on their nine-to-five jobs.

Steve, who'd introduced her to Hale and then refused to move aside when she wanted someone better.

Steve, who'd fought so hard to live he'd almost defeated her.

"What is it, duchess?" Hale asked as he came into the kitchen.

"They've said it looks like rain for the weekend," Wallis replied as she sprinkled the sweetener over her fruit.

An FBI investigation into a string of murders. Three murders didn't make a string, and three states didn't make it cross-country. Unless they'd tied all of them together. And if they'd done that, it was because her bitch of a daughter had opened her fucking mouth.

"If that happens, I guess we'll just have to spend more time indoors," Hale said as he sipped his coffee. "Or maybe we could catch a plane back to the Bahamas and celebrate our anniversary early."

It would be four months early, and the second time this year they'd celebrated their anniversary with the wild extravagance Hale insisted on. She'd finally found a husband who treated her exactly as she deserved, someone who made her think maybe it was time to stop climbing higher and enjoy the view. She'd begun to think maybe he was her last husband.

And now that dream was ruined.

That girl had always been a nuisance, and she was *still* causing trouble. And troublemaking brats needed to be punished.

Wallis sliced the grapefruit spoon into the citrus pulp. "Maybe we could go to Vancouver, or Whistler. I've always wanted to see the Pacific Northwest." *Especially with enough money in my pocket to see it in style.*

"I hate snow." Hale shivered and smiled. "You know that."

He had such a pretty smile. She was going to miss it.

"Then let's go to the Bahamas and live it up, baby."

Jeff shambled into the kitchen, yawning, scratching, and squinting in the early morning sun. Cass handed him a cup of coffee.

"Why are you up this early?" he croaked.

"I have to open the office today. What about you?"

"It's Evan's first day back at school after everything.

And summer school at that. We're putting him on the bus this morning, and then I'm going over to the State Police Headquarters in Hastings to talk about their new lab."

"Be sure and comb your hair," she said, grinning, "or they'll throw you in the drunk tank with the rest of the bums."

"Smart-ass," Jeff grumbled as he walked down the hall toward his office, combing his fingers through the tangled strands.

After a week of reviewing the first section of the training manual, he finally felt comfortable sending it to the supervisor at Quantico. After that, he sent his outline on new evidence procedures to Trish, his senior tech in Chicago. She would let him know if he'd forgotten anything. He scrolled through his email, seeing her name over and over—she certainly let him know about everything else.

An email from Tom Beckett, the social worker at the VA, stood out in the sea of fbi.gov addresses. Sipping his coffee, Jeff read the invitation to come lecture to Tom's students at the college in Hastings, who were studying deviant behavior. That could fun. He'd loved being in front of a class last year. One lecture wouldn't put him behind.

Bob had emailed to tell him the marriage license requests were processing, and that reminder dragged him from the computer to the board of victims' remains. The files that arrived earlier in the week had revealed what he'd thought—seventeen years of letters. It had also revealed something he hadn't expected. Each set had been sent from a different city: Atlantic City, Reno and Tunica. All the cities he'd flagged for the victims' gambling and for marriage license searches. It tied them all together.

The easiest solution was that the tipster, the beta daughter, was mailing them to those cities first and then they were being forwarded. It was old-fashioned, a technique used when people wanted their Christmas cards sent from Bethlehem or their Valentines sent from Romance. And it was damned hard to catch—the postal workers would never remember seeing the exterior envelope. It would have been thrown away. He'd asked Bob to alert them for new letters anyway.

Sure work was managed, he turned to Abby's profile.

I hate being like this. Those words had torn at him as much as her tears. He could still feel her shaking when she'd fallen into his arms.

"Having coffee with your girlfriend?" Cass teased from the doorway.

He ignored her. "Do you remember when we locked Jan in the closet?"

"How could I forget? Mom was pissed, and Jan didn't talk to us for a week. Why?"

"I think someone locked Abby in one."

His sister sat next to him. "Jeff?" Her sober tone caught his attention, and he turned to see her kind eyes, so like his mother's. "Why do you like this woman?"

"What the hell does that mean?" he snapped. "Just because she's—"

"My question has nothing to do with her. Why do *you* want to spend time with her?" She took a deep breath. "If it's just to solve the mystery of what made her this way, or to help her, then you're doing both of you a disservice."

He frowned at her. "When did you get so smart?"

"When you weren't looking. And my minor is social work." She grinned. "It's a good fit for a teacher, just in case."

Damn, she was a good kid. "Do you want me to answer your question?"

She shook her head. "I just want you to know the answer."

The alarm on his phone blared an annoying techno-jingle. Disoriented and deafened, it took him a good minute to remember how to turn it off. Once he did, he drained his coffee. "I have to get ready. See you after work."

There was no such thing as a quick shower anymore. It took twice as long to rinse the shampoo from his hair and then get the conditioner through it, and then he had to dodge the bottles as they clattered to the floor and rolled against his ankles.

Wet strands slapped his back as he dried, and rivulets of water trickled down his body, requiring him to dry again. His neck itched. With a sigh that was somewhere between comforting routine and resignation, he set to work trimming his beard. Sliding his hair behind his ears quickly degenerated to shoving into place and then to knotting it into a ponytail.

This had begun as a way to flaunt tradition while he wasn't tied to an office. Then it had become a useful way to hide what he was thinking. Now it took too long to be presentable, and the man in the mirror was almost unrecognizable.

Dressed in a sport shirt and jeans, with to-go coffee and his wet head cold in the breeze, Jeff drove down the hill and parked at the mouth of Abby's driveway. She and Evan were already waiting by the road. The little boy looked like he'd stepped out of a department store window, and his backpack was almost as big as he was. Both of them looked terrified.

"Hey, dude," Jeff crowed as he slipped the pack from Evan's shoulders and picked the boy up to mock wrestle, leaving him wrinkled, untucked, and with messy hair, but grinning.

Abby nailed him with a stern stare and reached for the boy, but Jeff took her hand and stood next her, whispering, "Leave him be, and hug him now."

"But the bus—"

"It'll embarrass him, Ab."

She knelt next to Evan and hugged him. "It's school. You've done it every day. Same school. Same kids."

Jeff took his turn, and Evan almost strangled him. The kid smelled like shampoo, soap and toothpaste, but he was still way too thin. Jeff would bet his paycheck that his backpack was half-full of lunch.

The bus rumbled up the road, and he pulled Abby away from Evan and to the car. "Let him do it alone."

She shoved her hands in her jacket, Jeff put his hands in his pockets, and they watched their boy hoist his pack and lunge up the steps. He wobbled and shuffled to a seat near the back and next to the window, but he didn't look out at them as the bus pulled away.

"Why did you mess him up?" Abby asked as Jeff walked around the car and opened her door. He waited until he was behind the wheel to answer.

"Because he looked like a nerd. No one's judging you by whether his shirt is tucked in."

"Will he be okay?"

"Yep," Jeff said as he dodged the ruts in the lane. "I talked to the school resource officer on Friday. Why don't you fix your driveway?" His phone rang, and he grimaced an apology for the interruption before he answered. "Hello?"

"We have a problem," Bob said.

"Hate to hear it," Jeff hedged as he opened Abby's door. "I'll call you back in a few minutes."

"Coffee?" Abby asked when he disconnected the call. "Since you drove me home."

He wanted to, but Bob was waiting with a problem. And Eric Freeman was expecting him to solve an argument. "Yeah, a whole fifty yards. That was really difficult." He winked. "I have to work today."

She nodded and waved goodbye as she backed away, but her smile faltered. He couldn't shake the feeling that she was disappointed, and he couldn't help but like it.

After navigating Abby's treacherous driveway, Jeff dialed Bob as he caught the highway toward Hastings. "Okay, boss. What's up?"

"Steve Peacock, older guy, well over six feet, went missing about six years ago. They found the body in Palo Duro Canyon last week. Same M.O. as your girl. And." Bob drew a deep breath. "The press found out about the connection. It broke on several stations this morning."

"Shit. How? Why are they interested at all?"

"He was some high-roller poker player. And one of the local cops couldn't wait to brag that they had an honest-to-god serial killer in West Texas."

"Fuck," Jeff snarled.

"I'll see that fuck and raise you another. There is no record of Abe Snyder or Ray Finch being married."

But they'd clearly been married. Everyone knew about

their wives. "So either they were common-law spouses," Jeff thought aloud, "or they got married overseas."

The accomplice had upped the ante. She'd targeted richer husbands with higher profiles, and had exotic weddings. She'd obviously gotten tired of living on the edge of society. Which should have made her easier to catch, but she'd chosen another old-fashioned dodge.

"Which leaves us with a global search," Bob grumbled. "I've got Amanda checking the popular destination wedding sites, but it'll be slow going with the international jurisdictions."

"Can you do that? Just assign your wife stuff?"

"I'm not going to lose my best analyst just because I married her. We'll call you if we find something."

It was past noon when Jeff returned from Hastings and drove through Fiddler to pick up lunch at Herb's. Sitting at the drive-in speaker, he watched his fellow diners. Teenagers from the high school crowded into cars, secretaries checked their watches to make sure they didn't exceed their lunch hour, mothers wrestled with small children.

"Hey there, handsome."

Jeff looked over his shoulder and up into the gleaming smile of Charlene Anderson, who looked like she was prowling a catwalk instead of a lunchtime drive-in. "Hey yourself. What's up?"

She handed him a flyer. "Drumming up last-minute business for the charity bachelorette auction and dance on Saturday. You should come. Your sister signed up this morning."

Of course she had, and he should probably go and

make sure Cass didn't scandalize the entire town. "Do all the single women come?"

"Abby has volunteered to take photographs through the whole thing," Charlene said with a wicked grin. "It'd be great if someone could get her to dance."

"That wasn't—"

"Bye," Charlene called as she walked away.

He scowled at the brightly colored sheet of paper and noticed the neat logo printed in the corner. Abby had designed it. She would work every minute leading up to the party, all the way through it, and then start over the next morning. She shouldn't work so much.

And that shouldn't be why he'd ask her to dance.

He slid the notice into his passenger seat and reviewed the menu before he pressed the order button. "Number three, with cheddar cheese, and a Dr. Pepper, please." He saw the last item on the menu. "And a veggie burger with fries and an iced tea."

"We'll have that right out," the voice crackled through the speaker.

Looking for a distraction, Jeff surveyed the notices board on the restaurant's outside wall. Little League Baseball sign-ups had started. He remembered the spring rituals of showing up at the field on Saturday morning and meeting the dads/coaches, tryouts for positions, first practices and pizza afterward, playing catch in the yard with his dad.

Jeff walked to the board and lifted a form from the basket, considering it carefully. Evan should play, but he didn't want to be the reason the kid avoided sports later.

The carhop walked out the door and to his car, frowning at the empty driver's seat. Jeff returned and dropped the form on top of the dance flyer.

"Twelve dollars, sir," she said, her smile wide.

He pulled out his wallet. "If I wanted sporting goods without going to Hastings, where would I go?"

"The dry goods section of the grocery store, in the basement." Her ponytail flipped and bounced as she turned her head and pointed to the sign dominating the middle of the block.

"Thanks," he said as he handed her the money. "Keep the change."

Fifteen minutes later, Jeff turned from the highway onto the road toward home. Gloves, bat, balls, burgers, drinks, paperwork, his jacket and his notes from the Hastings lab visit all shifted and slid against the leather, threatening to tumble onto the floor. They did it again as he bumped through Abby's washed-out driveway.

He carried lunch through the stable and back to her darkroom. Since the red light over the door was glowing, he knocked and waited. And waited.

The horses came to the stable door, curious about their visitor. But Abby didn't answer.

"Abby?" he called out and knocked again.

The light went off, and the door eased open. Abby peeked around it, blinking in the sunlight.

He held up lunch. "Wanna eat? I picked up a veggie burger at Herb's."

She stared at him, one eyebrow arched. God, she could say more with one expression than most women could say in thirty minutes.

"I can't eat both of them, and you do still owe me a meal," he teased. When she remained unmoved, he tried again. "You have to eat."

Nodding, she left the room and locked the door behind her. "How is your. Morning?"

"Good," he said as he fell into step beside her. "I went to Hastings and met with the Idaho State Police about their lab. They're rebuilding it and they want recommendations for equipment and procedures."

She unlocked her front door and stood aside, smiling.

"Hey!" he laughed, "my hands are full."

"You. Enjoyed. The lab?" she asked.

"I did." Jeff walked in behind her and set the lunch on the table. "They're a nice group of people, and I always like the science. The fries are probably cold. I had to make a stop on my way home."

Home. He cleared his throat. It didn't mean anything. It was just a word. He was used to making his home wherever he hung his hat, and his hat was here. Well, it was up the hill where he should be.

Abby dragged a cast-iron skillet from the cabinet and put it on the stove, heating it while she retrieved seasonings. "We can. Fix it. The. Parmesan. Cheese is in the fridge."

He dumped the fries into the pan, and went to the fridge for condiments. Juggling cheese, ranch dressing, and ketchup, he frowned at a covered bowl. "Is that chocolate gravy?"

"Yes. I made it. For Evan."

"It's been years since I had it."

"Profiling doesn't seem science-based," she said as the fries hissed and popped on the stove. "It seems more predictive than predictable."

"It is." He worked next to her, getting plates and napkins. "That's why the lab is a refuge. But both are puzzles with solutions. You just have to connect the dots."

Once the fries were crisp, they sat at the table and

ate them from the skillet, shaking them to cool them off while they juggled their burgers.

"I brought a baseball sign-up for Evan," Jeff muttered around a bite, "and I bought the equipment he'll need. I know he hasn't played before, but I'll work with him a little bit." He grinned. "I bought you a glove, too. We'll need an outfielder."

"Thank you," she said as she wadded up her trash. "And thanks. For lunch. I have biscuits. Would you like gravy for dessert?"

"God, yes."

While she worked in the kitchen, he moved around the living room, keeping one eye on her while he looked for clues to solve the persistent puzzle that was Abby—what existed past the rapid change of subjects and the willingness to talk about anything other than herself. She was from the South. She had to be. No one north of the Mason-Dixon knew about chocolate gravy. And from here he could see the kitchen curtains. In her clean, modern space, the bright white, country curtains with lilacs embroidered on the hem stood out. Next time he'd get her lilacs instead of roses.

There weren't any knickknacks, no photographs of people, no books other than ones from the library. She subscribed to *National Geographic*, *Time* and *Small Farm Today*.

"What?" she asked as she set the plate on the table.

"Nothing," he lied as he picked up the nearest book. *Persuasion* by Jane Austen.

"Don't profile me."

Busted.

"Sorry, force of habit," he said as he sat in front of

his dessert and took a healthy bite. Sweet gravy, flaky biscuits, butter. Oh yeah, she was a Southern girl.

Rather than confirming his guess, he kept eating until his fork scraped his plate. It echoed through the silent house.

They cleaned up their mess, and he walked her back to her darkroom. "May I come in? I'd like to see it."

"Didn't you see it already?" she asked as she walked through the door.

"It was dark," he teased, relieved to see her smile as she looked back at him.

The room was cast in shadows, and after his eyes adjusted he saw the darkroom of someone who hated small spaces, large and long, with her frame shop at one end, and a makeshift office at the other. Her processing center was in the middle. Photos cluttered every surface—framed ones of her friends that were obviously hers, and others that were clearly jobs. Prom, weddings, engagements, senior portraits—the perennial posed shots mixed with candid, playful pictures. "These are different."

She came to his side and dragged two photos forward. The prom photos featured the same couple. "Would you rather have a memory of this?" She tapped the stiff, posed shot. "Or this?" She called his attention to the couple dancing and laughing. "Everyone *thinks* they want the first, but when they look back on memories, they look at selfies or candid shots. They remember their first dance, or laughing with their friends.

"And when they're busy not thinking about the camera." She pulled a set of engagement photos forward. "You see how people really feel."

She went back to work, leaving him to continue his

self-guided tour past tools worn shiny with use, rocks and other interesting objects probably picked up on hikes, framed leaves, pressed flowers, poems tacked to the bulletin board. It was the color and chaos he'd come to recognize as Abby's brain.

As he thought about her mini-art class, he inevitably drew the comparison between the photos on her walls and the ones on his. The comparison between the two of them—he was always on the edge of the crowd looking for evil and ugliness, she was on the edge of it seeing happiness and beauty.

"I ran into Charlene at Herb's," he said. "She was drumming up business for the fundraiser. Are you going?"

"I'm working it," she said as she went to the other side of the room, putting distance between them. "Are you going?"

He nodded. "Someone should keep an eye on Cassidy. We could go together."

"We can't date," she said. As if to reiterate the point, she held the door open in a clear invitation for him to leave.

Jeff pulled his keys from his pocket and stopped in front of her. He kissed her cheek. "Okay, but we could drive together."

Her breath stopped on an inhale, pressing her chest to his. Her thigh trembled. She was like her skittish horses, afraid but wanting to trust someone.

He wanted to be that someone.

"We're going to the same place," he whispered as he curved his hand around her waist. He stroked her soft cotton shirt, intent on soothing her. "And carpooling is good for the environment."

The pulse leapt in her jugular, and he admitted that the petting was more about keeping her still as he pressed his lips to it. She sucked in another breath and wrapped her fingers around his shoulder. He stilled, waiting for her to push him away. Instead she tilted her head to give him easier access.

Dropping his keys to the floor, he tangled his fingers in her hair and held her still as he opened his mouth and sampled her skin. Dragging his tongue across her tendons, he reveled in the silky texture and, for the second time today, regretted having a beard.

Her nails scratched his scalp as she tugged him away from her throat and to her mouth, sighing in welcome even as he groaned in relief. As their tongues tangled and writhed, he nudged her legs apart with his knee. Abandoning her hair, he anchored his hand at the base of her spine and pulled her closer, sliding his thigh against her until she bucked against the friction.

Jeff pushed his hand from her waist up her ribs and covered her breast, letting her nipple press against his palm for a moment before he rolled it between his fingers and tugged, keeping rhythm with his thigh and his tongue. All the while, his hand on her back encouraged her to ride.

And she did, gasping against his mouth, drawing his tongue deeper, arching into his hand. Then she grabbed his ass and pulled him closer until he had her pinned to the wall and she wasn't the only one struggling for air as she started to tremble.

"Come, darlin'."

He lowered his head, and closed his lips over her nipple, sucking as though he could pull it through her clothes while her sweet cries echoed to the rafters. Once he could breathe, he switched places, leaning against the wall and holding her close. With his eyes closed and blood roaring through his ears, his other senses took over. Abby was shaky and pliant in his arms, and her perfume melded with the scents of hay, oil and horses.

"This will make carpooling awkward," she whispered.

Relief flooded his muscles as he laughed. "I believe we can handle it."

Chapter Fourteen

Jeff walked into the kitchen, his tie draped around his neck, as Cass tromped down the stairs. Her eyes went wide.

"Holy cow. Look at you."

"I'm gray," Jeff grumbled as he ran his hand over his shorter hair.

"You've been gray for a year. And it looks great on you or I would've told you otherwise."

"Gee, thanks." He rubbed his jaw and then consciously forced his hand down. He'd been doing that since he'd left the barber. It was weird, feeling skin against skin.

"She'll like it, once she realizes who you are."

"I didn't do it for her. It had become too much trouble, and the beard itched."

"Sure," Cass snorted.

"Besides, I can't look like that when I go back to the office so I might as well get used to it." He wagged an end of the tie at her. "Help me with this."

"Not a word about my dress?"

"It's purple."

"Plum."

"And it's too short, and too tight. No wonder you

couldn't walk down the stairs without sounding like a giraffe in a closet."

"Wow, thanks. That had nothing to do with the dress. It was the shoes."

Realizing she was almost at eye level, he looked down at her feet. Three-inch heels. "Tight hem, tall shoes. I hope you don't have to run for your life."

"In Fiddler?" she laughed as she looped his tie into a knot. "Who does this for you in Chicago?"

"I can normally do it for myself."

"Don't be nervous. We can smell fear."

"Ha-ha. Funny. Are you getting even for the giraffe comment?"

"Maybe," Cass muttered as she tightened the knot against his throat. "There." She stepped back and blinked. "Thomas Jefferson, you look like *Dad*."

Jeff gulped. He knew he did. Hiding it under the beard and hair had made it easy to forget, to block the memories. With the beard, his mother had relaxed when he'd walked into the room—he was no longer a reminder of her long-dead husband.

Rather than standing here reliving their family tragedy, he went to the refrigerator and retrieved the flowers he'd stashed. "We're taking Abby's SUV since we have to drop Evan with Faye. I'm walking down in a few minutes. I'll see you at the dance."

"You're taking her flowers?"

"Lilacs are her favorites," Jeff mumbled.

"Wait 'til I tell Mom," Cass teased as she walked past him to the door.

"Don't you dare. I've got my hands full as it is."

"Yeah, yeah…"

"Hey, Cassie?" Jeff waited until she faced him. "Thanks for everything. And you look great. Seriously."

"Thanks." She smiled. "See you at the party."

When Cassie's taillights disappeared, Jeff locked the house and walked through the gate into the pasture. The trail was easy to follow in the moonlight, but even in pitch dark he would've found his way. Between baseball practice and dinner, and then lunches with Abby, he'd spent more time in the valley than up here.

Yesterday he'd even carried his computer down there, and they'd shared her office. He'd worked all afternoon camped in her office chair, sipping tea and listening to music and to Toby's nails clicking on the hardwood floors.

The breeze picked up, and he shivered as it chilled the nape of his neck and tickled his bare face. He hadn't shaved for Abby, but he hoped she liked it…or at least didn't mind.

It was surreal, walking through a pasture in a tux, carrying flowers and worrying if his date would like his haircut. The whole thing was weird, if he stopped to think about it. And he'd been thinking about it all day, ever since he'd sent the next few chapters off for review and then emailed Colonel Freeman with his suggestions for the ISP's new lab. He was one step closer to finishing his job, to being ready to leave. And yet, not ready to leave at all.

He walked around the stable and through the yard toward the small house. Its windows glowed a soft yellow welcome. Evan pushed the living room curtains and waved wildly before disappearing. The front door swung open almost immediately.

"Hi! Do you think…" The boy's question died as his eyes widened and he stepped backward.

"It's me, Ev. I shaved, that's all." When the silence continued, Jeff sighed and smiled. "Our password is *werewolf*."

"You look way different," Evan said, grinning. "It's sorta weird."

"Gee, thanks." Jeff walked up the steps and through the door. "Now what do you want to ask me?"

"Do you think Faye likes Clue as much as you do? Or should I take another game?"

"Clue should be fine, and you need to take your math homework, too."

"Evan," Abby called from the back. "Do you. Have your. Pajamas?"

"Yes, ma'am. And my toothbrush."

She came around the corner into the living room and slid to a stop. "Hi."

"Hi." Jeff stood and stroked his fingers down his jaw. He wanted to reassure her, but he couldn't find the words. She was beautiful, clad in teal with a black wrap caught on her elbows and delicate heels on her feet. Jesus, even her toes were pretty. Her deep brown hair was sleek and straight. "Wow," he breathed.

"Who are the flowers for?" Evan asked.

Jeff stared at his hands. Right. Flowers. He took two steps into the living room and stopped, his nerves jangling under his skin. "Evan, why don't you go get in the car? We'll be out in a minute."

"Backseat, Ev," Abby clarified. "And buckle your seat belt."

"Hurry up," Evan called from halfway down the hall.

Jeff offered the bouquet. "I wanted to make up for last time."

"Do you always bring flowers to carpool?" she teased as she took them into the kitchen and retrieved a cut glass vase.

"I've never carpooled before, so I didn't know the rules. What about you? Do you always wear high heels?" He smiled when she shook her head. "Maybe we'll start a trend."

"How did you know I liked lilacs?"

"The kitchen curtains don't match anything else in the house. There had to be a reason you kept them." He smiled into her stare. "Never date a profiler, darlin'."

He hadn't known which color to get, so he'd bought them in every shade—white, lavender, deep purple and pink. The fragrance surrounded them, but she still lifted one flower to her nose and closed her eyes. Her dreamy expression reminded him of how she'd looked coming apart in his arms.

He'd plant her a forest of lilacs to see that look on her face every day. His body surged. He'd *put* that look on her face every day. Halfway to kissing her, he saw the tear clinging to her lashes.

"Hey," Jeff whispered as he lifted her gaze to his. "What's this?"

His heart twisted. He would put that look on her face. No matter how right this felt, he was leaving.

"Memories," she sniffed and dashed the tear away. "Are you ready to go?"

Leave her alone, Crandall.

"In a minute." He kissed her lightly. "You're beautiful, Abby."

She was, and it had nothing to do with her polished

clothes. He'd thought it every time he'd visited. He'd looked past her silence to see the humor dancing in her eyes as she shared a joke no one thought she'd heard, or when she found her friends funny but didn't tell them. She was intelligent, graceful and kind—and incredibly fragile.

"Thank you," she said. "The ladies won't know what to do with you. You'll probably dance all night." She traced his jawline with her fingers, tickling the skin. "You look so civilized."

"It's just an act." He winked. "Do you like it?" He'd sworn he wouldn't ask her that.

She kept her hand on his jaw. "The beard was comforting, but this way I can see your face."

"Is that a good thing?" He was vain. He'd admitted it years ago. But now it was humbling to admit that it mattered what she thought.

"Smile." She whispered the command.

"Are you always this bossy?" he teased as he obeyed.

"Damn. You're...*pretty*."

He wanted to kiss her, but he knew he wouldn't stop until they were naked and sprawled on the floor. Besides, she had a job to do.

The horn honked in the garage. And they had an impatient little boy in the car.

Jeff tightened the wrap around her shoulders and put his hand on her waist to guide her away from the temptation. "Thank you, but don't say that out loud. The guys would never let me live it down."

"Do you think he'll be okay?" Abby asked as they slowed to turn into the country club entrance. "He gets difficult if he's bored."

"He looked like he was moving in," Jeff teased. "Why didn't you just have a sitter come to the house?"

"They shouldn't be out there alone," she said. "Besides, all the girls old enough to sit will be at the dance."

"But a retirement home? Are you sure Faye's up to it?"

"The residents love him. And the nurses can help keep him safe."

Safe. She was always worried about his safety. "Andy's in jail, Ab."

"You never. Know what. Might happen."

Every case in his career was a study in what might happen. His adolescence had been the same. One day he'd been worried about summer league baseball, the next he'd been making sure his mother turned off the stove after breakfast. And he'd become obsessed about never being late for curfew and making her worry.

"Don't make him scared of his shadow. He needs to be a kid."

"Don't worry. I always act brave. Even when I have to kill the spiders."

They stopped at the back of the line and waited on the valet. "You're afraid of spiders?" What other small details didn't he know about her life?

She shivered. "All those eyes and legs, and able to go anywhere. They're creepy. And Evan hates them almost as much as I do. So one of us has to be brave. I'm the grown-up. That's my job."

"Speaking of." He took her hand. "How did it go with Tracy Hoover?"

Her fingers flexed in his. "I have a show in a month."

"That's a short turnaround."

"She had a hole in her calendar because someone flaked out on her, and I have the photos already." She fidgeted in her seat. "I don't want to chicken out, and I will if I have to think about it."

"You'll do fine," he assured her. "The entire town will make the trip."

At the door, Jeff handed the keys to the attendant and walked around the car, waving off the valet. He opened the door to see her smiling and reaching for his hand as she lifted her camera bag in the other. "You know, that's his job."

"No way in hell was I going to let him stare at your legs," Jeff growled. "That's *my* job."

He walked her into the bustling room and searched for friendly faces. Cass waved from one side of the room, surrounded by giggling girls. Gray waved from the other, sitting at an empty table. Another group waved, and Jeff stared hard before he recognized the patrolmen from the Fiddler P.D.

"Let's go sit with—"

"You go sit," Abby said as she slid her hand from his arm. "I have to work."

"Of course," he said, putting his fingers on her back and sticking close to her while she circled the room. "Where do you want to set up?"

"Close to the dance floor but at the edge of the room so I can move."

Gray's table fit those guidelines. Jeff nudged her in that direction, then pushed her when she resisted. "It's just a chair, Abby."

"You finally found a barber," Gray teased as he stood. "I wouldn't have recognized you if it wasn't for your date." He hugged Abby. "You, on the other hand, look marvelous."

"It isn't a date," Abby said, her words muffled by his shoulder.

Gray looked over the top of her head, arching his eyebrow.

They were dressed up, he'd brought her flowers, they'd found a sitter, and he'd driven her here—to a room filled with music and a buffet. It was a fucking date. "You heard the woman," Jeff said as he held Abby's chair.

"This thing is a whole lot more fun when you're married," Maggie said as she joined them. "No wonder everyone looks forward to it." Her smile spread wider. "Jeff?"

The general disbelief became a theme as the rest of the group arrived. Just as they got it out of their system, the lights flashed and the emcee called all the participants to the dance floor.

Abby elbowed him. "Go dance."

"In a minute. Do you want a bottle of water?"

She nodded as she raised the camera to eye level, and Jeff left for the bar. When he returned, he had to hunt her down by looking for the flash.

"Thanks," she said. "You don't have to wait on me."

"I know."

Rather than staying behind her, Jeff went back to the table and sat with the various members of the group as they came and went from the dance floor. And he had fun *not* looking for a date.

He slumped back in his chair. He hadn't looked for a date in about a year. It was difficult to recall his last one. Sheila something, maybe? She'd been a redhead, he remembered, because she'd reminded him of Gray's crazy ex, Shelby. More than that, she'd been…wrong. It just hadn't felt right to be with her.

It had felt wrong to be with anyone since the first time he'd held a door for Abby.

His heart thudded harder in his chest, and his stomach sank as he counted how many times he stared across the room when her camera flashed—eager to see her smile. *Aw, damn.*

When the lights came up for intermission, he had a plate of snacks at her chair, baiting her to sit beside him. "Do you have all the pictures you need?"

She nodded. "You aren't. Dancing."

"I will in a minute. Just figuring out who likes whom."

"How do you know that if you don't dance?"

He put his arm along the back of her chair. "You know that and you haven't danced." He leaned forward until they were almost nose to nose. "It's all about how close they get to one another." He dropped his voice. "How low they whisper." He ran his finger across her back. "How many times they touch each other when they don't have to."

Her eyes widened. "Jeff."

He sat straight and nudged the plate toward her. "Eat."

All through the intermission, he kept his hand on her back while they visited with their friends. When the lights flashed signaling the second round of dancing, he stood and offered his hand. "Dance with me."

The blood left Abby's face as she stayed in her chair.

"One dance." He tugged her to her feet and kept hold of her icy fingers. "What's wrong?"

"I don't know how."

He looked at the crowded floor and then met her frightened stare. Making a quick decision, he led her the other direction, into the hallway. They were alone, and the music was still audible.

Jeff kept her hand and put his other on her waist. "Put your hand on my shoulder." She was stiff in his arms, but all it did was call his attention to her muscles and narrow waist. "Relax, darlin'. It doesn't hurt. Close your eyes and listen to the beat. Hear it? One. Two. Three. Four." He counted over it a few more times and inhaled, getting a heady hit of her perfume. "Now. Back. Right. No. Go right with your left foot."

She stepped on his foot and struggled to get free. "I'm sorry. I can't. Just go—"

"You can do anything you set your mind to. Try it again. Back with your right. Step left—no right, with your left foot. Forward with your left. Step right—wait." He cringed as he stepped on her toes—again. "Left with your right." He exhaled and ran his fingers across the lace on her dress. "Hang on a minute. How are your toes?"

When Abby didn't answer, he looked down and became fascinated by how the low light in the hallway caught the colors in her hair as she shook her head. She was trembling under his hands. Certain he'd swung too hard again, Jeff took a small step backward and prepared to apologize. Then he heard her giggle.

"You're *really* bad at this."

He sighed in relief as he pulled her close. "I'm a little distracted." Even here, indoors and in the darkness, she smelled like sunshine. His jitters dissolved, fizzing until he was pounds lighter and years younger. He nudged her away. "Back up and watch." He looked into her eyes and mimicked the proper steps he'd been trying to coach her through. "See? Box."

"Oh! I thought they called it that because it looked like boxing."

"I guess it does." He offered her his hand, and some primal part of him roared when she took it without objecting. "Close your eyes. Find the beat. And… One, two, three four." He counted as they stepped. And again. Then he stopped counting and inched her closer. With every *one*, he closed the distance until there was no space between them. Her breaths warmed his neck in time with her heels tapping on the floor. Her back muscles flexed under his hand, her leg brushed his, her fingers tightened on his shoulder—and with every step his mouth watered as his heart thudded in time with the music.

By the time the song ended, she was still shaking, but she was smiling, too. "Thank you."

He gathered her close as the music started again. "You're welcome. Now, just relax and sway. Follow me." When she dropped her head to his shoulder, he smoothed his hand down her back and settled it at the top of her ass. He moved it higher when every twitch of her hips made his fingers ache to explore. It wouldn't pay to get distracted. He had questions to ask. "How did you get to this age without dancing?"

"Would you want to dance with the weird girl who never talked?"

"It's not so bad." His steps faltered as her words registered. School dances were a part of growing up. In his hometown, everyone's first dance had doubled as their first *date*. If Abby had never danced… Oh God.

He tiptoed into the subject. "The first girl I ever dated was Amy King. I was fourteen and we went to a freshman mixer. We spent the whole night across the room from each other, afraid to slow dance."

"She missed out."

"Not on the important stuff. She was my first kiss, too."

"Amy and I have something in common," she whispered.

Jesus, God in heaven. "Actually, you don't. Amy had kissed a lot of guys. She was *fast.*" He pulled away so she could see his smile. "It's one of the reasons I asked her out."

"Then I'm very slow."

First date, first dance, first kiss—first orgasm up against a wall in her stable. His blush flamed from his neck to his hairline. He'd picked a hell of a time to shave. It worsened when he thought about all the other firsts he'd experienced. Sex at seventeen had been a disaster since neither he nor his girlfriend had known much. But now? The first time with Abby would be incredible. He'd be the only—

There was a big difference between *first* and *only.*

"We need to talk, darlin'. Why don't we get Evan and go home?"

Evan was asleep when they got to the nursing home, and thankfully he stayed that way. Jeff divided his time between watching the road and watching Abby in the passenger seat. Her brows were gathered in a frown, like she was thinking too hard, and she worried the fringe on her wrap between her fingers.

He caught her hand and practically arm-wrestled her to keep hold of it. "*Slow* is nothing to be ashamed of."

She nodded half-heartedly as if she didn't believe him.

Of all the women he'd dated, she had the right to expect everything from him. Instead, she was sitting there stewing about how this was all her fault.

Jeff parked the car in the garage, and she slid out the door. "I'll open the house if you'll get Evan."

He was torn between going in first to make sure she

was safe and protecting her from straining her back by wrestling with an unconscious eight-year-old. In the end, he gave up and carried Evan to his room. After tucking him into bed, Jeff stared at the pictures lining the walls. He and Evan had taped photographs of the Chicago skyline and various landmarks around the room. While they'd labeled the names of the buildings, Jeff had told him stories about watching Cubs games in Wrigley Field.

Those games made him feel like he was in Chicago more than anything else in the city. They also made him realize what he was missing. Before it had been the guys with their gray-haired dads. Now Jeff's chest tightened at the imagined torture of going alone and watching families enjoy the game.

His apartment was indicated with a big blue arrow, and his office building was marked with a red one. He could walk the route from memory, knew where to get the best coffee, the coldest beer, and the greasiest pizza. Even here in the quiet, he could imagine the hum of his lab full of techs and equipment working to solve every mystery brought to them, researching to improve techniques. It was home.

Easing into the chair he usually sat in to read bedtime stories about hunting monsters, Jeff watched Evan sleep. It was the only time the kid was still and quiet. He was already so different from the bruised survivor in the hospital, and Jeff was proud of the role he'd had in the improvement. He'd been able to help a living person.

But the majority of the credit went to Abby, who'd worked hard to overcome her own nature to give the boy a home. He was a testament to her capacity for love, just like Butcher in the stable.

The thought of leaving this little boy—leaving her—

squeezed Jeff's lungs tight. He closed his eyes and rubbed his temples with his thumbs, trying to put his thoughts into order, trying to force logic and reason to function. It didn't work. *Aw, damn. Damn, damn, damn.*

Abby was waiting on him when he walked into the living room. He pulled an ottoman in front of her chair and sat facing her, wondering how to start.

She did it for him. "Please don't worry about this."

Don't *worry*?

"You kissed me and taught me to dance. I don't expect you to change your plans."

Why didn't she?

"I did more than kiss you." And he'd thought about little else but doing *that* again. Hell, he'd spent most of the evening imagining her naked. "Did I scare you?"

"Don't treat me like a little girl. I'm not naïve." She stood, smiling. "We're friends who got carried away."

He'd made a variant of her speech on more than one occasion, so he couldn't escape the feeling that she was patting him on the ass and sending him home. And he wasn't sure he liked it. At all. "What the hell is going on?"

Sure enough, she opened the door. "We had a great time, and you're going home. I'll send Evan up tomorrow for baseball practice." A chorus of night bugs came in with the breeze. "Good night, Jeff."

That sounded an awful lot like goodbye. Jeff stood and blinked at her, knowing he should be happy about the lack of drama, her understanding of the situation—but he wasn't. However, he recognized the stubborn tilt to her chin. If he argued now, she'd just dig in her heels. So he pushed the screen door out of his way. "Good night."

Chapter Fifteen

Abby stood on the edge of the river, listening as Jeff and Evan rambled along the border of the thicket, cracking sticks and stopping to talk about everything. It always took twice as long for them to make the trek, but she didn't mind waiting. Evan's persistent questions, his curiosity and his enthusiasm, warmed her heart. Jeff's patient, quiet answers, his laughter, warmed everything else.

She shaded her eyes in the late afternoon sun and watched as they appeared on the opposite shore. As with every day this week, Jeff's smile faded the moment he saw her. Knowing she had little time for her fix, she greedily stared at everything from the way the sunlight glanced off the silver in his hair, down his lean frame, to his sneakers.

This would be her last glimpse of him until tomorrow's exchange. He'd nod and wave, the way people greeted strangers, and then disappear the minute Evan was safe on her side of the water.

It was the way it was supposed to be. He wanted honesty, and she couldn't give it to him. He deserved it, and that made keeping it from him so much harder.

And, when she was with him, she forgot to be afraid. That would seal his fate.

No. This was better. Let him stay on his side, disappointed. Let him go back to Chicago and find some beautiful woman and have impossibly pretty children. At least he'd be safe.

Evan started across, hopping from stone to stone. Abby was intent on watching his feet when she realized Jeff was following him across. Resisting the urge to primp, she waited on him to arrive.

She scooped Evan into a hug, stealing some courage as she filled her lungs with the smells of summer only Evan would have. Sweat, dirt and the grilled burgers Jeff had made for lunch. He wriggled free and went to play on the riverbank, giving her no reason to delay Jeff.

His smile was as frail as she felt. "I have to go out of town for a few days on business, but I should be back in time for his game," he said, as if going through agenda items. "And he probably won't be hungry tonight. He ate his weight in burgers."

"Hey, Abby," Evan called.

"They smelled good," she said as she stroked Toby's soft fur, hot in the sunshine.

The smile vanished, and a blush crept up his neck. "You could've come. I bought veggie ones."

"Abby?" Evan asked.

She shook her head. "It's better this way."

"For who?" Jeff gritted the words out. "You can't tell me you like being exiled down here."

"Abby?" Evan persisted, tugging on her arm.

"Evan," Jeff barked. He put his finger to his lips. "Shh."

How many times had she seen Wallis make that same gesture? Over her stepfather's shoulder, across the room when they were in a crowd, as she'd dropped her off at school. Their own morbid code of secrets and threats.

"Don't do that to him," she snapped. Bending double, she looked the little boy in the eye. "Jeff and I are talking, Ev. It isn't polite to interrupt. What do you need?"

"Can I go start my chores?" he asked.

"You can feed the dogs, the chickens and the barn cat. And use the basket to get eggs. Come here first." She pulled the tube of sunscreen from her back pocket.

"Leave him be," Jeff grumbled. "He's already slicker than a greased pig."

She waggled the bottle at him. "It prevents skin cancer."

"I know that. But he'll probably get something worse from all the chemicals you're smothering him in." He snatched the bottle away from her. "Go on, Ev. Abby and I need to talk."

Toby pressed close to her, and Abby looked into his big brown eyes. It wasn't fair for him to fight Tug for food later. "Go with Evan, boy."

She watched him race up the hill, and soon the sounds of barks and giggles drifted back to her. Using the joy she got from that, she faced Jeff alone. "I don't. Interfere. With you."

He handed her the tube. "Sorry, but boys *need* a sunburn. A little pink won't hurt him." He grinned. "You must've had some kind of mother."

Abby's joints locked. "What?"

"I'm just saying, women usually mother the way they were—"

The summer after Connie's death, my mother *kept me from sunburns by shoving me into a closet and locking me in the dark. The rest of the time, she didn't give a shit where I was or what happened to me. I think she* wanted *something bad to happen to me. I think she prayed for it with every breath she didn't spend on herself.*

"I am *nothing* like her," she snarled. Too late, she realized the slip. For a man who studied behavior, she might as well have been wearing a sign.

"Shit," Jeff muttered.

Yep. Great big neon sign. *I had a lousy childhood.*

"Is that why you're doing this to me?" He stepped closer, his face softening as understanding lit his eyes. "Pushing me away, hiding from me? Because she—"

Bile boiled in Abby's throat. *I'm hiding because you're safer if I do. Take Evan and run before it's too late. Leave me alone.* The words danced on her tongue, leaving icy footprints. She was so tired of being alone, of being cold and isolated. She wanted to be normal, to have a lifetime of passionate kisses and sarcastic conversations. She wanted to watch Evan grow into the young man Jeff could help him become.

The words changed—*don't leave me, please help me*—but she swallowed them, too. He'd do it, she knew he would. That's what he did. But he'd pay for that help, and, even if he didn't, he'd resent her for as long as he lived.

"You were. The one. Who was. Upset." She glared at him when he shook his head. "I could see it in your face."

"There was a lot going on in my brain," he hedged as he shoved one hand into his pocket and ran the other back through his hair. "Abby, guys like me don't expect to be someone's first anything."

Guys like him. Guys who were used to more sophisticated women who had normal jobs and decent families. Women who hadn't been shoved in a closet and cheated out of affection. He deserved a normal girl. "I'm sorry," she said as she turned to leave.

"Wait a goddamned minute," he snapped as he grabbed her wrist. "We're in the middle of a conversation. Do *not* do that to me."

Everything was about what she was doing to him. What about her? What about how she felt empty and lonely without him to talk to? That she'd spent every day listening to him and Evan play in his yard? Or sat at her desk and stared at the overstuffed chair in her office, imagining him sitting there with his glasses perched on his nose while he worked? Or, like now, when a simple touch broke every defense she'd spent years creating, that she'd have to recreate once he was out of her life.

He was going to leave her changed. She'd known when she'd sat next to him at the dance, when she'd held the door for him to leave. She cared far too much to lose him. And she was going to lose him either way.

I'm doing this for you. I'm trying to be good and do the right thing. As right as I can manage, and you're messing everything up in my head.

Abby planted her feet and yanked her arm, so desperate to be free that she almost fell over when he snatched his hand back like she'd burned him.

"Shit," he muttered. "I can't even touch you right."

The look on his face broke her heart, and she reached for one last weapon in her arsenal. Limited truth. She'd remind him of the obstacles and let him know she really was thinking of him. "You did fine until you found out I was a virgin with a shitty childhood." She took a step backward. "You don't deserve this."

He pursued her, taking a step that mirrored hers, not

cornering her but giving her no quarter. "What does that mean?"

"You said it. Yourself. Guys like you." When his frown didn't fade, when he didn't walk away, frustration loosened her tongue. "You've dated a lot."

"Yeah. So?"

"You deserve a normal girl," she said. "Someone who can go to a party."

"Like you did."

"Someone who can dress up."

"Like you did."

"Who can spend time with your friends."

"Like you do."

"Who has a normal job."

He grinned. "Like you."

Abby swallowed a deep breath. "Who won't disappoint you."

"Like you." He closed the distance between them.

His faith in her stole her breath and tempted her to believe him, but she knew he was incredibly wrong. His fingers teased hers until she relented and let him take her hand. She couldn't help it—didn't want to help it.

"I was embarrassed, baby. I just sort of bowled into your life and coerced you into everything."

"I'm not a baby," she scolded. "I knew exactly what I was doing." He needed to remember that. She wasn't someone he could save.

"Duly noted," he said, smirking.

Before she could stop him, he covered her lips with his. Tingles shot through her body, like the first time she'd accidentally touched an electric fence. God, how she wished he could save her.

Just as she parted her lips in invitation, he lifted his

head. His lashes shaded his eyes as he murmured, "Kiss me first this time." He ran his finger back and forth under her chin. "Indulge your curiosity."

How the hell was she supposed to do that? But the longer she stood there, the longer he stared, waiting with his beautiful lips quirked into a half smile.

"It's just like killing spiders," he said. "Act brave until you are."

Well, first things first. She'd need something to keep her balance. She put her hands on his shoulders and let the cotton soothe her nerves before she traced her fingers across his collarbones. His Adam's apple bobbed, calling attention to his throat, and she ran her finger down his skin, then her hand along the column of his neck, petting him like she did Hemingway, skimming her fingers across his jaw and around his ear until she burrowed them into his hair.

Next she traced her tongue along the same path, delighting in the salty taste of him, the scratch of his stubble, and the way his hands shook on her hips.

"I like you without a beard," she whispered into his ear.

"Uh-huh," he panted.

She brushed an open-mouthed kiss against his lips, taking his breath deep into her lungs and letting it thaw a week's worth of loneliness. Another, then another, feeling him smile as his fingers slid to her ass and he tightened his hold.

When she relented, stroking her tongue against his, Jeff's entire body twitched. She withdrew and did it again, sampling the textures and satisfying their hunger. Only then did he move his hands, running them up her back, combing his fingers through her hair, skimming them along her jaws. He surrounded her, overwhelmed her, until all she knew was his gentle strength and the hard body against hers.

"Did you make up?" Evan called from the hill.

"Yeah," Jeff gasped as he pulled free. "Think so."

"Good," he chirped, his voice fading as he walked away.

Abby stayed in Jeff's arms, feeling him tremble—or maybe it was her. "Are we ever not going to do that?"

"Why? Would you prefer the distracted *not now, I'm working* sort of kiss?"

Yes. If it would leave her less hungry for him, less apt to forget why he should stay away. "Don't know. Never had one."

He sighed and pressed a kiss to her forehead. "I do have to work. I'll see you when I get back, darlin'. Be safe."

Abby watched him go, her forehead tingling even as he vanished through the thicket on his side of the river. Bird songs gave way to the first hums of insects at twilight.

She'd been wrong. That last kiss had been more devastating than any previous one. The normalcy of it, the sweetness, and the calm reassurance that he would be back. And the tempting notion that he worried about her was intoxicating. She could get lost in it.

She was lost in it.

At the end of the evening, Abby tucked Evan into bed and sat watching him sleep. She'd been insane to bring him here. The very act spoke to her success at hiding in plain sight, yet his presence made it impossible to stay concealed. It should have terrified her, but she'd never been happier. Or more tired. And she wouldn't have it any other way.

Even when she warred over plans for Christmas and the knowledge that they'd be separated by then. They'd have to be. Andy's trial would be over, he'd be in prison, and some normal family would want a giggling, smart, baseball-playing little boy. It would be best for Evan. She knew that.

But just for a moment, here alone in the dark, she imagined what life might be like. It wasn't hard, this fantasy. It was an extension of one she had all the time where everyone found out about Wallis and loved her anyway, where she didn't have to leave her home to avoid everyone's disappointment and anger at the secrets she'd kept. Now she added Evan to it. Their monsters were banished, and they were happy together here. And then she added Jeff and they became a real family—a mom and a dad, with kids, a dog and a cat. Well, lots of dogs and cats—it was *her* after all.

She turned out his light and rounded the corner. Toby ran ahead of her, growling, his hackles raised. As Abby reached the living room, the security light flashed on, flooding the porch and throwing the person stomping up the steps into shadow.

The grim reaper, come to collect.

Fighting paralyzing panic, Abby pushed her back to the wall, straining for breath. She snapped her fingers. "Toby, go to Evan."

The dog wavered between protection and obedience.

"Git," Abby shouted.

Toby ran for the bedroom, where Tug was already yipping and whining in fear. Evan peered around his door.

"Run."

The front door collapsed in a shower of splinters and the security alarm blared to life. Her world tilted on its axis as the noise deafened her. Already sick with dread, now she was dizzy.

"Run!"

She wheeled back to confront her biggest nightmare, only to come face-to-face with a rail-thin man. One look at his red hair and jailhouse-orange jumpsuit, and she knew he was Andy Gaines.

"Boy," he bellowed, lunging forward in a wild-eyed stagger. "Get out here. We're goin' home." He had cuffs around one wrist, and a gun in his other hand. He swiped it in her direction. "Shut that racket off, bitch!"

From the corner of her eye, Abby saw Evan vanish into his room. *Please let him go out the window. Please take care of him.* As further proof that she was beyond God's help, Evan ran back into the hallway carrying his hatchet. Toby stayed glued to his side.

"I said," Andy screeched, throwing a glass to get her attention, "turn it off."

"I can't," she shouted the lie. Their only hope was that Jeff would hear the deafening wail. "The door's broken."

Andy's stare focused on Evan. "Come out here. We're gonna have a talk about your mama. And then you're going to tell the police you saw it wrong."

"No," Evan screamed. "You killed her. I saw it."

"I won't have a child that talks back to me."

The last time she'd heard those words, Wallis had been breaking her ribs and she'd been helpless. She wasn't anymore. Abby closed her hand around the nearest weapon she could find—Evan's baseball bat. Recalling the few lessons Jeff had given her, she kept her eyes open, looked at where she wanted to hit, and swung for the fences.

The deranged man howled as the bat cracked over his shoulder. He wobbled but he didn't go down. Abby grabbed Evan as he rushed forward, hatchet at the ready, preventing him from barreling into the arms of their captor. Toby yelped as Andy kicked him aside.

Beyond him, she could see the blue lights careening off the treetops, getting closer. Andy leveled the gun at her, its barrel a gaping hole that took up her entire line of sight. Help would arrive too late. Abby curled around Evan and hoped she'd be enough of a shield.

The *ch-chunk* of a shotgun beat in counterpoint to the alarm.

"FBI!" Jeff bellowed. "Drop it."

"You won't shoot a man in the back," Andy sneered.

"Try me."

Abby blocked Evan's face, keeping him from watching, and squeezed her eyes closed. More people crashed up her steps and into the room. The alarm keypad chirped, and the house was filled with ominous, expectant silence. Andy's pistol clattered to the floor and he swore right before the cuffs snapped closed.

"You're hurtin' me," he howled. "I just wanted to see the kid."

"How the hell did he get out?" Jeff shouted.

"He kept whining about his back until we took him to the hospital," Chet explained in a breathless rush. "He broke free in the ER. We didn't have time to call and warn you guys."

Abby opened her eyes to make sure Evan's monster was out of her house, then she grabbed the boy by the shoulders and shook him. "I told you to run." Tears dripped down his chin, and she yanked him to her in a hard hug. "You scared me to death."

Toby slunk across the floor to cower against her, Evan trembled in her arms and Abby gathered as many shaky breaths as possible, reminding herself that it was her job to be the grown-up.

Jeff crossed the room in two long strides, knelt beside her and wrapped her in an iron grip.

"Everybody in one piece?" he asked, a hitch in his voice. "No one bleeding?"

Unable to answer two questions at once, she simply nodded. "Thank God you heard the alarm."

"And that Hank keeps a shotgun by the door." He rubbed her arm. "Let's get you guys up to my house."

She couldn't go up there. Tonight was living proof of the havoc she'd wreak on his life. "Jeff, I—"

"Darlin' you don't have a door."

"Take Evan." She struggled to pull away. "I'll stay here."

Jeff let her get far enough to see the grim determination on his face. "No."

"But—"

"No."

She glared at him, and he glared back. A cool breeze brushed her skin, raising goosebumps. It wasn't a big deal. She'd been colder and lived.

Jeff chafed his hands on her arms—banishing the chill. "I'm not leaving you here alone. If you stay, we all stay."

Stymied by the manipulative argument, shivering worse with every breeze, all she could do was nod in agreement. Jeff picked up Evan, who was holding a squirming Tug. "Let's go."

At the top of the hill, Cassie greeted them at the door with a hug and a yawn before she returned upstairs. Jeff led them to the master bedroom, where the bedding had been thrown to the foot of the bed. The pillow he'd been using was still dented. "Crawl in, you two. I'll sleep in the living room."

He tucked them in and Evan snuggled against her, still shaking and sniffling. Shock settled into her bones, and she jumped when Jeff touched her shoulder.

"I'm going to hell," he muttered as he lifted the blankets. "Scoot over."

The mattress dipped, rolling her against him, and his arm anchored her close. "Hush, baby. I'm right here." He rested his forehead against the back of her head. "You're safe." Evan hiccupped and burrowed closer, and Jeff moved his arm so he held both of them.

"You're safe, Evan. I promise. Close your eyes," Jeff mumbled. "You, too, Slugger."

She obeyed and he curled around her, his breath stirring her hair. "Now. Deep breath and exhale." His voice vibrated through her. "Relax your toes and feel them sink into the mattress. Deep breath and exhale. Now your arches. Deep breath. Exhale. Your heels. Deep breath. Exhale. Your ankles…"

Toby leapt onto the bed, gingerly picking his way over feet, sniffing until he found the right spot next to her. Abby stared out the door down the dim hallway and into the shadowy kitchen, relaxing until her eyes drooped closed and her head sank into the pillow.

She jolted awake, breathless, as if her body was punishing her for sleeping on guard duty. She'd been asleep hard enough that Evan had moved without her knowing, and long enough for him to have curled on the other side of the mattress, he and Tug both snoring. Toby was snoring, too. Jeff was her island of peace. She dropped her head to the pillow and closed her eyes. And snapped them open again when his thumb brushed the underside of her breast.

"Sorry," he whispered, but he didn't move the hand splayed across her stomach. It warmed her through the soft cotton shirt, relaxing her against him even as his erection prodded her behind. Her nipples hardened, and suddenly the flimsy clothes were too much.

As though he was thinking the same thing, Jeff dragged his fingers down her torso and stroked her lower abdomen before sliding his hand under the shirt. Skin to skin, Abby soaked in the heat and comfort even as she grew aware of every place on her body she wanted him to touch.

"I've wanted you in my bed for months," he said. "And here you are, with an eight-year-old, a border collie and a beagle. With my sister asleep upstairs. Did you hit Andy with the bat?"

Abby scrambled to separate her arousal from their conversation. "Uh-huh."

"Good hit." His erection lengthened, and he flexed his fingers, urging her backward. "I'll cancel my trip."

While that sounded like a perfect plan at the moment, she fought the urge to agree. He had a life, and he needed to keep it. "You can't do that. We'll be fine."

"Stay up here until your door is fixed. And I'll talk to Glen about moving the bastard to another town, and about patrolling out here. I'll check on you."

That was too much. The police shouldn't be out here, and he shouldn't get involved. "Jeff—"

"You scared the shit out of me," he said as he balanced his chin on her shoulder.

"You didn't seem scared."

"The shotgun helped." His soft laughter tickled her neck. "I've always wanted to do that."

"You'd never done it?"

"Abby, I'm a lab rat. We don't go on raids." He danced his fingers across her stomach, his short nails adding a thrilling bite. "You're so soft."

This was her family. A little boy who wasn't hers and this man she couldn't resist. And she was going to lose them both. Her fantasy was just that, and the thought crushed her worse than any blow Wallis had delivered.

Jeff kissed her neck. "You're thinking too much."

"Jeff—"

"Shh. It'll keep. Deep breath. Exhale. Relax your toes…"

Chapter Sixteen

Abby slid into a booth at the diner and met Maggie Harper's smile with a deep sigh. "Sorry I'm late. Evan had practice. I had to sign up for snack duty."

"How did that go?"

"Fine." It had. Eventually. The mothers, the real mothers, had all known each other for years. It had been nerve-racking to walk into the chatty group and have to make conversation, but she'd done it. "I have the first game."

"Friday?" Maggie asked, raising her eyebrows. "Are you sure?"

Abby understood her friend's doubt. She actually shared it. But the only other dates had been late in summer, and it didn't seem right to wait that long to help. Or to spend the summer worrying about it. Besides, she might not have Evan then.

"Yes." He was going to be normal, and she was going to fake it. Like killing spiders.

"You've had a busy summer," Maggie said, grinning. "How's it going otherwise?"

"Good." And it was. Andy Gaines was an hour away, locked in a tiny cell for twenty-three hours a day, and dealing with more charges than she could recite, including ones for kidnapping, criminal trespass and terroristic threatening. Evan was sleeping in his room again, without nightmares and with his hatchet under his bed instead of *in* it. They'd finally hit a rhythm in their routine.

"How's he doing without Jeff?"

"Fine. He video chats. They do Evan's math homework."

"How are *you* doing without Jeff?"

She missed him. A lot. Enough that she'd dawdled over repairing her door just to sleep in his bed and imagine him next to her. And enough that Maggie's twenty questions got under her skin. "Fine. Why are you asking?"

"It's conversation," Maggie hedged.

No it wasn't. Conversation for Maggie was generally about mutual friends, work, or the community. Abby crossed her arms and arched an eyebrow.

"All right," Maggie grumbled. "He dates a lot, Ab. And he's not the small-town farm-boy type."

"And I am?" Abby asked, ignoring that for the last twenty-three years she'd been exactly that. What would Maggie think if she knew about the years spent rattling around racetracks and casinos, about truck stop breakfasts and scrambling out bathroom windows to avoid paying hotel bills? About the hard lessons of death and secrets.

"I'm just worried you'll get hurt," Maggie persisted.

Just like I'm worried about you.

"You've taken on a lot, and things will change later. I know how much that can suck."

No she didn't. Gray had started out temporary but had become permanent. She'd never lost him. But *ev-*

erything in Abby's life was temporary, even the friend sitting across from her now, pissing her off by reminding her of her fate.

You'll be alone. Wallis's age-old taunt crept through her brain.

"So you can have Gray, and Char can have Kevin, and Tiffany can have Michael. But I can't have anyone?"

"That isn't what I'm saying. It's just that—"

"No one like him would spend time with me without a motive?" *People will use you and throw you away. You'd better learn to use them first.*

"Abby—"

You'll die, and no one *you've cried over will remember you.* "I'm supposed to end up like Faye? Alone in the nursing home, looking out the window, with no one around but other people's children?"

Maggie put up both hands. "Whoa. That is *not* what I'm saying. It's just—"

"I know he's going back to Chicago. I know Evan will be adopted." Abby balled her fist around her napkin. "It's *my* life. I know what I'm doing."

Sure she did. She'd wrapped her life around people who were moving forward without her. "Maggie, I'm not a little kid anymore." *I was never a little kid.*

"We love you. You know that, right?"

They'd love her until all the secrets came out, and then they'd be glad to see her go. She'd fade into Fiddler lore. The crazy woman who'd tricked everyone and hidden in plain sight.

"I know. And I love you, too." *You have no idea how much.* Abby lifted her purse onto her shoulder and stood, her appetite ruined. "I'll see you on Friday at the game."

She walked to her car and sat behind the wheel without starting the motor, staring out the windshield. Rather than seeing the shoppers on the sidewalk, she saw her past and every cruel, twisted fork in the road.

Bridget Simpson walked by, the greyhound at her side on its leash, and waved wildly. The sun glinted off her earrings. Abby waved back, noticing the patterns created by sun and clouds, listening to birds, traffic, and laughter.

In Fiddler, her silence hadn't made her an outcast. At every point, given a choice, she had picked the path that had created a life here. A life she wanted to keep.

There was no way to do it.

Abby sat in bed and flipped through the last three days' worth of journal entries. All the pages documented her dead-end conversations about how to unravel the mess of her life and give everyone what they wanted.

"Let's be honest," she said to Toby, who was curled at her feet. "So I can get what *I* want, and maybe have Jeff in my bed instead of you." She stared into soulful eyes. "No offense."

The only way to have what she wanted was to leave Buck in his shallow, nameless grave. She felt disloyal for even thinking it. The other option was to simply wait until someone came looking for the connection. Dishonest as well as disloyal.

Her phone rang, and her breath caught. No one in Fiddler called this late. They were all home with their families, curled up and safe. Except for Maggie and Gray, who were still at the bar. She leaned over and read the name on the screen. Jeff.

Despite tingling all the way to her toes, Abby didn't answer. Even though she ached to hear his voice, she had too much stuff bubbling in her brain, including how disloyal it was to keep secrets from him. Disappointment washed over her when the ringing stopped.

And, just like all those years ago, that first month alone when the house phone had been disconnected, cold silence settled over her, reminding her of what life would be like if she told him everything. Toby moved within petting distance.

The text alert dinged, and she couldn't stop her curious fingers from hitting the button.

Answer the phone.

It rang again. She let it go.

I'm going to keep doing this until you talk to me.

She typed the truest response she could muster. I can't talk tonight.

Then listen.

Maybe there was an alternative. Can't we just do this?

No.

Her resolve strengthened. He couldn't make her talk, not from long distance. All she had to do was shut off her phone.

The alert dinged again. Please.

Dammit.

The phone rang again, vibrating her fingers and amping her nerves. Why couldn't he understand? She connected the call.

"Why do you. Push me?" she snapped.

"Because you pull me."

Silence stretched between them until his deep exhale crackled through the line. "I miss you, Slugger."

That made no sense. "You call every night."

"And talk to *Evan*. Do you know what it's like to sit here and listen to you clatter around in the background but not see you?"

She did, because she stayed in the room just to hear his voice. "I miss you, too."

"You do?"

His audible smile curled her toes. The man was too much of a flirt for her own good. "Yeah. I have to open my own doors."

"Good. But I need to talk to Evan about his manners."

"No you don't." She grinned. "When I got to school this afternoon, I caught him opening the door for a girl in his class."

"That's my boy."

His boy. The line fell silent again. "Damn," Jeff breathed before he cleared his throat. "Why did you have to go to school?"

"I've been taking him and picking him up."

"He needs to be on the bus," Jeff said. "Don't make him afraid."

"Can't he be afraid?" she countered. "He's been through a lot."

"He has, but he needs to be a normal kid."

"Why do you think I'm doing all this?" she asked. "I have to take snacks for Friday's game, Jeff."

"That's not the point. He'll make friends easier if he's not isolated like—"

"Like me. I know that. But I'm not going to teach him to be some macho jerk who's all swagger and no substance."

"Like me?"

She'd give everything she had to see Evan turn out

like Jeff. "Don't put words in my mouth," she snapped. "I have my own. And what I'm. Trying to say is that. He gets to say when. He's afraid. And he gets to know people will listen."

"All right," Jeff sighed. "I get it."

"And he's going back on the bus on Monday," she informed him. "We'd already talked about it."

"I wish you were here." Jeff's voice had turned silky.

"You do?" Abby couldn't stop her grin.

"I like watching your face when you yell at me."

"Where are you? Can you say?"

"West Texas. I'm meeting with the local sheriff on a case." He yawned. "And I have a field trip in the morning, so I'd better get some sleep. Sweet dreams, Slugger."

She lost the fight against the tingles under her skin, the security that wrapped around her. Even at the other end of the country, he inspired it. She was wanted, missed even.

Wallis had been wrong about that. Maybe she had been wrong about everything else, too. Maybe there was a life waiting beyond all those secrets.

I'm a baseball mom.

Abby shook her head in disbelief as she and Evan dropped the cooler in the dugout. Evan had wanted to bring SweeTARTS, candy, popsicles and soda. They'd compromised with water, tangerines, apple slices and frozen squeezable yogurt.

She wanted to stay and make sure Evan was comfortable and that he fit in. She wanted to encourage him to do his best and be a good sport and not to worry if he missed a catch or struck out. But he was quickly surrounded by his teammates. Michael Marx and Nate Mathis, the coaches, winked and shooed her away.

Her walk to the bleachers was interrupted by greetings from parents she'd met at practices. Wrestling her bag full of camera gear, rain slickers and umbrellas, she fought the urge to run from small talk. Evan didn't need to be tagged as the boy with the weird mom—even if she was only temporary.

In the dugout, Evan kept his gaze on the crowd, and she knew he was looking for Jeff. She resisted turning to search for the Audi in the parking lot.

"I'm sure he'll be here if he can," Maggie reassured her.

Abby nodded and smiled. "I know. So does Evan."

The first batter walked to the plate, and the parents on each side clapped in encouragement. After two strikes, he hit a wobbly ground ball and made it to first base. The next two batters struck out. Evan was fifth in the lineup, and Abby prayed he wouldn't get a turn in this inning. Maybe the rain would start and they'd stop the game.

As the fourth batter came to the plate, Jeff scrambled up and sat behind her.

The clang of aluminum signaled a hit, and the runner easily made it to first. Two outs, runners on first and second. And Evan was up.

"C'mon, Ev!" Jeff, Gray and Maggie shouted and clapped in chorus.

Abby held her breath. How did parents do this every week?

Strike one.

"Good look. Wait for your pitch," Jeff coached as he

ran his knuckles up her spine. "Breathe, sweetheart," he whispered.

Strike two.

"Good cut!" Jeff yelled. "Watch the ball, Evan!" Under his breath, he muttered, "Clap, Abby. He needs to see you cheering for him."

His large hands rested on her shoulders, and Abby responded to the coaxing. She was glad of it when Evan looked over his shoulder to see his fan club. He stepped back into the batter's box and readied for the pitch. Jeff's grip tightened.

It tightened further when the clang rang out, sharper than the last hit. The ball shot past the infield and dropped between the outfielders. Evan was already halfway to first base. The throw to third was too high. Nate Mathis was signaling Evan around to second.

"Run, Evan!" Abby and Jeff shouted in stereo.

Stand-up double, one RBI.

"Woo-hoo!" Jeff whooped.

Gray and Maggie whistled their approval while Evan waved from second base. His gap-toothed smile was wide.

"Pay attention," Jeff said, pointing at the third base coach.

A new batter came to the plate, and Abby looked over her shoulder. Jeff leaned forward and kissed her cheek.

"Sorry I'm late," he whispered. "The rain slowed me down."

"We knew you'd come."

They relaxed into the game, laughing with the families and celebrating each run regardless of which team scored. Jeff draped his arm over Abby's shoulders and whispered explanations of each error and every good play.

In the last inning, with two outs, the Mathis Mariners were leading when the other team's best hitter came to the plate. His hit went high and deep, and toward Evan in center field. Abby squeezed her eyes closed.

"Watch," Jeff said as he shook her shoulders. "If he catches it, he'll want to know you saw him."

She pried her eyes open and watched the play. Behind her, Jeff whispered instructions.

"Watch the ball, Ev. Look it into the glove. You can do this. You can."

He did.

"Yes," Jeff yelled.

"Go, Evan!" Abby cheered.

His team cleared the dugout and surrounded him, lifting him to their shoulders. He was the hero of the game.

Jeff helped her scramble down into the crowd, and they were waiting at the dugout as Evan ran off the field and straight into her arms.

"Did you see me?"

"I did!" Tears tickled the back of her throat.

His smile was wide and bright, and he was covered in dirt and sweat. He was such a different boy already. He had friends and good memories. He was doing what normal boys did. She was doing something right for him.

Evan wrapped his arms around Jeff's waist, and Abby's heart grew two sizes when the grown man knelt to the boy's level. Jeff's smile was as brilliant as Evan's, and his hug was just as tight.

"I'm glad you got here," Evan said.

"Me, too, buddy. You did a great job! Just like we practiced."

"We all did a good job," Evan said. "I only got one RBI. Kyle Sullivan got three. Did you see Allie Logan? She's a good catcher…for a girl."

He walked between them to the crowd of parents and players. "Did Abby tell you I'm going to spend the night with Kyle? We're going to Herb's for pizza and ice cream, and then we're going to play games on Kyle's PlayStation."

Abby's courage faltered, slowing her steps as they neared the group. They were nice people, but she was used to standing on the edge of their lives, not being in the middle.

Jeff's fingers tightened on hers. "I'm right here."

True to his word, he kept her hand while she accepted celebratory hugs, introduced him to the other parents, and talked to Don and Melanie Sullivan and gave them her numbers in case there was a problem. After making sure Evan had money to pay for his share of food, she waved as he drove away.

"I hope he remembers his manners."

"They have an eight-year-old. They're used to it," Jeff reminded her as they walked to her SUV. "Relax."

Gray and Maggie joined them.

"You're a pretty good hitting coach, Crandall," Gray said. "I'll bet Mike and Nate wouldn't mind a little help. Even if it's temporary."

"You should," Maggie chimed in. "We never win the first game of the season." She turned her attention to Abby. "What are you going to do with a night to yourself?"

"Wine, bath, book," she lied. Tiffany always said that when she had time on her own. It sounded better than canning vegetables and missing Evan's endless questions.

As she climbed behind the wheel, Jeff closed her door.

"Do you need help with chores?" he asked.

She shook her head. A large, fat raindrop splattered on the brim of his cap. She turned the key in the ignition.

"Go before you get wet," she whispered. "Get some rest."

She arrived home to the sight of her anxious horses lined up at the stable door. While she'd outrun the rain, thunder rolled in the distance, and lightning split the darkened sky. Abby raced through the paddock and threw the door open. The herd trotted on her heels, threatening to knock her over.

After securing each horse in its stall, she calmed nerves where necessary before serving feed and checking water. The rain on the metal roof went from smattering drops to a noisy torrent. She opened the door to rivulets of mud and puddles in the paddock. Thunder now crashed immediately—sometimes simultaneously—after bright lightning. Toby left the doorway and curled on his bed in the corner, keeping a wary eye on the water inching over the threshold.

"Prince Prissy-Pants." The dog hated to get wet, and she couldn't blame him. It wasn't like he could hover under an umbrella.

Looking around the stable, she groaned. Neither could she. All her rain gear was in the car—in the driveway. For a moment, she considered staying in here. Then a stiff wind rattled the metal walls and roof. Thunder boomed overhead, and the lights went out.

Abby looked over her shoulder at the cavernous dark space and the hulking shadows. It didn't matter that she knew each item. The darkness and the cold made everything a threat.

Sucking in a deep breath, she stepped into the rain, slammed the door behind her, and bolted for the house. She was drenched in seconds, sloshing through mud in waterlogged shoes, and wiping her hair out of her eyes. After almost slipping and falling on her face, she gave up running for a resolute trudge. It wasn't like she could get any wetter.

Once in the house, she stripped from her clothes and left them in a neglected puddle before grabbing a flashlight and quick-stepping to her room. She chafed a towel over her skin and then pulled on her thick chenille robe and fleece-lined slippers to seal in the warmth.

After washing the ruined makeup from her face, she rubbed the towel through her hair as she crept through the dark house with a white-knuckled grip on her flashlight.

For years she'd struggled to light fires in the fireplace. Then Hank had helped her install a gas starter. Now it was just a matter of newspaper kindling, dry wood from the box on the porch, and a butane lighter.

As the wood crackled and caught the flame, Abby lit candles throughout the rooms she'd use tonight. The flickering light lengthened the shadows and gave the house a gothic glow, but at least she wasn't sitting in the cold dark jumping every time the house creaked in the wind.

She hung her clothes over the shower rod. The drips echoed through the quiet, making it sound like it was raining inside. The roof of their Alabama house had leaked, and it had infuriated Wallis to be cooped up with it while Ron was working. She'd lashed out every time she stepped in a cold puddle on the floor.

Abby used a dishtowel to mop the water she'd tracked in, and then relied on the batteries in her speaker dock and a soothing playlist to drown the sound and the memory. She picked up a book, but reading was useless in such low light. Left with nothing else to do, she leaned back in her favorite chair and closed her eyes.

The stillness made her toes twitch. No Toby, no Evan, and too many memories of what it had been like in those dark, frightening, early days.

She walked to the kitchen and pulled a pint of ice cream from the freezer and a spoon from the drawer.

A loud banging at her door stole her breath. The rhythmic pounding came again, and a flashlight danced in the window.

"Abby?"

The voice sent a hot tremor down her spine, to her hips, and lower. She pulled the curtain aside. Jeff was wearing a heavy rain slicker and the hood hung almost to his nose, shading his eyes but not his brilliant smile.

"Open the door, darlin'. It's cold out here."

He brought the chilly damp in with him, and Abby wrapped her robe tighter as she closed the door.

He pulled a bottle of wine from under his coat. "I knew you didn't have any."

Abby lifted her ice cream container. "Changed my mind." Watching his face, she reached behind her for another spoon.

"Vanilla bean? That's sorta bland, isn't it?"

"Not with the right toppings."

"Bowls?" he asked.

She wiggled the spoons. "Bite-sized sundaes."

While he rifled through the fridge, she got a tray and pulled her favorite toppings from the cabinets. To her cinnamon, peanut butter and Nutella, he added chocolate syrup, caramel sauce and strawberry jam.

"Those are very *normal* toppings," she said in mock disappointment.

"What would you suggest?"

She plucked the sriracha sauce from the fridge and balanced it on the heaping tray. He reached behind her and grabbed the can of whipped cream.

"I'm embarrassed that you own whipped cream in a *can*," he teased.

"Then I won't even tell you about the spray cheese Evan likes on his crackers."

She carried their feast to the fireplace and heard him open the hallway linen closet door. He came back with a quilt. "Hang on a second." He dropped to the floor, balanced himself against a chair, and spread his legs. "Come here."

He put her back to his front and covered their legs with the quilt. "You're freezing. Are you sure this is a good idea?"

"It's part of the fun." She pried the lid from the ice cream. "Hot and cold at the same time. Maggie and I used to do it at her house when she came home on Christmas breaks. I'd sit under a blanket and shiver while she told me about college."

"What did you tell her about?"

She stuck a spoon in the ice cream and added a dollop of chocolate syrup. "Canning tomatoes."

He opened all the lidded containers, and loaded his

first bite with strawberry and chocolate. "This is a great idea, changing flavors like this."

"I always thought so."

She settled in against him and watched the fire, and they ate spoonful after spoonful in silence.

"Try this," Jeff whispered as he hovered his spoon in front of her mouth. Hazelnut, cinnamon and vanilla coated her tongue.

It started a new game, introducing each other to new flavors. Abby finally loaded a bite with a dash of Sriracha and a coating of chocolate. He liked chocolate best. "Here."

Jeff hesitated for so long, she thought he'd lost his nerve. She was readying her tease when the ice cream plopped on her shoulder.

"Hey!" she squealed at the waste of perfectly good ice cream. If he didn't want it—

The protest died as he sucked the bite from her skin and then swirled his tongue to lick her clean. "That is good," he rumbled. The jars on the tray rattled, and his cold finger stroked behind her ear. "But how did you get Nutella back here?"

He used his tongue and teeth to torment her until Abby was panting, begging for him to move to other places. He caught her earlobe between his teeth, and his hot breath flooded her ear. "Fuck. You taste better than the ice cream."

Her robe gaped open as he tilted her. A cold drop of ice cream hit her other shoulder and the rivulet trickled down her back before he caught it against his tongue and devoured it in a long, flat lick that ended as he nibbled her shoulder. Reclining her against his shoulder and kicking the quilt away, he ripped his fingers through the loose knot at her waist and tossed the folds of the robe aside. He was hard against her hips, and his chest heaved with every breath.

More ice cream ran from her collarbone down between her breasts. This time he dragged his finger through it. Abby twisted, begging him to explore other places. Instead, he touched his sticky finger to her lips. "Open."

Beneath the flavor of ice cream and strawberries was the salty taste of him. She went from licking to sucking, encouraged by his legs writhing against hers.

"Shit," he panted as he pulled his finger free. "You're incredible."

Back against his shoulder, Abby closed her eyes and tracked the movement of his slick finger down her chest and abdomen as he nudged her calves with his heels.

"Open your legs," Jeff rasped in her ear.

Guessing his goal, she draped her legs over his ankles and felt her legs spread wider. His hand passed her navel, and she arched as much as possible. "Please."

His other fingers laced with hers as he slid his hand between her legs. Abby's senses centered on every stroke, every rub, every touch. Soft and slow, short and fast, flicking, fluttering. When screams reached her ears, she realized they were hers. She opened her eyes and stilled. She had one hand around his thigh and the other in his white-knuckled grasp.

"Don't stop now," Jeff gasped. He resumed his torment, this time sliding his finger inside her and out, dragging it over her center before reversing the path and delving back inside.

He freed his other hand and grasped her nipple between his fingers, rolling it and tugging in time to his strokes. Abby flailed for a handhold, something to ground her, and found his shoulder even as he spread her legs wider and the pressure changed.

Opening her eyes, she watched flames from the fireplace cast shadows across her body, throwing his hand on her breast into relief, and adding extra shadows as she flexed against his hand between her legs. He had three fingers buried inside her, pressing a spot she'd never known existed, as his thumb strummed her sensitive flesh.

Abby released her hold on his leg, only to grab his wrist and hold him captive against her as she shook, until her world went black.

She roused when Jeff shifted her to the floor. He stood and stripped his shirt over his head, and she marveled at his body as he continued to undress. His cock sprung free, and its thick length made her mouth water. Without thinking, Abby rolled to her knees, put a drop of hot sauce on her tongue, followed it with a large bite of ice cream and then slipped her lips over him.

"Oh *fuck*." Jeff burrowed his fingers in her hair as he pushed deeper and withdrew. He returned, deeper, groaning when Abby flexed her tongue against his salty, musky skin. His taste, as much as his response, drove her wild with hunger, with a need to satisfy him.

Instead of letting her, he pulled free. "Your turn."

After rolling on a condom, he joined her on the floor and gently pushed her down, following until he loomed over her. His kiss was sweet and sinful as he traced his fingers over her shoulders and arms, then her breasts and abdomen, and finally her hips and thighs.

The jars and bottles rattled, and then his fingers were back, slick and cold, tracing her collarbone, her nipples, her stomach. His hot tongue followed them, licking her before coming back to her mouth so she could taste the flavors on his tongue.

He trapped her nipple between his teeth and tongue, and she arched off the quilt, opening her legs and making room for him. The torment of his mouth was joined by a teasing set of fingers. Roll one nipple, suck the other, then switch. Over and over again until she was mindless underneath him.

He pushed her back down and shook the can of whipped cream, leering at her as he sprayed it from her sternum to her navel.

As he followed the trail, tickling her skin, evading her hands, humming in pleasure, Abby writhed, alternately giggling and whimpering. She was torn between pulling him up to kiss her and pushing him down her body, begging him to satisfy the ache he'd caused.

Spreading her legs wider, he pressed open-mouthed kisses to her thigh, traveling down to her knee, grinning against her skin when she flinched at the sensitive spot. Then he switched legs and traveled up again.

She remembered the scar only when she felt his fingers on her skin.

"It was a long time ago," she whispered. "Please don't stop."

He nuzzled the spot as if he could erase her memory of it, and then paused. His breath cooled the wetness already waiting on him. Then he licked it and curled his tongue into his mouth.

Her gaze locked on his heated one, and she saw the change from playful to hungry, saw him lick his lips and crouch—just like the wolf she'd always compared him to.

Grasping her hips, he held her down while he devoured her. The only thing Abby had for an anchor was him, so she dug her fingers into his shoulders and watched his muscles bunch and flex, stared at his dark head bent over her like she was dessert.

When he sucked her into his mouth, she abandoned his shoulders for his hair, begging him for more as her climax began anew. His fingers joined his tongue, and she shrieked something that sounded like his name as she shattered against his mouth.

He crawled up her body with a wicked grin and a gaze full of pride and satisfaction. His erection nudged her opening as he lifted her knees.

Abby sighed as he filled her. Sliding her hands up his shoulders, she tugged him down for a kiss and tasted herself on his beautiful lips and his sinful tongue. He withdrew only to return again, going impossibly deeper, and she gave up kissing him to watch him make love to her, to see him come undone.

But watching him, feeling the friction, brought her to the edge again. His heated stare locked onto hers, and she was soon arching to meet him, fighting to keep him deep inside her, begging him to take her to oblivion again.

The tempo sped, and the crack of the flames was joined by the sounds their bodies made. His hands on her hips urged her to the rhythm he needed, and his gasps grew to shouts and mingled with her cries of pleasure as they finally found peace.

Jeff collapsed against her shoulder. "Jesus, woman. Where'd you learn to do that?"

"Very funny," Abby grumbled as she ran her hands down his back, reveling in his strong, quaking muscles.

Satisfaction combined with relief and pride, giving her a fit of the giggles. While she shook in laughter beneath him, Jeff raised up on his elbows.

Once she could talk, she looked into his eyes, imagining the ocean behind them. "What?"

"You have the most amazing laugh," he whispered. "It makes me want to do this all over again."

"Maybe we should sleep first," she murmured.

"And shower." He stood and brought her with him. One warm hand curved around her waist. "Did I hurt you?"

No one in her life had ever asked her that question. Abby blinked away tears. "No. Shower?"

He stared at their feet, and his smile made her look, too. The ice cream had melted and all the toppings were scattered across the floor. The chaos continued to the furniture, which had been pushed out of the way. The rugs were bunched in wrinkled piles.

"Wow. We're messy."

He disposed of the condom. "Worth every bit of cleanup. I've always wanted to do that."

"The ice cream?" she asked. "You'd never done that?"

His smile was brilliant as he kissed her nose. "You inspired me. Now, help me find the lid for the peanut butter."

Chapter Seventeen

After their shower, Jeff sat on the living room floor with a towel around his waist and Abby sitting in front of him. He was still worried that she was too cold, or too shell-shocked to realize if he'd hurt her.

Because a nuclear blast could level Idaho and he'd never notice.

He pulled a dry towel through her hair before picking up the comb. Sectioning off a small portion, he began at the ends and worked his way up. Once at the roots, he combed down the entire length before drying it again and draping it over her shoulder. Then he divided another section and started again.

"Jeff—"

"Shh. Drink your wine. Are you warm enough?"

She nodded and stifled a yawn. Good. He liked taking care of her, and he knew now that no one in her life had ever done it. She deserved better than that, but she seemed to be embarrassed that her parents had neglected her. Thinking about her childhood made him think of his.

"I used to do this for Cass when she was little," Jeff said. "Mom was busy helping Ruthie and Jan with their homework, so it fell to me to get Cassie cleaned up and in bed."

"Then you did your homework?"

"Sure." He grinned. "Eventually. If I didn't have a new book."

"What did you read?"

"Detective fiction. I was fascinated with how they put the pieces together. And they gave me a chance to escape."

He ran the comb through her hair from root to end in long slow strokes, and picked up another section. Abby tilted her head back like an affection-starved cat.

"Why escape?" she murmured.

He kept his focus on the knots in her hair. The knots he'd put there while he'd made love to her. "Before my father died, I had a partner. Fishing, baseball, helping on my grandparents' farm—we did everything together. We talked about everything. He didn't treat me like a kid, but he let me be one. We teased my sisters until they squealed. He made my mother laugh even when she tried to be stern.

"Then he died," Jeff whispered. "And it was all *gone*."

"But you had other people."

"My grandparents cried whenever they saw us, and my mother moved through her day like an automaton. She forgot to turn off the stove, or the water in the sink, or to feed us. Ruthie and Jan were scared, and Cassie was too young to know what was going on. I was the man of the house. It was my responsibility.

"We settled into our new normal. We pitched in for chores, and we studied extra hard. Mom went back to work. And every night I listened to her cry while I read far into the night reaching the end of book after book where all the criminals were caught."

Abby snuggled closer, and he accepted the comfort. "How did it get better?"

"Cassie did it. The kid was a menace. She refused to be left behind. She'd sneak off and follow me everywhere. I finally gave up one year when she skulked after me when I went fishing, and I hooked her when I was casting a line. So I took her with me and she did everything I did. She was fearless. I swear she went a whole year with Band-Aids on both knees.

"And she pretty much demanded we attend every event. Dance recitals, gymnastics, plays, art shows—you name it, she did it. For the longest time we were the most somber row in the building. Then one day Cass flubbed a line onstage, and I heard Ruthie laugh. Cass did, too. She became the family clown after that."

"And your mother?"

"She got better once she knew I wasn't going to follow Dad into uniform. When I went off to college, Cass kept her occupied. She came back to herself after a while." He ran the comb through her hair and watched the chestnut strands flicker in the firelight. "You cut yourself, didn't you?"

Abby sat her wine on the floor and turned to face him. "Once."

"What happened?" A stubborn frown knitted her brows, but he refused to give in. This was important. "Please."

"It was my. First year. Alone."

The waltzing speech pattern was back. She only used it when she was nervous, and she almost never used it with him. He pulled her into his lap and wrapped his arms around her. "How old were you?"

"Eighteen." She dropped her head to his shoulder. "Everything. Was so hard. I was cold and afraid. And exhausted and lonely. And hungry. I was so hungry. It was Christmas. And I had a pile of presents from the Colemans, the Simons, the Mileses, the Mathises... *everyone*." She sighed. "And I didn't have anything to give them. I was poor." She leaned back and looked up at him. "Like Charles Dickens poor."

He wrapped her tighter as the images she conjured caused him physical pain. "So..."

"I got in the bathtub. I thought the femoral artery would be easier, but it's deeper than I thought. And I don't like knives." She fiddled with the tie on her robe. "And I realized Faye would find me, and that was a shitty thing to do to her. So I put duct tape on it and took a bath."

"Jesus," he breathed. What would she do after he left? What about when Evan got adopted? "Abby—"

"I never thought about it again." She kissed his cheek. "I'm not that person anymore."

Her denial only made her seem more fragile. He ran his hand over her hair.

"I only told you because you asked. I hate pity, Jeff."

"I can be sorry that you were in that situation without pitying you," he said as he tilted back to stare at her. "And I can be glad that you came to your senses. But, sweetheart, where was your family?"

A shadow flicked across her face, making her chocolate eyes impossibly darker. "My mother had left, and I would've rather starved to death than gone with her."

"But why stay here at all?"

"I'll bet you had tons of friends growing up," she said. "And you had your sisters. I had Maggie, and I didn't know how to do *anything.* At least here I had a home and people I trusted." She blinked up at him. "This is sort of a downer conversation for two people who just had amazing sex." She stood and offered him her hand. "Let's go to sleep."

They blew out all the candles in the living room and walked down the hall hand-in-hand. In her bedroom, he slid her robe into a pile at her feet. He wanted to sleep with her skin to skin, but he didn't want her to be cold—or nervous. "Okay?" When she nodded, he moved aside the quilts and crocheted afghans and watched her snuggle into the pile of pillows before he tucked her in. He stripped his towel and climbed in behind her—and tossed at least three pillows to the floor.

She surprised him by rolling over and kissing him, shy and sweet. "Thank you for staying."

He wouldn't have left her for all the money in his research budget. And not because of what she'd shared. Because he had no choice. Leaving her now would make him ache. "Why would you think I wouldn't want to?"

"*Cosmo* says guys don't cuddle."

He pulled her close and snuggled under the blankets as their shadows danced across the far wall. "*Cosmo* is full of crap. Good night, Slugger."

Hours later, he woke to a loud crack of thunder. The rain thudded against the roof and clicked against the windows. The power was still out, and the room smelled like hot wax.

The shadows flickered over Abby as she slept beside him. Most of her dark hair trailed down her back, but a few strands clung to the pillow. She was a study in contrasts—dark lashes and pale complexion, delicate brows and blunt, utilitarian nails, reserved with everyone else, but passionate with him. Her lips were swollen from his kisses, and his body twitched as he remembered them wrapped around him.

He slid from bed, almost embarrassed to see his cock at half-mast so soon. She was in his blood, under his skin, and he craved her.

He'd suspected it when he'd cheerfully considered shooting Andy Gaines in the back for daring to scare her, and again when he'd lain next to her alternating between watching her sleep and looking for later flights so he wouldn't have to leave her.

That had scared him so much he'd deliberately left her alone for most of his trip. It had been impossible to focus on chatting with Evan when he could hear her in the background. He'd missed her, and it had bugged the hell out of him that she didn't appear to miss him at all.

But she had. In that spare, direct way she approached everything else. As though it burdened him somehow for her to admit it.

Padding through the house, he added wood to the fire and checked the doors. Lightning cracked again, illuminating the stable and the paddock and throwing the trees into relief. He carried a glass of water back to the bedroom. Abby was leaning up on one arm, her eyes wide.

"I didn't mean to startle you," he said as he returned to bed. "Just a security sweep."

Her smile was shy. "I'm not used to having anyone in here, much less a naked man."

He offered her the water, and then became mesmerized by her throat as she swallowed.

"Thirsty," she whispered.

"Panting and screaming will do that," he teased. "So will hot sauce."

"Good thing I have lots of water." She slid her hand under the covers.

God help him, he backed away. "I didn't pack a supply of condoms, Ab."

"Look in the bedside table."

He slid the drawer open and found two boxes of condoms sitting side by side.

"*Two* boxes?"

"I didn't know which size you'd need."

He shuffled through the proper box, which was stuffed over the twelve count listed. She'd combined a box of plain latex condoms with more adventurous ones.

"How did you get these?"

"Amazon," she quipped. "A woman should be responsible for her own protection."

Did she have a subscription to *Cosmo*? "When did you order them?"

"After you left. I have Prime. Two-day shipping was free."

"This one glows in the dark." He looked over his shoulder and waggled his eyebrows. "Could be fun."

She shook her head. "Too much like Star Wars."

Laughter bubbled up from deep within him—honest, belly-shaking, face-creasing humor. "Well then, let me show you my lightsaber, Princess."

"You are such a nerd." The end of her sentence was lost in a fit of giggles and squeals as he lunged across the bed.

Pulling her under him, he rolled on a condom and slid inside her. He should take his time with her, he knew, but now he had two dozen condoms and a goal—to get under her skin. Her groan sent shivers through him, and he flexed against her, driving deeper, so she'd do it again. He continued the same slow pace, watching Abby writhe and feeling her hands on him. She alternated between wrapping her legs around his waist and sliding her heels against the sheets.

She looked down their bodies. "Oh my God."

He followed her gaze and watched his cock slide into her. And out, and in again. Her muscles gripped him tight. He looked her in the eyes. "Come to the dark side."

If watching her laugh had been sexy, *feeling* her laugh was his undoing. His orgasm crept from his feet up, shaking him in its wake and leaving him heaving for breath. His arms went rubbery, refusing to hold him any longer. Rather than crushing her, he collapsed to her side and pulled her with him.

This weird, stubborn woman was amazing.

And he loved her.

Wallis flipped through the pile of mail that had arrived while she and Hale had been in Nassau. One postcard stopped her cold. It was from the Hoover Gallery in Boise, one of Hale's favorites.

Still Life: Photographs of the Natural World by Abby Quinn.

The little bitch had stayed in Idaho. Probably in Fiddler at the godforsaken farm she'd loved. And apparently she wasn't starving if she had enough time to take gallery-quality photographs.

If she was still there, she was comfortable. If she was comfortable, she was talking. And if she was talking, she was a liability.

After carefully unfolding the edges of the postcard, Wallis put it on top of the mail and carried the stack to Hale's desk. Then she left and went to the spa for a massage. Travel was tiring.

When she got back to the apartment, Hale was home and the living room was full of red roses. "How's my Beauty?" he asked as he sipped his drink.

He had the prettiest smile. She'd miss it.

"How's my Beast?" she purred as she curled into him.

"A winner, as usual." He handed her the postcard. "This is the gallery where I found that landscape we sold last year for a huge profit. I talked to the owner while you were gone and she says this photographer is going to be huge. We could go to Whistler after that."

"I'd like that," Wallis said. "I'll start looking for flights."

Chapter Eighteen

Abby sat in the back of the lecture hall at Boise State-Hastings, watching students file in and feeling conspicuously overdressed. She and Jeff had agreed—she'd come listen to him guest lecture on their way to her show. That way, she didn't feel like he was doing something just for her.

That habit, the *I'll do something for you to keep you off the List* habit, was hard to shake. She might never get over repaying every kindness, keeping score.

At the front of the class, in his glasses, and a suit, Jeff looked like the typical hot professor. He was also overdressed. All of the women jockeyed for center seats and primped once they sat.

It did them no good. As Tom Beckett introduced him, Jeff looked up from the podium, stared over the top of every co-ed's head, and winked at her. She winked back. With him, she never minded keeping score.

"Thank you for coming this afternoon. I thought we'd start off by discussing two distinct types of aberrant behaviors—narcissistic personality disorder and anti-social personality disorder."

As he talked, Abby leaned back in her chair and closed her eyes. His descriptions of the disorders sounded like he was outlining life with Wallis, the monster who'd been banished under her bed. The sound of his voice, though, reminded her of every day over the last two weeks, every conversation, every yawn when he woke from a nap, every fishing trip with Evan. They'd formed a family—one that was about to be tested by real life.

His manuals were finished. His sabbatical was ending. And she still hadn't been able to tell him about Buck. Every morning she woke intending to tell him and filled with dread. Then Evan would laugh over breakfast, and Jeff would kiss her over lunch. And every night she went to bed a traitor filled with hope and forgetting to be afraid.

"As we progress to more serious disorders," Jeff continued. "We come to serial murders. There are fourteen other common traits."

As he recited and discussed each trait, Abby opened her eyes and leaned forward. Domineering mother, absent father, attempted suicides, intelligent, psychiatric problems, hate one or both parents, abused… Now she didn't recognize Wallis. She recognized herself.

That's silly. I'm nothing like her.

But earlier doubts, first stirred when Evan had arrived, now returned with a sickening hiss. What if one day everything was fine, and the next she was standing over his bloody body in the middle of the floor? Could that be possible?

Of course not. Wallis was always mean and hateful. Wasn't she?

"Can these traits lie dormant and then be triggered?" She heard the question before she realized she'd opened her mouth.

Jeff's smile doubled. "The homicidal triad appears early, but the rest usually do develop with age. And there are some lively discussions about whether serial killers are born or made."

Made?

"Are there cases where children of serial killers grew up to become serial killers themselves?" she asked over the thudding of her heart.

"Not that I'm aware of," Jeff answered. "However, many serial killers do have families and manage to hide their crimes for years."

"Do you really think their families didn't know?" a student asked.

"I think it would be difficult to live with someone who is hiding a secret that large without suspecting something," Jeff answered. "And I wonder at the complicity of silence. Of suspecting but not saying anything, or of being confronted with the truth and choosing not to believe it."

"What if. There wasn't. A choice?" Abby asked.

He tilted his head the way Toby did when she talked to him. When he didn't understand. "There's always a choice to do the right thing."

And just like that, Abby's fantasy of a happy ending crashed to the ground. There was no way he'd accept that *right* for her was relative. That she'd done what she could. That she'd sacrificed the truth he expected for the safety she wanted him to have.

She wanted to run away, but if she left the room he'd pester her until she ruined the precious time they had left together. Besides, they were in the same car. There was nowhere for her to go.

And no way for him to stay.

When the lecture ended and the lights came up, the students lingered to ask questions. Once they were gone, Abby walked down the steps.

Smile.

Jeff gathered his notes and shoved them in his briefcase. "You should come to all my classes," he teased. "I liked having you up there asking questions."

"I liked. Listening," she said. That much was true. She hadn't liked the answers, but she'd hung on every word.

He took her hand as they left the room. "Are you nervous about tonight?"

"Yes." The gallery show was a dream come true, but it was frightening leaving her anonymity behind. What if everyone hated her photographs? What if they didn't? What if she fell apart in a room full of strangers?

Jeff kissed her cheek. "You'll be awesome, Slugger." He stayed close. "And then I think I'm behind on the orgasm tally. You have some ground to make up."

Despite herself, she melted against him. Making love with him was addictive, and she was so, so tempted to claim a few more of those memories before she told him the truth.

When they arrived at the car, Abby stood aside and let him open her door. Every small kindness and affectionate touch were now torturous keepsakes.

They drove in silence and Abby watched out the window, counting the miles to her downfall. She had to tell him tonight. After the show. She wouldn't let him distract her with that disarming smile and his talented hands.

"Are you concerned about Evan repeating his father's behavior?" Jeff asked after a while.

She shook her head. "Evan's too kind for that." But Jeff's question reminded her to talk before he got worried. She didn't want to do this in the car. "Your sabbatical is ending, isn't it?"

"Yes." He squeezed her hand. "We have a few things to talk about after your show."

Yes. They did.

She was still holding Jeff's hand hours later as she stood in the corner of the gallery. Evan was fidgeting at her side, and their friends had gathered around her for support. She'd used them one last time to get through tonight. While she felt awful for stealing one last memory, she knew tomorrow everything would be different.

Despite her worry that no one else would come, the place was packed. Waiters wove through the crowd with hors d'oeuvres and drinks. The women dripped diamonds and the men wore money. And they were smiling.

"Told you so," Jeff whispered. "They love you."

The clink of silver on glass called her attention to Tracy Hoover. "I won't keep you, because I want you all to enjoy these lovely photographs—and take a few home." She paused for the wave of polite laughter. "But I want to introduce you to the artist."

Artist.

"Ladies and gentlemen, Abby Quinn."

The applause swelled, and Jeff's hand left hers, abandoning her in the spotlight. Abby risked a glance over her shoulder and saw him next to Gray, clapping. Pride shone in his eyes. For her.

Evan wrapped his arms around her hips, and Abby stooped to give him a hug. When she straightened, as the applause faded, she caught a glimpse of a face in the crowd. Short, severe haircut, stormy eyes, hard mouth.

No. It couldn't be.

Abby blinked, and the apparition vanished.

Tracy came to her side. "You look overwhelmed, dear. Are you good to meet a few people?"

Abby nodded. She could do this. It was part of her new life. No more isolation. But her feet wouldn't move.

A warm, solid hand rested on her back. Jeff. Remembering his pride from a few minutes ago, grasping it to hold for the lonely years ahead, Abby clasped Evan's hand and forced her feet to move.

"Hale," Tracy said as she touched a tall man's broad shoulder. "I'm so glad you could come in from Vegas. It's been too long since we've seen you."

"Since you've seen my money," the man said in a booming voice. His laugh reminded Abby of a sitcom laugh track. He was handsome in a totally phony way, as if someone had assembled him rather than let him grow. "Is this your newest find?"

"She is." Tracy's smile was encouraging. "Abby Quinn, this is Hale Riker."

"Mr. Riker, it's a. Pleasure," Abby said, hoping her hand didn't shake as he enveloped it in his sweaty, meaty grasp. "This is Doctor Jeff Crandall and Evan Gaines."

"And here comes my wife," Hale said as he looked over Abby's shoulder. "Wallis, love. Come meet..."

Abby lost the rest of his sentence. The woman smiling up at the showy art patron, the woman with perfect lipstick and wearing designer clothes, was no ghost.

She held out her perfectly manicured hand. "How

nice to meet you, Ms. Quinn." She bent double and took Evan's hand. "And you as well, Evan."

Abby resisted the urge to snatch the boy away from the grim reaper in Louboutins. She looked over her shoulder, but Jeff had moved away to answer his phone. "Excuse me," she gasped as she turned Evan away from danger. A taloned claw wrapped around her arm.

"We'll talk soon," Wallis threatened in the deadly quiet tone that had haunted Abby for years.

She scurried away with Evan, staying in the corner and watching the crowd, not daring to go to Maggie, terrified to go to Jeff. Stranded, isolated, alone—this was up to her. She had to come out of hiding *now*.

Keeping a smile on her face and her pace even and slow, Abby walked Evan to Jeff. He'd be safe here.

"Now? Bob, now's not...ha, ha. Very funny." He sighed and ran his hand through his hair. "Fine. An hour. Text me the details."

He disconnected the call and met her gaze. "I have to go."

No. He couldn't. She needed him to get Evan out of here.

"Please don't look at me like that. I feel like a jackass as it is."

"Jeff—" She hurried next to him as he joined their friends.

"I've been called out on a case," Jeff said to Gray. "Can you get Abby to the hotel?"

"Sure thing," Gray said. "Hate that. We were planning on taking you both out to celebrate."

They couldn't go anywhere with her. "Jeff, please—"

"Great." He knelt and hugged Evan. "I'll be back as soon as I can. Keep Abby safe." He stood and took her hand, tugging her toward the door. "Come with me for a second."

Abby looked over her shoulder. Wallis's gaze darted from face to face, and her smile curved in a deceptively pretty, delicate bow. Jeff shouldn't be holding her hand. He should just go. Run. Take everyone with him. Leave her here to face her fate.

She should have done it long ago.

Outside the headlights glared in the dark, and the city lights dimmed the stars. The world smelled like concrete and exhaust fumes. Jeff hailed a cab, and one stopped almost immediately.

This shouldn't be the way they said goodbye.

"Take the car," he said as he cupped her face in his hands. "I'll call you and we can get a room here when I get back. We need to talk."

He was never going to speak to her again. He'd hate her.

"God, Abby," he whispered as he touched his lips to her forehead. "Please don't cry. I'm sorry. I wanted to do this so differently."

So did I. "I love you."

No matter what happens, I hope he believes that.

He kissed her, her favorite kiss—sweet, hot, and hungry. "I love you, too." He stepped away, toward the cab, toward his safety. "I'll call you when I land. Enjoy your night. I'm very proud of you, darlin'."

She stood on the corner and watched him go. It was up to her to save him, to save Evan. Not with silence, though. She'd never be quiet again.

Abby walked into the gallery and froze. Evan was across the room, talking to Wallis as she walked from photograph to photograph. Forcing her knees not to shake, Abby joined them.

"Hello," Wallis purred. "Evan was kind enough to be my guide and talk to me about the pictures from your home in Fiddler, and his dad's job with the FBI. He's a very smart boy."

"He is." Abby smiled down at him. And he'd be safe to grow up. She'd make sure of it. "Ev. Why don't you go see Mr. Harper for a second?"

"Sure." He grinned at Wallis. "It was nice to meet you, Mrs. Riker. I'm glad you liked my tour."

Abby watched him go and, sure he was safe, wheeled back on her tormentor. "Leave him alone," she said in a hushed voice.

"I told you what would happen," Wallis scolded her. "This is your fault."

"It has nothing to do with me."

"You've made quite the life for yourself. Handsome husband, cute little boy, life on the farm," Wallis sneered.

"They aren't mine," Abby said, ignoring the whimper deep inside. "He isn't my husband, he isn't my little boy, that farm isn't mine. You made sure I never had *anything*."

"I was happy, and you've ruined it." Wallis narrowed her eyes. "You always ruin it. If you think you get your life at the expense of mine, then you need a history lesson."

Hale Riker's laugh rolled across the room, and Abby's stomach plummeted. "I won't let you do it. Not this time. It's over."

Wallis looked past her, and Abby knew what she saw. Evan and her friends, Tracy Hoover, enough people buying her work that she'd have money to put a new roof on the barn.

"It is," Wallis agreed as her gray eyes hardened. "You've made sure it's over."

For the rest of the evening, Abby stayed close to her friends and looked for a way to warn Hale Riker of his fate. Wallis never left him alone.

As the last patron left, Tracy Hoover's smile widened. "I told you you'd sell out my gallery. You should be very proud of yourself."

"Thank you," Abby said as she gathered her things. "I have to go, Tracy. It's been a long day."

"Of course. We'll talk next week."

Abby strode to Maggie's side and coaxed her away. "Can you take Evan for the night? I'm sorry to ask, but I..."

"You need a break," Maggie guessed. "We're happy to take him."

Gray loomed over his wife's shoulder. "I told Jeff I'd make sure you were safe. We'll follow you to the hotel."

Once she was alone in Jeff's car, Abby searched local hotels, looking for the fanciest ones in town. Wallis wouldn't stay anywhere else. She narrowed the possibilities to two and panicked when she realized one of them was where she was staying.

She called it first and wondered how she was going to stop the entire crowd from going in.

"Thank you for calling The Grove, may I help you?"

"Hale Riker's room, please."

The clerk was quiet for far too long. Abby could see the hotel looming in the windshield.

"We don't have a guest by that name."

Abby disconnected the call and punched the numbers that would seal her fate.

"Nine One One, what is your emergency?"

"Wallis Riker is going to kill her husband, Hale. They're staying at Hotel Forty-Three. Please stop her."

"You've overheard a fight?"

"No."

"A threat?"

Enough of one to convince her. "Yes."

"Is she armed?"

"No, but she will be." Abby was now parked in her hotel lot, and all her friends were staring at her, waiting on her. "She'll take him outside town, crush his skull, and leave his body to rot. Please, you have to believe me. You *have* to."

"What is your location, ma'am? We'll dispatch an officer for a statement."

No they wouldn't. They'd dispatch an officer to deal with the hysterical, depressed artist in the throes of a panic attack.

Evan knocked on her window, grinning and waving. "C'mon, Abby."

They'd put her in a psychiatric ward. No one would protect her family.

She disconnected the call, turned off her phone, and opened her door. Forcing her body to work, she took Evan's hand. "You're going. With Mr. and Mrs. Harper. Behave."

"Yes, ma'am," Evan yawned. "You'll come get me tomorrow, right?"

"Yes." The word stuck in her throat. She never lied to Evan. "And Jeff will. Be home. Soon."

They all got off the elevator on her floor and walked her to her room.

"Go take a bath and relax," Maggie whispered as she hugged her.

"We'll have breakfast tomorrow," Tiffany said.

"Sext that hunky man of yours," Charlene teased as she swept in.

Abby saved Evan for last. He threw his arms around her neck, and Abby hugged him hard, trying to memorize how he felt in her arms. "I love you, Evan."

"Love you, too."

She went into her room because that's what they expected her to do. Then she stood and listened for the elevator bell, for the hall to quiet. Cracking the door open, she checked to make sure everyone was gone.

Then she ran for it.

Hotel 43's lobby looked like a business park rather than a hotel, and Abby was sure it made her stand out as she sprinted to what she hoped was the front desk. A clerk smiled as she approached. "Welcome to Hotel Forty-Three. How—"

"Send security. To the Rikers' room. Now. Keep them. From leaving."

The young man's smile faded. "Ma'am?"

"Mr. Riker is in danger. Please. Hurry."

A man appeared at his elbow. His suit was perfectly pressed despite the hour. "I'm the hotel security, ma'am. May we help you?"

"Hale Riker. You have. To save him."

She could have screamed when the guard went not to the elevators, but to the desk phone and dialed.

"Mr. Riker? We've had a report that you're in danger." His smile widened as he listened. "Certainly, sir."

The smile disappeared when he hung up. "The Rikers are in bed. If you'll come..."

"No," Abby snapped as she turned on her heel. She wasn't going anywhere with that moron. Maybe Wallis would at least reconsider killing Hale if she thought people were watching.

Back in the car, she pulled into the shadows and faced the fact that no one was listening. Again. Worse, they'd get in her way.

She'd have to confess.

Gray was at the hotel. He'd believe her. And he was calm enough to explain it and make someone listen.

And it would leave Maggie and Evan unprotected while he dealt with her. Wallis would have open access to the people Abby had spent her life protecting. It would all be for nothing.

Unless Wallis had no reason to come to Fiddler. And she wouldn't if the police thought someone else killed Buck. If they thought his crazy, silent stepdaughter had done it. The state would save Evan. Gray would keep Maggie away from her. And Jeff would never come back.

It was the worst kind of lie, but she saw no other option.

It was dawn when she finished cleaning her house and sat down to print the letters she'd typed and saved years ago. One to Carter about the business, to Lex about her animals and the Humane Society, one to Faye thanking her for everything. And one to Maggie.

It took longer to write the one to Evan, because she didn't want to type it, and she didn't know what to say. Each attempt turned into pages of maudlin wishes and dreams. She burned each one and finally wrote what she thought he'd need to know.

This wasn't your fault. Mind Jeff. I love you.

Jeff's letter was worse. Her tears kept blurring her vision and ruining the ink. Those attempts went on the fire, too. She'd already told him she loved him, and now he probably wouldn't believe it no matter how many times she said it. The best she could do was answer his questions.

I'm sorry. Everything you need to know is in the attic.

Slipping into her boots, she went outside and began her chores. Her animals shouldn't suffer and starve until the police let Lex come get them. The routine soothed her nerves, and ended when she turned the horses out of the stable. Butcher came out last. The sun caught his silver mane and patchy pewter hair as he walked to her and nudged her shoulder.

"You'll be fine now, boy," she said as she scratched his ears and sent him on his way.

She looked down at Toby. "You will, too. I want you to stay with Evan and Tug." The sun burnt the fog from the pasture, highlighting the large maple tree between her house and Jeff's. Abby stared at it while she dialed.

"Chet? It's Abby. You and Chief Roberts need to come to my place. Bring a shovel."

Chapter Nineteen

Why wasn't she answering her phone?

Jeff disconnected his fifth call to Abby without leaving a message. He'd left four others. And in between those, he'd texted Gray to make sure she was safe.

Everything was fine, according to Gray. So why didn't she answer the fucking phone?

His taxi stopped at the door of the Jamestown, Kentucky, police department, and Jeff got out carrying his jacket and a brand new duffel bag full of the neatly wrapped, expensive as hell, personal items he'd purchased as he'd run through various airports in the middle of the night.

All to get here, when he really just wanted to be tucked in next to Abby, listening to her say *I love you* over and over again.

This trip had better be worth it.

He looked at the images on his phone. One marriage certificate between Beauregard Zachariah Archer and Wallis Elizabeth Perkins. And one birth certificate for Wallis/Betty naming her place of birth as Jamestown, Kentucky. Amanda was still scrambling for the daughter's birth certificate, but everyone had agreed that coming here was the best way to connect the dots.

Everyone but Jeff.

He opened the door and walked into the small-town PD. The patrolman at the desk lifted his gaze and frowned. They probably didn't get many new people.

"I'm Jeff Crandall," he said, waiting for recognition. None came. "From the FBI."

That changed things. "Doctor Crandall," the man said as he bustled around the counter. "Chief Frank Mullins. So sorry. I'm stuck at the desk while my sergeant takes his daughter to school." He kept walking toward the conference room. "You must've flown all night. Coffee?"

"That'd be great."

When the chief returned, they sat at the table and Jeff put his ten-dollar steno pad in front of him. "Chief Mullins, I'm here to ask about a former resident. Wallis Perkins."

"Wallis? You're here about *Wallis*?"

Maybe Bob had been right after all. "So you knew her?"

"Everybody in town knows her." The look on the chief's face hinted that Wallis was more notorious than noted. "Have you found her? I mean…like a body or something?"

Or something. "You believe she's dead?"

"She's been gone for thirty-two years. We've just assumed she met with a bad end. It wouldn't be surprising."

Jeff sipped the hottest, vilest coffee of his career. "Who's *we*?"

"Her family, her husband, or ex-husband I suppose. Given everything."

Jeff rubbed his forehead. He couldn't think. "Husband? Mr. Archer?"

"No," the chief drawled, frowning. "Ned Quinn."

Quinn. Jeff's world tilted with the name as the pieces of the kaleidoscope in his brain formed a horrible picture. "Did they have a daughter?"

This time the chief's mouth dropped open. "Are you here about Abigail?"

Something told Jeff he was very much here about Abigail. "Tell me what happened."

"It's sad, really. The Quinns are an old family around here, well liked, hardworking—good people. Ned married Wallis. She's from another good family. Smart girl. Pretty, too. And one night we get a call from Ned's mother. She'd found him in the kitchen with his head split open. And all he'd say was that Wallis had left and taken their little girl."

My father died when I was four.

"He's still alive?"

"Sure. Still lives on the old place outside of town."

"How do I find him?"

The Quinn homestead sat atop a small hill surrounded by a white, split rail fence. Two houses shared a large, shady yard and a view of the lake. And a lilac bush.

The man who came around the corner of the house pushing a wheelbarrow was tall, wiry and large-boned. His face was shaded by a Braves baseball cap. "Can I help you?"

"Mr. Quinn?" Jeff heard the squeaky crack in his voice and cleared his throat. "I'm Jeff Crandall. Chief Mullins called you."

Ned abandoned his gardening and strode forward, stripping off his gloves. "From the FBI, right?"

"Yes, sir," Jeff said as his outstretched hand was swallowed in a callused, firm grip. "May I come in?"

"Sure, of course." Ned opened the gate. "Agent Crandall, if you don't mind me saying it, you look like you've been up all night."

"Because I have, and please call me Jeff."

"Ned," the man said, smiling. "Would you like coffee? 'Cause Frank Mullins and I fish together. I've had his coffee."

"I would." Jeff followed Ned up the stone walk toward the house. "I was admiring your lilac. My grandmother has one."

"That's my mother's pride and joy. She used to have a whole hedge of them between the houses." Ned removed his cap and ran his hand through sandy-blond hair, which was streaked with gray. The movement revealed a nasty scar on the right side of his forehead from his hairline almost to his eyebrow. And deep, soulful brown eyes.

His daughter's eyes.

While Ned went for coffee, Jeff swept his gaze around the living room. How the hell did he start this conversation? *Your daughter is alive. How could you let that monster have her? What was wrong with you?*

A picture on the mantel caught his attention.

Walking closer, he stared at the yellowed photo. A little girl was astride a stick horse, her braids frozen in midbounce and her giggle immortalized. A shaggy black and white puppy was dancing next to her on his back legs.

Jeff heard the steps behind him, but he couldn't take

his eyes off the vision of his somber Abby—and he was sure it was her—happy.

"This is your daughter?"

"That's her. Only picture I have," Ned explained. "Her and her Toby. Wallis hated that dog, and I think it was just because it loved Abby more than her."

Jeff's phone rang, interrupting the story. Gray. He pressed Ignore.

"Did you look for her?" Jeff asked, trying not to snap. His search for a killer had led him here. What was Abby's role in this? *Do children of killers become killers themselves?*

"Everywhere I went. I finally hired a detective who tracked them to Boone, North Carolina."

Jeff viciously disconnected another call. "Go on."

"Her stepfather had taken her into Pisgah National Forest. Murder-suicide. She was just eight, and he'd left her out there so animals could gnaw on her bones. Who does that?"

"Was she alone?" Jeff asked the question he'd already guessed the answer to.

Ned frowned and shook his head. "She had a friend. Connie Dempsey. They've never found her. Why are you here, Jeff?"

Because I'm chasing a killer across the country when the answer was living next door. "Because I know your daughter." He pulled his phone from his pocket and displayed the photo he'd taken last night of Abby at the gallery, shyly soaking up the adoration.

Ned stared as tears ran down his face. "Where is she?"

"Idaho. I took that picture last night."

"She's beautiful." Ned tapped the screen when the

photo faded, then handed it back to Jeff in a silent demand that he unlock it. "I should have asked for my own DNA tests."

Jeff handed the phone back to him. "Is…the body still in Boone?" The police department there probably had a stack of letters. One for every year.

"I had her exhumed and buried here with her family." Ned's face changed from adoration to a frown. "Can you make this larger?"

"Sure." Jeff complied, and watched the frown morph to shock.

"Why is Wallis there?"

Her mother? Jeff stood over Ned's shoulder. "Where?"

"There." Ned jabbed a finger onto the screen. "I'd know those eyes anywhere."

She'd been in the same room with that monster and not said a word. She'd kissed him goodbye, told him she loved him, but not told him that. Why?

His phone rang again, and again he silenced it. As he fumbled to get the picture back, it buzzed in his hand. Enough was enough.

"What?" he growled.

"Finally," Gray growled back. "Where are you?"

"Kentucky. Gray, where's—"

"How far is Bowling Green?"

"How the hell… Ned, how far to Bowling Green?"

"Hour and a half."

Jeff repeated the information as his skin crawled.

"Get to Bowling Green," Gray commanded. "We're sending a plane. I'll call with details, and this time answer your fucking phone."

"Go pack a bag, Ned." Sure the man was gone, Jeff

walked to the fireplace and stared at toddler Abby. This was bad. He could feel it. "What's wrong, Gray?"

"Your girlfriend's just confessed to murder."

A litany of questions droned through Jeff's brain, overwhelming the engine noise as the executive jet touched down in Hastings. Thankfully, Ned had taken advantage of the droning hum and the leather seats and fallen asleep somewhere over Missouri. Up until then he'd been full of questions about his daughter, and Jeff was tired of hedging. He couldn't lie to the man, but the full truth wouldn't make things easier.

Jeff wasn't even sure if he knew the full truth, though he'd received a photo of Abby's birth certificate. Abigail Marian Quinn, born October 15, 1980, to Ned and Wallis Quinn. Wallis who'd been in Boise just yesterday, shaking his hand. Who'd dragged her daughter away from a large, loving family and…what? Tormented her until she became a monster herself? That's what he'd spent months believing. He'd never wanted to be more wrong in his life.

Glen Roberts was waiting next to the hangar.

"Where's Gray?" Jeff asked.

"He's with Maggie. They've got Evan with them, and Gray thought I'd be able to answer more questions for you. Besides, I can get you to town quicker."

The police chief looked past him, and Jeff remembered his passenger. "Glen Roberts, Ned Quinn."

"I'm Abby's father," Ned said as he offered his hand.

Glen's eyebrows arched to his hairline. "We have a lot to catch up on. Let's go."

After they were on the road, under the flash of red

and blue lights, Jeff asked the question he'd been unable to voice until now. "What happened?"

"She called me out of the blue yesterday morning and said she had information on Buck."

"Who's Buck?" Ned and Jeff asked in tandem.

"Her stepfather," Glen explained, glancing at Jeff. "Didn't you know that? She lives on his place. Has since he went missing almost twenty years ago."

Jeff's lungs shrank two sizes. "Did he gamble?"

"Yeah. Nothing too heavy, but he liked to play the ponies over in Tacoma. Anyway, he was buried in the field behind the house. Tree roots had gone through the body. Poor bastard."

All those faceless photos in his study swirled through Jeff's thoughts. Mother-daughter team. This couldn't be happening.

The traits he'd memorized, that he'd recited in front of her two days ago, were as easy to recall as his social security number. Intelligent child from an unstable family with a domineering mother and an absent father. Whether she'd admit it or not, life on the farm had kept her from achieving what she could. She hated her mother, who had abused her, and she had a list of phobias and hang-ups as long as his arm. And at least one suicide attempt.

Jeff rolled down the window to get some air.

Glen was still talking. "I got out there, and she led me straight to the body and told me she'd killed him. If I hadn't arrested her, I think she would have cuffed herself to the car."

Ned leaned up from the backseat. "Wallis did it. Abby couldn't have—"

"You haven't seen her since she was four," Jeff reminded him, and then immediately felt like an ass. "Ned. You need to prepare yourself." *We both do.*

The man shook his head, and Jeff recognized his stubborn expression. He was just like his daughter.

"Did you say Wallis?" Glen asked. When Jeff nodded, Glen exhaled a long slow breath. "See, that's the other part. This couple has gone missing from their hotel in Boise. The PD sent me a photo of the suspect, and it's…well, it's Abby." Glen shot an apologetic look at Ned. "And the missing woman's name is Wallis. Hale and Wallis Riker."

"Wallis isn't missing. She's running," Jeff said as they entered the Fiddler city limits. "Where are we going?"

"I thought you'd want to go to the jail, see about getting her—"

She was the last person he wanted to see right now. "I want to talk to Gray and see Evan. The kid has to be terrified."

"Okay, but you need to get on with it. We can't keep the Feds out of it for much longer."

"I'm the Feds, Glen."

"Guess you are," the chief snorted. "I keep forgetting that. Whatever. We'd like to get to the bottom of it first. I figured you'd agree with that, seeing as how—"

"She's confessed," Jeff reminded him. Truthfully, he needed the reminder, too—because his heart was soaring with the knowledge Abby had such loyal friends.

"Son, that confession is a load of shit, and you know it. Abby wouldn't hurt a fly, much less murder a man and leave him to rot in a shallow grave. No one thinks she did this."

The car was quiet for a few minutes. Jeff stared out the window as the countryside slid by at a dizzying pace.

"Who's Evan?" Ned asked.

"Our—her foster son," Jeff answered. There was no *our*. She hadn't shared anything with him. Hadn't trusted him. He'd told her everything, let her tempt him with the promise of peace, and she'd lied. Lied. And he'd been too lovestruck to see it.

"She has a child?"

The shake in Ned's voice indicated he was reaching information overload. This morning he'd woke with a daughter in a grave, and Jeff had dangled hope in front of him. A daughter, a grandson.

A suspected murderer and a temporary child.

They arrived at Gray's home, and Jeff walked in without knocking. Conversation led him to the kitchen.

"Badger, I'm not the best choice for this."

"She doesn't need a real lawyer, Graham."

"Gee, thanks."

"You know what I mean. She didn't do this. She—" Maggie looked up from her perch on a counter stool. "Hi, Jeff."

Evan bolted into the room, and Jeff dropped to his knees to catch the boy in a tight hug. Toby galloped next to him. Tug was close behind, scrabbling against the hardwood floor.

"Hey there, squirt."

"Abby's in jail," the little boy whispered through his tears. "She has to be cold in there, and she doesn't like the dark. Can you take her a light?"

"We'll ask Chief Roberts to take her one," Jeff murmured, fighting the knot in his throat. "Are you okay?"

"I miss her. Can you bring her home?"

He wanted to say yes more than anything, but he wouldn't lie to the boy. Abby would hate that. "I'll try," he said, now fighting to stay upright as the dogs bounded against him.

"Toby," Evan commanded in his little voice. "Down. Stay."

The collie went to the floor, and Ned gasped as he thumped into the nearest chair. The man had reached his limit, and Jeff needed to give him something good to hang on to.

"Evan, this is Ned. He's an old friend of Abby's from when she lived in Kentucky."

"She said her grandma lived there," Evan chirped as only a child could.

Ned's nod was shaky. "She still does."

"Oh, and she had a horse named Berry who slept next to her bed. Did she really?"

Tears streaked down the older man's face as he nodded.

Evan looked up at Jeff. "Can I come with you?"

"Yes." He wasn't sure which of them needed the comfort more. "But you have to do exactly what I tell you."

Gray walked them out. "Hold up a second, Crandall."

"Evan, go get in the backseat. I'll be right there." Once the boy was out of earshot, Jeff looked at Gray. "Yeah?"

"This ties to your case, doesn't it?"

Jeff nodded, and Gray's mouth thinned into a grim line.

"I'm her lawyer. You don't talk to her without me." He blew out a long deep breath. "This sucks."

"Tell me about it." Jeff spun on his heel and strode

to Glen's patrol car. He wanted a bottle of whiskey and a good sleep in a warm bed, but he needed answers.

As they left the Harpers behind, Evan crawled into his lap and Toby rested his head on the seat. Both stared up at him with desperate eyes. Even Tug seemed to plead. Ned turned around to watch them.

He needed everyone to quit expecting him to fix the pile of shit his life had become overnight. Some things couldn't be fixed.

One thing he could do. Wrestling his phone out of his pocket, he dialed Colonel Freeman with the ISP.

"Eric? It's Jeff Crandall. Any chance you're investigating the disappearance of Hale and Wallis Riker?"

"I'm on the task force. What can you add?"

"I think they're tied to a case I'm investigating." He closed his eyes and prayed he was wrong, that the feeling in his bones was weariness and not fear. "I'm fairly certain Wallis isn't a victim. I'd appreciate it if you could add an APB for her."

"I can try. Can you give me anything else to make my point?"

Jeff surveyed his audience, each member of which was paying far too much attention to him. "I'll call you back."

"Mrs. Riker?" Evan asked. "From the party?"

"You remember her?" Jeff asked.

He nodded. "When Abby was outside with you, I went to get a drink. Mrs. Riker asked me to tell her about Abby's pictures. She was nice. She wanted to know all about the farm."

Alarm bells clanged. "Did Abby see you with her?"

"Uh-huh. When she came back in."

So that's why she'd left him with Gray, an ex-agent

who would protect the boy like a hawk. Solving one mystery gave Jeff a bit of equilibrium.

"Did I do something wrong?" Evan whispered.

And just like that, Jeff was floundering again. "No, buddy. Abby's trying to keep you safe." Just saying it gave him a steadier footing. Her goal all summer had been Evan's safety. And it was normal thinking, normal behavior. Anyone faced with a murderer would protect the people they loved.

They parked at the top of the hill. Below them, the valley was peaceful. The horses grazed in the paddock. Jeff trudged up the steps, his entourage in his wake. Cassie opened the door and swept him and Evan into a hug.

"She didn't do this," she whispered.

"Cassie." He swung his arm behind him. "This is Ned Quinn. Abby's father."

"Ohmigod," she gasped as she moved aside and let them in.

Glen stayed on the threshold. "I'm going back to the station. I'll send Chet up here to…" He looked down at Evan.

"Watch us?" Evan asked. The boy was getting way too familiar with bodyguards for Jeff's taste.

"Yep," Jeff said as they walked into the house. Now it was his job to keep them safe. "Chet's going to watch you and Cass and Ned while I work."

As soon as Chet arrived, Jeff drove to Abby's home, cursing as he crept over her rutted driveway. Why the hell didn't she fix this? It took him twice as long to get—

He slowed and stared out the windshield as his headlights bobbed and swayed against the trees. As he drew closer, the lights careened off the house's windows, and then the porch. Damn. It was an early warning system. She would've seen anyone coming and had enough time to run.

He parked in front of the house and stood next to the car, looking at the security lights with a new perspective. He'd always considered the overly bright yard a symptom of her fear of the dark. Maybe she had another reason to be afraid.

The horses were still out in the paddock. As he approached, the motion-sensitive light over the stable doors blared to life.

"I'll bet you guys are confused," he whispered as he led them to their stalls. Butcher was last.

Jeff ran his fingers along the horse's coat. It was still thin, but it was shiny. The visible skin was healthy. His eyes were bright. Abby loved this horse, had virtually willed it back to life. Just like she'd done with Evan. So animals and children were safe, but adult men were fair game? Could she compartmentalize that much? For her whole life? And how did that explain *him*?

He fed the horses and then walked up the hill to put the cow in the barn and feed the cat, now expecting the security light to awaken as he approached. He got the eggs and put the chickens in their coop. And then he broke the window in her back door, let himself in, and disarmed the security system.

The house was a spotless shell without her and Evan in it, but without their distraction Jeff saw the space in a new way. Every room was arranged so she could see the door, every desk and bed was near a window. Even the mirror over the sink meant she could see if anyone was behind her. And her shower curtains were clear liners.

Everything she'd decorated with spoke to her personality, to her preferences for soft, warm fabrics and bright colors, but nothing was personal. He'd seen it as OCD, but maybe it was another way to hide. No one could see what was important to her. And she wasn't attached to anything, just like a kid who'd been on the run through their adolescence. On the other hand, Evan's room was a shrine to everything he loved. Toys for his dog, his baseball glove, his favorite books.

One by one, he searched every cabinet and drawer in her office until he sat back on his heels and stared at a new piece of the puzzle. In a box was a neat collection of envelopes, paper, and stamps just like his mother kept on her desk for paying bills and sending birthday cards. Except in Abby's kit, everything was sealed in plastic bags. And she'd added rubber gloves, bottled water and sponges. Everything she'd need to eliminate trace evidence from her mail.

He walked into her bedroom and sat on her side of the bed—the side nearest the door. It smelled like her in here. No one who smelled this sweet could be a monster. Could they?

The darkness and quiet settled around him as he closed his eyes and let his thoughts sift and stack. She'd been hiding down here in fear for years.

And she was making it easy to leave it behind. His fingers twitched with the memory of the scar on her thigh. Would she—No. She'd told him she'd never thought about it again. But she'd leave. Everything *not* here told him she wasn't expecting to stay. Whether she left or went to prison for the rest of her life, she didn't consider this her home.

Grabbing her pillow, he hurled it against the wall. She'd slept here, cuddled naked against him, cried his name as she came, and told him *nothing.* The down barrage continued, thudding against the wall and sliding to the floor, until he saw the envelope on the bed. His name was written across it in her precise, neat handwriting.

Great. Not only was she making a fool of him, now he was breaking in to houses and contaminating crime scenes. Pulling his phone from his pocket, he took a picture of the note where it lay, held the envelope on the edges and shook the paper free, and touched it as little as possible to pry it open. He took another photo before he read it.

I'm sorry. Everything you need to know is in the attic.

She'd known that he'd be driving himself crazy, and she was still leaving an enigmatic trail. Why couldn't she just fucking tell him?

How could she have done something so monumentally stupid?

The entrance to the attic was in her closet ceiling. Taking photos with each step, he reached for the handle and stopped. What the hell was waiting on him up here?

Jeff went up the ladder anyway, and wasn't surprised to find it totally empty except for a plastic crate sitting in easy reach. After more photos, he pulled it down the ladder, thumping it rung by rung, and sat it on the bench at the end of the bed.

It was full of journals. Year after year, page after page, painstakingly dated and kept in order. Early, cheap notebooks were full of cramped writing clearly meant to make the most of space, as if paper was scarce, later ones were nicer—colorful spiral ones, some covered in soft leather that was now shiny with use.

In the back, shoved and buried under the others, was a pink book covered with rainbows and unicorns. Loose pages were askew. The pages were dry, dark, and crinkled.

He sat next to the box. It was a little girl's diary, minus the lock. The thoughts of someone who wasn't allowed to have secrets. The finish on the cover was rubbed off in spots. He checked some of the others. All the early ones had the same wear patterns. She'd shoved them somewhere tight and narrow to hide them.

Inside the front cover, she'd printed her full name in precise block print with pink ink. *Abigail Marian Quinn.*

The corner of a picture peeked out from behind the loose faceplate. Jeff pulled it free. A redhead with a gapped-tooth smile and skinned knees had her arm around the shoulder of another child. A somber, thin little girl staring into the camera, her eyes wide. He could almost see her pulling away. The braids identified her as the same girl in Ned's photo, at least genetically. Emotionally, she was as far from that child as he could imagine.

He hesitated to turn the page. He'd tormented his sisters by reading their diaries. They had thrown a fit about him invading their private thoughts, as if there was anything private about what they wore to school or ate for lunch, or who they sat with.

The first page of Abigail Marian Quinn's first diary squeezed the breath from him. A stick person made of thick black lines had black hair that looked like thorns. Its mouth was open to reveal sharp teeth, red eyes were slanted into an angry glare. Yelling—no, screaming. The head was larger than the body. Leaning in to scream.

The hands were red. So was the page under its feet, obscuring another figure with fountains of red spurting upward from its head. More precise handwriting lined the top margin.

My mommy is a monster.

Hours later, he sat in his office chair, the journals spread out on the table behind him as he alternately studied the profiles of his suspect and the woman he loved. Every time he turned his head, the world spun on its axis and the coffee churned in his gut. He'd quit counting the cups at midnight.

Toby dropped to the floor at his feet with a sigh.

"Tell me about it," Jeff grumbled. "And don't look at me that way. I *am* trying."

"Are you talking to the dog?" Cass asked from the doorway.

He spun and faced her. "Why are you still up?"

"'Cause you are." She pointed at the stale sandwich and greasy potato chips and glared at him. "You didn't eat."

"Not hungry."

"Not tired either?" she sighed when he ignored her. "Jeff, you have to sleep. You'll make yourself nuts."

He was already nuts. He dropped his head into his hands and forked his fingers into his hair. "Cassie, she was a happy kid. She was a little girl with braids and a puppy. She had a family." He waved at the line of victims. "And that monster made her live with this." He leapt from the chair and pointed at Abby's profile. "Do you know what hyperthymesia is?"

She shook her head, tears already in her eyes.

"She remembers every day of her life. Every day, just like it's happening in real time. She carries—" he pointed at the grisly photos "—that around with her. And she'd rather be in fucking prison than ask me for help, and for the life of me I don't know why."

"You have to help her."

"I don't help people." He gritted the words between his teeth. "I convict them."

"You know, one of the meanings of conviction is convincing someone."

Jeff blinked at her. "Of what?" He crossed the room in two quick strides, and put his hand on his suspect profile. "She fits this. Do you understand that? What if she—"

She walked to him and put her hands on his shoulders. "This is Abby. Vegetarian, animal-rescuing, foster mother Abby. She argued with you about Evan having a rabbit's foot on his keychain."

"Hale Riker is dead," he said. "I got a text from the ISP an hour ago. They found him in the foothills outside Boise. Abby and her mother end up in the same room, and another husband dies. That cannot be a coincidence." He wrenched away from her and prowled the room. "She showed up at their hotel, insisting they check on him, and twenty-four hours later he's dead."

"She didn't do this," Cass repeated.

"It is my *job* to look at the evidence without skewing it, Cassidy. I have to consider every shitty angle." He ran his hands through his hair, resisting the urge to pull it out. "Why didn't she trust me to help her? One word, all it would've taken is one four-letter word. One syllable. And she couldn't fucking say it."

"She didn't—"

"Leave me alone. Let me think."

She closed the door behind her, and Jeff sat on the table, staring at the butcher paper-covered walls. He'd spent the summer profiling the woman he loved—twice—but he'd learned more in the last twenty-four hours than he had in months. And he'd learned none of it from her.

He was responsible for facts. And the cold, dry facts were that she'd confessed to a murder, and her mother, through violence and neglect, had spent years crafting her into a perfect killer. On paper anyway.

Jeff looked at the photograph on his wall, at the silvery tree in the dawn light. Abby wasn't paper. She was the woman who'd built a life from nothing and still managed to see beauty everywhere she looked.

I would've rather starved to death than go with her.

He stood in front of the wall of evidence. Every letter had started seventeen years ago. Abby had been nineteen years old, on her own for the first time. Cold, poor and suicidal. And without her mother. She'd escaped, only to live in a prison of fear.

The broad, vertical stroke on his board labeled 1999 stood out. Now he knew the trigger. Abby's disastrous Christmas at eighteen, and her suicide attempt. She'd come out of that bathtub committed to catching her mother. The letters had begun the following year. Except for Buck. Why leave him a secret until now?

And she hadn't killed the other ones. She'd spent the last twenty-three years in Idaho. She hadn't known about them until she'd seen Hale Riker at the gallery. And she'd immediately taken a drastic step. A huge, stupid, drastic step.

Jeff, please...

She'd kept trying to get his attention at the gallery, but he'd been focused on his job. He'd written her tears off to disappointment, but they weren't just that. She'd been afraid, and he'd left her there.

He picked up his notebook and began scribbling questions. He was violating every rule of his training, but he was going to have to go into an interrogation without knowing everything.

Abby was going to have to fill in the blanks.

Chapter Twenty

Abby walked down the hall with Max holding one elbow and Chet the other. The cuffs and manacles jangled with every clopping step in the oversized flip-flops, making her sound like a horse being led to the starting gate.

Except this wasn't a start, it was a finish. And she didn't feel like a racehorse. She felt like one of her horses—cold, exhausted, hungry and terrified. Even without a mirror she knew she didn't look much better.

Her jumpsuit was stiff and scratchy and so large it scratched her more. The short sleeves left her arms cold. And Charlene had always said no one ever looked good in orange. At least the shackles at her waist cinched it in a bit.

Even though they'd finally given her a hair tie this morning, she'd given up on braiding it because her fingers shook. As a result, the strands slipped free, tormenting her neck and reminding her of the kudzu that had grown over everything in Alabama. It had always been pretty in the spring, but in the fall the leaves had come off and made it depressing and creepy.

They opened a door, and she saw Jeff at the table. It was reflex to reach for her hair, to straighten it. But the chains stopped her. When they jangled, his gaze snapped to hers.

There was nothing soft about his glare, and his glasses made it worse. His mouth was set in a grim line and his jaw was rigid. He was in a dress shirt and tie, and his badge hung from a lanyard around his neck. He hadn't come here to see her. He was working.

He was trying to scare her. He thought she couldn't lie to him. He should know better by now. Her whole life had been a lie. She'd been doing it so long it was like breathing. This was just another lie.

It was all she could think to do. If Wallis was bent on ruining her life, and she did it first, where was the fun? Wallis could visit her in prison and torment her from the other side of the glass. Maggie would be with Gray. Evan would be with Jeff. It would be over in a few minutes, and no one would be the wiser.

Surely Wallis knew by now. A crazy woman in Idaho with a body in her pasture had to make headlines. Didn't it?

Gray was here, too—standing beside Jeff. He smiled. "Hello, Abby. Are you okay?"

Fighting tears, she nodded. "M-Maggie?"

"She's worried about you. Why don't you come in and have a seat?"

It could have been any other day, any other meeting. But when she moved, her shackles rattled and her steps shuffled. It wasn't any other day, and she might as well get it over with.

Chet closed the door behind her, and the click echoed through the silent room. Abby walked to the only other chair and risked a glance at the two-way mirror behind Jeff. Instead of her reflection, she saw the paper taped to the wall. She spun, got tangled in her chains, and grabbed the table for balance.

Photos cluttered the chart—Beau, Ron, John, Walt, Connie, Buck—in life and in death. Their homes, their graves. Below those were her letters. Every other space was scattered with notes. Wallis's photo leered down at her from the topmost level. It was like some twisted family tree.

"No."

She heard the scream before she realized it had come from her. Fighting her shackles, not caring that she lost her useless shoes, she struggled to the door and wrapped her hand around the cold handle. But it was locked from the outside.

Memories overwhelmed her. Bicycles, ice cream, fishing, lightning bugs, camping under the stars. Every happy memory ended with the look on their faces as they'd realized what was about to happen. Remembered sounds hammered in her ears—squishy thuds, shovels hitting rock, closet doors slamming. Her skin stung from long-ago abuse, stealing her breath as she squinched her eyes closed and put her hands over her ears, heedless of the chains biting into her. Her chest hurt so she knew she was screaming, but she couldn't hear it. She also knew she was falling, but she couldn't stop it. Her bones were coming apart.

Strong arms caught her and held her tightly. *Jeff.* He hauled her against his chest, and his voice rattled her cheek as he stroked her hair. Eventually, his words soaked in.

"It's okay, Slugger. I've got you."

Someone had finally listened. *He* had listened.

The realization renewed her sobs. This couldn't come

at his hand. She'd dragged him into her private hell and forced him to dance with the skeletons crowding her closet.

He tilted her chin and wiped her tears, giving her a good look at the shadows under his eyes and the pity in his gaze. He shouldn't pity her. These people were dead because of her.

The weight of the chains vanished and she was able to breathe. Jeff handed her a handkerchief and draped his jacket over her shoulders before sliding her favorite socks over her icy feet.

"Better?"

She nodded, and he helped her stand and step over the pile of shackles. Two chairs were waiting on them, both facing the board.

"I'm going to sit with you and we're going to talk," he said.

"And I'm your attorney," Gray explained, looking at her like she was a wounded animal. "You stop if I tell you. The federal prosecutor has given you immunity, on the condition that you didn't actively participate in any murder once you reached age eighteen. Do you understand?"

She nodded and cleared her throat. "Why?"

"Why immunity?" Jeff asked. "Because no one believes you did this." He bent until he met her gaze. *"No one."*

"How's. Evan?"

"He's at my house with Cass. He's worried, but he's safe." He drew a deep breath. "Are you ready to start?"

You know what I'll do if you tell.

"I'm. Not. Sup-sup-posed. To. Tell. She'll. Be. M-mad."

"You don't have to be afraid anymore, darlin'."

Was it really over? He'd said Evan was safe. He wouldn't have said that if Wallis was still loose, would he?

"Beau died when you were seven. I've never met a child strong enough to wield a roofing hammer on a grown man." He wrapped his fingers through hers. "Tell me a story, Abby."

She looked into his dark green eyes, fringed with those impossibly thick lashes, and gripped his hand. "My. Mother. Did it."

No grim reaper appeared. The world didn't shear in two.

"Keep going," Jeff said, nodding in encouragement.

"She took. Casino. Jobs. And they were. Regulars. They were always older. With-without families. I was bait."

"Single mom, sweet kid?" Gray asked.

Abby nodded, but never took her eyes off Jeff. "They got married fast."

She nodded at each photo, eager to eulogize each of the men who'd loved her. "Beau taught me to ride a bike and took me with him to town. John tried to learn sign language so we could talk because she'd told him I was deaf. Ron took me fishing and shopping for new school clothes. Walt was kind, but he was totally wrapped up in Wallis."

"Why did she kill them?"

"Because of me."

"What do you mean because of you?"

"She thought they loved me more than her," Abby whispered.

"And you were there?" Jeff asked, resting his forehead against her hair.

She nodded, her tears renewing. "We'd go. Camping. And she'd—" Abby hauled in the deepest breath she could manage. "She'd stab them in the back. Through a lung. When they couldn't fight anymore, she hit them in the head."

The chorus of memorized thumps echoed again, and she put her hands over her ears while she curled into Jeff's side. She wanted to stop, to not think about it, not remember. But she had to. This was what she'd wanted—justice for all these people—and she had to be brave enough to finish the job. She sat straighter and wiped her tears away.

"Except for Walt and Connie. I was locked in a closet."

"Why are they different?"

As she stared at Connie's third grade photo, memories played across Abby's vision like a horror movie. "Because I'd told Connie that I'd had another daddy in Kentucky but he'd died. Wallis heard me, and she and Walt took Connie home."

"Dear God," Gray murmured.

It was easy to narrate a movie—that was telling a story, not *telling*. "Wallis had her monster face on when she ripped my locket off my neck. I loved that locket. My father had given it to me, and I'd put my first Toby's picture in it because I missed him. I'd worked so hard to get it the right size and not cut off any of his face or his ears.

"Everyone thought I was lost with Connie, and I could hear people in the house. But Wallis told me I had to be quiet or she'd be mad. When we left in the middle of the night, she shoved me in a box and put me in the trunk. When she let me out, we were in Ohio."

Jeff's arms tightened around her. "So you were quiet."

"I made a promise. No one else was going to get hurt because of me. I stayed out of the way and kept quiet. I didn't make any friends." She looked up at Gray, willing him to understand. "Until Maggie."

"Then Buck saw Wallis hit me. He was going to tell. He was going to keep me and send her away. I was so happy. So she killed him."

Freedom surged through her veins, loosening her tongue. It felt so *good* to talk. To quit worrying that she was saying the wrong thing. "After Maggie was in college, I told Wallis I was staying here. I promised her I'd be good, but she was so mad. Toby, my other Toby, and I fought so hard, but she won. She always won. She killed the only thing I had left that loved me and made sure I understood what would happen if I told her secret to anyone."

Gray swore again.

"And then everyone started helping me—teaching me things, hiring me, inviting me places. I had to protect them. They couldn't know—"

"I think they do, sweetheart."

She frowned at him. "Really?"

"Not specifics, but I'm guessing Hank doesn't keep a loaded shotgun by his door for squirrels." He cleared his throat. "So you sent letters?"

"I *had* to tell, but it had to be. Anonymous. Or Wallis would've come back."

She wiped her eyes and caught a glimpse of the other end of the chart, visible over Jeff's shoulder. More photos scattered that end, unfamiliar faces and places, no letters. Jeff followed her gaze.

"Abby—"

"No." She pulled away from him and stood. "She was supposed to *stop.* I wasn't there." She walked to the photos and stared at them through her tears. "They're dead because I didn't say anything. Aren't they?" She looked back at Jeff. "*Aren't they*?"

"They're dead because she killed them." He walked to her and put his hands on her shoulders. "Darlin', this was never about you, not really. It was the money. She killed them for their money. And she'll pay for it."

Abby walked the length of the wall, looking at each entry and remembering. She stopped at Connie, at the gravestone identifying her as Abigail Quinn. "This isn't my grave." She looked up at Gray. "Wallis showed me a grave with a big angel on it. She told me no one would miss me."

Jeff joined them. "Your family moved the grave to Kentucky." He cleared his throat again. "Your first Toby is buried there, too."

"He is?" she squeaked. "They kept him?"

"They did. He lived to be old and gray headed." He took her hand. "Do you remember your family?"

"Papa liked to garden. He was always outside. And he loved to sing. 'Blackbird' by The Beatles was his favorite song." She looked at him, hoping against hope. "Can you prove Wallis killed him?"

Jeff pulled her to a chair and knelt in front of her. "What can you tell me about the night she took you away?"

"He was on the kitchen floor all bloody, reaching for me. But he quit moving." She tried to remember anything else that would help. "They'd had a fight." That wasn't much. She met Jeff's stare. "Wallis always told me he was dead. Maybe you could get her to confess."

His fingers tightened on hers. “She lied, Abby.”

She shook her head. Wallis lied about a lot of things, but she’d never once lied about killing someone.

“That was the reason for the grave,” he continued. “So he’d think *you* were dead and quit looking.”

The door opened, and a lean, older man stood there, his face wet with tears. “Abigail?” His soft voice washed over her, bringing with it laughter and lilacs and sunshine.

No one had called her that since she was four. She’d been named for her grandmother, who had loved her and made her favorite cookies and taken her horseback riding.

Papa? It couldn’t be her father. He was dead.

He walked into the room. “Your middle name is Marian, and you thought you were named for the animated fox in the Disney movie.”

They’d watched that movie together over and over because she’d liked the idea of talking animals. She’d even made Evan watch it just to relive the memory. She looked down at Jeff, watched him nod.

She looked up again, meeting the man’s gaze and recognizing *her* eyes staring back. Saw the wheat-colored hair—no longer bloody. “Papa?”

He took the chair beside her and wrapped her in a tight hug. Caught between him and Jeff she was warmer than she’d been in over thirty years. Free and safe, and loved.

“Now what?” she whispered.

“Now you go home,” Gray said. “Hug Evan, take a shower—”

She looked at Jeff, confused. Surely she’d never have Evan with her again. “But the headlines—”

“We kept everything quiet,” he explained. “No one knows anything.”

Rather than comforting her, the favor began a new panic. "What about Wallis? You have her, right?"

"Not yet."

She looked around the room. Not only was everyone important to her now involved, they were unprotected. And her father… Wallis would never forgive her for this reunion.

Warn them, her conscience commanded. *Don't hide. You don't have to anymore.*

But she knew what they'd do. They'd rush to the house, straight into danger. Jeff, Gray and Papa…and Wallis would hurt them all. And then she'd go after Evan, Maggie and Faye. And then, God only knew. Abby thought about the strangers on Jeff's chart. Wallis would never stop. Not unless someone intervened. *You have to be brave.*

"Can I use the ladies' room?"

Jeff helped her to her feet. "You don't have to ask. You're not a prisoner."

Oh, but she was.

Abby walked out of the room and across the hall on quivering legs. Trapped in the ladies' room, she paced in front of the mirror and considered her options.

She could walk out there and put everyone in danger, or just walk out. The first wasn't possible. She wouldn't do that. But the second… No. It wasn't good either. She didn't want to leave her Papa here, thinking she didn't want to see him. She wanted to ask about everyone she could remember, see whether he still lived in the house she dreamed about.

And walking past Jeff was almost impossible. He was like a magnet for the truth.

Gray couldn't take her. He needed to be here to protect Maggie in case Wallis made it to town.

So…she'd have to run for it. In an orange jumpsuit, with no car. She'd have to steal a neighbor's car. She didn't have a choice.

This was a shitty option.

Angie Cooper, the dispatcher, came in with a sack. "We thought you'd be happier in your own clothes."

Maybe God liked her a little bit after all. "Thank you."

Once she was alone, Abby stripped and changed, then tipped the envelope up. Jeff's car key slid onto the vanity, sparkling in the light.

Calling on years of dodging restaurant checks with Wallis, she twisted the jumpsuit into a rope and tied it to the door and then to the nearest faucet. It wouldn't keep anyone out for long, but she didn't need much time.

Holding her breath, she shoved her foot through the glass and kicked the screen loose. The alarm stole her equilibrium.

"Goddammit! Abby!"

Jeff. She couldn't let him catch her. All her life she'd done the wrong thing. *This* she could do right. She could protect him. "Get away from me! Leave me alone!" Ignoring the glass snagging her clothes, Abby climbed out the window and sprinted across the yard. The Audi was parked on the curb, and she didn't hesitate. The engine roared to life and she punched the accelerator, spinning the wheels and fishtailing away as her crowd of protectors ran out of the police station's front door.

Icy calm crept up Abby's body as she stopped the car at the mouth of the driveway, out of view from the house and crept across her silent yard. She didn't have much time. Either Jeff would figure out that Wallis would be coming for *her*, or he'd come to yell at her for stealing his car. Wallis had to be stopped before he got here.

The horses all trotted to the fence, the chickens clucked and squawked, and Jane's bell clanged in the pasture. This was her home. Her life. She belonged here. Why the hell was she sneaking around her own home? Steeling her nerves, she tromped up the steps and through the open front door.

Wallis looked over her shoulder with a sneer. "Welcome home, daughter. We've been waiting on you."

Beyond her, Cass and Evan were in tears on the sofa. Cass's cheek was one large bruise, and her lip was split open. Evan was cradling Tug in one arm, and his other had a deep gash from elbow almost to wrist. Blood soaked his shirt and his jeans. Toby stood and took one halting step, whimpering and limping.

"Down, Toby," Abby said. "Good boy. Stay." Sure her dog was safe, she turned to Wallis. "I'm not your daughter. Never was."

The air smelled like gas and the stove hissed from the kitchen. Dear God. She was going to blow them up.

"Close the door."

"Do it yourself."

Wallis kept a wary eye as she circled to the front door, closed it and bolted it shut. And stayed there. Abby cursed her temper. She'd put Wallis between them and their quickest escape route.

"Why is there crime scene tape in the field?"

"Because I told them where Buck was," she said as she straightened to her full height. "I told them *everything*." She walked in front of Cass and Evan. "You're not going to hurt anyone else."

Wallis slapped her, hard. Despite the ringing in her ears, Abby didn't go down. She was finally big enough to stand up for herself. Instead, she kept her hands at her sides and turned back to look at the paper doll who used to be her mother.

"Oh, but I am. Do you know what you've cost me, you whiny bitch? I *loved* Hale. He treated me like a goddess, and I was *happy*." Her face was mottled red and pink. "And you ruined it. Just like Walt. You couldn't keep your mouth shut, and I've lost the man of my dreams. This is all your fault."

Remembering Jeff's words, Abby shook her head. "No, it's not. You're greedy and selfish. You always have been, and you always will be."

The punch in her stomach doubled her over. Wallis snatched her hair, lifting her head and leaving her short of breath. Spittle dripped from her lips, and a kitchen knife glinted in the sunshine. "You don't talk back to me, girl. And you don't tell me what to do."

Abby lunged forward, knocking Wallis off balance. "Run!" The word ended in a shriek as the knife sliced across her back.

Wallis was already past her, chasing Cass and Evan and the dogs into the hall. Abby grabbed her around the calves, toppled her to the floor, and climbed on top of her. As they fought for the knife, Wallis wriggled around to face her, spitting and scratching like the demon she was.

Abby held on, clamping her knees to Wallis's ribs and feeling them heave and give with every rage-filled scream. Her clothes ripped and tore under the clawed hands and taloned nails, and she wrapped her hands around the monster's neck and squeezed. Power surged through her as Wallis's eyes bulged and her screams faded to gasps. Kicks became heels thudding and scraping across the floor.

What the hell was she doing? She was *nothing* like this monster, and nothing could make her that way.

Abby released her prey and vaulted over her prone body. She ran to Evan's room and slammed the door. They didn't have long. She threw a chair through the window and pointed. "Git."

Toby obeyed, but the humans stayed frozen in place. Abby shoved Cass at the window as Wallis threw her body against the door. "Out."

Once safely outside, Cass reached for Evan. Abby lifted him and Tug, screaming as the clots on her skin broke open and her shoulder locked in place. He helped her by climbing the rest of the way on his own. His hatchet clattered to the floor.

His eyes were wide. "You're next, right?"

The door gave behind her just as the house buckled in a deafening roar. The timbers above them cracked and groaned. Abby's head hit the windowsill as she covered Evan's hand with hers. "I am," she lied. "Don't look back."

Wallis's shriek echoed through the room, giving Abby just enough time to deflect the blow she'd watched so many times. Rather than driving into her back, the knife slashed across her ribs and arm. It was followed by a hard knee meant to hammer the pain home. Losing her breath, Abby sagged against the wall.

Wallis reached for the window. No. She wasn't going to chase Evan the rest of his life. Jeff would find him and make sure he was safe. It was Abby's job to stop the spider.

She head-butted Wallis, feeling the perfect nose squish and wetness coat her scalp. As Wallis staggered backward, Abby grabbed the hatchet and swung upward, blindly, from the floor. Then she braced herself for the return blow.

It didn't come. Wallis's empty gray eyes were large in her face as she dropped to her knees with the hatchet buried in her temple.

I didn't mean to, Mama. I'm sorry. Please don't be mad. Please don't...

Abby's knees buckled as she sank to the floor in the smoky room, as if they were finally sharing a mother-daughter moment.

Flames licked toward the door and crept across the ceiling, and Abby's eyes drooped. Heat singed her skin, and smoke burned her lungs. She should get out of here. She would. In just a minute.

Chapter Twenty-One

Jeff lowered his arm and gaped as splinters rained across Abby's front yard. Flames lapped at the roof and smoke bellowed from the front windows.

No.

Everyone turned wide-eyed stares to him, as if he knew what to do. They were shouting questions he couldn't hear over the ringing in his ears. The vacuum trapped him inside his quaking bones with the scream building in the back of his throat.

No.

It was all he'd been able to think since she'd left the interrogation room, when Eric Freeman had called with the news that Wallis had been spotted in Hastings. Then the alarm had blared through the police station and the bathroom door had been blocked. And Abby had stolen his car.

He'd known then where she'd go, what she'd do…and he'd shut the word inside himself as they'd raced after her. Now, he was splintering apart, just like her house.

Movement caught his attention. Evan was running for his life, his face covered with soot and tears, and his clothes a bloody mess. Jeff caught him in a bear hug and held on even as the little boy struggled to get free.

"It's me, buddy," Jeff said. "You're safe."

Evan turned a wild-eyed gaze up at him and then crumpled. Cass was next, falling against his other shoulder. No one else came around the corner.

Jeff pulled Cass away and looked into her wide eyes. "Abby?"

The only word he could make out stopped his heart. *House.*

He shoved Evan at the first set of hands and pushed Cass into the next, and ran for the backyard with Gray at his side. The ringing in his ears faded, only to be replaced by his pounding heart and his heaving breaths. Those stopped altogether when he didn't see her in the backyard. She was still in there. Smoke poured from the window.

"Stay out here," he barked at Gray as he righted the chair under the window. "Catch her when I push her through."

He swung into the window, blinded by thick, acrid smoke and kicked his foot in search of the floor. Instead he hit something that bobbled back to rest on his foot. A head.

Jesus, what was he going to find in there?

Sucking in a breath of fresh air, he dropped to the floor. Smoke and fumes burned his eyes and coated his nose. Swinging his hand in front of him, he touched a leg and then felt up the body until he reached an elbow. He grasped a thick hank of long hair. Abby.

Pushing her up the wall, he shoved her into Gray's waiting hands and then clawed his way out. Dropping to all fours, he coughed and wheezed as he fought for fresh air and wiped the tears from his eyes.

Abby wasn't doing that. Gray was already at the corner of the house, bellowing across the yard for a medic.

"*No*," Jeff roared as he scrambled across the grass. Putting his hands over her sternum, he pumped by instinct. The first downward push soaked her shirt collar in blood.

"Gray!"

His friend slid next to him. "Christ." He stripped off his shirt. "Where?"

"Her neck, I think."

Gray applied pressure, and Jeff pushed again. Abby's ribs cracked under the pressure, and Jeff winced. But she didn't. And blood spread across her jeans and the grass beneath her.

He was killing her. He pulled his shirt over his head and shoved it at Gray. "Her ribs, too."

Another push revealed another hole.

"I'm out of hands," Gray said.

Jeff put his lips over Abby's cold, sooty ones and breathed, felt her chest heave in response, but just the once.

"Don't you do this to me," he shouted as he forced her heart to pump. "You hear me, you stubborn woman?"

The EMTs ran around the side of the house. As they took over CPR, Jeff dropped to the ground, his lungs burning and his arms shaking.

"Breathe," Gray muttered beside him. It took Jeff a moment to realize the command was aimed at him.

"Get Evan out of here. He doesn't need to see her like this. Ned, too."

Gray nodded and stood. "I'll bring your car to the hospital."

Alone, Jeff sucked in a shaky breath and counted the slices in Abby's clothes. She hated knives. And she'd had no one between her and the monster—nothing to protect her except a flannel shirt.

"We're ready," the EMT said as they lifted Abby to a gurney. Jeff ran beside them, through the silent yard, past the horses standing guard, to Toby, who was waiting next to the ambulance.

Jeff stroked his head. "I'll take care of her, buddy. You mind the stock."

They bounced and jostled down the lane, the blood bag swaying on its IV pole, the alarms pealing because her blood pressure was too low. Artificial breaths rasped through the cabin along with the EMT's rhythmic counts of chest compressions.

When his breathing labored, Jeff stepped in, glad for something to do. "Let me."

He straddled her waist and started compressions, counting out loud as he went. All the while, he stared at her face, tracing his gaze across the arch of her brow down the turn in her nose and along the bow in her lips, which were tinted blue. Her lashes were singed, and under all the soot her skin was too pale. "Don't give up, Slugger," he muttered as he pushed her sternum and felt her ribs give.

Halfway to town, they switched again. Which meant, when they arrived at the hospital, Jeff wasn't on the gurney that raced down the hall. He was alone, half-naked, cold, and covered in filth and blood, while she left him again.

His rubbery arms still shaking, he leaned against the wall and fought for breath. He'd lost count of how many times she'd disappeared on him, how many times he'd chased her, caught her only to lose her again.

"I want Abby!"

Recognizing the watery scream, Jeff pushed himself upright and sprinted into the small emergency ward, stopping only to steal a scrub shirt from a pile of clean uniforms. At the end of the aisle, he brushed the last curtain aside. Evan was curled at the head of the gurney, his back flat to the wall while he cradled his wounded arm. The blood combined with the dirt, mud and soot stuck to his orange-and-white shirt, and tears streamed in rivers until they reached the delta of his chin.

His stare was wild and bright. "Not you," he screamed, curling tighter. "Abby!"

Ignoring the nurse and fighting to keep the gurney steady, Jeff climbed onto the bed and wrestled with the terrified boy.

"Stop it, Evan."

"Mama!"

Using his body, Jeff weighted the little boy against the mattress as the doctor barked commands for sedatives.

"I *hate* you," the little boy howled, bucking underneath him.

The rest of his sentence was muffled as Jeff held his mouth closed, forcing him to inhale the medication. When he let go, Evan dissolved into sobs.

Pulling the child into his lap, Jeff let him cry until the sedative took effect. Evan's head drooped against Jeff's chest, and his sobs diminished to tears and hiccups.

Taking the supplies from the nurse, Jeff cleaned the wounds and then held Evan's thin arm in his hand while the ER doctor conducted his exam.

"Are you going to duct-tape them?" Evan murmured. "Abby said she did that."

"No, buddy. No tape." Jeff's heart banged against his ribs and his throat closed off. Abby…duct tape plastered in her bloody hair, cold and alone in the bathtub, working up the nerve to cut her femoral artery.

Abby in jailhouse orange, telling that horrible tale, stealing his car, running from him…

Abby limp in his arms, her ribs giving under his hands, her lips cold against his.

Abby… Abby… Abby…

"There we go, all done," the doctor whispered.

Evan twisted his arm, looking at the bandage. "It doesn't even hurt. I guess it will, huh? Like the last time I was here."

"Yeah." Jeff managed the word.

"You didn't even tell me not to cry." Evan looked up at him.

Jeff wiped his hand across his face, clearing the moisture into his hairline. "You can if you want to."

"I was so scared," Evan said, cuddling closer.

"Me, too."

The little boy was still for so long, Jeff thought he'd fallen asleep. He shifted to lay him on the gurney.

"It's my fault," Evan said. "I told her where we lived."

Jeff tilted Evan's chin and stared into his saucer-like eyes. "It was *not* your fault. She was a bad guy."

"Abby was really brave," Evan whispered.

She had been brave. And stupid. And stubborn. Why did she always have to do everything on her own? Why didn't she trust him?

Evan yawned and snuggled closer. "She's gonna get better, right?"

"Yes." She would, through sheer stubbornness alone. She'd fight through hell for this little boy. She already had. She'd battled for everything in her life. Alone.

Go away. We can't date. Leave me alone. Hell, she'd

thought he'd moved another woman in with him after their horrible first date.

How many times was he going to risk losing her because she didn't trust him? How was he going to handle it if he lost her?

"Are you leaving now?" Evan mumbled. "Like in *Jack Reacher*."

Jack Reacher? Seriously? She slathered the kid with sunscreen but she let him watch vigilante movies?

Before Jeff could answer, Evan's eyes closed. Jeff's heart stuttered, and he focused on the little boy's chest, refusing to blink until he saw it move in a deep, even inhale. He sat and watched Evan sleep, all while creating nightmare scenarios that left Evan in the house, a victim of a monster. But it didn't even have to be a monster. It could be the perfect family who took him away. And there wouldn't be a damn thing to do but stand aside and watch him go. To lose him, too.

Jeff put Evan on the gurney and pulled the sheet to his chin, tucking him in and making sure he was warm. The little boy didn't stir, even when Jeff ruffled his rust-colored hair. At least the sedative had made goodbye easier for one of them.

He walked into the hallway and faced a tiny, empty chapel.

Dark paneling and a slate floor were lit by low lights designed to look like candles at the prayer rail. An arched ceiling was decorated with delicate curved beams. The cross was suggested by lighting, rather than actually constructed, and angels stood in opposite corners—one hiding her head beneath her wing as she prayed, the other kneeling.

Jeff went to the rail, dropped to his knees, and bowed

his head, covering his ears with his hands. It didn't muffle his memories of her wails when she'd come into the interrogation room, of the explosion, of CPR. They mingled with Evan's screams. Someone knelt beside him and put a hand on his shoulder. "Jeffy?"

Cass. He'd forgotten about his baby sister. He lifted his head. "Are you okay?"

She turned to him, and the lights glanced and flickered over the bruises mottling her face and arms. Their mother was going to freak out. He hadn't protected his family. He'd introduced Cass to death and danger. He'd led a killer straight to her and left her to fend for herself.

"Don't look so stricken," Cass scolded. "It could've been much worse. Abby was an Amazon."

"She *died*, Cassidy." He ached in places he hadn't known existed. "And Evan… God, Evan… I swore—" His voice broke. "I swore I'd never…"

Cass squeezed his shoulder. "She's going to be fine. Come sit with us. They're all worried about you."

"I'll be there in a minute."

She left, and he glared at the angel kneeling in prayer. No way in hell was he going to that waiting room. He wasn't going to sit there and remember the first time he saw her. He wasn't going to wait for her to wake up and push him away. Or worse, have her not wake and then die a little bit every day.

Leaving the chapel, he turned his back on the waiting room, strode out the door and found his car where Gray had parked it.

When he passed the city limits sign, he ignored the ache in his heart and the itch in his brain.

Chapter Twenty-Two

Abby kept her eyes closed and wiggled her toes up Toby's body until she found his ears. His tail thumped her other leg.

"You let me sleep late," she scolded. Wait, was that scratchy voice hers? And the noise. Was Evan watching a movie?

Dr. Simon to the ICU. Paging Dr. Simon.

Keeping her eyes closed, Abby stretched out her arm and felt air instead of the other side of her large mattress, and she was at an angle. Antiseptic smells burned her nose. Hospital. She was in the hospital.

Her lungs tightened, and the beeping in her ears sped. Last thing…what was the last thing she remembered?

Explosion. Pushing Evan out the window. Wallis. The hatchet. She opened her eyes and stared at the ceiling tiles.

"Abby? Honey?"

She turned to the soft, sweet voice and froze as she met a familiar gray gaze. Oh God. Wallis wasn't dead. She'd made it up. Hoped for it so hard she'd created a reality.

Pain sliced through her as she tried to escape. Toby's head weighted her feet, keeping her prisoner. Maybe *she* was dead, too. Maybe she and her monster mother were going to be forced to spend eternity linked—

"Please don't be scared," Wallis said. No. It wasn't her. Abby struggled to catch her breath. Wallis's eyes had never been that kind. It was a Wallis clone—a defective one. "I know it's scary. I'm your aunt Susannah. Suzy. Ned just went down the hall."

She was still talking when Ned walked in the door. His smile split his face. "Abigail."

Papa. The man she'd spent five minutes with before she'd broken out of jail. He came to her side and took her hand. "I'm sorry Suzy scared you."

Rex Simon barreled through the door, only to relax when she met his gaze. "Welcome back, Abby. Let me check you over, and then you have a crowd waiting on you."

Her chest was bruised from her collarbone to her diaphragm, and her ribs were wrapped. "What happened?"

"They had to do CPR until they could get you here, and they broke a few of your ribs in the process. We've reset them. Good news is we fixed those crooked ones. You shouldn't hurt anymore." He smiled grimly. "In the long run anyway." He finished his exam. "I'm going to keep you for a few more days and make sure you don't pull your stitches loose. No arguing. Who do you want to see first?"

Jeff. "Evan."

"Cue the red tornado," Rex said as he opened the door. Evan galloped in and scaled the bed frame to get to her.

Ned stepped forward to stop him, and Abby waved him off. The little boy could break every bone she had. "Hi, sweetheart. Are you okay?"

"Yep. I've been staying with Cassie."

Not with Jeff. Abby called on years of hiding to keep her smile in place. "Really?" She stroked his bandage, remembering his bloody wound. "How's your arm?"

"I have stitches. Jeff helped me get them."

Breathe, Abby.

"Good for him. I think I have stitches, too."

"You do." Evan hugged her gently. "I'm glad you're okay, Mom. I knew you'd save us."

Tears burned her eyes, and she brushed them away as he sat up.

"Is it okay if I call you that?" he asked quietly, his stare uncertain. "You feel like my mom."

"And you feel like my little boy," she warbled. "I like it."

"Okay, good. Mr. Mathis was about to take me and Toby to the park. Can I go?"

"Of course. Remember—"

"My manners," he said before he kissed her cheek. "I love you, Mom."

"I love you, too, Ev. Would you ask Cassie to come see me?"

Evan galloped out, Toby on his heels. Ned and Suzy—her father and her aunt—each squeezed her hand before they left, too. Her heart broke all over again when Cassie came into the room, but her resemblance to Jeff was only part of it. "I am so sorry."

"Me, too," she said as she swept in for a hug. "He's a—"

"None of that." She didn't want to talk about him.

"I'll have a great story to tell my kids," Cassie teased. "Evan and I can't wait to have you home. And we can talk all you want then. Right now, Maggie's pacing the hall."

Cass left and Abby sagged against the pillow, fighting pain and exhaustion. She'd been awake for ten minutes, for pity's sake. She couldn't go to sleep now. Though she considered faking it to keep from facing Maggie.

She watched her oldest living friend walk through the door and across the room. Solemn-faced and quiet, Maggie sat on the edge of the bed. Abby fidgeted with her blanket, unsure of where to start.

"How are you doing with the whole *this is your life* thing?"

"My aunt Suzy scares me," Abby admitted.

"She's nice. You'll like her. Your dad is quiet, like you. He's been spending a lot of time with Faye, and he likes to read. He loved that awful *Edgar Sawtelle* book." Her teasing faded as her lips trembled. "Abby…"

"I couldn't let her hurt you," Abby sobbed as she clasped her friend's fingers. "I'm sorry."

Maggie squeezed back, her grip almost painful. "You have nothing to be sorry for. Now." She wiped her eyes with her free hand. "Graham needs to talk to you. Are you up for it?"

Abby nodded, and Maggie handed her a tissue as she kissed her cheek. "I'll tell him not to take too long."

"Bossy woman," Gray teased from the doorway. He stopped Maggie on the way out and held her in a loose embrace as he whispered in her ear.

The sweet picture made Abby ache in places that had nothing to do with stitches and broken ribs. She looked away until the breeze from the door cooled her sheets and a chair grated across the floor.

Gray's smile was thin. "Hey, Ab."

Abby held up her index finger. "Send me a bill."

His smile widened as he nodded.

She extended a second finger and tried to keep her emotions in check. "Thank you."

He nodded again, this time scratching his nose and clearing his throat. "Your house is gone."

"My servers are off-site. The rest of it is just stuff. What about my animals?"

"They're fine, and your darkroom is in one piece. I've started the insurance claim. And I've talked to Deb and Hank. They're good with you staying on the hill. They were planning to stay gone longer anyway."

"Uh-huh," she drawled.

"They were, I swear. And I negotiated a reasonable rent. Which you can more than afford because Tracy Hoover's check came yesterday. Your notoriety has put you in high demand. She's eager to talk to you about a permanent collection."

"Notoriety?" she squeaked.

"You single-handedly brought down a prolific serial killer who was related to you. The networks are pestering the hell out of me."

"How long have I been out?"

"Two days," he said, winking. "I'm very efficient. Anyway, I've told the reporters no comment. Celia and I have had a long talk about Evan, and she's interceded with CPS. He can stay with you on the condition that both of you get counseling. Agreed?"

"Of course." She'd been cooped up in her own head for so long, it might be exhilarating to talk to someone else. Since Jeff—"I'm glad I gave you my power of attorney."

"Next time warn a guy," he scolded before he drew a deep breath. "Abby—"

She looked out the window, eager to delay the inevitable. The colors outside were so bright. Blue sky, green grass, all the flowers bobbing lazily along. It seemed perfectly right and terribly wrong at the same time. "Can you contact the Dempseys and see if they'll talk to me? And I need to arrange a funeral for Buck."

"I'll take care of it." The chair squeaked as he shifted. "Abby—"

"He's gone, isn't he?" She looked back at him. "It's what everyone *isn't* saying."

He nodded once, quick and sharp.

"It's understandable." She patted his hand. "I'm fine." When her statement sounded more like a whimper, she cleared her throat and blinked to banish the tears. "Really."

Jeff walked through the door of his apartment and dropped his bag in the entryway. He was home. After two days of driving himself to exhaustion, after months of being surrounded by other people's stuff, he'd expected it to feel better.

It would. It was like driving once you were used to public transportation—everything felt unfamiliar until instinct kicked in. He'd get back into his routine, and everything would click into place. He'd get back to his life.

He crossed the living room and opened the drapes. The sun glinted off the windows across the street. Beyond the skyscrapers, his little sliver of Lake Michigan glittered. The change in color disoriented him. He was used to trees, to green.

That wasn't your life.

Laundry. He always did laundry after a trip. He dumped the bag into the washing machine and stared at the clothes he'd bought because everything he'd been wearing when he'd left had smelled like smoke, dirt, blood and Abby's gardenia perfume. He'd left those clothes somewhere in Montana, where he'd stopped because he had to sleep. And then he'd bought pills because he couldn't sleep alone.

Not your life.

He turned back to the apartment. Now what. Clean? The place smelled like bleach, Pine-Sol and furniture polish. There was nothing for him to do except stand here and miss the smell of garden soil, horse and the lime and sugar body wash Abby had kept—

He should call his mother. He always called her when he got home.

"Call Mom."

Calling home, his phone chirped, happy to do him the favor.

No. No. No. He punched the stop button with every denial, cursing the flight of fancy that had prodded him to program *her* number with *that* name. He'd done it in the middle of the flight to Kentucky, when he'd stared out into the darkness and plotted their future.

Before she'd run away from him and died.

He dialed his mother the old-fashioned way.

"Hello?"

He stretched his face into a grimace. "Hi, Mama. I'm—" he forced the word up his throat "—home."

"Oh, Jeff."

Those two simple words hollowed him out, undermining everything he was trying to rebuild. He should have known Cass would call her. His breath stopped as he slammed his eyes closed. "I have to go."

"Love—"

He'd apologize later for hanging up on her. Right

now, he needed to unpack his gear…except that it was in Idaho. He'd run away and left classified material in a rental house.

Sucking up his courage, he dialed Cass.

"Hi." His baby sister made that one word sound like a condemnation. It's one of the things he loved about her—she never hid how she felt.

"I need you to box my stuff and—"

"Gray called the Boise field office, and an agent picked everything up to ship back to you. It should be waiting in your office."

Why did it feel like he was breaking up with his sister? "Okay, thanks. How's Evan today?"

"Right now he's playing catch in the park with Nate Mathis."

Jeff's fingers twitched, aching to feel the leather glove and the seams in the ball. "Good. Would you tell him I'll call tonight?"

"Sure."

He should go, but he couldn't bring himself to hang up the phone. And he couldn't bring himself to ask what he wanted to know more than anything.

"She's awake," Cass volunteered.

Jeff dropped into a chair that was stiff from disuse, closed his eyes, and raised his face to the ceiling. "How is she?"

"Awake," Cass repeated. "Why would you care any—"

"Cassidy Renee," he barked, his hands shaking. He was like a junkie desperate for a fix. "Please. Has she—"

God, he was a vain SOB. Maybe Cass wouldn't fill in the right blank.

"You are a self-centered bastard, you know that? You

ran away, and all you want to know is if she's crying her eyes out, begging to see you."

"Yeah," he grunted as he sagged in his chair and prayed for it. He'd go back on the next flight. He'd spend the rest of his life chasing her around and milking cows. If she wanted him there.

"She says she's fine. Evan says he's fine. *You're* fine. I'm fine. Everybody's fucking fine." She hung up on him. It's how every phone call had gone for the past two days—talk to Evan, fight with Cass.

As he sat in his cold, stiff chair, in his sterile apartment, the walls closed around him and the clouds cast dark shadows across the floor. No dogs clicking across the floor, no cowbells or contented chickens, no wind through the grass. No Evan asking a string of endless questions. No Abby humming along with her playlist.

Jeff pushed himself upright, tossed his head and welded his spine straight. He could call his sister back and apologize, but he'd done that the first night and she'd yelled at him for an hour. He really couldn't go through that again. He could call the hospital…

He marched out the door and took the stairs, all twenty-six flights, rather than wait on the elevator. On the street, the crowds and noise of Chicago surrounded him, and he joined the throng for the two-block walk to Bailey's.

The bar was packed. Wall-to-wall people yelled to be heard over the deafening sound system and tripped over each other in the semi-darkness. Jeff moved away from the door and stood on the edge of the crowd, looking for a path to the bar.

His favorite bartender saw him and waved wildly, beckoning him forward, but he couldn't move. The crowd, the noise, the darkness—everything pressed on him, making him dread the path strewn with faceless revelers who stood too close and laughed too loud.

He waved at the woman behind the bar, turned around and left it behind in favor of relative fresh air and comparative quiet. The farther he walked, the less he could feel the music pounding through his feet, the more peaceful—and the more lost—he felt.

After two blocks, he turned onto a quiet street. Here the buildings were older and families left restaurants, waving goodbye to the proprietors. Jeff walked down a set of concrete steps and through an ornate wooden door.

The Japanese restaurant had been a lucky find one night after a hard day at work. And Jeff had kept it a secret from everyone. It was quiet, and spare, and everything was art.

Shiro Matsume, the owner, bowed low and then stood upright, his smile twinkling in his weathered face. "My friend, it's nice to see you again."

"Thank you." Jeff bowed in return. "May I sit?"

Shiro followed him to a table. "Would you like sake?"

"Tea?" Jeff suggested.

Shiro nodded. "You look hungry. I'll bring soba noodles."

He returned minutes later with two bowls of soup, two cups and a pot of tea. He took the opposite seat and picked up his chopsticks. "Where have you been?"

"Idaho," Jeff said as he poured their tea.

"You visit Idaho a lot. Do you have family there?"

Yes. "No, not really."

Shiro arched an eyebrow.

"I have friends there who are like family," Jeff admitted, suddenly wishing he'd agreed to sake. "But it doesn't matter. I don't think I'll be going back."

Shiro looked up from his bowl as he spun a noodle around his chopstick.

"There's a little boy, but he's not related. Not really." It felt wrong to even say that. He fell into silence.

"Little boys generally have mothers," Shiro hinted.

"He does—" Jeff stopped the contradiction. "He does. They live—lived—next door."

"And you miss her?"

Miss her. People *missed* buses, but they just waited for the next one. There was always another bus. There wasn't another Abby. Her absence left a hole where all his internal organs were supposed to be. He nodded. "But she doesn't trust me."

"And running away helps build this trust?"

"I didn't run away," Jeff objected, ignoring his headfirst rush to the state border. "She kept telling me to go away—running away from *me*. So I just— Look. She's the one who confronted a murderer rather than asking me to help her."

"And she was hurt?"

Every time he closed his eyes he saw her blue and still on a gurney racing toward the operating room. "Yes. And it wasn't the first time."

A family came into the restaurant, and Shiro excused himself to wait on his new customers. Jeff finished his meal alone, and went to the register to pay.

Shiro handed him his change and a small bowl, blue as the night sky with gold seamed through it in irregular patterns.

"It's called *kintsugi*," he said as he traced a golden line. "Google it."

Chapter Twenty-Three

"And that brings us to today."

Having finished her tale, Abby sat back in the Adirondack chair on the porch, wincing as her bruises and scars came into contact with the wood. Her friends sat across from her, and past them she could see into the valley where Cass and Evan were doing all the chores. The foundation pilings were the only reminders of the house that had been her home.

For the past month, she'd spent hours talking. To Tom Beckett from the VA, whom she'd selected as her therapist; to Celia about Evan's progress; and to Reverend Ferguson about forgiveness. No matter how many times she'd talked about her past, this last confession, to her friends and their husbands, was the one she'd been dreading. She'd be strong enough to live without them, but she didn't want to. She was already living without too much.

"You're expecting us to just get up and walk away, aren't you?" Charlene asked. "I can tell."

It wouldn't have surprised her. She'd spent her life planning for it. "I lied to you." She looked at the semicircle of weepy wives and shell-shocked husbands. "I lied to all of you, and I put you in danger because of it. I can't expect you—"

"How could you think we wouldn't love you?" Tiffany scolded.

"I had a body in my backyard." Abby looked at each one of them—sitting still, talking like it was a normal Sunday afternoon—sure they were losing their minds. "I lived my life in casinos and racetracks, dodging the police. My mother was a murderer."

"And you lived in fear, alone down there, putting yourself through hell to keep us safe," Faith said. "You damn near died stopping her. So I think you deserve a little love and forgiveness."

She stared at Nate, waiting for him to be the voice of reason. She should have known better. His grin widened. "I'm still getting used to hearing you talk."

Everyone was getting used to it, even her. Wallis's death, telling the stories, and Buck's funeral had all freed her. She still locked the doors, but she no longer locked up her words. She didn't have to keep Wallis's secrets anymore.

Because Wallis was gone. Dead and buried in Kentucky, her bones charred and a crack in her skull the width of an axe blade. Killed by her only child, who'd spent the last nineteen years wishing she was dead. Out of all the wishes to come true…

Abby struggled to her feet, anxious to walk away from the memories that haunted her whenever she was still.

"Do you need help?" Maggie asked, already halfway out of her chair.

"No, just—"

It was no use. Gray was holding the door so Maggie

could follow her into the house. The simple act, the reminder of Jeff, broke Abby's heart just a little bit more. And that pain made her angry.

"You don't have to help me," she said once she and Maggie were alone.

"You're welcome," Maggie quipped. "What's going on?"

"I just need a pain pill. I can do that myself."

"Beyond that."

Abby hobbled deeper into the house, out of the crowd's earshot. "I killed someone, and you guys want to act like it's a party."

"You saved a whole bunch of people, and you got justice for several others," Maggie said. "We thought you were going to die. So, yeah. We're a little glad you didn't."

She hadn't died, but she wasn't living either. Everything was foggy and cold while she was haunted by the dead and the living. She slept in Jeff's bed, she lived in his house, she sat in his chairs.

"Have you talked to him?"

She didn't need to ask which *him*. No one mentioned him by name, but everyone asked in some way or the other. "He Skypes with Evan every night."

"But you don't—"

She never talked to him, but God how she wanted to. It was torture to hear his voice and not see his smile. But he never asked for her, and she was afraid to come into view—worried she'd see pity, or worse, in his eyes. "He chases monsters for a living. He doesn't want to be dragged into my freak show in his spare time. He left. I expected him to do it."

"Ask him to come back."

"People leave, Maggie. You know that. They take

your heart, and your faith, and your trust, and they leave. You get used to being happy and safe, and then you aren't anymore, and you have to start over and be—" Abby shoved the words back down her throat. It was traitorous to even think these things, much less say them out loud.

"Alone in a closet?" Maggie pressed. "Stuck by yourself? Afraid?"

"Yes," Abby snarled. "They all promised to stay. They told me they loved me, and they left me alone with her. They weren't strong enough to stand up to her. They made me do it, and *he* sees that ugliness every time he looks at me. And I won't…" she sobbed. "I can't…"

Maggie cradled her against her shoulder. "You need to be brave, Ab. He's worth the risk. *You're* worth it."

"Are you going to spend the night here again?"

Jeff looked up from the file he was reviewing to see Trish Phillips, his assistant director, lounging in the doorway. Past her the lab was empty, and past those lights the hallway was dark. "I haven't spent the night here in years. Why are you still here?"

"Because I didn't know if you'd need me while you ran tests to confirm results that have already been confirmed twice."

"I'm not doing that," Jeff lied, hoping she didn't hear the centrifuge whirring in the far corner of the lab.

"Uh-huh."

Damn. The woman had ears like a bat.

Trish sat in the chair opposite him and craned her neck for a view of his laptop. "Are you watching that video again?"

He minimized the email, stopping Evan's last baseball game mid-inning. It didn't matter. After a week of rerunning it, he knew every RBI, every whooping cheer. "Go home. Harry will kick my ass if you're late for dinner."

Instead of leaving, she settled in. "Not until you admit that you don't want to go home."

"I'm busy reviewing reports." He swept his hand at the stack on his desk. "What did you do while I was gone?"

"You can rubber-stamp those and you know it," Trish scolded. "You miss her, Jeff. You watch those videos for Evan the first time and for Abby the other fifty." When he didn't rise to the bait, she sighed. "Why don't you come for dinner with me and Harry?"

"Thanks, but no. I'll go home as soon as these tests are finished. I promise." It was a lie. He knew it and so did she. Truthfully, he couldn't stand to see Trish and Harry together, or Bob and Amanda. He'd quit calling his sisters because the domestic din in the background made him yearn for something he couldn't have.

He got part of it with Evan and Cass on Skype calls, but it wasn't enough. No matter when he called, no matter how often, no matter how badly Evan wobbled his tablet, Abby was a phantom.

The videos were worse. He knew she shot them. She wouldn't have left that to someone else, and Evan lit up only like he did around her. It was like watching them be a family without him.

But she never spoke. He'd caught himself turning up the volume on his laptop just to hear her breathe. It was a sickness.

He walked Trish to the elevator and then returned to his silent, empty lab. He'd always enjoyed being alone here at night, and the pleasure had doubled now that his team walked on eggshells for fear he'd collapse into a brokenhearted mess.

His cell phone rang, and he checked the number. An Idaho area code glared back at him in clear, well-lit numbers. With shaking fingers, he connected the call.

"Hello?"

"Jeff?" The booming, deep voice dashed his hopes. "Eric Freeman. Are you still working?"

"Yep. How's it going, Eric?"

"I just got out of another meeting where my techs did nothing but argue about their lab. I'm going to take your advice and start looking for a new director."

"Best thing," Jeff said as he juggled evidence bags and check-in sheets. It was still early. He could clear one more report off his list. "If your current guy can't manage the team now, it won't get better with the new facility."

"Would you like the job?"

Jeff dropped the bag he was holding. "I didn't recommend you fire him so you'd hire *me*."

"You're the perfect fit for this, and you already like Idaho. Do I have any shot of getting you away from the Feds?"

Great. The only person who wanted him back in Idaho was a six-foot-six, balding highway patrolman.

Jeff looked around the dark, empty lab. It was church-quiet and full of all his favorite toys. Full of people he enjoyed working with.

He ought to just say no and get it over with. It was an easy word. *No.* And with it, every door he'd left propped open would slam closed. Maybe he should let them do that.

"Let me think about it."

Chapter Twenty-Four

The video chat icon flashed, and Jeff maximized the window. He expected Evan's wide grin and sunburned nose, instead Abby was fidgeting in the chair. Her brief smile lifted only one corner of her mouth. "Hi."

She was too thin, too pale. No makeup, thick braid, sweatshirt. She was the most beautiful woman he'd ever seen. "Hi."

Scents flooded over him—gardenias, fresh hay, peppermint. Tastes followed—sour apple, sweet tea, butter, caramel, sriracha. His tongue twitched in vain, and his fingers danced in a frustrated search for her skin. "Is everything all right?"

"Umm, no." She gulped. "Yes." She sighed and shook her head while she rubbed her neck. "Maybe."

"What's he done?"

"Not him," she sighed. "Me. His birthday is in a few weeks. Remember?"

"He's told me every time we talk. He even sent me a Google reminder for my calendar."

She missed the humor. "He asked me if he could have something special, and I told him yes without hearing what it was." She glanced at the screen. "I should have known better, but it's been a rough year and I wanted him to have a special day."

"What's he want?"

If she rubbed her neck any harder, she'd rip open her scar. "He wants to come to Chicago and see you."

The back of his throat itched. "Really?"

"He's going to ask you, and I didn't want it to be a surprise. I've tried to explain that you might be busy. So you can always tell him—"

"Is he there?" Evan asked as he ran around the corner of the table. The video feed shook. Abby stood, her nervous smile flitted across her lips, and she disappeared.

"Hi!" Evan's greeting was drowned out by crashes and thumps. The dogs snarled and snapped offscreen.

"No need to rush, Ev. Be careful." *Go away. Let me talk to Abby.*

"I wanted to show you this." His wide smile was obscured by a piece of paper. A bright red A- was written within a circle at the top of the page. "Look at my math test. Isn't that great? I did what you told me, I took my time and counted on my fingers if I had to."

"I'm proud of you, buddy. How's everything else?"

"We're starting soccer. Mr. Harper's our coach because he used to play a lot in school. Did you know that?"

Jeff nodded. "I—"

"And Mr. Anderson is going to teach us basketball. He told us yesterday at baseball practice. It's not going to be hard like on TV. The basket is lower to the ground. And it's not even cheating to play that way."

"Evan, don't interrupt," Abby chided. "Manners, remember?"

Jeff soaked in every syllable as he imagined being

there, helping Evan with homework, going to soccer games, fishing on Sunday afternoon.

The little boy rolled his eyes. "Yeah."

"Yes, ma'am," Jeff scolded. "And don't roll your eyes."

"Yes, sir. I'm sorry, Mom. That was rude."

Mom. Every time Jeff heard the word, his chest hurt. They'd done something good. If nothing else, Evan had people who loved him.

"Thank you." Her smile was audible, and Jeff's ache doubled. Abby had someone who loved her. Someone she *let* love her. She wasn't alone.

He was the only one who was exiled.

"Have you been fishing?" Evan asked.

Jeff shook his head. "Not since I've been back."

"Don't you live by a great big lake? Doesn't it have fish in it?"

Jeff held his breath. She'd lose her shit over this. "I don't have anyone to fish with. Why don't you come visit?"

"Really? Could I? It's my birthday, remember? Could I come then? I don't have school yet."

"Perfect. Abby and I will work it out. I'll see you in a few weeks."

"Wait 'til I tell Kyle. He didn't think I'd get to do it. His dad moved away, too, but he never wants Kyle to come see him."

Dad.

Jeff cleared his throat. "Yeah, well. You're coming to see me, and we're going to have a great time for your birthday. I hear Abby tapping her foot, so go on to bed before she gets mad at me."

"G'night," Evan said as he waved with both hands. "I'll talk to you later. Love you."

Now he couldn't breathe. "Love you, too, squirt."

Evan slid from the chair, and Jeff stared at the vacant spot as he strained to hear the murmurs in the background. Steps thudded up the stairs, then Abby appeared on camera. If possible, she looked more nervous than before.

He couldn't do a damn thing about it from here. He never should have left her. He should have fought for her, even if it would've meant fighting her.

"You didn't have to—"

"I want to. Please?"

Her lips were thin and tight, but she nodded. "I'll send you the details."

"Abby!"

Jeff sat up in bed, gasping for breath and drenched in sweat. He kicked the sheets, then resorted to tearing them away when they became more tangled. When he could stand, he walked to the kitchen on shaking legs and got a glass of water. It took five minutes for his hands to quit shaking as he talked himself out of the nightmare.

She was well and whole and safe. He'd just talked to her. The gravestone wasn't hers, not anymore. They hadn't reused it to bury her adult body in Kentucky where he couldn't reach her. She hadn't died alone in a cold rain.

But she had died, and every night those memories haunted him. Every night it was a different type of loss, but it didn't make it less real. She'd left him alone, and she'd done it on purpose.

He was tired of being alone. He was tired of being afraid.

He sat on the edge of the bed and dialed the one person he knew who could help him.

"Hello?"

"Ruthie?"

"Jeff? Is something wrong? Is Mama okay?"

He checked the time. "Damn. I'm sorry, I didn't realize the time."

She cleared her throat and juggled the phone. He could mark her path through the house by listening to the closing doors and her shuffling steps. "It's not like I've never woke you. What's up?"

"How do you do it?" he asked as he fell across the bed and stared at the ceiling.

"I do everything well," she snorted. "What are we talking about?"

"Clayton. Jason."

"Oh *that*. Is this about Dad?"

"He left us alone." He would have never admitted that if he was fully rested and in the light of day, but here—tired in the dark—it was easy. "He died because he rushed in without backup to be a hero."

"He did."

They'd hashed this out for years, always on opposite sides. This time it was his turn to be angry and hurt. "So how do you not worry every day?"

"I had to accept that anything could happen," she yawned. "Clay could get hit by a bus or get sick. It's out of my control."

"But he's not pushing firemen out of the way so he can run into burning buildings. He wouldn't leave you."

"Not on purpose, no. But he would save me. Since he's not trained to do it, he'd probably get hurt. But… he loves me, Jeff. How am I going to stop him?" The squeaky rocker she'd inherited from their grandmother screeched in the background. "Could *she* have stopped you?"

"No. But I'm trained—"

"So was Dad," Ruthie stated.

"You're supposed to tell me I'm right, you know?"

"Then you should've called Jan."

He lay on his bed and listened to her rocker squeak. "I ran away."

"Then run back, moron. Can I go back to sleep now?"

Chapter Twenty-Five

"He said he'd meet us by the taxi stand." Evan craned his neck around the passengers milling in front of them. "Do you see it?"

Abby shrugged her bag onto her shoulder as Evan dragged her through baggage claim at O'Hare. Sweat slicked her skin—the cold sweat that preceded nausea—and dread slowed her steps. The feelings had been her constant companion all day, through flights, layovers, turbulence and crowds. But now it was so much worse. Because Jeff had said he'd meet *Evan* at the taxi stand. He didn't know there was an *us* coming.

She spotted the sign just as Evan slipped from her grasp.

"Jeff!"

Rather than intruding, Abby lifted her camera, capturing the reunion and drinking in the sight of the man in her frame. Jeff's smile was as broad as Evan's. In a Cubs cap, a rain slicker, jeans and sneakers, he looked like a college jock instead of a professor. Through the lens, she watched the moment he spotted her, saw confusion give way to shock. Wide-eyed and slack-jawed, he darted his tongue across his bottom lip and braced his hands on his knees. And she resisted the urge to run to him and knock him to the floor, to cling to him and beg until he forgave her. Because he would, and she'd vowed every five minutes all morning that she wasn't going to do that to him. Not unless he asked her to.

He walked to her and stopped just out of reach. "Hi."

"Hi." She could do this. She'd practiced it. "I won't. Intrude. I'll get a. Hotel. And meet you on. Sunday." She swallowed the words she wanted to say. *I'm sorry. I love you. Please come home.*

"Okay," he said as he slid his fingers between the luggage strap and her shirt. "At least take the taxi with us."

Sparks cascaded under her skin, opening wounds she'd thought were scabbed over. They'd itched every day while she lived without him in the house on the hill, eavesdropped on Skype conversations, and worked in his office. And she finally admitted that this trip was a way to scratch them, to see if they still bled. After all, sometimes you scratched and the old tissue just flaked off.

She should have known better. Under Jeff's wary gaze, she felt like she was hemorrhaging internally.

"How was your flight?" he asked as they walked to the door.

Evan answered for her. "It was cool. A lot of the time we couldn't see the ground, and it looked like snow. But then it started to storm, and the plane jumped and bounced. Mom was scared, but I took care of her."

"Good man." Jeff held the door for her, and she risked a deep breath just for the familiar smell. She shouldn't have, because then she wanted to burrow into his jacket and never let go. Somehow she kept walking to the curb, where she climbed into the waiting cab and put Evan next to her, using him as a shield. He stayed there for all of two minutes before he scrambled over Jeff and climbed to the window, craning his neck. "Gosh, look at all these cars. Have you ever seen so many people? We flew over the lake. There have to be some great big fish in there. Did you rent a boat? Do you know what's in all these buildings?"

"Seat belt, Ev."

"Mind your mom." Jeff scooted closer to her and put his arm across the back of the seat. His warmth threatened to erode all of her convictions, especially when his breath tickled her ear. "I wish I'd known you were coming. I would've planned differently."

She'd been afraid to tell him, afraid he'd say no. "I won't hover. Gray gave me a list of places to see."

His hand closed around her shoulder. "Are you going to look at me at all?"

It seemed like she'd done nothing but stare at him. She tilted her head and looked into his mossy green eyes. "There was a. Two-hour. Layover. In Den- Denver." Inhaling deeply, she plowed forward on the exhale. "Can you imagine *Evan* alone for two hours?"

His smile was brighter than she'd remembered. How was that possible? "The terminal would never be the same. We're stopping by the lab first. Would you like to see it?"

She should just stay in the cab and keep going to a hotel. Gray had given her the name of the one closest to Jeff's building. This was the perfect place for their weekends to diverge, for her to make good on her promise not to hover. "Yes. Thank you."

"Hey, Jeff!" Evan tugged on his sleeve. "What are they building over there?"

He looked out the window. “I don’t know. What do you think it is?”

“A heliport. We saw one of those on a movie last week. Remember, Mom? Don’t you think it looks like a heliport?”

She leaned across Jeff to look out the window at the sea of concrete, glass and asphalt, swimming with people and vehicles. The building concerning Evan zipped by in a blur. “Maybe.”

“And that one there.” Evan pointed at something else. “That looks like the building from *Mission Impossible*. Do you think it is?” He kept asking questions until Abby became more interested in sightseeing than staying on her side of the car. Then Jeff’s hand slipped to her hip, and she forgot about Chicago entirely. He was strong and whole, and his heartbeat drowned out Evan’s monologue. She let herself listen to the strong, rhythmic thud, remembering all the times she’d curled against him while he slept and vowed to do whatever it took to keep him safe. And she had. Even if she was empty for the rest of her life, he’d be free.

“Abby?”

The question rumbled against her ear, and she realized she’d gotten too close, stayed too long. He was tense against her, as though he was afraid of her and unsure of how to untangle himself. Embarrassment heated her skin even as tears burned her eyes.

“Sorry,” she said as she straightened and moved back to her side of the car.

He looked like she’d hit him. “Abby—”

“We’re here, sir,” the cabbie said.

Letting Evan monopolize Jeff’s attention, she stayed quiet and apart from him through the metal detector and into the elevator. When the doors opened to a room full of equipment, long tables, and white-coated staff, Jeff stopped them next to a row of lockers. He stowed their bags and retrieved two lab coats. He gave the smallest one to Evan. "This is for you to wear so we know you work here. And it keeps stuff on your clothes from contaminating evidence."

He helped her into a coat and straightened the lapels. When he stayed close and kept his hands on her shoulders, she looked up into his uncertain gaze.

"Abby—"

"What's this do?" Evan called from the middle of the room, interrupting him.

Jeff left her to continue the tour, and Abby tagged along as he talked about every machine and introduced each technician. She gave up on the science and watched Jeff work. For the first time today, he relaxed. He was *her* Jeff—laughing, teasing, listening to Evan's questions and answering them without talking down to the little boy. She knew firsthand how good he was at what he did, what it meant to him, and now she got to see what he meant to his staff. This was where he belonged, and he'd stayed gone far too long. Because of her. Letting him go had been best.

"Is this the famous Evan?" a happy voice sang. It belonged to an equally happy, pretty woman in a lab coat and glasses who put her hand on Jeff's shoulder a second before she put her arm around him. "And you must be Abby." She extended her hand. "I'm Trish Phillips, Jeff's assistant director. It's a pleasure to meet you."

Jeff had told her about Trish, the woman he trusted more than anyone on his team. He'd said she was a smart, funny, capable partner. He hadn't mentioned that she was pretty.

Trish stooped to Evan's level. "I've worked up an experiment just for you. Wanna come play?"

Evan looked up at her. "You're coming, too, aren't you, Mom?"

She wanted to run the other direction, away from this perfect woman Jeff spent so much time with, but Evan suddenly looked frightened. She knew how he felt. "You go play. I'll be right here where you can see me."

For the rest of the afternoon, she sat on a stool and watched Jeff and Trish tease and laugh with each other. He didn't look at her like she was going to fall apart or like he wanted to run away. They shared a passion.

Abby made herself smile at the young woman who approached, made herself join a conversation rather than run the other way. This was the downside of her ambush—coming here and seeing him, answering the *what if* questions that kept her up late and woke her early. In those dawn hours, she'd promised that she'd be brave enough to tell him how she felt and see what happened. But now she didn't need to do that. This is what had happened. She'd found her bravery too late. He'd moved on like she'd hoped he would, like she dreaded he had.

So she smiled at another technician, shook another hand, and ignored the man in the corner, living happily-ever-after without her.

He wanted to kiss her so badly his tongue hurt, and he could still feel her head against his chest, her hip under his hand, smell her hair. But now she was firmly on her side of the car, staring out her window so all he could see was her crooked ponytail. Was she really just here to escort Evan?

"Did you not like the lab?" he whispered. "Did someone say something?"

She shook her head. "It's easy to see why you like it there, and Evan had fun. It was nice of Trish to include him."

Jeff couldn't even remember what experiment Trish had done with Evan. All he'd been able to think about was Abby across the room, talking to his team. He'd wanted to pull her away from everyone, lock his office door, and kiss her until she let him come home.

When they coasted to a stop, Evan scrambled from the taxi. He tilted his head back and turned in a circle until he lost his balance, a goofy grin on his face. Jeff remembered feeling that way when he'd first moved here. Now he rarely looked up.

"Ev. Get your bag," Jeff said as he helped Abby to the sidewalk. He took Abby's luggage and slung it over his shoulder. He'd keep it with him if he had to sleep curled around it. She wouldn't go anywhere without her camera.

Once inside, he toured them through the lobby before walking for the elevator. The mirrored walls let him glimpse his patchwork family. Abby surreptitiously shared Evan's curiosity about the surroundings. That was good, wasn't it?

He lifted Evan to the panel. "Push the one that has twenty-six on it."

They emerged onto his floor, and Evan ran into the hallway, only to turn back in confusion. "Where's your sofa?"

Laughter bubbled free. "In my apartment, dude. This way."

He opened the door, and stood aside. Evan walked in and looked around. "I thought it would be bigger."

"Evan!" Abby scolded.

"I know it's not as big as your house, but I don't spend a lot of time here. I'm at work most of the time. You've got your own room though. Wanna see it?"

Keeping a tight grip on Abby's bag, Jeff gave Evan a tour—including battling the wind and rain on the patio so they could see the traffic crawling like ants on the street below. They returned to the living room, where Abby was looking at his bookshelf.

God, he loved seeing her here. The walls didn't seem so close, or the shadows so dark.

"You have a PlayStation!" Evan said. "Can we play?"

"After you unpack."

When Evan ran off, Abby turned to him and reached for her stuff. Jeff shifted away from her. "Stay. You can have the bedroom. I'll take the sofa. It folds out." She dropped her hand, but she shook her head. The lonely, lost look in her eyes reminded him of that first spring morning when she'd surprised him in his yard. He looked like that every morning now when he stared into the mirror.

If he had to fight dirty, he would. "Do you really want to be alone in a strange city?"

A silent war raged across her face, down through her shoulders to her fingers. "I'll take the sofa."

He wanted to smell her perfume on his sheets, but he'd compromise. He surrendered her bag as Evan came back into the room. "Great."

Sprawled on the floor, he and Evan started a game of video baseball. Jeff missed too many important plays by looking over his shoulder to watch Abby on his sofa, Abby reading a book, Abby in the kitchen.

"You're not even swinging," Evan scolded. "I'm gonna win because you keep staring at Mom."

Heat burned his ears as he focused on the television. "Demon child."

"Devil Dad." Evan giggled.

Jeff blinked, staring at the red hair muted to bronze by the cloudy day.

They began another game. Trash-talking devolved into distractions, nudging became tickling—which turned into wrestling until bacon smells made their stomachs growl.

"All right, you hooligans. Come to dinner."

Evan leapt to his feet. "Great. Winning makes me hungry."

"Careful there, son. I won't bait your hook on Saturday."

Son. Warmth spread under his skin. It doubled when he joined Abby in the kitchen. While she danced between stove and sink, he pulled dishes from the cabinets and handed them to Evan. It was the routine they'd followed so many nights during the summer. "You didn't have to cook. We could've ordered in." He picked up the salad bowl and carried it to the table. "But I'm glad you've made yourself at home."

Evan wriggled in his chair as he chewed on his BLT. "So what are we gonna do this weekend?"

"Tomorrow we're going to the Field Museum to see their dinosaurs. And we're going to a Cubs game on Friday, and fishing on Saturday. Other than that we can do whatever you want. Or whatever Abby wants."

If he'd known she was coming he would have planned

something for her, *with* her. Just the two of them. He had a list as long as his arm of places he wanted to show her.

"Okay. Did Mom tell you we had to go see the judge?"

"No." Jeff drawled out the word as he looked at her. She stayed focused on her salad.

"It wasn't anything bad," Evan explained. "Andy was there, too."

"Your dad?"

"He's not my dad no more. The judge told him he couldn't be since he tried to kill me."

"Are you all right with that?"

"Uh-huh. We had our first basketball practice last week…"

Evan told stories about Fiddler through the rest of dinner and then while they did dishes, and then until Jeff tucked him in. Listening helped distract Jeff from the water singing through the pipes as Abby showered.

When he walked out of the bedroom, she was sitting in the middle of the fold-out bed in the dark, or what passed for dark in Chicago. She was staring at the photograph of their tree.

"That looks good here," she murmured. "It glows in the dark."

"Which is why I hung it there." Jeff walked to the window and stared at his shadow stretching across the mattress, as if even it was reaching for her. "I'm glad to have it. I hear your work is outside my price range now."

She ducked her head. "Being notorious has a few advantages. Tom Beckett wants me to come talk to his class."

"Really?" What would she do if she knew Tom had

emailed him to see if he wanted to join the teaching staff in Hastings? "Are you going to?"

She shook her head. "Not yet. But my thesis advisor asked me to teach a photography class. I think I'd like to do that."

Her words were coming easier now, but she had the blanket gripped in her fist. "Where's Toby?"

"He's home. He gets to be a dog now most of the time." She smiled a real, honest smile that broke his heart. "He's very confused."

He wasn't the only one. "Will you be okay out here?" *Please say no.*

She nodded. "It's comfortable, thank you."

Comfortable, hell. There would be a bar across the middle of her back and the mattress wasn't much thicker than a ham sandwich. "Sure." He fell silent, content to watch her in his space, until he realized that her smile had vanished while she was looking at the photographs of his family. "What?"

"They look very nice—normal." She sighed. "Ned wants us to come to Kentucky for Christmas and meet everyone, but I'm not sure. I'm not used to having a family."

"You have Evan. He calls you Mom. He still calls me Jeff."

"He'll try *Dad* out for a bit to see if you correct him. Then he'll ask."

Silence grew between them, and it pressed against Jeff, making him want to say and do everything that would scare her off on her first night here. He pushed himself away from the window. "Good night."

"Jeff?"

He was halfway across the room when he looked

over his shoulder, hoping she'd say what he wanted to hear.

"I'm going to adopt Evan. You and Trish can't take him. I'll fight you with everything I have."

Chapter Twenty-Six

She'd expected him to be angry, but she hadn't planned on his thunderous expression as he marched back to the bed and yanked her from under the blankets. They were to his bedroom before she found her voice.

"What do you think you're doing?"

"We're about to have a fight, and I don't want Evan to hear it." He pulled her into the room and shut the door before he released her. *"Trish?"*

"Well, it's sort of obvious you two are involved." She moved to the far corner of the room, putting as much distance between them as possible.

"That would be news to her husband." He ran his hand through his hair and stared at the ceiling. "God, Abby. What's it going to take for you to trust me?"

She put her hand over her mouth, too late to remove her foot from it, but soon enough to prevent worse damage. Dammit. He'd always made it too easy for her to say what she thought.

When he looked at her, he'd aged decades. "You thought I'd just move on?"

"You left." He'd come back to his life. He was *supposed* to move on.

"Because you told me to," he snapped. "Over and

over again. A guy can only hear that so many times before he pays attention."

"Since when do you pay attention to anything I say?"

"When you'd rather die than stick around."

"You were there?" She'd never asked about what had happened after the explosion. She'd been afraid of the answers.

"Who do you think broke your *fucking* ribs?"

He sagged against the wall, drawn and haggard, struggling for breath as though he was deflating in front of her.

All those plans to keep him safe, to take the punishment so he didn't have to, because she couldn't bear to see him hurt. It had never occurred to her that he'd share it anyway. What had she done?

She raced around the bed to reach him, cradling his jaw, heartbroken yet relieved to finally touch him. "I'm so sorry."

He dropped his head into her palm, begging for attention much like Toby did, and she gave it. He shuddered under her hands as she ran her fingers through his soft hair.

"I broke you," he whispered. "I *broke* you."

Abby put his hand on her chest, pressing it flat so he could feel her heartbeat. "I'm fine, baby."

He opened his eyes, and his haunted stare stole her breath. "Why didn't you let me help you?"

"Because you would have run in there to save me," she said, keeping one hand over his. "And she would have hurt you." She traced her thumb across his cheek, relishing the stubble contrasting with his soft skin. "I couldn't let her do that."

He yanked her to him, plastering them together as he

sealed his lips over hers. It wasn't a gentle kiss. Every hot, hungry stroke reached places she'd hidden since she'd collapsed in her burning home. When she tried to pull away, he bracketed her face and burrowed his fingers in her hair, forcing her to stay where she wanted to be anyway.

But now more than ever she was sure he'd never see beyond their past. She wrapped her fingers around his thick wrists and pulled.

"No," he growled against her lips before he kissed her again, softer this time. Teasing her, tasting her like she was his favorite ice cream topping, until she was holding onto him and tasting him in return.

She had to stop this. Using the last bit of her will, Abby tugged his hands away.

"Why?" He rested his forehead against hers. "One good reason."

"I'm trying to do the right thing. Please don't make it hard."

"How is me here and you there *right*?" She wriggled to get free, but he held onto her. "I want to come home, Abby."

His whisper broke her heart. "No." She dropped her head to his shoulder. "I won't let you give up your life because you think you have to take care of me." Her sobs wracked through her. "I won't be selfish with you anymore." Despite her words, she wrapped her arms around his waist and held tight.

Eventually Jeff stood straighter and nudged her to the bed, walking without letting her go. When she sat, he knelt in front of her and dried her eyes before swiping his hand down his face. "God, we're a pair, aren't we?" He combed his hand through his hair. "I am moving. They've offered me the job as the lab director for the Idaho State Police, and I'm taking it."

She shook her head. "You can't do this." She put her hand over his mouth to stop his argument. "How are you ever going to look at me and not see stitches and duct tape?"

He plucked a bowl from his nightstand and put it in her hands. Under the light, the irregular gold seams sparkled, giving the simple piece a unique beauty.

"It's called *kintsugi*," he explained. "The Japanese developed it as a way to fix broken pottery. For them it's a way of honoring the history of the piece." He ran his thumb along her inner thigh, scorching her through the flimsy cotton of her pajamas. "It makes it more beautiful." He brushed his lips along her hairline. "Stronger." He kissed the still-red scar on her neck and dragged his mouth up her skin until he reached her ear. "Precious."

He slid his hands under her shirt, around her ribs and up her back, tracing the long, bumpy scars and keeping her still when she would have squirmed away. "I would give anything to never have you hurt—past, present, or future—but you are beautiful to me because of your life, Abby, not in spite of it. I never should've left you." He kissed her again, his lips clinging to hers. "I love you."

"I love you, too." *Love.* It was such a small word for such an all-consuming feeling.

"You have to promise me something," Jeff said, keeping her close and resting his forehead against hers. "From now on, we rush into trouble together. Okay?"

He didn't want to take care of her or make her give up taking care of him. Happy tears pricked her eyelids as she nodded.

"And since I'm already on my knees, why don't you

go ahead and agree to marry me? That way we can sleep together without scandalizing our little boy."

"That's the worst reason to propose," she scolded gently.

"Wouldn't know. I've never done it before."

"But you've always wanted to?" It felt good, normal, to tease him.

Jeff shook his head. "You inspired me." He closed his warm fingers around her trembling ones. "Marry me," he repeated in a husky whisper.

Abby's heart soared, and the most joyous word she'd ever felt danced on her tongue, but she was too overcome to say it. All she could do was nod and surrender to another thorough kiss.

When Jeff pulled back, his smile was wide and brilliant, and laughter had replaced the wariness in his gaze. "Say the word, darlin'."

"Yes."

* * * * *

Chapter One

A guy walks into a bar...

Every lame joke Graham Harper could remember flitted through his brain as he stood just inside the door of Orrin's Bar. He was as tired as those overused punch lines.

Maybe the joke was on him. "Why don't you come early? I could use your help," Nate had said. "Bring your stuff."

So Gray had spent five days in a moving van with all his portable belongings, like a turtle. The worn suspension rattled every bone in his body, and the springs in the seat had been poking him in the ass since Montana's eastern border. All in the name of friendship.

The bartender looked away from her conversation with a group of patrons who towered over her. In a relaxed T-shirt and overalls, she would have passed for an urchin from *Oliver Twist* if not for her skin's golden glow and the stylish pixie haircut. Her smile sparkled, as did her eyes. And that hair—honey, cream and platinum—he'd only met one person with hair like that.

"Hi, Gray. Welcome back. Want a beer?"

Only in Fiddler, Idaho, could he be absent ten years and be treated like he'd only gone around the corner.

He walked to the bar. "Hi, Maggie. Nice to see you. Shiner Bock, if you have it. Bottle's fine."

She put one in his hand, and the cold, dark glass numbed his fingers. Gray tipped the bottle, closed his eyes and let the icy, bitter beer wash down his throat for the first time in almost two months. When condensation dripped to the bar, Maggie slid a coaster and a napkin in his direction.

"Don't I even get a hug?" he teased with a wink.

"You're Nate's friend," she said, echoing his tone. "He can hug you."

This joke was as old as the others. Maggie Mathis, his best friend's sister, was always friendly, always warm and welcoming. And in all the time Gray had known her, she'd hugged him exactly once.

"Nathan!" she yelled over the rumble of conversation. "Gray's here!"

The man winding through the crowd shared his sister's smile, but years of working outside had bronzed his skin.

Nate and Maggie Mathis. The wonder twins.

"You always were a sneaky bastard." Nate's grumble was diffused by a laugh.

The trademark cackle was as large a part of Gray's college memories as his degrees. He'd heard it before he reached his assigned dorm room on the first day of orientation. As a Nebraska farm kid on a scholarship, Gray had been overwhelmed, already worried about his GPA and balancing his class schedule with work-study. Nate, the trust-fund baby from Idaho, had been planning a party to break the ice.

Gray braced himself for a hug like a half-nelson. Instead Nate hesitated, with a tentative smile and a raised hand. His gaze darted from one of Gray's shoulders to the other.

Like I'm broken.

"Don't hit the left one," he muttered under his breath and forced a smile.

Shoulder to shoulder, halfway between a handshake and a hug, Nate whispered, "Do me a favor and just play along. I'll explain later."

Oh shit, not again.

"Guys!" Nate's bellow silenced the crowd. "This is Gray Harper, best friend, best man, and our new business manager. Make him welcome, please."

Business manager? What the hell?

"Nate." Gray stooped to whisper, "What the fuck is going on?"

Nate dragged him across the room without answering. "You remember Kevin and Michael, don't you?"

"Of course." He stuck his hand out to a Nordic giant in wire-rimmed glasses. "Nice to see you again, Kevin."

"It's about time you came back," Kevin answered. "We thought we pissed you off."

Michael was next. He'd always been the most reserved of the group, but his callused grip was warm and his smile was as wide as Nate's. "Welcome back."

Their reunion was interrupted as a well-meaning but chaotic mob milled around the table while Nate yelled introductions over the din. Gray ignored his aching shoulder, spinning head and stiff smile as the crowd overwhelmed him. Maggie brought them refills and shooed everyone away.

"Don't scare him before his first day." She clucked after the men like a mother hen. "And Fred Drake, take off your hat. Your mother taught you better manners than that."

A petite redhead weaved through the crowd. Gray recognized Faith Nelson, Nate's fiancée, from the photos Nate had emailed over the last year.

"Gray Harper, Faith. Nice to meet you."

She ignored his outstretched hand and snatched him into a hard hug. Despite losing his breath as pain lanced from his shoulder to his ribs, Gray warmed to the first person in months who hadn't treated him like he was fragile.

As the tide of introductions waned, Gray surveyed the room. Warm yellow walls brightened the walnut floor and the matching trim around doors and windows uncluttered by the traditional neon beer advertisements.

Maggie held court behind a large oak bar, and red caps emblazoned with the Mathis logo crowded every surface or hung from chairs. There wasn't a waitress. There weren't any guitar solos screaming from a jukebox. The air was crisp, as if the windows had been open until the day had cooled in the sunset. No one was drunk. This was the weirdest bar he'd ever seen. But then, the Mathis family had always been unconventional.

Every college summer, instead of touring Europe or sunning on the beach, the twins had worked in the family quarries and lumber mills. Their only true vacation had been two weeks in July when their friends had flown in to play. Gray had come from his parents' farm to join Nate and his childhood buddies, and Maggie's college roommates had come from wherever they lived when they weren't on campus in Seattle.

Maggie's smile caught his attention, just as it had during those summer adventures. He drained the last of his beer and walked to the bar, winding through the friendly crowd, for another round.

Glassware and liquor bottles lined the shelves facing him. Framed photographs documented years of celebrations. One was of an older couple standing where he and Maggie were now.

Maggie followed his stare. “That’s Orrin and Faye Coleman, the bar’s original owners. He died a few years ago, and she’s in assisted living across town. You’re renting their old house.”

Before he could ask why he needed a house, Nate clapped him on the left shoulder, and Gray’s knees shook. He wasn’t sure if it was from pain or fear. Neither was good.

“Let’s go see your office.”

He was swallowed by a dark hallway, and Gray’s throat constricted as his stomach churned. The ceiling fan cooled the sweat on the nape of his neck. *It’s just a hallway, Harper. Get a grip.*

He put one foot in the shadows, then another. Step, breathe. Step, breathe. Once he was inside the bright office, Nate closed the door. The men dropped into opposite chairs in front of a desk that managed to be imposing and understated at the same time. Gray’s head fell backward as he drew a deep breath and waited for his knees to quit shaking.

“Now that we’re alone, how are you? Really,” Nate asked.

On top of being drenched in a cold sweat, Gray imagined creaks and squeaks in his joints. Every morning he looked in the bathroom mirror to see if the screws in his shoulder and ribs had ruptured his skin while he slept. When he slept.

“It bothers me less every day.”

He needed to start keeping a list of the lies he was telling. At some point, confession would be in order.

"You scared the shit out of me," Nate scolded. "How does a white-collar FBI agent get shot anyway?"

"Raids and arrests are part of the job, and money makes suspects as desperate as any other criminal." *Especially mousy accountants committing investment fraud with money they skimmed from the mob.*

Nate shifted in the chair and bounced his fingers against the upholstered arm. "How much longer will you be on leave?"

"Until I can get through physical therapy without a spotter." *And until I can prove I'm not addicted to Vicodin and can see a closed door without thinking I'm in a cage.*

"A month." Gray's conscience twinged. "Maybe two."

"Is Shelby coming out later? After talking to her so much while you were in the hospital, I'm looking forward to meeting her."

"No." Gray sighed as he stared at the ceiling. This was another confession he avoided. "We—I—ended things about a month ago."

"Damn. I'm sorry."

Gray waved off the concern and changed the subject. "Why am I here two months before your bachelor party, and why the hell does everyone think I'm coming to work for you?"

There was a knock at the door a second before it opened. Maggie thrust a box at him. "You'll need these. I've labeled them to make it easier." She held up a small key ring. "There's one for each door and the office. The larger ring has all the quarry office keys." She lifted a second bundle. "These are your house keys. The garage door opener is in here, too. And I've put the lease on your desk. Nate insisted on month to month in case you don't like Faye's house. But if you don't, you're screwed because it's the only place to rent in town."

She was gone as fast as she'd come.

Enough was enough. He faced Nate. "What. The. Fuck."

"She has a stalker."

A familiar jolt of adrenaline fired through Gray's system as his brain seized the first puzzle pieces of a new case. It felt good until he saw Nate's tense jaw and shadowed eyes. "Are you sure?"

"Flowers have arrived every Monday for six months from some anonymous bastard. The accompanying notes are creepy as hell."

"Define *creepy*."

"They start out sweet—'I think you're pretty' sort of stuff. But they end with promises to come get her or be the last person she sees." Nate's ease had evaporated and taken his smile with it. Now his eyes were sharp and his jaw muscles gathered at his ear. His elbows rested on his knees, and his fingers were steepled together. He perched on the edge of his chair as if he was prepared to leap into action. "It's clear he's following her around, watching everything she does, and just *waiting* for some signal. And I can't—"

Gray put up a hand to stop Nate's typical headfirst rush. "Usually it's someone you know."

Nate snorted. "Dude, we know *everyone* in Fiddler, and I can't imagine any of them would do this."

"Is it always the same florist?"

"Our *only* florist. They're ordered through FTD and Teleflora."

"Payment?"

"Prepaid gift card."

"You can't get a judge to issue a warrant?"

"I've tried. Since he hasn't approached her, they don't

consider him a threat and I can't ask for special treatment."

Despite belonging to the wealthiest family in town, Nate and Maggie had been born with shovels in their hands instead of silver spoons in their mouths. *No special treatment* was the family motto.

"How's she handling it?"

Nate shook his head. "She refuses to suspect anyone or to change her behavior. The police department tries to watch her, but she ducks them. I suggested a bodyguard, and she quit carrying my favorite beer for a month. I'm afraid to suggest a security system."

Gray frowned. "She's never been irresponsible."

"Yeah, but she's always been independent. She thinks she can figure it out on her own. That if the guy knows her, he won't hurt her. He'll eventually come forward," Nate grumbled. "But something's not right. It's gone on too long."

Gray remembered the family who'd welcomed him, the friends who'd laughed with him during those college summers. Maggie had always been the bright spot at their center. The girl who brought *Anna Karenina* to the lake, wouldn't camp without a sound system and doted on her family but rolled her eyes when they weren't looking. Memories of her had followed him home each year and haunted him until Christmas break. She'd been off-limits on so many levels for more reasons than he could count. And he'd counted them—repeatedly.

"How can I help?"

"Find this guy while you're here?" Nate's raised eyebrows added to the plea.

"Aww, shit. Nathan, despite the badge and the gun, I'm basically a tax attorney. It would make more sense for me to be involved if he was embezzling to buy the flowers."

Nate persisted. "I don't know what else to do. I've tried. The police have tried. In a town this size, it shouldn't be difficult. Maybe we just need a set of fresh eyes." His grin was lopsided and brief. "And I know you can't resist the challenge."

Gray shifted positions and wondered if the creak he heard was the chair or his battered shoulder. Challenge and adrenaline aside, he wasn't up for this. "Nate—"

"She's the only family I have. I'm in the middle of wedding plans, a honeymoon, and being a newlywed. Not to mention work. I can't be everywhere at the same time, and *everyone* deserves my full attention. Besides, I *suck* at details. You know that. If she gets hurt because I—" Nate stared at a spot on the floor. "I need someone I trust to look out for her, without her knowing they're looking out for her."

Gray's head throbbed as Nate's cockeyed plan came into focus. *Business manager, office, house.* "You're a moron. You know that, right? This will never work. She's got all the brains."

"She's been after me for a year to hire a business manager. We're spread too thin, and it's only getting worse."

"So I've suddenly left a career in law enforcement to manage quarries?"

"I've never told her about the FBI. As far as she knows, you're a tax attorney with an MBA and you've been working in Chicago since she last saw you." Nate leaned forward in his chair. "You're the only person I trust with her."

Gray had seen Nate this tense only once, on the darkest day of the twins' lives. That convinced him more than anything else Nate had said. So did Maggie's laughter filtering through the door.

"Okay, I'll try. But I get to say when I'm in over my head."

Nate dropped back into the chair, and his deep exhale ended in a wide grin. "Thanks. Glen Roberts, the police chief, is the only other person who knows why you're really here. He'll give you access to whatever you need. Oh, and Faith knows. Can't keep a secret from my girl."

Before he signed the lease, Gray read the first page. The rent was criminally low, even by Fiddler standards, and Maggie was his landlord. Great. She'd get wind of this scheme and he'd be homeless.

Wait. I have a home. In Chicago. Where my job—my real job—is waiting on me.

"What have you gotten me into?" he grumbled.

"Hey! It beats watching the History Channel and reading detective novels. It'll be fun—you know, once she's safe and I'm married."

"Once she's safe and you're married, I'm going home. When exactly does the *fun* start?" Gray asked as they stood.

"It won't be all work," Nate said. "You know us."

He returned to Faith's side without a backward glance. Gray sat at the corner of the bar and watched Maggie, who was in the middle of a quiet conversation with a mountainous man. Though her words were inaudible, he relaxed under her attention. It reminded Gray of the last time he'd visited Fiddler.

Ten years ago he'd flown in to attend a double funeral. Ron and Ollie, the twins' father and grandfather, had died when their private plane had crashed in a storm.

Everyone in town had hovered over the siblings, intent on helping. Instead, Maggie had comforted each of them, bending her head in conversation, hugging them, sending them home with leftovers. When they'd been with their closest friends, Nate had been the shaky one. Maggie had let him lean on her while she'd whispered in his ear.

Realizing he was staring, he wondered who else might be watching her, or worse, watching *him* watch her. He looked up, hoping to catch an unguarded gaze in the mirror. He could be done with his job in five minutes and then relax until Nate's wedding.

There wasn't a mirror. His gaze flew to where she was working with her back to the room, oblivious to who was behind her or what was happening. She smiled as she walked over.

"Do you want another?"

He did, but now he was working. He couldn't drink on the job. "Water?"

"Sure," she said as she delivered the bottle.

Nodding his thanks, Gray left his post and walked past Nate's table. Taking the chair in the far corner of the room, he watched every man with new suspicion. Early patrons left for home and were replaced by others who, given their clean clothes, had gone home first. Who spent too long at the bar? Who stared too hard?

He also watched her, getting past the curiosity she'd always inspired and recalling his objective observer skills. That's what let him see the change in her when no one was looking, the way her smile faded and her gaze shifted from man to man in suspicious assessment. Then she'd catch someone looking and flip a switch, softening her grip on the towel in her hand, tossing it over her shoulder and forcing her smile to sparkle. Just like the funeral, hiding in plain sight.

Damn it, Nate was wrong. She wasn't ignoring the threat. She was terrified.

Squaring his shoulders and straightening his spine, Gray forced away his warm memories of Fiddler and counted how many times she put on her carefree mask.

She was wearing it a few hours later when she laughed and half-pushed the last persistent patron out the front door. Gray was exhausted just from watching her and relieved when the forced smile faded. Wanting to give her peace, he joined Nate and Faith in cleaning tables and turning chairs.

She went down the hall, and her voice drifted behind her. "Gray. I hope you don't mind, but I put sheets on the bed and stocked your kitchen with some basics."

"Thanks," he replied as he handed Nate the chair and conducted reconnaissance while she wouldn't catch him.

Empty, the room told a better story. Years of elbows had worn dull spots in the bar's finish, and generations of work boots had mottled the brass foot rail. The floor was scratched from patrons who'd tracked in sand and gravel, and the leather cushions on stools and chairs were shaped to each occupant's behind. They loved this place. Did one of them let that carry over to obsession with her?

"The guys and I will help you unpack tomorrow," Nate said. "There's a company truck in the garage. The keys are in the ignition."

Gray nodded. This was surreal. Five days ago he'd been a wounded FBI agent recuperating in Chicago. Now he was posing as a business manager and moonlighting as a bodyguard. To keep from laughing at the lunacy, he indulged his curiosity. "I don't think I've seen a bar with a ten o'clock last call, especially on Saturday," he called down the hall.

The clatter of mops and brooms and the squeaky wheels of a bucket almost drowned out her answer. "The guys are tired after a long day of work or chores. We're open 'til midnight on Fridays, but otherwise we close early. We don't want to make anyone miss work or church the next morning. That's not why we're here."

Next to him, Nate silently parroted the last sentence, ending on a wink.

Gray snorted and shook his head. "That's an interesting philosophy."

"Are you laughing at me?" Maggie asked, as she dragged the broom across the floor and whacked her brother with the handle. "Or is Nate mocking me again?"

Gray was glad to see the honest humor behind her smile. It vanished when someone knocked on the front door. An officer walked in and over to the group without waiting on an invitation. "Everything okay? I saw the lights."

"Everything is *always* okay, Max," Maggie drawled. "I just closed. Can't clean in the dark."

The younger man stared at Gray, clearly assessing. Gray stared back, noting the man's wide stance and the hand resting on his sidearm.

"You're new," the patrolman said.

"You caught him," Maggie said. "He came to kidnap me and I talked him into mopping the floor first." She pushed the man's shoulder, but he remained immovable. "Seriously. He's a friend of the family. Ease up, RoboCop."

Max stayed put. "Nate, do you need me to hang around?"

"No." Maggie bit the word out, and then softened it with, "thanks anyway."

She shooed him out, locked the door and returned to them, her chin tucked to her chest and her shoulders square as she charged toward her brother. The twins had always argued in identical fashion—deep breath and jump in.

"Call off the babysitter brigade," she said.

"If you'll let me hire someone to watch you," Nate countered.

"A *bodyguard*? Nathan! I'm surrounded by men who treat me like their little sister."

"Dammit! You're *my* sister. You're my responsibility. I let you down once."

Her head snapped back like he'd struck her. "I'm my own responsibility. You've heard Glen. Flowers aren't against the law. They can't do anything unless it escalates."

Gray's molars ground together as heat climbed his neck. He'd be talking to the police chief first thing Monday. The judge would be next. Nate might not ask for special treatment, but Gray would call in every favor the family had accumulated over the years. No one was going to get close enough to harm her.

"I'm sorry, Gray. You're probably exhausted, and now you've walked into another—"

Her sentence stopped on a sharp inhale, and he dropped his lashes to hide his eyes. Too late.

She wheeled on her brother. "You told him, didn't you?"

"He needed to know what he was getting into."

"He's not *getting into* anything. These guys would never hurt me." Her shoulders squared. "I'm tired of policemen following me around. At this point, I don't know who the boogeyman is and who he isn't."

Nate's posture mirrored hers and Gray stepped between the siblings to stop the brewing fight, as he'd done several times before. The worst, until now, had been when Maggie had narrowly defeated Nate in a dump truck race and he'd accused her of cheating.

"Maybe it's not such a bad idea to have more eyes on the place," Gray reasoned. "You're worth a lot of money."

Guilt washed over him as Maggie's eyes darkened and her chin dropped. He tugged the broom from her hands and nudged her onto the stool he'd pulled closer.

"What is it?" Putting a hand on her shoulder, he found all curves and no sharp angles. In worn cotton and denim, she was the human equivalent of his favorite blanket. He wanted to burrow his fingers into the softness. Instead, he squeezed gently. He knew full well the fragility of the bone under his thumb. "Tell me."

"Money?" she echoed his whisper. "I don't want to think about one of my friends terrorizing me for *money*. I don't want to think about one of them doing it at all. I can't."

She trembled under his fingers as a shadow flitted through her eyes. For a moment, she looked the way he felt going down a hallway. Then her mask came back. She had to be tired of fighting.

Gray handed her the broom. "Let's finish so you can get some rest."

They completed their chores in silence, and Nate and Faith left for home. Certain Maggie was safe for the night, Gray entered his new address into the GPS. Shifting into gear and pressing the accelerator made him whimper. The first pothole sent his shoulder into a spasm, curling him over the wheel.

The air-conditioning wheezed until he gave up and rolled down the window. It was cooler outside anyway, and the air was clean. After ten years in Chicago, he'd almost forgotten the crisp bite of country air. He'd certainly forgotten the quiet. Ghostly shadows of rail and barbed wire fences bordered the road, and behind the barriers empty fields hinted at livestock occupants. Wide dirt lanes interrupted the fences and led to large, well-lit houses peeking from behind massive trees.

In five hundred feet, turn left, the GPS bleated.

"Shit." He slammed on the brakes and listened as his possessions crashed into the front wall of the container. His motorcycle would probably be in pieces.

He turned left when commanded to do so and braced for a rutted lane. Instead the tires crunched on fresh gravel, and the tracks were so straight he could have removed his hands from the wheel.

Hardwood trees towered over the driveway. Behind the trees, a rail fence separated the manicured shoulder from wild pasture. The jagged peaks of the Sawtooth Mountains loomed in the distance.

The lane opened into a lawn. The stone house blended into the foothills, and its wide windows overlooked the front yard. Window boxes overflowed with early flowers, and lights shined as if someone was expected home.

Parking in the garage, Gray swung the door open and peered inside before stepping into a kitchen with slate floors, oak cabinets and stainless steel appliances. It melted into a living room full of large, comfortable furniture draped with crocheted throws. A stone fireplace dominated the far wall, and thick wool rugs warmed hardwood floors. Windows and French doors showcased an expansive view.

He switched on all the lights to check two extra bedrooms and a guest bath. The other end of the house was the master suite. A huge bed mounded with pillows faced another wall of windows and French doors.

The master shower was straight out of a high-end spa. Without hesitation, Gray stripped and climbed in. The temperature was easy to learn but the dials for the jets were more confusing. Eventually he found a combination that left his muscles weak with relief.

After his body was relaxed, he reduced the pressure and then stopped it altogether in favor of a soothing, warm rain. Standing under the water, he considered his options.

The smart thing would be to go home now. Except for Nate's worry…

Besides, he owed it to Ollie and Ron. Nate's grandfather and father had always treated Gray like another son. They'd shaped his adult life almost as much as his own father, and he'd never had the chance to tell them.

Thinking of them took Gray back to their funerals, where he'd sat behind Nate, next to Kevin and Michael, and watched the twins hold hands so hard they'd both had bruises. But they'd never cried.

Gray had seen Maggie's composure crack once, and only then because he'd walked into the kitchen pantry in search of paper towels and met her tear-filled gaze. She'd barreled into him, wrapped her arms around his waist and hung on for dear life.

At twenty-five, never having experienced loss, he'd had no idea how to help. He'd patted her on the back simply because he'd had nowhere else to put his hands.

Now he was different.

How could Nate be oblivious? Gray had seen the twin telepathy work firsthand when Nate had been tossed from a final exam in Nebraska for cackling at a joke

Maggie had heard in theater class—in Seattle. Why didn't he see how her body language changed when no one was looking?

Which, granted, wasn't often. Those men watched over her like a daughter or a sister. But if she caught them doing it, she cracked a joke and offered them a refill. One large man had carried a case of beer from the backroom, and she'd thanked him but shooed him away, swatting him with her towel and telling him he'd worked hard enough this week. Even with the patrolman she'd hidden behind sarcasm and scolding as she'd pushed him out.

She won dump truck races, consoled everyone else rather than dissolving into tears and worked alone behind the bar. If she knew he was here to guard her, she'd fight him every step of the way to prove she wasn't afraid.

In the end, her fear swayed him. He knew a thing or two about being afraid. About hiding.

Lying made his job more difficult, and it made him feel like shit, but he'd do it. To protect her, he'd lie.

Acknowledgments

Every time I mentioned writing a book, my mother always said, "Just don't write one about me." I couldn't resist dedicating this book to her—the mom who is the complete opposite of Wallis. Love you, Mom!

My stepfather is like Doctor Doolittle, and he inspired Abby's homeopathic approach. He's also the inspiration for all her fabulous stepdads. I couldn't be luckier.

A while back, I told my best friend a plot idea. Since then, she has been Jeff and Abby's biggest supporter. Patti, this one's for you.

And for Connie, who really, *really* wanted to be a dead body.

There's my crew of regular supporters, critique partners and beta-readers. They have held my hand through my sophomore jitters. Thank you, Cheryl, Carrie, Sherry, Melinda, Brynn, Kari and M.A.

Thank you, Kiss of Death, the RWA's Mystery/Romantic Suspense chapter. Their month-long class on profilers and serial killers helped me find the voice for this book.

Thank you, DSRA, The Ink Spot, Sisters of Suspense, Not Your Usual Suspects and (again) the Kiss of Death. Every writer should surround themselves with the best they can find, because you get inspiration in the company you keep. You are my inspirations.

Thank you, Kerri Buckley, for your patience, help and good humor. As always, I'm in awe at my sheer good luck to work with you.

Thank you to Heather, Stephanie and the team at Carina Press. I appreciate you more than all the cookies available on Amazon Canada.

And for Greg. I couldn't do this without my adorable husband who makes me laugh and has the prettiest smile of any man I've seen in real life.

About the Author

Like most little girls, I always wanted a horse. I actually had a pony when I was very young. His name was Toby, and he was too wild to keep. I sobbed when we sold him—until my dad promised me a Dr. Pepper.

As a small-town country girl, I have done enough farm-related chores to be glad I don't have to do them every day. However, my parents' small farm is one of my favorite places to be.

I am lucky enough to have an incredible group of friends who help me shop, give me advice, make me laugh and remind me of what is important. All of them are embodied in the women of Fiddler.

For as long as I can remember, I have loved to tell stories. Writing them down for others to read is the best job I've ever had.

That said, writing this book was scary. In addition to the normal sophomore "what if I blow it" jitters, this book pushed me out of my comfort zone. The subject matters were dark at times, and I wanted to make sure I was respectful of those topics while still writing a story about survival and hope. To tell that sort of story, with two very quiet characters, I had to learn new skills and write in a new way.

Every book teaches me a lesson about writing. This one taught me to get out of the way of the story.

(By the way, chocolate gravy is a real thing—and it is awesome.)

Mia

Web: authormiakay.com
Facebook: facebook.com/authormiakay
Goodreads: goodreads.com/author/show/14437835.Mia_Kay

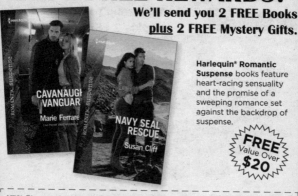